Y0-BDF-202

Grace & Peace,

Rennie G. [signature]

This book is inspired by and dedicated to
the memory of
Caremeanearseal McCreary

This book and any success is especially dedicated
to Ma, Daddy, Day Day, Uncle Joe, Iris and Aunt
Mel, with the ancestors now, supporting, guiding
and loving me always.

To God goes all the Glory

one

February 1939 was *cold* in Smedley, South Carolina. I was only seven years old, but I remember it like yesterday. In fact, I can remember back to before I was two years old, if the recollections of my momma and daddy are right.

See, I remember I loved Mr. Red Comb, an old rooster we had that used to strut around in our yard so big and bold and cocka-doodled any ole time of day or night that he pleased. Mr. Red Comb was a real rascal that gave everybody a fit, specially our three hens. I guess I liked him best because you had to earn his affection. He was too smart to fall for just a few breadcrumbs or cooing. After I scattered bits of corn or bread, Mr. Red Comb used to squawk and scold and flap his wings, chasin' away me and anyone else in his yard. Then he would gobble up half of what I put down and strut around a while longer darin' anybody to make a move. It wasn't until afta he perched hisse'f up on a fence rail for a little afta-dinner snooze, was it safe to venture back into the yard. Mr. Red Comb made me laugh til I ached, fussin at me. Momma would laugh too, but I think she was really laughin at me. Daddy would laugh and say, "Ah'm gonna keel me one onnery ol' bird."

Come that Thanksgivin, the firs' one I can recall, we had mo' food on the table than I ever seen in my life; yams, cabbage an greens, corn, turnips, carrots, an chestnut/apple cornbread dressin stuffed inside a juicy, gold bird. We ate til we all look like Momma, who awready had a big ol' belly from carryin my sister, Bertha. I axed could we always eat like that an Momma said, "Ever'time the crops is good as this year's."

The next mornin, I went to feed the chickens. Afta I scatter all the meal, the hens come-a runnin. I look all around surprised cause ain't no Mr. Red Comb. I call to Momma in her garden, "Momma, whure Mista Red Comb?" Daddy start laughin on the porch an say, "We et 'im yestiddy!"

I said, "No we din't," an laughed along at his old joke. Then daddy stopped laughin an said, "Yes, we did." I looked over at momma standin in her little patch of garden lookin at me all sad, like she was bout to lose me. Then I knew that that juicy, gold bird from yestiddy was Mr. Red Comb.

I knew it was true, but I couldn't say it because that would make daddy a murderer. So I shook my head real slow an said over and over, "No we din't. No we din't! No We DINT!NOWEDINTNOWEDINT!!!" I start kickin an punchin out at ev'ythin, I couldn't see nuthin though, cause my eyes was clenched tight. Then daddy scooped me up in his strong arms. His long legs got him off the porch an up to me in no time. He was tryin to rock me like a cradle, but I wa'nt havin none of that. He killed Mr. Red Comb! He was tryin to splain, but there was no explanation for killin my loud, proud, feathered friend.

It seem like I was mad at daddy for forever. But I forgave him that Christmas when he gave me the best present I ever got, then or sence. It was a li'l walnut chair with a cane seat that he carved an wove an painted hisse'f. On the back, he painted a beautiful rooster flappin his wangs an shakin his red comb that was shaped like a crown.

Years later, I told momma that no other gift ever made me feel as good as when I got that li'l chair cause I knew daddy was really tryin to give me back Mr. Red Comb an earn my affection again. Momma said, "How you member all that? You wa'nt even two years old!"

So tha's how come I *know* I remember back to before I was two.

An February 1939, Smedley, South Carolina was colder than Siberia. I was seven, my sister Bertha was five an the twins, Daniel an Samuel, was two. Our job that winter was stuffin newspaper an old rags in the cracks round the windows, the doors an in the walls to try to keep the drafts out. Momma knitted wrappin strang an twine t'getha to make us extra "socks" to wear over the patched up ones we awready wore that somehow always sprung another hole. We exercised to keep warm. We did a lot of jumpin jacks an loft relays, cause they was best to get our circulation to circulatin. Mos'ly what we ate that winter was plain oatmeal an sugar tits, a piece of cloth soaked in sugar water. But sence we couldn't afford no sugar, we really sucked on wet rags an make-believed they was sugar tits.

We had so much fun runnin an jumpin in the house without gettin yelled at an make-believin our oatmeal an wet rag dinners was somethin else, that we probably never would'a realized how bad-off we was, if it wa'nt fer Mr. Tucker an thangs gettin so much better.

Mr. Tucker was the oldest man I knew. He was older than my daddy, who was older than my momma. He was maybe thity-nine or forty years old! He owned a lot of land, like millions an millions of acres, wit all kinds of trees on 'em that always needed choppin an splittin or plantin an prunin. It was hard work that took a lot of people an sence he was all alone in the world, he had to hire hands to he'p. He came over to our house wit daddy one day an afta that, ev'ythang changed forever.

It was always a good time when Mr. Tucker showed up to the house. Daddy would get a good payin job, if only for a li'l while, or he would be paid for the last job he did. He din't just hire daddy eitha. Momma would wash an mend his clothes an we would get his hand-me-downs. I know daddy wished he coulda got some of Mr. Tucker's warm flannel shirts or stiff denim coveralls, but daddy was too big. He was bout three feet taller than Mr. Tucker an daddy's back an chest was so wide, it woulda took two of Mr. Tucker's shirts sewed t'getha to cover 'em. But Mr. Tucker had a bigger belly. It was round an hard like momma's when she was carryin babies. Bertha an me would wear his t-shirts like dresses an his wool shirts an sweaters like coats. Momma wore some of his shirts too, like jackets, an she split his pants legs open an sew 'em back t'getha for a skirt. His raggediest stuff she pieced t'getha makin quilts or stuffed into our

5

pallets. If she knew he was comin ahead of time, momma always fixed an extra special supper puttin the fat back, ham hocks or trotters that she been savin, in the greens. A lotta times Mr. Tucker would brang over a beef tongue or a rabbit for momma to make an we eat like it was Sunday.

Mr. Tucker always gave me an my sister an brothers cashews, pecans, walnuts or apples from his trees. Sometime he gave us peppermint balls or gum sticks. An sometime, he gave us the spare change in his pocket, less he only had one or two coins, then he give that to me bein as I was the oldest.

I liked Mr. Tucker like people like Santa Claus, cause tha's what he was to my family an me.

****

One of my favorite things to do was to make up stories bout the pretty strangers inside the mail order cadlog.

"This lady name is Callie an she is rich, rich, rich. She got all the fancy clothes in the world, see?" I say flippin through the pages. "Even her bloomers an brassiers got lacy frillies, see?" Me an Bertha be out on the porch lookin through the Sears Roebuck mail order cadlog at all the pretty people an thangs we could never imagine, even when we din't have to imagine 'em cause they was right in front of our face.

"Who dis?" Bertha axed pointin to another lady. "Her bloomers is fancy, too."

Bertha thought I knew the real story bout 'em cause, for some reason she thought I could read. Momma an daddy couldn't even do that! I never told Bertha I could read, but I never told her I couldn't eitha cause then she wouldn't listen to me.

"Tha's her evil neighbor, Sadie," I said.

"That ain't none a her name! You just sayin that cause you don' like cousin Sadie!"

"Her name is too Sadie! It say so right here!" I pointed to some letters neitha one of us unnerstan. "They more than one Sadie in the world. You thank you the only Bertha?"

That shut her up, so I went on.

"Sadie break into Callie house sometime an steal her clothes when she gone. But Callie don' never notice nuthin missin cause she always buyin other stuff. Callie buy a hunnerd dresses ev'yday, see?" I would flip the pages an each one would have three or four yellow-haired women on it. They din't always look like the same lady. But sence Bertha din't axe, I made out like she was the same one.

"Who dat?" Bertha axe pointin at some knobbly-kneed man.

"Tha's Callie brother, Jasper. Him an his sister go ev'ywhure t'getha." That was an easy one cause ev'y one'a them pages got 'em somewhures... on a beach, at a party, in the park.

"There ain't but one problem, Jasper like Sadie. Sometime he tell her to come go wit 'em." I say that cause a lotta pages got all three of 'em t'getha.

"Callie don' look like she don' like Sadie."

"She smilin for her brother," I said. "She know he like Sadie an she don' wanna hurt his feelins. So on the ou'side she smile, but on the inside she hurt cause..." I flip the pages to the long fancy dancy dresses. "See this here dress Sadie got on? That was Callie favorite one! She had it special made an when she seen Sadie in it, she knew she stole it. But she couldn't tell Jasper that the girl he love is a thief."

"Why not?" Bertha axe lookin at me like this was the silliest story in the world.

But it wa'nt a silly story. It was mines. It happen to me all the time bein as I'm the oldest. Mama an daddy always tellin me to give somethin I want to Bertha or my brothers cause I'm older an I got to take care of 'em. Like the wagon daddy useta pull me round in when I was real li'l. I loved gittin pulled round the yard in that cart. Then me an Bertha got pulled, then all four of us was pulled til we got too big to all fit an daddy say I had to get out.

"Why?! Why I got to be the one to get out?! I was in it firs'!" Samuel was whinin an squirmin round cause he couldn't get all the way in an tha's why daddy said I had to get out in the firs' place.

"Out now, Alice. I ain't gonna say it again!"

I got out, but I was so mad I thought I was gonna bust my gut! I stomped over to the outhouse but fore I could even get inside, I was upchuckin my breakfast on the walk up to the toilet. I taught myse'f to throw up all my bad feelins an thoughts to get 'em out of me. Mama said if you keep bad thangs hidden inside, afta'while they make you ugly an sick.

Mama was hangin laundry an heard me retchin. She was too li'l to pick me up, so she come wit a warm washrag an cleaned me up right there, then she axed me t'come he'p her git supper started.

It seem like daddy cut the wagon ride short that day cause before the biscuits was mixed good, he was settin at the table sayin, "You got to make a zample of yose'f so the li'l ones be bettah."

I said, "Why I got to be the zample?"

Daddy look real strong at me cause chirren not s'poze to question grown folk, I awready know that. He say, "You bettah stop smellin yerse'f, girl. You the zample cause we say you the zample."

Mama try to make it better. She smile an say, "You my firs' born! The firs' always got to lead the way."

I din't want daddy to thank I was jes smellin myse'f, meanin I'm feelin grown an can challenge my parents. So, I studied my shoes an axed real soft, "If you need a zample to get bettah an the firs' always gotta be the zample, who my zample then?"

Daddy knew I was tryin to unnerstan this time, not just bein fresh. He put me on his knee an brush my hair wit his hand an said, "You listen to yer mama an me. Tha's how you know how to be a good zample."

Then mama, bein mama, brought the church into it. "It's like Jesus. He the zample for the world. We cain't always have what we want. Life ain't like that fer nobody, an it specially ain't like that for us. We got to share an make sacrifices so thangs get bettah for ev'ybody. God taught Jesus that, then He let his only child lose his life to save the world. You hear me, Alice? God give up His son to save the world. Yer daddy jes axed you to give up a seat in the wagon so yer sister an brothers could ride. That wa'nt such a big thang, now was it?"

She smiled, then daddy smiled, so I knew I was s'poze t'smile too, an I did. Then she laugh an daddy laugh, so I knew I was s'poze t'laugh an I did.

"What d'you thank Jesus did when his Daddy told him that He was gonna let him be killed?" She axed. "You thank he stomped round in the yard, cryin an throwin up?!" The three of us really whooped it up in the kitchen then, imaginin Jesus throwin up his guts by the privy.

Then mama got ser'us again, "Nooo. Jesus jes said, 'Okay Daddy. I love You an I know You know wha's best.' Then he went on out there an let hisse'f git lied bout, stabbed in the side an nailed to a cross. He knew Judas would double-cross him. He knew Peter was gonna lie bout not knowin him three times fore the cock crowed. But Jesus let all that go cause his Daddy taught him not to fuss over ev'y li'l thang. The more you give, the more you git. Jesus knew that afta he died, he was gonna come back in three days. Then he knew he was gonna live in heaven wit his Daddy whure he could he'p ansa the prayers of good people."

Mama kneeled down to where I was sittin on daddy's lap, took my hand in hers an said, "All prayers git ansa'd, you know. God always provides for people wit givin, unse'fish spirits. It might not be t'day. It might ain't got nuthin to do wit ridin in a wagon. But somethin good is gonna happen to you sooner or later, for lettin Samuel ride in yer place." She kiss my hand an put it on her cheek for a minute, then she got up an finish mixin the biscuits.

I swear, Mama coulda been a preacher ef she wanted t'be. She tole the best Bible stories. An she din't mak'em all scary like in church whure they got you screamin an burnin in fire forever if you do one li'l bad thang. Mama always helped me feel bettah an unnerstan stuff, kinda. I still din't know what a zample was, but I din't mind bein one anymore.

"Callie cain't tell Jasper his girlfriend is a thief cause that would hurt his feelins."

"What about her own feelins?" Bertha axed, really gittin mad. "Tha's her best dress Sadie stole!"

"Bertha, it's jes a dress. She git a hunnerd mo ev'yday, member?" That calm Bertha down some.

"Callie don' wanna hurt Jasper, cause he might run away an she cain't git another brother."

"Well now, tha's a rail nice story you tellin there, Miss Alice!" Mr. Tucker said standin in the screen door. He brung a duck over earlier that mama stuffed wit apples an onions. Now there was some good smells comin out the house.

"Alice read to me mos ev'yday!" Bertha said.

"Miss Alice read to you?" Mr. Tucker axe, comin ou'side to get a bettah look at the book. "Tha's a right nice thang for you t'do, Miss Alice. Lemme see tha'there book."

I thought he was gonna tell Bertha that I was just make-believin wit her, but he din't.

"You a right smart girl, readin a big ole book like this an you ain't never been to school. Thank how much smarter you be ef you did go to school. I thank I'ma talk to yer people bout that. Would you like to go to school, Miss Alice?"

"Yessuh, I wanna go to school!" I always did wanna go to school. I never knew nobody that went, but I thought all the people that live in the

9

mail order cadlogs musta gone. I figgered tha's how come they had so many pretty thangs an went ev'ywhure in the world.

"Okay, then I'ma talk to yer people bout puttin you in school. Now you gurls clean up an come on into supper, it's a good one." He smile an give me back the book fore goin back inside.

Tha's how I wound up bein the firs' one ever in my family t'go to school. Ef this was my good thang to happen, Samuel could keep my seat in the wagon, Hallelujah!

two

"Alice!! Did you just shove LeRoy in the face?" I know I made Miss Johnson tired, but these boys was bout to wear me out, always tryin t'hold my hand or touch me an callin me they wife.

"He was tryin' to kiss me Miss Johnson!" I barked.

"I did not ask you *why* you shoved him! I was questioning *what* I saw. Did I see you shove LeRoy in his face?"

"Yessum," I said, quietly seethin.

"That is not nice, Alice. That is not the way I allow young ladies to act. You know that."

"I leab him alone ef he leab me alone!"

"*Leave.* You will *leave* him alone if he *leaves* you alone. *Leave*, got it?"

"Yessum." I mumbled, still mad cause she could repeat my words, but miss the whole point.

"LeRoy, why don't you leave Alice alone?"

"I love her," he said wit an eager grin, then blushed an hugged hisse'f real tight while the rest of the class laughed an pointed at him.

I 'ont know what *they* was laughin at! Ha'f the boys in the room do the same thang for the same reason when Miss Johnson ain't lookin. The other ha'f pro'bly want to, but is too chicken-hearted. All of 'em ceptin Isaac. Isaac ain't never writ me a note or try to touch me, but I ketch him studdin me alla time. I been in school almos a year an it been like that sence my firs' day. All the boys write me love notes, pull my pigtails an say thangs like, "We gone get married." Cept Isaac. They even kiss my books or my coat when they ain't in the mood to git slapped, cause I slap 'em ever chance I git when they try to touch me. I hate it! I don' want all these li'l snot-nosed, peasy-headed boys kissin me an makin goo-goo eyes. But, I was learnin this was my fate, bein as I was the mos beautiful girl in the world.

I'm the smartest, too, the way I figger. See, the school was two rooms, one was fer primary grades an the othern was fer secondary. I started school late bein almos eight years old, but I caught up fast. It he'ped a lot to have the li'l girl in my firs' real book named afta me. She was Alice from Alice an Jerry. I was so excited to read bout a girl wit my name cause a course, I make-believed she was me. I could hardly wait to see what I was gonna be doin next.

Truth is, Alice was really not very interestin at all. Jerry did all the fun stuff. Even Jip, the dog, seem to have more fun than Alice. But I still got goosebumps make-believin somebody had writ a book bout me.

I was so good in school, the teacher made me her helper. I he'p her teach the younger grades an the slower kids in my class when I was through wit my own work. Bertha was s'poze t'come to school later this year. I knew she would ketch up fast, too, cause I was awready teachin her at home ev'ythang I learn.

Daddy an momma wa'nt plannin on alla us goin to school. Our family wa'nt real big, compared wit other peoples. One of the reasons folks had so many kids was so they could he'p out on the farm when they got big. Mr. Tucker din't have a family, bein as he was all by hisse'f, but he did all right cause he made enough money to hire other people. That worked out good for ev'ybody cause sometimes farms wouldn't do so good causa no rain, or bugs or bad seeds or somethin else that din't have nuthin to do with alla the hard work put into it. It was only cause Mr. Tucker kinda made us his family an kep daddy workin that we was all able to git book learnin.

"LeRoy says he loves you, Alice. Isn't that nice?"

"I 'ont care if he do or don', long as he don' be tryin to kiss on me!"

I din't believe Miss Johnson din't know that, as smart as I thought she was. I thought she shoulda been tryin to teach me bout bein a zample or somethin. I thought maybe I'd brang it up afta school, if I wa'nt in jail for killin me one a these peasy-heads!

****

"I like bein yer he'per, Miss Johnson," I was washin the blackboard afta school right before sprang break.

"I like having you for my helper, Alice."

"My daddy an mama say I got to be the zample for my sister an brothers so they can do bettah. My sister, Bertha gonna be here come September an I 'ont wanna be still fightin wit these here boys in class cause if Bertha start fightin an say she got it from me, then I'ma git in trouble for bein a bad zample."

"Example."

"Huh?" Here I am pourin out my heart 'n soul an Miss Johnson up here tryin to correct my words. Was she even lis'nin to me?

"You said *zample*, but the word is *example*. I think that you are probably a fine example for your siblings. I know you're a good example for this class. That's why I made you my helper."

Ha'f the time when Miss Johnson be splainin thangs, I 'ont know what she be talkin bout. I always got to look up some of her words in the dictionary to know what she said. But it's always worth it. I am not a zample. I am a example an I am a good one for the class an my siblings... whatever those are.

"But nobody's perfect and fighting seems to be your biggest fault."

"But I...!" I started to protest, but then she quickly splained.

"I'm not saying the fights are your fault. I realize that you are striking back in self-defense against their amorous assaults. But I cannot condone violence of any kind. So, you need to find an *acceptable alternative* to repel the affections of these young men."

Lawd a mercy, what she jes say? I wonder whure Miss Johnson from. She don' talk like nobody I know. Anyway, I 'ont know nuthin she said past "I'm not sayin the fights is yer fault." So I axed her, "What kin I do?"

"Talk to them."

"I do alla time! I tell 'em, *Don' be kissin on me or I'ma bust you in yo head!*"

"Try another approach," Miss Johnson said. "Tell them if they stop touching you, you will let them sharpen your pencils or carry your books. Use kindness instead of threats."

"But they always touchin on me cause they say my skin so pretty, or my hair so pretty. They not gonna stop til I ugly up."

"You are a very pretty girl, Alice," she said. But I could tell by the way she said it, she ain't b'lieve it. "But I think *all* of the children here are real beauties. In time, when these young men realize that you are seriously not interested, I'm sure they will befriend some of their other pretty classmates."

I ain't for shore, but I thank she jes said these peasy-heads is gonna stop fallin all over theyse'f fer me one day an go somewhure else. That be fine wit me, the sooner the bettah!

****

"You know why the boys don' run afta you anymo?"

Mabel Gaye like to always be up in somebody bizness. I was jes finish takin my turn wit the double dutch at lunch break an I wa'nt studdin nuthin, but how I migh'could git me a swig a somethin cold fore class start again. Mabel come up on me even fore I could ketch my breath. She pro'bly thankin I'm too tired to ansa right off cause I was bent over, huffin an puffin an sweatin like a sharecropper. But the truth is, I was shocked. I never thought bout these boys lessin they was tryna force theyse'f into my space, an sence they wa'nt, I never thought of 'em.

Fine'ly, I looked at Mabel standin wit her hands on her hips an cuttin her eyes at me like she thank I'm bout to be mad. She had a pretty little chocolate bunny-face wit big, wide set eyes an a little bunny nose. Her mama always put her hair in two tight little braids on the side of her head wit rubber bands on the end an they hung down like little skinny bunny-ears. I always wondered if they wa'nt too tight an maybe tha's what make Mabel's big eyes pull up on the ends like a Chi'nee.

"You wanna know why?!" Mabel axe me when I ain't say nuthin.

14

I really din't care, but she wanna tell me, tha's fer shore. It was over two years sence my talk wit Miss Johnson bout this very subject. I laughed a li'l cause Miss Johnson was right, as always. I wanted to run an tell her right then that the boys was courtin Mabel Gaye now, Hallelujah!

But instead I said, "Why?"

"Causa Alberta Carter!" Mabel jes bout spit at me.

I knew it was true, too. Alberta had wavy-curly brown hair an grey eyes. She was pale all year-roun an when she talk, it sound like a whiny song. "Stop it, stop it, stop it," she say when the boys rub her face or arms. Anybody wit ha'f a brain could tell she like all that pettin an fussin over her. Well good, bettah her then me.

Mabel was still up in my face though. She musta had somethin more to say, I figgered.

So I say, "What?"

"You wanna know why the boys are after Alberta an not you?"

I din't care, but Mabel wa'nt bout to let me be til she said all she come to say.

So I axe, "Why?"

"Cause Alberta is yellower then you are!!"

Time stopped.

I seen Mabel skippin away from me, but it was like ev'ythang was movin real slow an quiet.

Yellow? Tha's it? I'm yellow? Not beautiful, or smart, or fun... I'm jes yellow?

Then I member how I knew Miss Johnson din't mean it when she told me how pretty I was. She pro'bly wanted to say, "Alice, you jes yellow, tha's all. They be another girl lighter'n you come by directly."

All the rest of that day I thought of all the people I knew where the man was dark an his wife was light, or the other way round. Seem like nearly ev'ybody was a two-tone match, even my own daddy an mama. Is that why they was t'getha? Is that why Isaac stare at me?

Mabel Gaye was the prettiest girl I know. I got big feet an hands. I ain't hardly got no chin an what li'l I do got come to a point wit a dent in it. Plus, I always thought darker skin made you look young an rich cause it don' wrinkle. An it shine when the sun ketch it. An it feel like velvet. I only thought of myse'f as the mos beautiful cause the boys acted like I was. Now they fallin all over theyse'f fer ol' homely Alberta. They don' care that I'm smart, or can cook, or that I run like the wind in a footrace. They ain't never once care nuthin bout pretty little Mabel.

It was all so sad an stupid. It made me want to puke!

three

I was drainin the maple outta trees jes like Gretchen, the li'l pilgrim girl the younger kids was readin bout in school. It was hard an heavy work come time to switch a full bucket wit an empty one, but I din't know whure Bertha run off to. I tried to take it down by pullin it up by the handle, but that ain't work. So then I pushed it up from the bottom. It was heavy! I was holdin it round the middle an it was pushin into my stomach. I tried to walk, but it was too heavy. I got a great big cramp down in my gut, then I stumbled an fell an the edge of the bucket hit my crotch real hard before it spilt down my legs makin 'em feel warm an sticky. The handle musta broke off when I dropped it, too, cause layin curled up on a soft patch a leaves I could feel that wire handle stickin into my side.

"Bertha! He'p me, Bertha! Bertha!" I called. I tried to kick my legs, but they was stuck t'getha wit the syrup. Ev'ytime I called out or moved, I felt that wire handle poke my gut. I was too skeered to pull it out cause I thought I might bleed to death. I stayed curled up on my side, holdin my stomach callin to Bertha kinda soft.

"What'sa matter Alice? Alice? Alice?"

I heard her callin from behine me, then I felt her hand on my shoulder shakin me.

"Alice?... wake up. You sleep. Alice, wake up."

I woke up. Dawn was jes breakin an the light comin into the loft from the window washed ev'ythang in a pale blue-gray. I was full awake an I knew wa'nt no wire in me, but I still felt it stuck in my gut an my legs was still sticky.

I moaned an rocked quiet-like so as not to wake the twins cross the room. "Go get mama, Bertha. Somethin wrong. I feel a hot coal burnin in my gut!"

Bertha eased the covers back to git out from our pallet or to take a look, one. She kinda choked an said, "Wha'chu do Alice? Wha'chu do?"

I turn round slow to look at her an seen her eyes all bugged out lookin down at somethin on me. I looked down an seen blood all over ev'ywhure.

"Oh sweet Jesus, no. NO!" I screamed. I rolled over real slow, feelin round my sides an back to find out whure I been stabbed, all the while callin on our lord, "Sweet Jesus, I been stabbed! I been stabbed! Oh God, no no No No NO NONONO!!"

I don' know when Daniel an Samuel got up. I know nobody coulda slept through my racket. By the time mama an daddy was up the ladder an got the lantern lit, all us kids was cryin an screamin.

Mama was so calm an sure, that it made alla us calm down some. All she say was, "Nate, take the boys downstairs please."

Afta daddy an the boys lef', she told me to take off my gown an checked me fer cuts an stab wounds. Then mama smiled an said, "You not hurt, baby girl. You jes growin up."

"Huh?"

"This yer firs' monthly. You got to be careful round boys an not play so rough anymore, cause you can make babies now. Ev'y month, you gonna bleed fer bout a week until you too old to have babies."

"But somethin *wrong*, mama. It hurt bad. I thank somethin inside done come loose."

"Growin up hurts, baby. Yer breasts are gonna git tender an sore an start growin. Yer face might break out in puss bumps, too. But tha's jes alla part a growin up."

"But Alice ain't but twelve, mama," Bertha said lookin confused.

"Tha's right. Mos women start they monthlies when they bout twelve an keep havin 'em til they bout fifty. It's gone be yer turn soon, Berth."

"Nuh-uh!" Bertha said scrunchin up her face.

Mama jes shook her head an give Bertha a little crooked smile an say, "Go heat up some water for yer sister's bath."

****

"Happy Birfday to you!"

The biggest an best birfday I ever had was when I turned the big thirteen! Mama say I was a woman four months ago when my monthly start. But wa'nt til my age had *teen* in the number, did I feel any older. Thir-*teen*! Fine'ly a teenager, o boy, oboyoboyoboy. I had a real party an ev'ythang! Mama always baked a cake an Mr. Tucker always come by a course, cause if it wa'nt for him, there wouldn't be no presents.

But for the firs' time, seem like all my cousins was over to the house an I got to invite some of my school friends, too. Mama made two big pots of pumpkin stew wit lots of chicken cause Mr. Tucker brung over four. I made a pile a biscuits an cornbread muffins cause everybody always say I make the best there ever was. Mama made two kindsa desserts, five pecan pies an three a my favorite kinda cake, pineapple upside down. Afta we et, I opened my gifts. I got more presents than alla my other birthdays an Christmases put t'getha! I got a brand new red coat wit a black velvet collar. I got three skirts, two dresses, two blouses an a pair a saddle oxford shoes for school. Mama knit me two sweaters an a scarf. Plus, I got a mess a new underwear wit matchin brassieres. I ain't never had nuthin spankin new jes for me! We always got hand-me-downs or mama made us *new* thangs outta hand-me-downs that she took apart an resewed back into somethin else. Now I had me nuthin but new stuff. Stuff nobody else ever owned or wore before. Stuff I would hand-me-down to Bertha one day. I felt like I musta died an come back as Callie from the Sears Roebuck Cadlog!

19

"Alice, thank Mr. Tucker fer this here feast an alla these nice presents you got t'day," daddy an mama said. They stood smilin side by side next to whure Mr. Tucker sat in the rocker.

"Oh, thanky, thanky, Mr. Tucker. Much 'bliged to ya, sir." I was still sittin on the floor almos buried wit all my new stuff an the boxes an wrappin paper it all come in.

"Don'chu jes love that man?" Ant Betty axe me sittin over in the windowsill. "Ain't he jes the best?! You need to thank him better'n that, Alice. Go on over there an give him a nice big hug an a kiss!"

Ev'ybody smiled then an said thangs like, "Kiss that man!" An "Oooo chile, Mr. Tucka give *me* all them thangs, wouldn't nobody have to tell *me* what t'do!"

Mr. Tucker sat in that rocker lookin all embarrassed. He gimme a funny smile, look more like an apology. Then he open his arms an his eyes beg me to come to him.

I got up an he smiled so big. He puckered his lips an I give him a quick peck an a big hug. Ev'ybody clapped an some of the li'l boys whistled an whooped.

"You my little princess, Miss Alice." Mr. Tucker say to me. That made daddy an mama an them Oooo an Ahhh.

"You my St. Nick!" I said an ev'ybody laughed.

****

Afta that, the grown folks danced, played cards an drank corn in the house. The li'l kids played hide 'n seek in the yard. An me an my friends went to the barn.

My cousin Lillie was drankin a pop out the bottle. When she was through, Sylvester took her bottle an said, "Y'all wanna play?"

The other boys started laughin an pokin each other in the side. Alberta an Mary snickered behine they hands.

Me an Mabel looked at each other like, *What they talkin bout?*

So I axed, "What y'all talkin bout?"

"Spinna bottle, birfday girl," Sylvester said grinnin an tossin the bottle up an down in the air.

"How you play that, Sylvester? An why you grinnin like a chesir cat?!"

"Daggy baggy bloomers, Alice! You thirteen an you ain't never spinna bottle?!" Alberta blurt out like she was Queen of Spinna Bottle.

"Easy Berta, this Alice birfday." Thomas say to Alberta all soft an smooth puttin his arm round her neck. "Sylvester, show Alice how we spinna bottle."

"C'mon y'all, make a circle."

Ev'ybody stood in a circle with Sylvester in the middle.

"Y'all sit down," Sylvester said.

We sat down an Sylvester put the bottle on the ground an spinned it round. When it stopped, the neck was pointin tween Mary an Jesse. Sylvester ain't never stop grinnin, he jes bend down an spinned it again, splainin, "It gotta point clear to somebody, an when it do," the bottle stopped an pointed at Janey, "the spinna get a kiss."

Ha'f of us said, "Ugh!" or somethin like that. But Janey got up an kissed Sylvester smack dab on the lips, then spinned the bottle herself. I guess she knew this game.

Alla sudden Daniel come runnin in the door an scampered behine a bale a hay.

"What'chu sneakin in here fer boy," Thomas said, "git on outta here!"

"I not sneakin! I'm hidin in the hide n seek!" Daniel called from behine the bale.

"Well, go fine some other place to hide an tell them other li'l snotnoses you playin wit, the barn ain't no hidin place fer y'all."

Daniel jump up hotter'n a poker shoutin, "This ain't none a yer barn, Tommy! I ain't gotta listen to you!"

"It's yer sister's birfday," Sylvester said real nice. "Don't be se'fish an mess up Alice special day. Gone now, Daniel." Sence Sylvester talked quiet an nice, Daniel lef'.

Ev'ybody had moved around when Daniel an Thomas was yellin at each other, so nobody knew who the bottle was pointin at. Janey spinned it again. It pointed at me. I got up an kissed Janey on the cheek, then spinned that Grapette bottle an it pointed to ol' bad-breath Rickey. I spinned it again real quick an said, "It was tween Rickey an Mabel."

"No it wa'nt!" Rickey fussed.

"Was too!"

"Wa'nt."

"Anyway, I awready spinned it again."

"It's *her* birfday y'all," Mabel said. She got up an took the bottle. "She ain't gotta kiss Rickey ef she don' wanna. It *was* pointin tween me an Rickey, but more at me!"

While ev'ybody was still raisin Cain, Mabel kissed my cheek an got the game goin again.

It wa'nt so bad as it seemed like it coulda been at firs'. Mos people give li'l pecks, but sometimes there was a long, sexy kiss. Alberta an Mary would kiss anybody, so Rickey got a few pecks. I was glad for him cause I ain't never wanna hurt his feelins. It kep soundin to me like Daniel or somebody had snuck back in, but I was jes spooked hopin my mama an daddy wouldn't find us playin a sex game.

What I wanted more'n a little bit was to get a big, sexy kiss from Isaac. He nearly six feet tall an black as the lake at night, wit bright, straight, white teeth an deep dimples when he smile, which ain't very often. He don' act like the other boys. He quiet, he smoke an he real smart. I thank he older, like maybe fifteen, cause he came to school even later'n me. But we in the same class.

I thank he like me, too. He always lookin at me. It make me nervous an gimme a warm rush when I ketch him lookin at me, like somebody alla sudden turned up the sun.

Mary's spin ended up pointin at him. She tried to give him a big kiss, but he made it a little peck. Then he looked right at me before he spin that bottle. Afta that, I couldn't look at him or nobody. I dropped my head, closed my eyes an prayed to the bottle to pick me. Mama told me once that all prayers git ansa'd.

Somebody say, "Go on girl, wha'chu waitin fer?" That broke the quiet. Then I felt a nudge in my side an that made me jump. I opened my eyes an looked at the bottle. It was pointin straight at me! I couldn't hardly b'lieve it. I looked up an caught Isaac slippin a candy in his mouth fore walkin over to me. He was smilin so big an had his hand out to he'p me up. I felt the sun rain down on me inside that barn, when I knew it was twilight ou'side.

He slowly pulled me up an drew me to him. The smile moved up from his lips into his eyes. He brushed my lips wit his one, two, three times. Then he wrapped one arm round my waist, an the other one braced my back wit my head restin in his hand. He pressed his lips to mine. His mouth slowly worked mines open, then his peppermint tongue slipped tween my lips.

I din't know if I like swappin spit like that. I do know if anyone a the other boys had tried it, I'da hauled off an hurt'em bad! But Isaac taste so good. Fore I know anythang, he slipped the peppermint into my mouth. I sucked on it a li'l an slipped it back into his. I could hear the kids laughin an jokin, some was countin like they was tryin to time us. Yet an still, I felt like it was jes the two of us all alone in that barn, on this farm, in the world.

Til I heard a angry shout, "Wha'chall thank y'all doin?!" I felt Isaac bein snatched from me at the same time I was pushed back so hard I fell down. All the other kids was scramblin to stand up an lookin skeered. It happen so fast. In the middle of the floor Mr. Tucker was tryin to punch Isaac. He was punchin at his face, his stomach, anywhures at all, but Isaac easily blocked ev'y punch.

Afta he got tired of blockin, Isaac grabbed hold of Mr. Tucker's wrists an jes held him steady. Mr. Tucker tried to stomp Isaac feet an kick his legs, but Isaac jes step back or step around wit'out ever lettin go a his wrists.

"Lemme go boy!" Mr. Tucker near bellowed like a bull.

"You gone stop ef I do?" Isaac was cool as a cucumber.

"Lemme GO!"

"You gone stop?"

I 'ont know how long that went on. Fine'ly Mr. Tucker say, "Lemme go NOW, boy, an I won't kick yer ass!"

He talk real big, but he was sweatin an pantin all hard like he done awready been in a fight.

Isaac unnerstan Mr. Tucker jes tryin to save face. So all he say is, "Promise?" He din't point out that Mr. Tucker couldn'a kicked his ass ef he was twenty-five inches taller, twenty-five pounds lighter an twenty-five years younger!

Mr. Tucker so tired, he jes nod his head.

Isaac let him go an looked over to me, still sprawled out on the floor in shock. The smile was still in his eyes when he bend down to he'p me up.

Tha's when Mr. Tucker broke his promise.

"Don'chu touch her!" He cried an drew back a fist.

Isaac pulled me up quick, then turned round jes in time to ketch Mr. Tucker's fist in his open palm like a ball in a mitt. Then Isaac squeezed an squeezed an bent Mr. Tucker wrist backwards til he yelped an dropped to his knees.

"Don' break my hand. Please! Don' break my hand!"

"You gone stop?" Isaac was still cool, but not like before. The smile was gone outta his eyes. He wa'nt beatin Mr. Tucker up. He was beatin him down an din't care no mo bout savin his face.

Tears started rollin down Mr. Tucker's chubby cheeks, "Ah promise, son."

"I ain'chur son!" Isaac snapped an bent his wrist a li'l mo.

"Okay! Okay! Okay!" Mr. Tucker pleaded, "Ah promise!"

"Yer promise worth bout two dead flies, ain't it Tucker!"

"Ah swear fore God, Ah stop," he said in a raspy whisper.

I felt bad for Mr. Tucker an proud of Isaac who behaved more like a grown-up then the grown man he brought to his knees. I din't know what t'do when Isaac fine'ly let Mr. Tucker go. Mr. Tucker was like a gran'daddy to me an I felt like I should he'p him, even ef he did brang all this on hisse'f. He din't do no more'n my mama an daddy woulda done ef they had walked in on me gittin a long, sexy kiss. I wanted to go to Isaac, too. He the one felt like my hero. But I din't thank it be right for me to thank him for beatin down the man that felt like my gran'daddy.

Sence I ain't know what to do, I ain't do nuthin. Isaac was the firs' one to leave the barn. He din't rush out or look at anybody. He jes walk on out like it was time to go. Ev'ybody else stood round for a minute lookin kinda dumb an he'pless like we was at a fune'ral an Mr. Tucker, still crumpled over an cryin in a heap on the floor, was who we come to mourn. Ain't nobody know what to say or even whure to look. Afta'while, we jes lef', filin out one by one. I was the last one out. I look back at him jes before goin, but decided it was best to leave him be. He look so embarrassed earlier, when ev'ybody was teasin me to give him a hug an kiss. I figure, he be a lot more embarrassed now.

****

Afta we lef' the barn, ev'ybody stood in the yard watchin the kids play hide'n seek. We was all lookin at the kids, but I thank ev'ybody was seein the same thang as me, Mr. Tucker on the barn floor, an was wondrin what was gonna happen next. A noise in the bushes behine us made us all jump an look at the barn. I thank we all thought it was Mr. Tucker comin out fer round three, but it was jes li'l Verdell tryna hide before Tiny reach a hunnerd.

"I'ma go on home now, Alice," Ruby said easin on away. "Nice party. Happy birfday,"

"Wait up Ruby! I walk you home," Sydney called to her. "I'ma go too cause it's dark an dangerous an she ought'na be alone. I had a good time, Alice."

"I migh'swell go now, too," Mary say.

Then Jesse, "Thanks Alice."

Then Alberta, "See y'all Monday."

One by one, they all said g'bye then run off to ketch up wit ev'ybody else high-tailin it away from me an my troubles.

Isaac musta gone on home right afta he lef' the barn cause he the only one I ain't see go.

I was jes standin there lis'nin to the li'l kids playin in the dark. I always loved to hear li'l kids laugh. They sound like the windchimes of the Widow Petty to me. I was standin there lis'nin to they musical laughter when somebody grab my shoulders kinda rough an say, "Gotcha!"

I screamed.

It was Bertha. I skeered her when I screamed.

"Wha'chu screamin fer, girl?!" Bertha axe me.

"It's dark out here, I ain't know it was you! You can git yerse'f hurt like that, Berth."

"Well, you know it's me now, so calm down. Momma an daddy wanna see you in the house."

I prayed the ground would jes open up an suck me in. It work before. Not even a hour ago, I prayed to the bottle an it pointed at me. But ef my prayer was ansa'd this time, the ansa was no.

"Wha'chu waitin fer, Alice? Daddy an mama wan'chu now!"

I figger the ground wa'nt gonna swallow me up t'night, so I went.

"Alice?" Momma call to me soon's I come through the door.

"I know you havin fun wit yer friends, but yer other guests is bout to leave."

I jes stood there starin like a deer in headlights. I ain't know what she want or what I was s'poze to do.

"What do ya say, Alice?" Mama axed, facin me an dartin her eyes from side to side to let me know she talkin bout these folks in the room. Here I thought she was wantin me to say how sorry I am bout Mr. Tucker, and I was jes bout to, too. But he ain't nowhures round. That was my guilt, not my mama.

"Oh!.... Thanky, all y'all. Y'all made my firs' day as a teenager real special. I'ma always member it."

As they pass out the door, ev'ybody gimme a little hug or kiss me on my cheek or forehead. Some of the ladies, even though they smilin, look to me to be kinda sad. Firs', I'm thankin they know bout Mr. Tucker.

Then I'm thankin, lookin at me remine them a how much growin up kin hurt. Then I'm thankin, they pro'bly look to me like I look to them.

I know I'm smilin too, but inside I'm sad. I know somethin they don' know an it ain't good. We all jes lef' that old man in the barn by hisse'f layin on the floor. I wonder ef he still there, or ef he lef', or ef he waitin for ev'ybody t'leave before he come tell on me. My best birfday ever, jes become my worse, an it all jes make me feel sad.

I'm also thankin, why is some of these ladies lookin at me so sad? What they know that I don' know that ain't good?

four

Ain't nobody never say nuthin to me. Mr. Tucker come over the next day reg'ler as rain. It was Sunday an he always brang some kinda meat. We had enough leftovers from yestiddy an mama plan on heatin that up. But Mr. Tucker walk in wit a rump roast an that made mama squeal! We ain't had one of them sence the firs' time Mr. Tucker come to give daddy a job.

We went to church an when we got home, Bertha an me he'ped mama cook an set the table. Afta we et, we sang songs. Then the twins, Berth an me read the poems we was gonna hafta know by heart for poetry week in school. Afta'while Daddy said we oughta go out an play before the sun go down. But when we was leavin daddy remind me, "You a young lady now, Alice. You jes watch yer brothers an sister."

I din't quite git that. Was I s'poze to sit on the porch an watch Bertha an them run round, whoopin it up in the yard like I was fragile or sick or old? I mean, I wa'nt even a whole two years older'n Bertha! 'Sides, I wa'nt on my monthly right that minute, an even ef I was, I woulda still had to take gym at school.

Anyways, I sat on the porch steps an watched 'em race. They wanted to see who could touch the chinaberry tree firs' runnin in from the road. The twins ain't had a fat rat's tail of a chance of beatin Bertha. It was cute watchin 'em try, though. Afta bout a dozen tries, they got tired of that. They wanna go down by the creek out back an see who could catch the mos crawdads.

Daniel so silly, the lease little thang kin make him forget what he set out to do. We git down by the creek an there was a coupla bullfrogs jumpin round like the water was hot. Daniel crouch down an tried hoppin like them, then Samuel, then Bertha. She made us all crack up cause she look more like a grasshopper wit them long legs a hers.

I din't feel like sittin round jes watchin the fun anymore. I said, "Le's run another race an give Bertha a exter challenge... like *ME*!"

The twins jump up an down shoutin YEA! Bertha stood to the side bein quiet an lookin kinda curious. I thank the twins thank I was gonna have Bertha to ride me on her back or drag me holdin onta her ankles or somethin. I told Samuel to take off his t-shirt then I tole Bertha to stick in her lef' foot, while I stuck my right foot through the neck of it. We pulled the bottom part of the shirt up over our knees an tied it. I said, "Me an Bertha three laigs against y'alls four!"

It took Bertha an me jes as long to git back to the startin line as it did for us to git to the finish cause we was still tryna git our wrapped two laigs to move like one. So really, it was a race now tween the twins. In the beginnin, we kep fallin down. I din't want Bertha to git hurt sence this was my idea, so when we was fallin, I pull to my side an that make Bertha mos'ly fall on me. Afta'while, I got me a big thigh bruise an I skinned the palm a my lef' hand purty good. Yet an still, it was more fun this way. Lease we all laughed more.

We run from the creek to the strawberry patch up aways maybe twenny times or more. I felt so beat up an tired afta runnin like that, I couldn't wait to wade in the creek. We took off our socks an shoes an was steppin from rock to rock, make-believin we was indians fishin fer supper.

Daniel had him a stick, call hisse'f gonna spear fish wit. We kep teasin him, "Daniel! Spear this here crawdad!" An Daniel would try, wit his silly se'f, splashin water all over the place an gittin mosta the rocks wet an slippery. Sence I'm the oldest an the biggest, I led the way through the creek wit no perticuler place in mind.

"Daniel! C'mere spear this here can a beans!" I 'ont know what made me t'say that, but we laughed so hard Samuel blew a big ole fart. He always fartin when he laugh or git excited an it ain't no joke! It smell like dirty mildew socks or garlic mornin breath, only worse.

When Samuel farted we all screamed "PeeeeYouuuu!" an scramble to git away. But the rocks was all slippery from Daniel splashin wit the spear fishin, so we was slippin an slidin around. I jes got myse'f up on one big rock wavin my arms round tryna ketch my balance an fore I know anythang, Bertha done plop her big foot down on my rock an it slid out from her an knock into mine. I loss my balance an land face firs' smack dab in the middle of the creek. That water was cold, cold! I turned over, but stayed sittin in the water cause it feel good on my thigh bruise an on my hand where I skinned the palm. Daniel, Samuel an Bertha jes stood there starin at me like they wanna say, "Oooo, you gonna git it!" or "Girl, git out that water fore you ketch a death a cold!" But they ain't say nuthin. I was the firs' one to talk.

"Bertha, you kin do a full split!"

Ev'ybody look at her then. Even she look down and her eyes git big cause she ain't know she was all sprawled out like that.

"Y'all he'p Bertha git up wit'out none a y'all fallin in the creek. I got t'go wring my clothes out fore we head back."

****

Mama seen us comin through the backyard an say, "There y'all is. I was jes bout t'call y'all. Mr. Tucker fixin t'leave. C'mon give him a hug an kiss g'bye."

The twins kissed him on the cheek an got bear hugs. Then Bertha give him a quick li'l shy hug an pecked his cheek. Ain't nobody see I was soakin wet yet cause it was kinda dark ou'side. Mr. Tucker puckered up his lips an like yestiddy, I give him a little peck. But to me, yestiddy was differnt, bein as it was my birfday. I hope he don' thank this s'poze to be the way I kiss him alla time bein as I'm a teenager now. Anyway, afta the peck, he spread his arms all wide. I had'ta hug him, so I did.

"Omigosh! Thaniel? Grace? Y'all know Miss Alice here is soakin wet?! Why you so wet, Princess? Go on inside now fore you ketch yer death a cold!"

I was jes bout to go inside, but mama grabbed me back an start feelin all over my clothes an hair, "Why you so wet Alice? Look, yer hair is turnin back an ev'ythang!"

"Alice," daddy was tryna stay on simmer, but I could feel his boil startin to bubble. "What I say when y'all firs' went ou'side? Din't I say fer you jes to watch, Alice?

"Yessuh, y'tell me to jes watch."

"Then how you git wet? Wha'chu been doin?"

"Nate," mama said, "let her git inside an out them wet clothes fore you preach, okay honey?"

Soon's I git in the house, Mr. Tucker leggo a yelp an say, "How you cut yer laig, Puddin?"

I couldn't see nuthin fer my skirt, so I liffed it up an seen a cut dribblin blood jes b'low my knee. It was jes a li'l thang, not too deep or nuthin. But I migh'swella had my laig cut off the way ev'ybody went on bout my thigh bruise. It was big an red an purple an blue. It look like a storm brewin 'neath the skin.

"Wha'chu been doin, Alice?" Daddy start up again.

"I fell inna creek."

"She was tryna he'p me," Bertha pipe up right quick talkin fast. "Samuel blew a big fart an me an Daniel was runnin away from him. But the rocks was slippery an I slid into a full split tween two rocks. Alice come tryna he'p me, but she slip an fell in the creek. It was a accident... Really!"

I could tell daddy wanna say more, but he din't. Bertha ain't like a lotta li'l sisters I know, that tell stories to try to cause confusion fer fun. She look out for me better'n I do for myse'f mos times.

"You a young lady now, Miss Alice. You gotta promise to stop hurtin yerself...promise me, Princess?" Mr. Tucker say.

I'm thankin, *Wha'chu got to do wit anythang*? Ef I din't hafta hug an kiss you, pro'bly wouldn't nobody even know I was wet. An ef my daddy an mama ain't tell me to promise them, why you thank I gotta promise you?

But I know what I'm s'poze to say, so that's what I say, "I promise."

'Sides, I thank I'm really hearin him say somethin he ain't said. Like he tryna bargain wit me, ef I don' hurt myse'f no mo, he won't tell bout the barn. So I promise. But I wa'nt *tryna* hurt myself an ef it happen again, it jes happen.

****

Mama, Bertha an me cleaned the kitchen afta Mr. Tucker was gone an daddy an the twins went to bed. When we finish, mama had me sit down an she put ice wrapped up in a rag on my thigh bruise. She say, "Us girls gotta look out for one another." She look up at me then over to Bertha sittin side me at the table an add, "But lookit who I'm talkin to. Y'all awready know that! Y'all want some tea?"

We said yeah, so she put the kettle on to boil. Bertha try to he'p, but mama shoo her away. So we jes watch her put the leaves in the pot to steep an set the cups out fer us. Afta'while, she put the milk an sugar out an strain the tea into our cups. Then she fix all three teas the way she know we like it, light 'n sweet.

We sippin our tea, thankin our own thoughts when alla sudden mama say calm an kinda quiet, "Y'all have fun down to the creek t'day?"

We wa'nt spectin that. We sprayed our tea all over the table an mama. I look all bug-eyed over to Bertha an she lookin back all bug-eyed at me. Then we both look over at mama. She makin funny little noises an it look like it painin' her, tryin so hard not t'laugh. There's tea spray all over mama face, in her hair, an all over the table. She got tears comin down her face while she laugh an she holdin her sides. Soon, me an Bertha is laughin an cryin an holdin our sides like her.

Ain't nobody say nothin else that night. Wa'nt nuthin else to say afta *Us girls gotta look out for one another*. We all know that, an *tha*'s a promise.

five

"Roses is red. Violet's is blue. Candy is sweet an it make a good treat," Henry Thompson said for poetry week in school, then bust out laughin like it was a joke.

"Henry, uhm... that was nice, but these were supposed to be poems written by someone else." Miss Johnson say.

"Franklin writ this'un, not me!" Henry said pointin at his best friend.

"Well, I guess I didn't make myself clear. I wanted you to learn a poem that was *published*. I'll accept this one today, but I want you to find another poem in the library and read it to the class tomorrow." She said fore lookin at her watch.

"Okay, that's it for the primary grades. We'll break for lunch and hear from the upper class students this afternoon."

All the grades in one classroom now, sence it's spring an a bunch of kids had to drop out to he'p wit they farms. Mos the kids still in school is here causa Mr. Tucker. More'n likely, they daddy is workin his trees an gettin paid cash money. Wa'nt but a few ways a makin cash money round Smedley: Sell yer crops, sell bake goods, make an sell corn likka, work fer Mr. Tucker or hire yerse'f out to white folks an take care of they house an kids. Ev'ybody ruther work fer theyse'f or work fer Mr. Tucker, but he ain't needin that many people alla time. So we was exter lucky my daddy is purt near a reg'ler em-ploy-yee. Isaac lucky that way, too. I hear tell ev'ybody in his house is big an strong as a bull, even the womens. Isaac daddy is purt near a reg'ler wit Mr. Tucker, too, bein as he kin do the work a three or four mens. So Isaac git to go to school much as me.

Sence my birfday, Isaac ain't shy bout talkin to me. We spend mos all our lunches talkin bout this an that. He real smart, too. Even smarter'n I thought at firs'. Even smarter'n me! He jes so quiet before, ain't nobody know cept maybe Miss Johnson.

One time I axe him, "How come you don' be Miss Johnson he'per?"

"Cause thadda take time from my readin." He say, "Ah'm tryna read alla books in the liberry."

"Git out! What fer?"

"So I know ev'ythang anybody round hear could know, ef they was t'take the time."

"An then what? Afta you know ev'ythang there is, then what?"

"Then I got mo possibilities. All book learnin do is give you mo possibilities. Ef it wa'nt no school, ev'ybody in Smedley be a farmer or be married to a farmer. Miss Johnson got book learnin an she a teacher. An I 'ont b'lieve she studdin gittin married."

"Miss Johnson don' count. She ain't from round here."

"Why you say that?"

"She don' talk like she from round here."

"Could be cause she went to college an learn to talk bettah."

"You smart an I ain't dumb, but we don' talk like her."

"Ev'ybody that talk like her ain't smart, Alice. An ev'ybody that talk like us ain't dumb."

"Yeah, but I still don' thank you should talk bout her ef she ain't from round here."

"Ef she from round here or not don' make no never mind. Womens from round here ain't my point. Seem like womens ev'ywhure git married mos'ly cause they thank they need somebody to take care of 'em. But book learnin make you to know differnt. An ef you know bettah, you do bettah. Booker T. Washington was a slave. He got book learnin an started *his own* school! They teachin black mens how to fly planes in his school down in Tuskegee, Alabama right now. An them black pilots is kickin all kindsa butt in this here war.

"Bessie Coleman wanted to fly. But wouldn't nobody in this country teach her how cause she was colored. So she went to France to learn. *An* she had to learn *French firs'*! She did it though. An she the *firs'* American lady to git a international license t'fly. She even got hers fore Amelia Earhart, that white woman you hear s'much bout."

"I ain't hear bout no Melia Earhart. I 'ont hardly hear nuthin bout the war. I fergit we in one sometime!"

"Well, don' fergit. Don' fergit nuthin. School is a blessin cause knowledge is power. Tha's how come in slavery times they kep the slaves from book learnin. Tha's how come Jim Crow the real president. We ain't got enough schools or teachers or books or heat inna winter or patches in the roof inna rain. I ain't jes talkin bout in Smedley eitha, I mean *nowhures*. That ain't no mistake. It's on purpose. Maybe tha's why I be readin ev'ythang. We got to learn what all need changin, befo' we kin change it."

"But'chu know so much awready."

"I don't know nuthin, nexta what I'm gonna know. But I know one thang...you still owe me the resta my kiss from spinna bottle," he say then pucker his lips all up, his eyes laughin at me.

"Boy, go someplace!" I push his arm an ack like I ain't studdin him, but he know tha's all I thank bout half the time.

Tha's the way Isaac be doin. We be talkin bout one thang, then he quick change it to somethin else... usually that spinna bottle kiss. I thank he like to make red roses blossom in my cheeks an t'hold my hands so he kin feel the tremble he put there.

****

That afta'noon, we git to recite our poems. I thank ev'ybody favorite one was Isaac doin "When Malindy Sing" by Paul Laurence Dunbar. It was so beautiful cause it wa'nt jes bout us, *it was us*. Wit'out apology. *Our* language, *our* rhythms, raw an real, wit all our possibilities. Ev'yone a us know Malindy. She our mama, our antie, our sista... Malindy was us.

Afta he was through, I tole Isaac I wanted me a copy, so he recited it for me while I writ some down.

When Malindy Sings
"G'way an' quit dat noise, Miss Lucy
Put dat music book away;
Wat's de use to keep on tryin'?
Ef you practise twell you're gray?"
You can't sta't no notes a-flyin'
Lak de ones dat rants and rangs
F'om de kitchen to de big woods when Malindy sings
You ain't got the nachel o'gans
Fu to make de soun' come right,
You ain't got de tuns an' twistin's
Fu to make it sweet an' light
Tell you one thin now, Miss Lucy,
An' I'm tellin' you fu' true
When it come to re'l right singin'
T'ain't no easy thin to do.

Afta Isaac was done, Miss Johnson say, "That was excellent, Isaac. Class, you should know that Paul Laurence Dunbar was chosen to participate in President McKinley's inaugural celebration and when requested to perform one of his *lively poems*, he chose to recite 'When Malindy Sings.'

"Dunbar was a brilliant poet who is best known for his works written in the so-called *Negro* dialect. But it's really a *southern* dialect, isn't it? Everyone here in Smedley speaks the same whether they're black or white or green or grisly. Dunbar wrote in this dialect as an art form. But he spoke and wrote *High English* or the *Queen's English*, also. One of my favorite Dunbar poems goes like this...

We wear the mask that grins and lies,
It hides our cheeks and shades our eyes,
This debt we pay with human guile;
With torn and bleeding hearts we smile.
And mouth with myriad subtleties.
Why should the world be over wise,
In counting all our tears and sighs?
Nay, let them only see us, while
We wear the mask.
We smile, but, Oh great Christ, Our cries
To Thee from tortured souls arise.
We sing, but oh the clay is vile
Beneath our feet, and long the miles;
But let the world dream otherwise,
We wear the Mask!

We spend the rest of the day talkin bout differnt poems an the power a words. Sylvester recite the words to *Amazin' Grace* like it's a poem. Tha's my favorite song cause mama name is Grace an even though she jes awdinery, she purty amazin to me. Yit an still, I'm surprise Miss Johnson say tha's okay fer Sylvester to say words to a song. She say lyrics is poetry too. She say my poem, *The Creation*, was a good example of how pow'ful words is. The Book of John in the Bible say, "In the beginnin was the Word, an the Word was wit God, an the Word was God..." She say ef you a Christian, then you b'lieve the Bible is the book of truth. *The Creation* show how ev'ythang come to be from God's sayso. Same thang fer Roscoe's poem, *Somebody Said That It Couldn't Be Done*. Words kin hold ya back, too, an keep ya from doin thangs ya oughta do an they kin make ya do thangs ya ain't got no bizness doin. She say ya gotta be strong enough an smart enough to ignore devil talk an do wha'chu know is right.

School seem to always end real quick. But then, I couldn't wait fer afta school eitha cause then it jes be the two of us an Miss Johnson talk to me bout whatever I want, mos'times.

****

"Wha'tuk ya so long?!"

36

Isaac like to skeer me silly steppin out from behine a tree when I was walkin home from school.

"Boy...You bettah stop creepin an peepin behine trees like that! Less'n you lookin to git hurt."

"Who gonna hurt me...you?" He took my books an walked side me. "Wha'tuk ya so long, I was worried."

"Me an Miss Johnson was talkin."

"Bout what?"

"Lot'sa thangs. Y'know how she said we need to always do what we know is right? Well this afta'noon, she say even doin wha'chu know is right ain't mean you safe. She say they sayin millions a Jews in Yerp been kilt in this here war jes cause they Jews. She say millions an millions of colored peoples been dyin righ'chere in this country from slave days up to now jes cause they's colored. Folks don' say that though. They make up lies bout colored mens rapin or reckless eyeballin some white woman an them lies gits 'em hung or burnt to death!"

Isaac start lookin hard an mean an skeered at the same time.

"But ain't no white mens ever been charged wit rapin no black womens in America. An we wear the proof of they crime wit our light skins an light eyes an strait kinda hair that we be callin *good*. Miss Johnson say she kin be kilt t'marra jes fer teachin us what she did t'day!"

"A lotta what she say remine me of wha'chu said at lunch."

"Readin the same books might cudda gimme the same idears," Isaac say.

"It might cudda. I was still thankin she from somewhures else. So I axe her, 'Whure you from, Miss Johnson?' I don' know what make me to axe that. It jes pop out.

"'I was born jes ou'side a Macon, Georgia,' she say. Then she splain she move wit her family to Detroit as a li'l girl in the Great Negro Migration Nawth. She move here to Smedley seven years ago when she gradiate from school an found out there was a need fer colored teachers inna south.

"I axe her ef they gotta lotta colored teachers up nawth?

"She say naw. But the only reason she got a education is cause her family moved nawth. She say she wanna give the same vantage to chirrens who family din't, or couldn't, move nawth.

"I axe ef tha's whure she learn to talk.

"She say, 'Schoolin, in perticuler college, demand tha'chu speak english the way it's writ.' She say she kin talk jes like alla us, an she do when she ou'side a school. She do that fer purtection. Cause ef she don', some people in town migh'would thank she was bein up'ty an had fergot her place. She say that fergittin yer place is the main reason they lynch in this country, an they do lynch colored *womens*, too."

Isaac walk me home an we talk bout kids we know or hear bout that was kilt round here. Titus was only twelve when they found him beat up an drowned in Pritchard's pond. Emmanuel was fifteen an Butchie was nineteen when they was hung by a crowd that tuk pitchers an serve food, like they was at a picnic.

Isaac say he seen some of them people in the pitchurs righ'round here. No wonder he look so mean an skeered. We got quiet afta that an I start feelin mean an skeered myse'f.

Afta I git to the walk lead up to my house, Isaac gimme back my books wit'out a word an kep on down the road.

****

I was thankin s'many bad thoughts bout s'many thangs afta Isaac lef' me, my stomach was threatenin to empty itse'f any minute. I axe mama could I work in the garden so case I git sick, I wouldn't mess up her clean floors.

I was pickin beans off the stalk when I heard a big commotion out in the fron'yard. Daddy come racin in the drive, kickin up a dust storm an blarin the horn on the truck Mr. Tucker borrowed him.

"Gracie! Gracie-girl! C'mon out here!" Daddy was callin to mama.

Mama come out fussin, "Nate you know I'm tryna git suppa onna table! Wha'chu want?!" But'chu could tell she was jes as curious to fine out what he was raisin Cain fer. Afta I heard the front do' slam, I come round to the side of the house an watch from there.

Daddy was standin wit his chest all puffed out wit one arm wrapped round Isaac like he was his long, lost son or somethin.

"I wan'chu meet Ikey here. He is one strong, brave bugger what jes save mah life! Y'hear me Gracie, this boy here done jes save mah life!" He said that twice an ruff'd Isaac hair, an Isaac look proud an shy. I notice how big Isaac really is fer the firs' time. He stood almos as tall as my daddy. He ain't quite as big, but he shaped the same wit a wide chest an the tee-ni-niest l'il waist, round bubble muscles in his shoulders an arms, an great big hands.

"Well, I'm please to meet'cha Mr. Ikey. An I'm happy you done saved my Nate here. I don' know what I would do wit'out him. Y'all c'mon into the house now, an you kin tell me over hot peach cobbler bout how ya come to be a hero, Mr. Ikey."

Oh boy, I thought, now I'ma hafta figger a reason fer me to be inna house so soon, ef I'm gonna git to hear this here juicy story.

I was out there a minute or two tryna figger how to snag my finger, but not too bad, jes so's I could run inna house to clean the cut. When alla sudden mama come callin me, "Alice! C'mon to the house."

I wa'nt sure ef this was good or not, so's I took my time an brung ha'f a basket a beans.

"Wha'tuk ya so long, Alice?" Daddy axe me wit a big grin. "Ikey here say he know you from school."

"Yessuh. Hey Ikey," I try to keep from laughin at *Ikey* so's daddy wouldn't know I'm funnin him.

Isaac smile an say, "Hey," but his eyes is laughin an sayin, "I'ma git'chu later!"

"Is a small world, I tell ya." Daddy start t'tell his story. "I work wit Ikey daddy over to Mr. Tucker's mill, choppin an haulin them trees. Ikey here the spit of his daddy, too. Big an strong as a bull!

"Now I was drivin on down Tenderfoot road when alla sudden three youngins pop out from nowhures chasin a bicycle rim wit they sticks. They ain't never lookit me. They jes a chasin that rim on out into the road. I had to swerve to keep from hittin 'em. Y'all know Tenderfoot jes a narrow road. When I swerve, the truck slid down the bank there an I come near to drownin myse'f in Copper Crick. I'm stuck there knee deep inna mud watchin Mr. Tucker tars sink lower an lower an lis'nin to them youngins spin they rim on up the road. Alla sudden, I look up an Ikey here standin at the back a the truck pointin my rifle dead center of my head. I froze thankin, 'Why Freeman wanna kill ME?!' Cause he the spit a his daddy an tha's who I'm thankin he is.

"Then he shoot!

"Blood an wet chunks a flesh splat my face. Then the whole body of that cottonmouth snake fall out the tree onto my shoulder. I like'ta peed my pants! Ikey had jes shot the haid offa that serpent what was hangin offa the branch right over me, only I ain't know 'twas Ikey yet.

"I say, 'Freeman, ya jes save my life! How you know I was heah?'

"He say, 'How you know my name?'

"I kin see now that he ain't who I thought he was, so I tell him bout Freeman over to the job an he tell me tha's his daddy. I tell him my name then we gits back to the truck. Ikey put a buncha dry sticks an leaves an thangs neath the tars an he'p me push it on outta alla that mud. I be layin there right now, dead at the bank a that crick, ef it wa'nt fer Ikey!"

Mama was heatin up the cobbler all this time, but afta daddy finish the story, she ain't wanna serve dessert fore supper. She axe Isaac to stay fer supper an promise it be ready in thirty minutes, but Isaac say he got to git home an work the fields some fore the sun go down cause they ain't had much luck wit they crops this year.

Mama invite him to come back t'marra. Daddy say ef he come right afta school, he put him to work fer some of our crops cause our'n been real good. Isaac like to fall offa his chair, but he say that be fine.

Afta he gone, mama like to fall over too, from daddy tellin stories bout how we had good crops this year. Ev'ybody work hard. God give us all the same sun an rain. Ev'ybody seeds come from Mr. Charles gen'ral store. So ain't nobody have no better luck wit they crops this year then anybody else.

But daddy quick say, "How come I cain't thank that boy proper fer savin my life, Gracie? Ain't my life worth a few beans an onions?!"

That was the end of that. We all agree daddy worth at lease a few greens.

six

Afta that, Isaac come by mos days. He do all kindsa jobs round the house. He fix the roof an him an daddy rebuilt the porch wit lumber from the mill. He made toys fer the twins outta wires an sticks, whatever he find. The boys love him like he the best toy of all. Daddy an momma love him, too. Sometime daddy give him firewood, or they go huntin an daddy let him take all the game, steada veg'tables. Sometime mama fix a soup or dessert for him to take home.

There's a lot more kids in Isaac family, so ev'y li'l bit he'p, even ef he jes eatin wit us so's they kin split his share at home. But he the oldest like me, an they need him to work at home an do the same thangs fer them that he do fer us.

I could tell daddy really depend on Isaac bein round. He give him money when he kin, too, cause Mr. Freeman wa'nt gittin no more work over to Mr. Tucker mill. That make daddy hafta work harder an longer hours, but he git a li'l more money so's he kin give some to *Ikey*.

****

A month er two go by like that an then Isaac stop comin to school.

"Why ain'chu been t'school?" I axe him comin into the field whure he been plowin wit Lazybones, our mule.

"My daddy ain't been to work fer Tucker in ten weeks. He need my he'p bad now. We fix cars t'getha t'make cash money. Comin here is a blessin cause it he'ps out my family a lot, wit food an stuff. Tha's why I come. Fer that, an t'see you."

He said the las lookin me straight in my eyes an he look more ser'us then when he near to broke Mr. Tucker hand.

I din't know what t'say or what t'do. I jes stood there like a ninny, blushin from my sca'p to my toes. I guess he seen how nervous he make me, so he eased up some.

"Cause ya still owe me the resta my kiss from spinna bottle," he say an puckered up.

"Boy, go someplace!" I push his arm, then scratch Lazybones on the neck b'fo I run to the house. Isaac laughter floatin behine me like a feather on a breeze, soft an loopy.

****

Mama made a big pot of stew for supper. I was sittin at the kitchen table doin my school work an mama axe me to call Bertha inside. When Bertha come in, mama tell her t'go git Isaac.

I say, "Mama, how come you ain't axe me t'go git Isaac?"

"Cause you busy doin yer school work, Alice," she say.

That ain't make no sense to me. She stop me from doin my work t'go call Bertha. She coulda save a step an jes have me to call Isaac, but I ain't say nuthin.

When Isaac come, mama say, "We gonna eat a li'l later t'night, Ikey. Nate an Mr. Tucker workin to the mill a li'l late, so we gonna wait fer them, okay?"

42

"I thanky m'am, but Ah'm gonna hafta go on home. I promise poppa I he'p him wit Mr. Hawkins truck. He promise t'have it fix by day afta t'marra. But I 'preciate the offer."

"Well, I fixed a mess a stew. I'ma pack some up for you an yer family. When it's done, I have Bertha t'come git you."

"Thanky m'am. I be through plowin directly," he say to mama, then steal a look at me b'fo goin back ou'side.

"Bertha, come he'p me pack up some of this food fer Ikey," mama say.

"I he'p you mama," I tole her, "I done writ all I'ma write t'day."

"Well, you kin clean yerse'f up an set the table fer yer daddy an Mr. Tucker then. Bertha, c'mon now. Don' make me say it twice."

Me an Bertha do what mama say, but we lookin an talkin to each other in signs, knittin our brows an shruggin our shoulders. We don' know wha's goin on an we jes keep sayin that over an over to each other wit our eyes.

Afta'while, Isaac come in wit'out mama sendin for him. He say, "Lazybones back in his stall an the tools inna shed. I pro'bly cain't come t'marra, but maybe the next day I kin."

"Thanky there s'much, Ikey. Ef you wait, Nate be glad t'run ya home."

"Ef I mosey on now, I be there directly." He collect the food mama put out fer him an say, "Thanks agin, m'am. Bertha. Alice." An leave. He seem sad to me, but he migh'could jes be tired.

Not ten minutes later, Mr. Tucker come huffin an puffin through the door. "Wha'chu doin walkin, Mr. Tucker? An whure Nate at?" Mama axe.

"He see that boy come from here an give him a ride home," Mr. Tucker say like *that boy* ain't brang him to his knees squealin like a pig, not too long pass now.

"That don' splain why you walkin," mama say.

"Ah tole Nate I walk on t'the house an he kin take that boy on home."

"Why'nt you jes go wit'em?"

"We was righ'chere, jes barely up the road a piece. I ain't wanna go so far out the way when we was righ'chere."

"Well, sit yerse'f down an take a load off. Alice, pour Mr. Tucker a cool drank."

I start to pour him some water, when mama jump all over me like it's poison!

"Not water, Alice, give him a ice tea!"

"That there water be jes fine now, Miss Alice," Mr. Tucker say an smile for the firs' time sence he come in the house.

It hit me then that he jes bout always smilin an happy lookin, but he ain't happy now. I know is causa jes seein Isaac. I cain't wait for this to all be over.

When daddy come home, he wash up an bless the food then we all gits to eatin.

Mama the best cook in the world I bet. Lease she the best in Smedley. Her stew wit my biscuits make ev'ybody near to hurt theyse'f, eatin like it's they last supper. Ain't nobody got room f'dessert, but ain't nobody wanna turn down mama's baked apples wit cream. So we tuk a li'l break in the fron'room.

"What that boy name you carry home t'night, Nate?" Mr. Tucker say nice an easy.

"Tha's Ikey, Freeman's boy. I thought you'da knowed that! He the spit a his daddy."

"Yeah. He did look famil'er," was all he said at firs', then he axe, "What he doin over here?"

"That boy a real life saver! I got yer truck stuck inna mud down by Copper Crick a while back. They's a cottonmouth water moccasin hangin offa branch right over me bout to bite my head off. That boy come from outta nowhures an shoots that snake outta that tree. Then prac'ly push yer truck on out that mud by hisse'f!"

"Well, he shore sound like a life saver to me... But that don' splain what he doin here t'nite, Nate."

Mr. Tucker tryna sound like he don' care, but you kin tell he do. His lips is jerkin in the corners whure he tryna smile, but don' really feel like it.

Daddy musta notice somethin wrong cause he stop soundin so happy bout Isaac. "Well, he save my life that day. He real strong an he stop by from time t'time an he'p me wit the heavy work round here."

Then daddy say somethin real strange, "I thank him an Bertha might be sweet," an he give a li'l wink.

"*WHA*...?!" Bertha stop what she bout to say, cause we wa'nt raised to disagree or even question our parents. But it's too late cause Mr. Tucker heard her.

"That true, Bertha? You an Ikey Freeman sweet on each other?"

"Who ready for baked apples an cream?" Mama axe an pop up t'the kitchen all of a sudden, like she ain't hear Mr. Tucker axe Bertha a question… one I wanna hear the ansa to, too.

"Ah'm still too full, mama. I'ma go t'bed," Bertha say.

"Me too, mama," I say.

"You girls kiss Mr. Tucker g'night fore ya go upstairs," daddy say.

Bertha peck him on the cheek an give him a hug. He lookit me an puckers up, but I peck him on the cheek like Bertha an give him a hug. He lookit me kinda funny an glance quick at daddy.

Daddy say, "Alice, di'ja kiss Mr. Tucker g'night?"

"Yessuh, I did," I say to daddy. Then I say to Mr. Tucker, "G'night Mr. Tucker, suh."

A quick li'l somethin cross his face, like pain or anger. My stomach start feelin like it's grindin an my mouth taste sour in the back like I'm bout to be sick. I kiss an hug my daddy an mama real quick an go on up the ladder even fore Bertha.

When Bertha come up, I'm standin by the winder lookin at the moon. She come stand by me an don' say a word. Afta'while I ask her, "You sweet on Isaac?"

"Nah...ugh! He nice an ev'ythang, but I 'ont want that boy!" I give a li'l laugh an poke her in the side t'make her laugh. I knowed she say that. My stomach churns start feelin bettah. Afta that, we jes standin in the winder watchin the night. Then Bertha axe kinda quiet, "Why you thank daddy say that?"

"I 'ont know Berth. I 'ont know."

Daniel an Samuel come up afta'while an we still jes standin in the winder.

"Wha'chall do...?"

"Sshhush. We ain't doin nuthin," I said. "Y'all go on to bed now." For some reason I ain't want mama an them downstairs to hear no talkin or nuthin up here.

While they was gittin ready for bed, the twins start chantin real soft, "Berth an Ikey sittin inna tree, k-i-s-s-i-n-..."

"Y'all shet up an go on to bed now!" Bertha liked to bark they heads off. They laugh then, cause tha's jes what they wanted.

****

45

We was all tucked away in our pallets an had been for a while. Ev'ybody was sleepin cept me. I know cause li'l as they is, the twins got snores awready. An Bertha grind her teeth when she sleep. I ain't heard no talkin comin from downstairs, but the lanterns still lit, so they must still be up. I ain't never hear the truck eitha, so Mr. Tucker must still be here. It been a strange day. I wonder what it mean?

seven

Daddy ain't work in a month of Sundays, but the weather was so nice an all the time the farmin an schoolin an he'pin to raise my *siblings* (which I found out mean my sister an the twins) took up, I ain't pay no tention. I was fixin supper an he'pin the twins wit they take-aways one day, when daddy come bustin through the door.

"Alice, you git yer li'l fast tail out chere...Righ'*NOW*!" He say, then he bust right back out.

Bertha looked over her shoulder an gimme a look like wha'chu do? I give her a li'l shrug cause I 'ont know, then I told the twins to keep doin they take-aways til I git back.

Daddy was down by the chinaberry tree pacin back an forth tryna keep his temper, but I could see he was losin it. When he looked up an seen me comin, he jes stop dead in his tracks.

"I wan'chu to tell me bout wha'chu was doin in the barn on yer birfday."

Daddy was jes standin there wit his knuckles planted on his hips lookin real strong an talkin kinda low an soft, but it was a lot skeerier than ef he was yellin an pitchin a fit. I was so skeered I couldn't talk. I jes stood there takin turns studdin his face an his chest.

"I awready done heard one side. Now I wanna hear yers. Now, Alice!"

I fine'ly made myse'f say, "We was playin spinna bottle."

"I heard y'all was doin a li'l more than jes spinnin a bottle."

"Well, afta the bottle stop, the spinna git..."

"I know how spinna bottle is played!" He say b'fo I could finish.

I'm wondrin two thangs now, how he know bout how t'play spinna bottle an what did he hear we was doin?

"We wa'nt..." I started again.

"*YOU* Alice! I axed Wha'*CHU* was doin! I ain't axe bout yer frien's!"

"I was kissin a boy...but only cause the bottle stop on me."

"That ain't all you was doin...was it?"

"It is too! I 'on't know who tellin you stories, but tha's all I did.... kiss a boy!" I din't mean to sound so fresh, but somebody tole my daddy a big ole story an now he was mad at me!

Daddy stood there lookin at me. He ain't say nuthin bout me smellin myse'f or nuthin, so I know he thankin bout somethin else. I thank he b'lieve me. But somethin botherin him. Afta' while he axe, "What happen afta y'all kiss?"

"Well... Mr. Tucker run in b'fo it was over... He pull us apart an I fell down. Then he try to wail on Isaac... it was him I was kissin... but Mr. Tucker couldn't git in a lick. He promise to stop tryin to fight Isaac, but that was a story cause afta Isaac let'im go, he took another swang. Isaac caught his fist b'fo it hit him, an make him stop for real, then Isaac leave. Then ev'ybody leave."

"How Isaac make Mr. Tucker stop fightin *for real*?"

"When Isaac caught Mr. Tucker fist in his hand that last time, he wouldn't let it go til Mr. Tucker stop fer shore."

"How he know Mr. Tucker wa'nt gonna break his word again?"

48

I din't wanna git Isaac in trouble, but I couldn't lie eitha. I thank the truth cain't hurt him cause he ain't do nuthin wrong, but I still ain't wanna say nuthin.

"What he do, Alice? Did he beat him up?"

"Nah he ain't beat him up." I wanna say, He beat him down, daddy. He made that old, fat, story-tellin man kneel down to him an beg fer mercy! Tha's what I wanna say, but I din't.

"Then what he do, Alice?"

"Y'know how big an strong Isaac is. He ain't gotta do nuthin to skeer n'body. Mr. Tucker was tryna beat him up an he couldn't an he know he couldn, but he kep tryin. I thank he fine'ly stop cause he was embarrassed. Isaac ain't hurt nuthin on him, cept his feelins."

Daddy lookit me a long time, but I could tell he thankin bout what I say an I thank he b'lieve me. Then he axe, "What bout his hand?"

"He migh'ta hurt that some. But he wouldn'a tetch it at all ef'n Mr. Tucker ain't told a story an swang at him again."

Daddy ain't lookit me afta that. I was studdin the roots of the chinaberry stealin looks at Daddy, who look like he was studdin a spot in the sky for a minute or two. Then he take my hand an we walk back to the fields. We strollin hand in hand thout sayin nuthin til we git jes pass the house.

"Mr. Tucker a pow'ful man in Smedley. He got a lotta land an a lotta money. He hires he'p to git alla his work done, tha's how much land he got. He kin hire anybody. We all need the work, an he seem to faver me. He gimme exters, too. Like when he borrow me his truck, even ef I ain't at work. Tha's a exter faver. He ain't gotta do that. It he'p us out alot an we cain't have it wit'out him. Fack is, we wouldn't have much a nuthin wit'out him.

"Is a busy time righ'now down to the mill, but I ain't work there for near to a month. So I walks over there to fine out ef I could git some work.

"He say, 'I kin use a good man er two, but you done choose yer side.' I ain't know whut he talkin bout, Alice. Then he tell me bout y'all bein inna barn on yer birfday.

"Now I b'lieve ev'ythang you tole me, Alice. But you gotta unnerstan, that man thought we was laughin at him behine his back.

"I like Ikey. He been a big he'p round here. An I thank you right bout Mr. Tucker, he pro'bly jes embarrassed. But ef I gotta choose tween

49

a pow'ful boy or a pow'ful man... an it seem like I do gotta choose... then I gotta go wit the man that been takin care a my family like we was his.

"Wha'chu want me to do?" I axe daddy.

Daddy lookit me like he lookin righ'through me. He look like he got a whole lot t'say, but he don' know how t'say it. He look kinda tired. But more'n that, he look...sad.

There it is again. I cain't remember the las'time I done seen so many sad lookin grown folks not at a fune'ral as I have since I turn thirteen, startin wit my birfday. The longer we standin, the sadder an tireder daddy look. I jes wanna hug him an tell him ev'ythang gonna be awrigh'... but is it?

Afta'while he say, "Ain't nuthin fer you t'do, Alice. It's fer me to do. I jes wanna hear yer side so's I could git the whole pitchur. You gimme that, an tha's all ya cudda done. You a good gurl. Y'always was. Gone back an finish he'pin yer brother's."

"I wanna he'p you."

Daddy smile an hug me fer that. "Y'always he'p me an yer mama, Alice," he say, "Y'always do. Now gone back an he'p yer brothers."

I went back, but I was more confused then ever. What did daddy hafta do? An what bout Isaac? He need t'go to school, smart as he is, *an* he need to work. What he gonna do ef daddy gotta choose, an it cain't be him? Mr. Tucker shore ain't gonna hire him. Seem like I kin do somethin, but what? I feel like ev'ythang is my fault even though I cain't figger out what I done. It's my fault Isaac ain't in school an daddy ain't workin an Mr. Tucker feel embarrassed. But ef I pologize to Mr. Tucker, he pro'bly thank I'm jes doin it to he'p Isaac... an maybe tha's all I would be doin, too. So what kin I do?

Right now, I kin finish he'pin Daniel an Samuel wit they take-aways.

****

Daddy went back to work at the mill.

Isaac stop comin by, but I see him in the liberry mos anytime I want. He say Miss Johnson tell him he could teach hisse'f ef he jes keep up his readin. I give him the lessons Miss Johnson give us ev'yday. He end up teachin me mos times. He tell me I take good notes. He copy'em down, then he splain to me bout his unnerstandin a what all I writ. It be perfect to what Miss Johnson splain, but bettah. Maybe cause it's my second time gittin the same lesson, but I unnerstan it even better afta Isaac through.

50

That he'ped *me* in school. Miss Johnson tole me I was doin so good, she was gonna put me on a fas'track. She gimme lotsa science an math that she ain't give t'nobody else. She tole me I oughta thank bout goin to college when I gradiate.

"I cain't go to college, Miss Johnson. My family ain't got no money like that!"

"You are such a smart young lady, Alice. I bet you could get a scholarship, if you applied."

"Even ef I did, my family need me to he'p them at home afta school. I'm shore my daddy an mama ain't gonna lemme go."

"Then why do you think they send you and your sister and brothers here? There are very limited opportunites for young, educated, colored people in Smedley. Surely they understood that before they sent you here. You'll be a much bigger help to them once you get a college education and can get a good job somewhere."

"But what bout when I'm gone? How kin I spect them to make do wit'out me?"

"Oh, *now* I see. *You* don't want to go to college because *you* think that your family won't be able to get along without you. That's all you had to say, Alice. You don't want to go."

"But I do! I do, Miss Johnson. I jes know my family..."

"Don't you worry about them. Concentrate on your studies for now. If you're interested, I'll get some applications for some of the Negro colleges in this state, okay?"

"That be fine, Miss Johnson. I Thanky."

eight

Puttin me on the fas'track, put Isaac on it, too. I don' know ef I'da made it wit'out Isaac. But we did real good t'getha for almos a year.

The war end an the Depression been over but ain't none of that seem to make a differnce in Smedley. Ev'ybody jes keep doin the same thangs we been doin, til that one day.

That one day I go to the liberry an Isaac sittin there lookin like the cat what ate the canary. I use'ly slide my papers over to him an he start right into copyin, but t'day he slide a book over to me an tell me to read the page he mark. It's a book of poetry by his favorite poet, Paul Laurence Dunbar. Isaac put bracks round a piece of this one poem call "Sympathy":

"I know why the caged bird sings, ah me,
When his wing is bruised and his bosom sore
When he beats his bars and he would be free;
It is not a carol of joy or glee,
But a prayer that he sends from his heart's deep core,
But a plea, that upward to heaven he flings –
I know why the caged bird sings!"

"Tha's beautiful, Isaac. Why you want me to read that part?"

"I want you to read alla it. I'm givin you that book, Alice."

I looked at the front an back an seen it wa'nt a liberry book. Then I said, "Thanky Isaac. I'ma read this whole thang. But you mark this part righ'chere. Why you want me to read this part, now?"

"Cause *I know why the caged bird sings*. We all jes caged birds round here, Alice. We ain't doin what we want. We thank we doin what we kin, but we jes doin what we been allowed t'do. What you really wanna do Alice?"

"What do I wanna do?"

"Yeah. Ef you din't have nobody an nuthin else t'think bout, then wha'chu wanna do?"

"Right this minute?"

"Yeah, right now."

"I wanna finish my lesson wit'chu."

"An afta that...?"

"Miss Johnson tole me I be ready to gradiate in May. I wanna go to college afta that an be a teacher or a nurse."

"Tha's good. How you gonna do that?"

"I'ma try to git a schola'ship. Miss Johnson said she gonna git me some apple-cations."

"Miss Johnson is right too. She gimme a list of colleges, but I ain't got no time t'be waitin t'hear from'em. I gotta git outta here real soon. This is one bird gonna fly the coop."

"Whar ya goin?"

"I 'ont know. But ef I leave, I b'lieve Tucker would hire poppa over to the mill again an thangs a be a lot eas'er on my family."

"Why you thank that?"

"Tucker hire yer daddy again afta yer daddy tole me I couldn't work to y'alls house no mo."

I ain't never thought bout that. Isaac ain't never complain to me all this time we been studdin in the liberry bout his family tryna make do. He ain't come back to school, so's I know thangs wa'nt great. An even afta daddy an me talked about spinna bottle in the barn, I jes know daddy went back to work. I ain't never thought bout what he said or did to git there. Now Isaac sittin here tellin me somethin that shoulda been somethin I been done knowed sence ev'ybody else do. But I ain't pay it no mind.

The worse thang is findin out how stupid I am. I jes set there wondrin to myse'f how I git to be so dumb. I guess Isaac thought I was thankin a somethin else cause he still tryta he'p me puzzle it all out.

"C'mon Alice, you know that fat, ol' man still mad at me for kissin you inna barn."

The way he say that make it sound like somethin else. I wanna make shore he unnerstan jes what make Mr. Tucker so mad. So I said, "He ain't do no more'n daddy or mama woulda done ef they'da caught us."

"Maybe...but that ain't the point. Tucker the only free bird in Smedley. Ev'ybody do what *he want* an what *he say* cause ef you don', he make yer life hard... real hard.

"I'ma leave. I'ma try to git a job at one'a these schools Miss Johnson writ down for me, then I'ma try t'take some classes cause they free ef you work there."

"Isaac, that be so good! You the smartest person I know, even smarter'n Miss Johnson! Least when you splain this work, I unnerstan it bettah."

"You oughta come go wit me, Alice."

"Huh?!"

"We kin work an go t'the same school."

"Isaac, I'm fo'teen!"

"Miss Johnson say you kin gradiate in May. I kin teach you what li'l you don' know. Git outta here, Alice. Come wit me."

I was shocked! Isaac axin me to go wit'em woulda seem sudden anyway I heard it, but I was exter su'prised bein as he was still wantin me to go when I jes foun'out how dumb I was.

But I ain't say that.

I said, "I cain't jes up an go like that right now. I wished I could."

"I wished you *would*. Watch an see ef poppa don' git hired back to the mill soon's I'm gone. You watch an see."

"When you goin, Isaac?"

"I 'ont know. Soon... but not b'fo I git the resta my spinna bottle kiss," he say real sly-like an come leanin into me wit his lips all puckered up.

"Boy, you bettah go someplace!" I say pushin him away an blushin like a strawberry.

****

Isaac musta lef' that night or the next. Ef I'da knowed he was gonna go wit'out me seein him again, I woulda give him the resta his spinna bottle kiss right there in the liberry. I woulda hold on to him so hard, I migh'not a leggo. He mighta *had* to take me wit him jes cause he couldn'a got me offa him...ef I'da knowed.

But I din't.

nine

That Sunday, Mr. Tucker brung over a fat goose for dinner an mama roasted it til it was a copper penny brown. She boiled fresh cranberries in orange juice an sugar, then chilled it on a ice block. She call it cranberry sauce an that was some gooood stuff! I made potato salad, mashed yellow turnips an biscuits, a course. Bertha cook strang beans an corn. We had bread puddin wit peaches an raisins an vanilla sauce for dessert. We was so stuffed, we couldn't barely move when we finished. We all jes set there at the table with dopey, sleepy grins not even able to move for bout twenny minutes. Afta that we all went t'the front room.

Me an Bertha was playin the card game "Go Fish". The twins was playin wit they stick soldiers Isaac made 'em. Mama was knittin a scarf. Mr. Tucker was whistlin an playin checkers wit daddy. Afta'while, Mr. Tucker start talkin bizness to daddy.

"T'marra gone be real busy, Nate. I'ma make you the fo'man for choppin down all the timber in the nawth'west q'water. You have back-up in the mawnin, but come the afta'noon ya on yer own. I'ma put Freeman in charge of clearin out all the cut trees."

"Freeman comin back?" Daddy axe soundin surprised an happy.

"Yep. He gone start t'marra."

"Y'oughta hire his boy, too."

"I migh'woulda done that wit all the work we got comin up. But I heard Ikey lef'," he said then looked over to Bertha an axe, "Bertha, di'ja know yer beau done gone away?"

"Who say he gone?" Daddy axe zactly what I wanna know.

"Freeman. Tole me yestiddy that he ain't seen him sence late Thursd'y."

"I hope he okay," mama say soundin kinda skeered. "It don' seem to be Ikey's ways to up an leave thout a word. I jes hope that chile is awrigh."

"Oh I'm shore he awrigh," Mr. Tucker said soundin too happy to cover up his mean streak, I thank. "Big, young, strong, smart boy like that! He pro'bly jes found another life t'save an latch onto. Ain't that right Nate?" He give a little chuckle, but we all know he jes makin fun bout what daddy tole him las'time bout how Isaac come to be here.

Daddy ain't say nuthin fer a spell. He set there lookin like he studdin the checkerboard, then he say, "I hope so...I hope so."

Ev'ybody was kinda quiet afta that. Only sound in the room was Mr. Tucker whistlin, an I found that perticulerly ear'tatin'. God bless Bertha for breakin all that up.

She axe the twins an me, "Ain't y'all tarred a bein cooped up? Le's go ou'side an play somethin."

Daddy say, "Is gonna be dark purty soon, but y'all kin go ou'side fer a short spell. Alice, ya jes watch now, ya heah?"

"Okay daddy." I ain't much feel like playin no way.

When we gits ou'side, I come to fine out Bertha ain't wanna play nuthin neitha.

The twins was runnin an jumpin up an down like puppies axin, "What we gonna do? What we gonna do?"

"Le's go in the back. Me an Alice gonna time y'all runnin a leap frog race."

"Huh?"

"Jes go round back," Bertha say an we all went.

She tole Daniel to crouch down in the field an tole Samuel to leap over his back then crouch right down so's Daniel could git up an leap over his back then crouch right down.

"How's thadda race?"

"Y'all do it over an over an ya git bettah each time. Y'all tryna be faster each time. Y'all be racin to beat yer own record."

The twins start moanin an groanin, "Tha' don' sound like no fun! Tha' don' make no sense!"

"Jes do it. Y'all have fun afta'while," Bertha say, then she crouch down in a li'l ball an say, "Y'all come leap over me firs', then jump over each other!" They did, an was back to bein silly li'l puppies again.

Bertha an me set in the grass a li'l ways away to talk. Ev'y now an then, the twins yell, "How'zat?" an Bertha say, "Bettah!" or "Real good!" or "Y'all must be tar'd, y'all gittin slow!" But we wa'nt payin 'em no mind. We was talkin.

"Di'ja know Isaac was gonna go way?" She axe me.

"Yeah, he tole me. But I ain't know he was gonna go so soon."

"Whur'd he go?"

"I 'ont know. I 'ont thank he knowed ahead a time eitha. He say he had to go so's his family could do bettah. He tole me to see ef Mr. Tucker don' hire his daddy back soon's he gone.... An he did! I wonder why?"

"Cause Mr. Tucker like you an he wanna perteck you."

"That don' even make no sense! Perteck me from what? Isaac ain't no bad boy!"

"Nah, he ain't no bad boy. But he ain't no yellow boy neitha. Mr. Tucker always did like you bettah cause you yellow. He pay you mo tention then any of us. You git mo gifts an stuff on yer birfday. Even when we was li'l, he give you mo pocket change then us. Cause you bein light-skin an all, he like you bettah."

"Oh Bertha, tha's stupid!"

"It is stupid, but is true."

"It ain't true! Jes cause some people thank it or say it don' make it so! Do *YOU* thank yellow people is exter special?"

"Nah."

"Well then, SEE?! It ain't so. Per'od!" I was so mad, I ain't know what t'do. How we git to talkin bout that stupid stuff anyway? I wanna talk about Isaac an whure he coulda gone off to.

We jes set there afta that not talkin or nuthin. I thank Bertha thank I'm mad at her, but I wa'nt. I was mad at the rumors people make real by talkin an ackin like they real. Mabel was the firs' to brang it to my tention wit Alberta an her sorry se'f bein treated like a beauty queen. Now I cain't hardly trust ef somebody bein nice to me cause they like me or ef they faver me jes cause I'm lighter'n them. Plus, ev'ybody seem to thank the same thang cept me. How I come to be of a differnt mind then ev'ybody else? Why I don' know what ev'ybody else seem to know? My own sister thank like ev'ybody else, who taught her that?

Isaac said we is all jes caged birds round here. Ain't nobody doin what they want. We thank we doin what we kin, but we ain't. We jes doin what we been allowed to do. Now I'm wondrin WHO *allowin* or *not allowin* us to do stuff? WHO make the rules ev'ybody follow round here?

Now that I know what was makin me so mad, I ain't mad no mo. Anyway, I wa'nt never mad at Bertha an she oughta know that. I looped my arm in hers an axe her what I jes axe myse'f.

"Who make the rules ev'ybody follow round here, Bertha? Why we follow somebody else rules? We need to make our own rules, don'cha thank?"

Bertha was tryin, but I kin tell she ain't know what I was talkin bout. She was jes happy I ain't mad at her no mo an she don' wanna change that so she gimme a quick li'l grin an say, "Yeah. We need to make our own rules."

She ain't got no idea what she talkin bout. She jes happy we talkin.

Watchin Bertha, I unnerstan a li'l bettah how we git stuck bein the way we are. Caged birds jes go along to git along. We set low goals ef we set any goals at all. We ain't try'na be happy. We ain't even gotta unnerstan nuthin so long as we all gittin along. Free birds is the ones makin all the rules fer ev'ybody else.

We need to make our own rules, but firs' we gotta be free.

****

I was still good in school, but I had to work a lot harder wit'out Isaac t'splain thangs to me. Miss Johnson gimme a buncha apple-cations for differnt colleges one day afta school round about Feb'rary.

"Here Alice. Fill these out now, so I can help you if you need it, then I can mail them on my way home today. I want to make sure you progress and develop at least a little of your potential You have so much in so many areas."

I know Miss Johnson thank a lot of me. She show it all the time. But I never know why. An wit gradiation jes a few months off, I wanna know what all these p'tentials is she say she see.

"Why you do s'much for me, Miss Johnson?"

"I don't do so much. I don't do nearly enough, it seems. I'm slowly losing each one of my students here, as I had fully expected. But they're not getting ahead. They're getting pregnant!"

I guess she talkin bout Mabel leavin school to have her a baby last year. An Janey and Gladys both lef' early this year wit big bellies. Lease Janey gonna marry Lucas. Even Sylvester an Thomas lef' school t'take care of they new babies wit girls that ain't never went to school. So my guess is she talkin bout them.

"Of course I realize that not everyone has the same talents, so I can not and do not expect the same things from everyone. But as a teacher, I want more for all of you. Otherwise, why go to school...to graduate and marry and have babies and farm?"

Tha's what mos girls be talkin bout mosta the time, who they like an ef they thank they boyfriend is gonna marry 'em afta they git outta school. Sence I ain't have no boyfriend, I was jes mos'ly lis'nin, but I use'ta be thankin bout Isaac like that b'fo he went away. Now Miss Johnson make it sound like tha's the dumbest thang in the world to do, to be worryin bout gittin a nice man an makin a good home. I don' see nothin wrong wit it. I'm thankin maybe tha's why she ain't got no husband.

I axe her, "You thank marriage an babies an farmin is bad?"

"No, not at all. It's just so... ordinary. I don't say that to be condescending, but that's what most people do here anyway, without an education. Almost everyone in the world eventually marries and starts a family. So what's the big deal? Once the family's begun, there's little time for anything else. You'll be swamped with the tasks of providing. Providing food, clothing and shelter to your dependents and trying to teach them how to be independent. You may make sacrifices to send them to school, hoping they'll get ahead, only to watch them repeat your same pattern of babies, marriage and struggle. Where's the progress in that? I'm trying to give you the tools you'll need, not just to make a living, but to make a life!"

What she say remine me a what Isaac said bout book learnin givin you mo possibilities. He said the same thang bout girls jes tryna git a husband too cause they thank they need to. She remine me so much of Isaac that I'm lis'nin to her, but I'm missin him. I wonder ef Miss Johnson the reason he lef'. Did she tell him bout his p'tentials that was so big an plen'iful? Did she tell him not t'be studdin me alla time an to thank bout the big ol' world an how he migh'could see some of it?

Nah, I don' thank she tole him that last part cause he axe me t'come go wit him. But I figger she did tell him what she tellin me now, an that make me keen to listen.

"To make a life, Alice, you have to have vision. We limit our growth when we limit our dreams. And we tend to dream small when we discover the many boundaries set to harness our strides and achievements."

"What kin ya do bout somethin holdin you back?"

"Don't accept the limitations someone else gives you. We limit ourselves enough with fears and doubts. If you find yourself against a fence you didn't put there, climb over it, tunnel under it, find a way around it, or blast through it. It's a lot easier said than done, but it's my best advice. Be bold. Be brave. Be true to God and your heart, Alice. Be true to God and your heart."

Well, there it was! This musta been the very same thang she tole Isaac cause he shore blasted outta here! I still wish I coulda gone wit him, but ef I could do it all over, I know I wouldn't. Isaac lef' to make thangs better for his family. I gotta stay a li'l while longer to make thangs easier fer mines.

****

"Alice! Alice!" I heard mama callin me to the fron' porch. I was in back takin down the laundry.

"Yessum?" I called, high-tailin it t'the front.

Mama was standin there on the porch holdin a letter in her hand. She was studdin it hard like ef she look long enough she migh'could read it afta'while. Ain't nobody never write to us cause the folks mama an daddy know cain't read jes like they cain't. Mos folks we know what got letters was when they people got kilt in the war. The gov'ment writ 'em to let 'em know. So I guess to us, letters is kinda skeery t'git. When I come round the side a the house, she hold it out to me like it migh'could bite her, "What this fer?"

I looked an seen it was from a college an I got nervous an excited.

"Oooo mama tha's for me! I filled out some apple-cations t'go t'college. This from one of 'em."

"College?! Alice, you cain't go to no college! We ain't got that kinda money!"

"It ain't gone cost y'all no money. I'ma only go ef I git a schola'ship, that mean the school a pay fer me t'go there."

Even though I was still excited an I awready splained to mama how I migh'could go to college fer free, I could see mama was still worried. Maybe she ain't unnerstan bout a schola'ship, or maybe she don' trust that I kin git me one. But when I read that letter, I seen this school wa'nt gonna gimme jack.

I was so hurt, I ain't say nuthin else til she axe me, "Well, di'ja git that schola'ship?"

"No m'am," I said. "But this was jes my firs' ansa back." I sent out bout ten or more that firs' week. But I was still dis'pointed.

I thought mama would stop lookin so worried an maybe be sad fer me, but I swear mama look glad bout it. That make me wonder bout what I tole Miss Johnson in the firs' place, bout I cain't go away to school cause they needs me too much righ'chere at home.

ten

Miss Johnson tole me not to worry bout not gittin a schola'ship fer ev'y apple-cation. She say she was proud of me even ef I ain't git no schola'ship to nowhure. That make me feel bettah bout losin in my firs' letter back, but I still ain't know bout leavin at all ef I do git one, sence mama look so worried bout me goin away.

Other letters start tricklin in. They ain't all turn me down flat. Some of 'em offer a parta one, so I could jes pay some money an the school pay the rest. But sence we ain't got no money to spare, I gotta git a full schola'ship or not go at all.

Mama an daddy seem t'be glad when I tell 'em I still cain't go an sence I'm jes happy when I git offers fer a piece a one, we's all happy.

Til that one day.

We jes bout ready to siddown to eat. I was pourin water when mama brung out a letter an put it on the table by my place.

"I guess this another one a yer apple-cations, Alice," she say.

We was all use to 'em by now, so I wa'nt excited or nuthin. I din't even open it righ'then. Afta we et, daddy axe me wha' that letter say an then I member it, even though it was in my face all dinner long.

I open it an near to faint.

"Omi'gosh! Omi'gosh! Omi'gosh!"

"What is it, Alice?" Mama axe.

"Omi'gosh!" I say.

"Alice wha'chu omi'goshin bout?" Bertha axe tween laughin at me.

"Omi'gosh!"

Then Bertha take the letter an read it herse'f.

"Omi'gosh...ALICE! OMI'GOSH!!" Bertha pop up, turnin over her chair then she grab my hand an pull me up, then we jumpin round the kitchen doin a Omi'gosh dance. Then the twins start jumpin round jes cause we was.

"Wha'chall pitchin a fit about?" Daddy an mama say lookin at us real funny, like they was curious or amused.

"Alice got it! Alice got a *full* schola'ship!" Bertha fine'ly yelped.

"Omi'gosh!" Mama say, an stand up slow like she in a dream. "Omi'gosh, Nate?"

Daddy set there lookin so stunned. He look strong an weak an skeered an...strong all at one time. I was standin there thankin how I always like the way daddy could look s'many ways all at one time when he said… almos kind, "You cain't go to college, Alice."

"Yes I kin, daddy. It ain't gonna cost y'all nuthin!"

"No. You cain't go baby," he said again, quiet but strong.

"It's true, Allie, you cain't go."

Mama near skeered me ha'fta death. Ain't nobody call me *Allie* but mama, an she only call me that maybe twiced in my life. It woulda been okay, her callin me Allie, since this a special occasion, ceptin mama an daddy was tellin me this ain't no special occasion. This a mistake.

"Why I cain't go to college ef it's free, mama?" I axe bout chokin on a big ball that jes growed in my thoat. "Daddy?"

They ain't say nuthin.

Bertha an the twins was quiet now waitin for an ansa like me.

Afta'while Bertha axe, "Why cain't Alice go to college ef it's free?"

Daddy say to Bertha, but he starin straight at me, "Alice gonna marry Mr. Tucker."

"WHA...?!! Mama? Mama? MAMA?!"

I do like daddy jes done, I'm axin mama, but I'm starin straight at him. I'm waitin fer my daddy to laugh an tell me how he was jes teasin me.

I'm waitin to hear my mama laugh an say somethin like, "Nate, don'chu be playin round like that! Look now, you bout to make Alice have a stroke like ole man Cletus."

But I don' hear nuthin. Ain't nobody laughin. Ain't nobody move.

Afta'while daddy stop lookin at me. He look down at his empty plate, quiet an sad. Tha's worse then him starin at me cause it make him look guilty, like he jes got caught doin somethin bad. I looked over to mama, when daddy dropped his eyes.

Mama try'ta smile, but I kin see pass that. She look like I feel. She might could even feel worse then me, knowin this they choice an they ain't never give me no choice. But mama ain't say none of that. She try'ta smile an act like this s'poze t'be happy news for me.

Mama say, "Allie, Mr. Tucker done fell in love wit'chu the firs' minute he seen you. He hire yer daddy reg'ler right on the spot an start brangin us thangs an givin us favers til we promise t'make you his bride when you grown. He the only reason y'all is goin to school right now, y'all know that. Bertha an the boys kin go on t'college an git good jobs an thangs, but'chu don' need that cause you ain't never gonna hafta work a day in yer life!"

She give a big ol' chesire cat grin, but I know her heart is bleedin. I kin see righ'through all of her proud, peacockin, mama-a-the-bride-to-be shuckin an jivin.

She wish they ain't give Mr. Tucker they word all them years back, but they did. And we all know they cain't take it back. When you dirt poor an all you got is yer word, then yer word is yer bond. You don' give it lightly. You don' give it at all ef you thank you cain't keep it.

"Mr. Tucker promise that afta y'all is married, he gonna put a new roof on this ol' house. He gonna put in some 'lectricity an plumbin an add a bathroom so's we won't hafta go ou'side t'the toilet or bathe in the kitchen no mo. Bertha gonna git her own bedroom. Yer daddy gonna be made the permanent fo'man, so's the money comin in'll be reg'ler, steada sometimey."

I couldn't move. I couldn't feel nuthin. Maybe I did have me a stroke like ol' man Cletus. I kin hear mama talkin, but she sound like she far away, like I'm drownin inna lake an she standin on the shore talkin away cause she cain't see I'm drownin. Lawd, I'm thankin, what real good thang is gonna happen t'me this time for tradin my dreams… my Life… so's my family kin git some home improvements? Then mama ansa'd.

"But'chu the real lucky one! You be livin in that big house up on that hill wit alla those rooms lookin down on alla us lowly, common folk in the valley. No mo hand-me-downs. You ain't gonna hafta do nuthin less'n you want to. You kin even hire a cook an a maid, ef you want! An you kin hire somebody to drive you round in one a his fancy dancy motorcars."

I couldn't b'lieve she b'lieve that. *I'll be the Lucky One?!* Locked away in some big ol' house on a hill wit Mr. Tucker?!! When she gonna laugh? When she gonna git to the punchline so we kin all laugh. She don' even see me standin here drownin. But daddy do. Tha's why he couldn't keep lookin me in my eyes. I look back to daddy cause he was my only hope. I tried callin to him, but I could barely whisper, "Daddy? Daddy?"

"Yer daddy an me done had to work ev'yday of our lives. You know how we slave jes t'make do. You ain't never gonna hafta work like that. You gonna be Mrs. Tucker, the firs' colored lady of Smedley!"

****

Afta you die, you unnerstan ev'ythang.

An when you unnerstan thangs, really unnerstan, cain't nuthin make you mad no mo cause you seein thangs fer what they are, not for wha'chu want 'em to be. You kin feel happy or sad or sick or calm, but you cain't git mad at nobody or nuthin cause you unnerstan. Tha's the nature of unnerstandin.

I know this for a fact cause April 5, 1947, I died when my daddy look straight at me an tole Bertha I was gonna marry Mr. Tucker. I din't stop breathin an drop down on the floor or nuthin like what mos dead people woulda done. But I died fer real all the same. I felt alla my insides dry up an git sucked down into a deep dark hole somewhures inside me. POOF! I was gone.

What was lef' standin there still look like me. It move an sound like me, but it was jes a shell of me. It was the house I use to live in, but not no mo. I was gone. Dead. An full of unnerstandin.

I unnerstan why Mr. Tucker call me princess an why, even when he givin alla us somethin, he always give me exter. He was treatin me like I was a whore of Babylon he was payin fer way ahead a time. I unnerstan why he hate Isaac s'much an why he fire Isaac daddy from the mill an why he hire him back afta Isaac leave. I unnerstan why daddy make b'lieve that Bertha an Isaac sweet on each other, cause he know ef Mr. Tucker thought it was me an Isaac that was sweet, then he was gonna lose his job... which he did. I unnerstan why mama always had me to wait on Mr. Tucker. She was tryna git me useta the idea sence they done awready plan for me t'do it for the rest of my life. I unnerstan why, sence I turn thirteen, ev'ybody remine I'm growin up an I need to ack like a lady an Mr. Tucker always pucker up fer a kiss on the lips an why I ketch s'many grown folks lookin at me real sad-like, cause they know what li'l freedom I got was runnin out an maybe I remine 'em of theyse'f right b'fo they freedom got took. I wonder ef tha's why Isaac tell me to come go wit him when he go. I wonder ef tha's why Miss Johnson tryna git me into college in sech a hurry. I thank, yeah...they pro'bly awready know what I'm jes now findin out, an that make me wonder fer the umpteenth time how I git to be so dumb. I unnerstan mama an daddy ain't mean no harm. I unnerstan they ain't thank they was sellin me or tradin me or sacrificin me fer they ownse'f, even though they was. They was hopin I would 'preciate Mr. Tucker bein a pow'ful man in Smedley as much as they did, an maybe I would thank of marryin him as a blessin for me like it been fer alla us all these years. I unnerstan ef I din't marry Mr. Tucker an I went off to college or ef I runned away, my family would be hurt real bad, not only for the he'p that would stop comin, but for Mr. Tucker tryna collect on his debt come due. I unnerstan my family couldn't never pay him back an it would kill all of 'em. I unnerstan I wouldn't, I couldn't, let them all suffer jes to save myse'f cause I was taught a thousand years ago what I was gonna hafta do t'day: *"You my firs' born! The firs' always got to lead the way...You got to make a zample of yerse'f so the li'l ones be bettah... We cain't always have what we want. Life ain't like that for nobody, and it specially ain't like that for us. We got to share an make sacrifices so thangs get bettah fer ev'ybody."*

We wa'nt raised to disagree or even question our parents. It's that last what make me t'know I was gonna marry Mr. Tucker.

And it kill me.

****

I ain't say nuthin to Miss Johnson bout me not gonna be goin to college. Sometime she axe me ef I got anymo ansa's an I mumble somethin, ha'f the time I 'ont know what. I know she musta knowed somethin cause she ain't say nuthin like, "Wha'chu say, Alice?" when I mumble to her. Afta'while she stop axin me all t'getha.

Afta school, even afta I done done alla the afta school chores Miss Johnson gimme, I ain't wanna go home an hafta ack pleasant to ev'ybody. That was the worse part, tryna smile at daddy an mama when I was havin s'many bad thoughts. I stayed sick to my stomach an wouldn't hardly eat nuthin cause it was jes a waste wit me throwin it up not too long after I et it. I ain't hate my parents, but I ain't like 'em neitha. I ain't want school t'ever end. But come mid-May, it did.

That last day, I washed the blackboards an swep the floor an straightened the tables an chairs an books. I did ev'ythang I always did an somethangs I ain't never done t'try to make this day last fo'ever. Miss Johnson was there the whole time at her desk up front. She ain't say nuthin an neitha did I. I thought it was a strange g'bye for us, sence this was always my favorite part of the school day for years. This the time I had Miss Johnson all to myse'f an we would talk bout any an ev'ythang. Now here is our last day t'getha an ain't neitha one of us got nuthin to say.

When I was through wit alla my chores, I set real quiet an still in the back of the room an stared out the window, tryna to keep from losin my mind.

I don't know how long I set like that, but afta'while Miss Johnson start talkin to me.

"Alice, you are the smartest young lady I have ever known, or can imagine. You are one of my favorite people in the world. From your very first day in school, your eagerness to learn and your bright eyes, so full of trust in me to teach you, won you a special place in my heart and in my prayers. I came back to the south to teach and do whatever else I could do to help every child break free from their sub-standards of living. You became my greatest hope and promise for a better tomorrow. You aren't just smart, you are bold. You are brave. You are kind and giving and forgiving. You are a selfless leader who naturally and eagerly tries to help others to rise..."

While Miss Johnson talkin, I kin hear her walkin slow, up to me. I hear what she sayin, but I'm hearin it differnt from the way she sayin it. It sound like a eulogy to my ear. I know I'm dead, but she sound like she know it, too, and she tryna praise the chile I was an mourn the woman I won't never be. I'm hearin her like she givin a chu'ch sermon, "Alice was a smart girl, uh-huh. She was bold an brave an kind to her neighbors. Amen? Amen! She was the hope an promise of her teacher, Lawd!"

Hearin it that way, in a quiet room like a fune'ral chapel wit one quiet voice full of strength an sorrow, goin on bout a promise tha's been broken an a hope tha's been kilt, I start to lose myse'f. Tears fill up my eyes an spill down my face in two li'l streams that meet neath my chin an drip into my lap. My face is scrunchin up an my lips is twistin an tremblin from tryna hold back a pressure risin inside of me, a pressure that grow heavier wit ev'y word Miss Johnson say.

She touch my shoulder an say, "I couldn't love you anymore if you were my own daughter."

I cain't hardly hold myse'f t'getha no more. I feel like I'ma pop!

But she keep right on talkin cause she don' know how heavy her words weigh on me, "I heard about your pending marriage, Alice..."

I threw my head back an a high pitch wail come out from way deep inside, jes like a kettle screamin out the exter pressure from the water boilin inside of it. I screamed an screamed an screamed wit'out takin a breath fer minutes, then I sunk to the floor an screamed some mo.

Miss Johnson was tryna hold me up, but I was like a floppy rag doll an bein almos her size, I was too big fer her to handle. I could see what she was tryna do an I could still hear her talkin, but I couldn't he'p her. All the strength I had I was usin to scream my head off.

Miss Johnson rubbed my back an say, "I know your mother and father mean well. I know you'll listen to them because you are an obedient daughter. I'm sure Mr. Tucker truly loves you, who doesn't? Still, I cannot let this happen. This is not India or China where arranged marriages are accepted and expected. I am coming to your wedding, Alice. And when the minister asks if there is anyone who objects to your marriage, I will. I will object!"

When I hear that, I sit up an lookit her. I wanna make shore I done heard what I thank I done heard and I ain't gone all the way crazy. Lookin in her face is almos like lookin in a mirror cause her face is kinda scrunched an her lips is tremblin an she got tears streamin down her cheeks that meet under her chin, too. But her eyes is full of fire an I know she mean it when she say, "I will!"

I hug her real tight an pray to God that He gonna let Miss Johnson make ev'ythang awright. But all I kin git out is, "PLEASE! PLEASE! PLEASE...!"

"I will!...I will!...I will!" She promise each time.

That prayer an promise is the only reason I was able t'venchally go home an ack pleasant.

eleven

Mr. Tucker weddin day was set for the Sat'day afta I gradiate. Mr. Tucker din't come round fer that whole week, but he kep sendin thangs over to the house. One of the thangs he sent was a weddin dress, I thank it was his mama's. It was way too big fer me. It woulda been too big anyway, but sence I wa'nt eatin nuthin much sence findin out bout my weddin, it really swamped my skin an bones. Mama thought she could take it in, but it was too much cloth to bunch up in the seams so she cut it down to fit me an almos had enough material lef' over to make a second dress.

"Alice, you gonna disappear ef you don' eat somethin. You want me t'fix ya some supper? I kin make somethin special fer you."

I ruther disappear, I was thankin. But I said, "Thanks mama, but nah."

****

It was s'poze to be a small li'l ceremony in the house. Mama an daddy jes tole a few friends an family. But word a mouth spread faster'n a plague an come that Sat'day, they so many people comin over brangin pots a greens, cabbage slaw, chicken stew, ambrosia fruit salad an whatnot, daddy an mama had to quick change it t'be ou'side in the field.

Mosta the people was waitin ou'side, but they was a mess a womens in the house fussin over me like I was bound fer glory. I ain't say nuthin to nobody cause I was skeered ef I open my mouth, the lump stuck in my thoat would spew out all over ev'ythang. I did look nice, even ef I was skinny as a poker. I jes stood in the mirra starin, but not lookin at myse'f. I was seein what mighta been, me an Isaac studdin our college books t'getha or me bein a teacher an sendin ha'f my check home so daddy ain't hafta work at Mr. Tucker mill no more. I was seein what shoulda been an lis'nin to the Prayer Promise of wha's to be, the song Miss Johnson an me writ, "Please! I will. Please! I will. Please! I will."

"Gurl, you done played yer cards RIGHT!" Ant Betty say fluffin my dress.

But Miss Barnes figger somethin else. "You look a li'l pee-ked Alice," she say. "Yer face all drawn like one a them starvin chirrens they have in LIFE magazine... or like one a Miz Mackey's kids."

Some of the other ladies laugh, but she was ser'us. "Shush up y'all now! Alice don' look well to me. Alice, you feelin awrigh'?"

I wanna tell her zackly how I'm feelin, but I ain't say nuthin cause she ain't really wanna hear bout how I feel, none of these womens did. They so happy fer me an my family an Mr. Tucker. They only wanna hear that I'm happy, too. But I couldn't give 'em happy. Stony silence was jes bout as pleasant as I could be righ'then.

Ain't nobody seem to notice or even care that I ain't ansa. They still buzzin round me like bees in a hive. Rubbin red rouge on my cheeks an lips, puttin lotion on my hands, complimentin how small my waist an how high an firm my bosoms is. Mama in the room, but she ain't flittin round me like the rest of 'em. She was quiet as me, ceptin she do ansa when somebody speak to her. Bertha in the house, too. She been quiet an sulkin like me ever since daddy say I'ma be Mr. Tucker's bride. I figger her an Miss Johnson is the onliest people to know an care bout how I really feel.

Miz Mamie Jordan come in the house wheezin' sayin, "Well, it's pass time to git this hitchin started (wheeze wheeze) Wha'chall waitin fer?!"

They all look round at each other, then start movin to the door, cept me.

Bertha come up to me in the mirra an say, "You look beautiful, Alice." Then suddenly poutin an strugglin to keep the water in her eyes, she whine, "You so lucky."

B'fo I know anythang, I done spun round an slapped that chile silly. *WAP*! cross her one cheek, then *WAP*! backhand slap cross the othern. Then I turned round an glared at all them womens dressed in they Sunday best, darin anybody wit my eyes to say anythang. I musta looked like a rabid dog cause tha's how I felt an ain't nobody say nothin, not even mama. They pro'bly thankin ef they do, I slap them, too. They pro'bly right.

I look over to Bertha holdin her face an lookin at me wit her wide eyes full of fear. I couldn't b'lieve she ain't know! I couldn't b'lieve she that stupid! But lookin at her cringe from me, I know it's so. That broke my heart worser'n anythang. A picture of Jesus nailed on the cross flashed in my mind. Ef I ever had a doubt b'fo, now I know fer shore it's true that part bout Him bleedin on the cross an lookin down at his killers an sayin, "Forgive them Father for they know not what they do." They really don' know!

Bertha up here jealous! Ant Betty thank I planned all this! Mama thank her an daddy done me a faver! All 'ese women buzzin round is really happy fer me! They really don't know! Or maybe it's me. How I come to be of a differnt mine then ev'ybody else? Why I don't know what ev'ybody else seem to know? My own sister thank like they do, who taught her that?

I wanna scream so bad, but instead I reached for Berth. She jerked away like she thought I was gonna hit her again, but I hugged her close an whispered savagely in her ear, "Do *you* wanna marry Mr. Tucker?"

Her head snapped back from me an her face got all twisted like she smell somethin that stank, then she start shakin her head from side to side. "Nuh-uh!!" She say.

"Me neitha," I shot back.

Her big eyes got even bigger, her mouth drop open an her lips start movin like she wanna say somethin, but she not shore what or how. She look like a fresh caught fish gaspin for water.

Ant Betty axe, "Kin we go now...?" Then she lookit me like she hope I ain't gonna snap.

"NO!..." Bertha say.

"Yeah," I say cuttin her off. "Yeah, we kin go now." Then I walk pass ev'ybody wit my head high an proud, my Prayer Promise song singin in my head, holdin me up, keepin me strong.

****

Ou'side, ev'ybody was standin round in a big circle. Daddy come take my arm an lead me through the people. They move t'eitha side of us like the Red Sea partin fer Moses. Up front was Rev'ern Pritchard wit Mr. Tucker dressed in a shiny black suit fit fer a fune'ral.

The rev'ern axe early on, "Who give this woman to be wed?" I jumped thankin it was Miss Johnson turn t'save me. I looked for her in the crowd an found her close t'the front on my lef'. She gimme a li'l nod an I smile for the firs' time that day.

Daddy say, "I do," an he kiss my hand lookin deep in my eyes, then he give me a li'l smile fore he step back away from me.

I stand there lookin at my father wondrin what jes happen. He do his eyes t'make me know I should turn round. When I do, I see Mr. Tucker grinnin at me an the lump in my thoat growed so big it almos choke me. I had t'keep my eyes on the rev'ern to keep my insides inside.

I couldn't hear nuthin the rev'ern say cause I was lis'nin fer Miss Johnson to stop all this. Rev'ern Pritchard goin on an on bout good times an bad, health an sickness, bettah or worse, then he axe me ef I will.

Ef I will what? I don't know what he talkin bout! I din't say nuthin.

"Er-rah, Alice...honey?" Rev'ern Pritchard kinda whisper to me an lookit me like he searchin fer somethin, "Say, '*I will*.'"

I'm purty shore we pass the part whure Miss Johnson s'poze to save me. I ain't know what t'do. I feel like cryin or screamin, but I don't wanna git daddy an mama in trouble wit Mr. Tucker. Plus, I could be wrong. Maybe the part fer Miss Johnson is a li'l later on, but I ain't wanna say "*I will*" nuthin. I was jes standin there feelin lost an trapped an a li'l mewlin sound escaped from me.

Well, that was good enough fer Rev'ern Pritchard, he say, "Good, good!" Then he make a li'l joke, "Miss Alice jes wanna make shore. Tha's good cause this a big step." Some people give a chuckle.

Next thang I hear is, "I now pronounce you man an wife!"

WHA'?!! HOW THA' HAPPEN?! I turn round lookin for Miss Johnson. I see her, mama, daddy, Ant Betty an a few others fussin mongst theyse'f. I lookit the rest of the people an they seem to be li'l pockets a commotion here an there. Lookin at 'em all gathered like that, I notice fer the firs' time they's quite a few couples whure the womens is wit old mens. The Thom'sons, the Williams, the Clays, the Millers, an mosta these womens is lookin sad. Even Mrs. Petty, the widow woman some calls The Black Widow, is lookin at Mr. Tucker like she wanna scratch his eyes out. I see how young an pretty Mrs. Petty look an seem to member some story goin round bout her husband bein old but not sick an he migh'coulda died fore his time. B'fo now, the onliest thang I kin member bout Mrs. Petty is her pretty musical wind chimes.

"Le's simmer down now, please," Rev'ern Pritchard say tryna quiet folks, "We ain't quite through. I'm shore Mr. Tucker here wanna kiss his bride!"

"Alice?...Princess?" Mr. Tucker give a li'l tug to my arm an call to me from far away. I turn an see him smile then pucker up an pull me to him. I quick turn my head to look fer Miss Johnson one mo time, the Prayer Promise screamin inside my brain.

Mr. Tucker end up kissin my cheek when I turn my head. I look back at him an feel a real bad sick stomach comin on. I turn to run, but Mr. Tucker start runnin side me like we doin this t'getha. When I git near t'the edge of the crowd, Mr. Tucker ketch my arm to keep me back or somethin an I cain't hold it no mo. I vomit all over his shiny black fune'ral suit.

twelve

I 'ont know what happen afta that. I blacked out or somethin, cause I woke up in my daddy an mama bed. I wa'nt shore at firs' ef it was days, hours or minutes later, but mama was wipin my head wit a cold, wet rag an Miss Johnson was fannin me. Some other ladies had took my shoes off an was rubbin my feet an rushin round doin a buncha other stuff I couldn't see.

When I try to open my eyes I heard mama say, "Oh, my baby comin round now. Git her some water...thanky." I felt my head bein liffed up an a glass put to my mouth. "Don'chu swallow, Alice. Jes swish it an spit in this here bowl," mama say.

I swished an spit three or four times, then she jump up to git me some mo water. Miss Johnson stop fannin an bend down t'say in my ear,

"You are *NOT* married, Alice. You did *NOT* say 'I will' and you did *NOT* kiss him."

I start to axe, "Why din't you...?"

"The minister never asked if anyone objected," Miss Johnson say quick, *almos* b'fo mama come back wit mo water.

"There was more'n a few ladies out there ready to spoil yer big day, Alice." Mama sounded like she tryna hold her temper, but some of it ooze out tween ev'y other word or so.

"I told Rev'ern Pritchard to leave out that part bout speakin now or fo'ever holdin yer peace. Over ha'f these folks wa'nt axed t'be heah in the firs' place! Who they t'be objectin to somethin they shouldn'a been at to begin wit?!"

Ain't nobody say nothin to her tellin them they wa'nt invited, but ain't nobody leave neitha. I thought it was only jes Miss Johnson to save me. But from what mama say, an from what I member bout the sad lookin ladies an the li'l commotions breakin out when the minster say we man an wife, I know they was a lot mo people on my side then jes Miss Johnson. That make me feel bettah, even though now, all the people jes ack like ev'ythang is right as rain.

When Bertha come an stood at the bottom of the bed, Miss Johnson kiss me on my fo'head an go to Bertha. They talk fer a minute then Miss Johnson turn an wink at me an leave. Bertha come an hold my hand.

"I'm so sorry, Alice. I din't know!" She say. "I din't know!"

"Shush up, Bertha. Ain't no 'pology never need t'be spoke tween us."

"I feel so stupid,"she say.

"I feel stupid bout lotta thangs, Berth, mo an mo ev'yday. I thank it jes mean we growin up. Y'know how you thank y'know ev'ythang til somethin happen t'teach you differnt? I thank the longer you live, the mo y'gotta *unlearn* til y'come t'the end an ev'ythang be jes a big blank, then God teach you what all you need t'know."

"Miss Johnson say you ain't marry Mr. Tucker. Ain't nobody hear you say 'I will' an everybody know you ain't kiss him."

"That don' make no di'fernce, Bertha. I still gotta go wit him fer the same reason I went through alla this t'day, daddy an mama."

Bertha start to protest, "Daddy an mama? But they..."

"One time, you said Mr. Tucker did s'much for me cause I'm yellow. But that ain't why. See daddy an mama promise him he could marry me when I growed up ef he give our family favers righ'now. Mr. Tucker been payin way ahead a time fer this day. Ef I 'ont go wit him, daddy an mama gonna hafta pay him back. How they gonna do that, Bertha? They cain't do that."

"We kin move nawth," Bertha say, "an daddy kin git a good fac'try job an pay him back ev'y penny!"

"Mr. Tucker don' want money. He awready got a mess a money."

"But..."

"No buts, Bertha. I died the day daddy say I cain't never go to college. I unnerstan thangs I hope you don' never hafta. Y'all gonna git a new roof here, an plummin, an a bathroom wit runnin water, an a toilet that flush. You gonna git yer own room, Bertha. Y'all kin go to college ef y'all wanna. Do it. Live yer life. Don' thank about me, I died. Enjoy yer life, yer freedom, yer plans. Do it!"

"I wan'chu to..." Bertha start to say.

"I will, through you. But only ef you do it."

I ain't feel no bettah, but I felt stronger. Strong enough to go out an face all the people that come to watch an celebrate, or to protest, this weddin that wa'nt.

****

"You feelin bettah, baby?" Daddy axe me soon's he see me comin outta they bedroom.

I give him a nod an try'ta smile.

Miss Myrtle quick brang a plate a food over to me, "You ready t'put some meat on them bones?"

"No ma'am...please," I tell her, tryna keep my sick stomach down.

I look round fer mama an found her in a corner lookin more loss then me. She look up alla sudden an seen me. She try'ta smile, but she lookin so sad, like she thank she done loss me. I go over to her an pull up a chair b'side her an jes set holdin her hand, not sayin nuthin.

Afta'while, Mr. Tucker come in the house wearin a differnt suit an lookin round fer me. I see him an daddy talkin, then daddy point over to me an mama sittin in our quiet li'l corner.

"Princess, you feelin bettah?" Mr. Tucker axe rushin over t'me.

"I feel stronger, thanky."

"Strong enough t'go greet the guests?" He axe smilin an puttin his arm out fer me to take.

"You go on. I migh'can join you directly."

He look a li'l disappointed, but he lef'. When he gone, I felt my thoat lump ease up some.

****

I feel like a ghost. I'm jes watchin ev'ybody talk, laugh, argue, eat, sang, dance, come an go, but I ain't there like them. I'm on the ou'side lookin in at 'em.

I unnerstan why ain't nobody fussin bout this afta'noon, too. Ev'ybody thank they won. The ones that woulda objected, know I ain't say "I will" an know I ain't kiss Mr. Tucker. They figger we ain't married, so there ain't been no weddin to object to. An the ones that want the weddin t'happen see I ain't sayin nuthin bout not sayin the vows or sealin 'em wit a kiss, so they figger they won cause ef I ain't fussin or fightin, why should they? So ev'ybody happy cause ev'ybody thank they won.

Now they leavin an all of 'em sayin how proud they are of me, cause I did or din't marry the man, dependin on what *THEY* want. I feel like laughin an I feel like cryin cause it's so funny an so sad how they happy fer they ownse'f wit'out even thankin bout me.

Only the widow, Mrs. Petty, ain't ack like this a vic'try fer her. She gimme a li'l hug an say, "Yer a strong girl, Alice. You be okay," then she leave.

Afta'while Mr. Tucker come over to me an say, "Princess? You ready t'go t'yer new home?"

I ain't say nothin or even lookit him cause I know he ain't really wanna know.

Mama say, "Mr. Tucker, Alice done had a big day an she been done had a bad spell a sick stomach all day long. Kin she jes spend this firs' night here at home wit..."

"It's okay mama. I go on over to Mr. Tucker's. Wha's the differnce in t'night or t'marra night... really?"

I couldn't b'lieve I said that, but I unnerstan why I did afta I did. Ef I claim I'm too sick t'go right now, fer a night or a month or even years, venchally I gotta go an that'll mean I'm well enough to. Then Mr. Tucker be in charge fer the resta my life. But ef I go now an tell him I'm sick t'night, or fer a month or fo'ever, I stay in control.

That man ain't never gonna force hisse'f on me. Ef he do, it's gonna be two black widows in Smedley.

****

We drive on off to his house on that hill. It take maybe twenny minutes t'git there. It's a big ol house on a li'l hill. It look like a hotel next t'the house we jes lef'. It's gotta porch upstairs an down an tall, tall pillars. Lookin at it remine me of them plantations, not s'long ago, whure we all woulda been slavin away, Mr. Tucker too.

When we gits t'the front door, he wanna carry me inside, but I quick put up my hand an say, "Don' touch me. I'm still feelin real sick."

He s'happy to have me there, he take off his coat jacket, open the door an drop it down fer me to step on.

"Please pick yer coat up, Mr. Tucker," I say as calm as I kin, when that ain't nuthin like I feel. "I done spoilt one of yer good suits t'day awready wit my throw up, member?"

"Awww, tha' don'..."

"Please!" I said again a li'l stronger cause any minute I thank I migh'would scream the truth: I don' wan'chu to be ackin like this some romantic evenin cause it ain't! It's my worse nightmare. You is Satan done bought my soul a long time ago an is jes now brangin me to live wit'chu in Hell fo'ever! So pick yer stupid coat up off the flo'. I ain't none a yer wife! I'm yer slave! Whatever I do here won't be fer you, it's fer my family. You gonna be payin them fo'ever fer buyin me!

But I ain't say none of that, I din't hafta. He pick his coat up an I walked into a grand white hall wit a wide staircase in the middle leadin up to a big balcony upstairs. Downstairs, doors open off it on both sides. The firs' door to my right was a sittin parlor. Cross from it was a dinin'room. Next to that was a game room wit a wall a likker behine a big pretty bar. Cross from that was a liberry wit a ton a books. Next to that was a sun parlor. An cross from that was a kitchen. An that was jes the firs' floor!!

"Princess, you kin go whur'ever y'wants an change anythang cause it's yers now, too. But'chu look a li'l peek-ed an I thank y'oughta lie down... the bedrooms is upstairs."

I went upstairs whure there was five doors off the balcony. The firs' two rooms from the lef' was bedrooms. The next was a sewin parlor. The next was a big ol bathroom. An the last was another big bedroom that look bigger then the other two bedrooms put t'getha. This one look used, too.

80

The bed was made, but there was shoes on the floor an stuff on the dresser.

"I'm gone sleep down there in that firs' room. Thanky Mr. Tucker."

"They's plenny room in this'un fer both of us, Princess."

"Mr. Tucker, I gotta bad sick stomach. I thank I be more comfi'ble down there. By myse'f."

He lookit me a minute like he tryna see ef tha's true. I ain't hafta ack sick. Jes the thought of him an me in the same bed make me turn pea soup green.

"Well okay, ef you thank you be mo' comfi'ble." He say real sad-like, "But you doesn't hafta call me Mr. Tucker no mo, Princess. My name is Luthern. It make me happy ef you call me that, or L.T. like some a the boys down t'the mill call me."

He give a li'l smile to show me how happy that would make him.

But I ain't wanna make him happy. The thought of bein married to this fat, old man, even ef he is rich, jes make me wanna die.

Mama said ef you keep bad feelins inside, they kin make you ugly an sick. Holdin onto bad feelins kin make you mean, too. That meaness kin feel like strength when you use it to hurt people you wanna hurt.

I wanna hurt Mr. Tucker. I wanna hurt him so bad by bein so mean to him til he don' want me no mo an he let me go wit'out makin my family pay him back. Tha's my plan. Bein mean don' make me happy, it make me strong, an I hope soon it'll make me free. I ain't plan this, it jes now come t'me. But it feel like it migh'could work. An any plan is bettah then none.

So I lookit him standin there pleadin wit his eyes fer me to be his friend ef not his wife an I say, "G'night, *Mr. Tucker*," b'fo walkin to my new bedroom at the other end of the hall.

thirteen

True to his word, my family got a new roof an Bertha got her own bedroom. New stairs replace the ladder goin to the loft. The 'lectric an plummin was takin longer, but pipes an wires was scattered in the yard ready to git installed. An a tub, a sink an a toilet was in crates in the room they added on fer a bathroom. We still go by daddy an mama's on Sundays t'go to chu'ch, then stop by they house fer a big dinner afta. I go some weekdays too, to he'p the twins wit they schoolin, lease tha's what I tell Mr. Tucker.

Mama an me be in the kitchen cookin an mendin clothes. We don' talk that much an when we do, it's almos always her tryna splain why they done to me what they done. This perticuler Monday we was peelin taters when mama start splainin again.

"Alice, me an yer daddy married each other outta love. We was young an din't know nuthin ceptin we jes had to be t'getha. We was doin awright strugglin long til y'all babies start comin. Ev'ythang change then. We ain't never have enough a nuthin then. I couldn't go lookin fer work cause who gonna watch the babies? We couldn't pay nobody. I had yer daddy pass the word that I could sew an make dinners fer people, but'chu see, mos people do that for theyse'f round here. An the han'ful a white folks that don', got they he'p livin in wit 'em. So that ain't send us no work t'speak of.

"One day yer daddy was workin over to the mill an he invited Mr. Tucker to dinner that evenin. I ain't know nobody was comin so's we ain't had nuthin special, jes some okra stew wit rice an biscuits. Mr. Tucker carry on like he was eatin the finest food ever cooked. He axe me ef I sew as good as I cook an I tole him, 'Oh yessuh!' So, he send me a mess of clothes to wash an mend.

"You's jes a baby then an winter was comin early seem-like. So sometime he send enough wood to cook an warm this ol cabin fo' months. He was always a blessin to alla us."

I say, "Mama, you done awready tole me alla this..." cause I ain't wanna hear bout what a gift from God Mr. Tucker is.

"Well, I'm tellin you again, so listen!"

It's not mama's way to snap like that, so I tried my best to listen.

"When you start growin into a long leg li'l Miss an you talk so good an he'p wit yer brothers an sister so good, Mr. Tucker took notice.

"He pleased as punch right now, cause the hard workin, thoughtful li'l girl you was, is now the woman you is. He always braggin bout how ya coulda axe fer he'p in that big ole house, but you does all the cleanin an cookin an thangs yerse'f. An you's a much better cook then I ever been! Ev'ybody love it when you sends over them strange an tasty meals. Mr. Tucker say you done switched the rooms round some, too, an he like it bettah. He been livin in that big place by hisse'f an knowed it inside out. Now when he walk in a room spectin to see one thang an fine a whole nother thang, it be like a special surprise, like a gift. It don' take much to please that man."

It's right what she say bout me doin all the work. But I ain't doin it to be a good wife or nuthin. I do it cause fer one, cause I ain't never been a stranger to hard work an it don' bother me none. I kin make b'lieve I'm still at home he'pin mama wit the house chores an forgit about where I really am an why. Ef I don' keep busy, I got time to thank bout what my life coulda been an tha's what makes me ugly an mean to Mr. Tucker. Ef somebody else was cookin an cleanin steada me, I would have too much time studdin my sitiation. So I keep busy as best I kin.

I cook big beautiful suppers, way too much fer jes the two of us. I stuff pork chops wit mushroom/onion cornbread dressin an stuff my baked sweet potatoes wit cabbage an greens. I mix crawdads an sausage in my okra stew to make gumbo to put over rice. I put a pecan praline toppin on my sweet potatoe pie sometime, an I make mixed fruit pies steada jes one fruit. I put pears in my apple pie an my berry pie got strawberries, blueberries and blackberries. I make pecan/pumpkin butter fer our biscuits, tha's somethin special ef I do say so myse'f. I would be a fat somebody ef I could hold ha'f of this food down, but I still throws up from time to time. I send alla our exter food home to mama an them, so tha's what she talkin bout when she say *strange an tasty meals*.

An I did switch the downstairs all around t'make mo sense to me. Like I thank the dinin room needs to be close to the kitchen, but that mean I was gonna hafta move the gameroom. Now I ain't want the gameroom in the front of the house, so I put the liberry there an move the gameroom to whure the liberry useta be. I ain't let nobody he'p me neitha, cause I wa'nt tryna git done in a hurry. I want my work to last. Plus, sometimes I say I'm dog tired steada sayin I got a sick stomach when Mr. Tucker invite me to his room.

"It seem like sech a tur'ble thang to you," mama still talking. "But they's lots a weddin's been made tween a man wit good prospects an the family's of li'l girls the man thank he migh'could wanna marry. Sometime the man find another wife b'fo the girl is growed up an the family don' owe him nuthin. Sometime somethin happen to the man, like he lose alla his money or he have a stroke or he die or somethin, an the family don' owe him nuthin. Sometime the young girl grow to love that man like he love her an they woulda got married anyways.

"We ain't never wish no harm on Mr. Tucker. I guess we was hopin he woulda found somebody else, cause it seem like yer growin up was sech a long time away. But you growed up faster then some folks blink. Then we was hopin you woulda loved him like he love you. We though'chu migh'coulda been doin jes that too, til Isaac come long."

I try not t'thank bout Isaac, or even say his name. It move me t'my bones an I jes wanna cry. I try not to thank bout what he might be doin, or what we woulda been doin ef I hadda gone wit him. I read the Dunbar book he gimme alla time. Somethin in ev'y poem kin make me member

84

him, ef I let it. I ain't finish the book yet fer readin some of them verses over an an. They's one in perticuler, "Lonesome", whure I put *Isaac* steada *Mother* an *to college* steada *a visitin* an *to make his life anew* steada *to spend a month er two*, but it's still Lonesome:

The shetters flap more lazy-like
n'what they use to do
sence mother's gone a visitin
(*sence Isaac's gone to college*)
to spend a month er two
(*to make his life anew*)
we've killed the fattest chicken
an' we've cooked her to a turn
we've made the richest gravy
but i jest don't give a durn
far nothin' 'at I drink er eat,
er nothin' 'at I see
the food ain't got the pleasant taste
It use to have to me
They's somep'n stickin' in my throat
ez tight ez hardened glue
sence Isaac's gone to college
to make his life anew

That poem splain jes how I feel.
"...ain't the way we raise you," mama say.
I ain't hear her cause I was thankin bout Isaac. I jes caught a piece of that last part. "Wha'chu say, mama, my mind driffed."
"I say do you member what the rev'ern say yestiddy, bout..."
How kin anybody ever fergit what the rev'ern say. Even ef you don't like what he sayin, you gotta 'preciate the way he be puttin on an performin. He be preachin, then right in the middle he axe ev'ybody what he say t'make shore he ain't lose nobody. Sometime he axe two or three times, to make shore ev'ybody answerin, an not jes a few. It kin be real entertainin. Watchin Rev. Pritchard preach is the closest thang to real live theater we got in Smedley. Yestiddy the rev'ern was perticulerly lively in his show:

85

"God made Adam. Then while Adam was sleepin neath a tree, God took one a his ribs an made Eve. Whure Eve come from?... From Adam's rib, tha's right. He coulda scooped up a whole nother heap a clay an shaped that woman. He coulda made her firs'. Afta all He God, ain't he?... He kin do whatever He want! Ain't that right? I say, ain't that right?!... Aw'right than! But he ain't do that, did He?!... NO! Tha's right. He made the woman second an he made her from man. Why you thank He done it like that, huh? I'ma tell you why! He done it so's it be clear that the woman is SECOND to man AN she ain't nuthin wit'out a man sence she come from him! Oh Yeah!! Now, y'all womens is havin all the babies, so some a y'all thank that y'all should be firs'. But that ain't how God planned it, now is it? I say is it? I cain't hear y'all! Oh now don' git mad at me, I ain't writ the book! Man is s'poze to lead an the woman is s'poze to follow, see?

"The firs' time Adam give Eve a chance to lead, wha'she do?! Y'all know wha'she do! She led him to the forbidden fruit an had him eatin thangs he ain't have no bizness eatin... tha's why we die! Why do we die? Causa Eve an her persnickety se'f, tha's right! She ain't know nuthin bout takin the lead, but she still gonna sit up there an tell somebody wha' to do... An Adam done it!!

"See now, tha's the other half, Adam done it! Y'all mens got yer own mind, don't be lis'nin to yer wives. Make her listen to you! Tha's God's plan. Hey, don'chu git mad at me! I ain't writ The Bible, I jes preach on it.

"Now I done pointed out that some womens thank they should be firs' cause they havin the babies. They say, 'Ah'm the one brangin new life.' Yeah, well y'all brought us death, too, member that! Git on off y'all high horses, cause now see, I happen to know that some a you womens is refusin to make babies cause you ain't gitten yer way.

"But ef you is married, you MUST SUBMIT TO YER HUSBAND! You ain't got no choice! Ef you is married, you must what? C'mon now, some a y'all is holdin back. Ef you is married, you must what?! You Must Submit! Tha's what! Now ef you ain't married, you ain't got no bizness raisin yer skirt an droppin yer pants lessin you takin a bath or bout to use the toilet! Oh Yeah!"

I read the Bible for myse'f when I want the real message, but I like goin to chu'ch to hear Rev. Pritchard's lively swang on thangs an yestiddy was purty lively.

"Now, like I say," Mama still talkin afta I come back from my mind driffin again, "...it ain't none a our bizness, Alice, cause you growed up an married now. But Mr. Tucker done tole yer daddy how you been sleepin down the hall since y'all been t'getha an tha'chall ain't never... well,... y'know... been t'getha. Not in the fo'teen weeks y'all been married. Tha's mean on a man, Alice. Plus, y'hear what Rev. Pritchard say yestiddy, you must submit. The good Lawd know that ain't the way we raise you, Alice."

"Wha'sa matter mama?" I axe mama jes as calm as kin be, I ain't raise my voice or nuthin. "Mr. Tucker tell y'all lessin I move into his room, y'all ain't gonna git yer 'lectric an plummin put in?"

Mama couldn'a look more hurt ef I'da slapped her silly like I slapped Bertha on Mr. Tucker weddin day. She stop lookin at me, like it hurt her eyes to see me. She drop her head down over the taters in her bowl an it look like she was prayin for 'em or somethin. Afta'while, she git up an go to the sink an start sniffin at the sink like she jes caught a cold.

"We ain't never mean you no harm, Alice," she say in a quiet, shakey voice. "We done said we sorry to you ev'y way we knows how to. You gotta lotta bad thoughts an feelin's, an they makin you ugly. You done turn ugly on Mr. Tucker. Now you gittin ugly wit yer mama, too? I don' hardly know my own daughter no mo!" She broke down sobbin at the sink.

I was too stunned to move at firs', then I put my bowl on the table an goes to her. "I ain't mean to hurt you, mama. I ain't mean nuthin by it," I hugged her best I could. "I ain't jes ugly, mama, I done got mean an cold-hearted. I cain't he'p it. I don' wanna hurt you or nobody, but it seem like tha's all I kin do now."

Mama lookit me then start backin away, "Omigod! Omigod, what we done done to our baby?" Mama look more skeered of me then before I tried to splain. "Who are you? WHO ARE YOU?" She start to wailin. "WHAT WE DONE DONE TO OUR BABY?! OMIGOD!! OMIGOD!!"

Wa'nt nothin I could say or do to make thangs right. Mama ain't wanna hear nothin I got t'say an she ain't want me touchin her. I felt so bad I start cryin, too. I sunk to the floor an start beatin on my thighs, then start kickin an beatin on the floor. I wanna beat the devil outta me cause ain't nobody but Satan make they own mama cringe an shy away from 'em like that.

I ain't even know I was carryin on like that til mama start rockin me in her arms tellin me it's gonna be awright. I ain't never done nuthin like that b'fo, but here I was pitchin a fit. I musta look jes like some of them li'l spoiled chirrens I seen actin up in the streets when they ain't git they way.

Now I'm wondrin ef them kids be actin like that cause they tryna beat the devil outta theyse'f. Or do they be actin like that cause they know what I jes found out, tha's the only way to git mama's attention. Lawd knows, that ain't the way I been raised. I feel like I'm shore nough losin my mind.

But I ruther lose my mind then lose my mama. I decide right then, next time Mr. Tucker invite me to his room like he do, I might go wit him.

I decide right then, too, I must shore nough be crazy.

fourteen

Mr. Tucker ain't know bout what I decided cause I ain't tell nobody or nuthin. Far as he know, I wa'nt bout to be goin to his room over mines down the hall no time soon. So's he ain't bother to invite me again til roun'bout November.

Fall is still got nice weather cause the heat is soft an snuggly. It ain't bearin down an smotherin like it be in the summer. Summer be like a big moo cow sittin on yer chest, but fall is like a li'l purrin kitten curled up in yer lap.

I was sittin ou'side on the upstairs porch enjoyin the mild weather one afta'noon when Mr. Tucker come out to me an say, "Tha' was some good dinner you fix this afta'noon. Ya know, I'm partial to chicken livers. It was rail good, thanky Princess."

I ain't say nuthin cause I ain't got nuthin t'say an I ruther jes sit quiet then to make a li'l small talk jes to be talkin. He stand there for a minute like he waitin for somethin, then he hand me a light sweater an say, "The temperture s'poze to drop down in the forties later on today. I brang you this sweater so's you don't ketch yer death. Ef you wanna hot toddy while you settin ou'chere, I fix you one."

"A hot tea be nice, Mr. Tucker. Thanky."

Somethin I notice bout Mr. Tucker, he cain't lookit me when he wanna invite me to his room, like it make him nervous or uncomfible or somethin. He always be busy doin somethin when he brang it up.

Afta'while when he was brangin me my tea, firs' he brang out a li'l table to put it on. When he was settin that up next to me he say, "It might be bess fer both of us, Princess, ef... sence it's s'poze to git so cold... It might be best ef... we sleep in the big bedroom...

"...t'getha."

Then he quick go t'git the tray wit the tea stuff on it.

When Mr. Tucker come back carryin the tea tray I say, "Yeah, that migh'could be best."

He drop that tray. "Ya thank?!"

"Well, sence it's s'poze to be so cold an all."

"Yeah...yeah...yeah," he say then quick start pickin up the mess he made of the tea.

He brung me some fresh tea an wit it he brung another chair so's he could sit on the porch wit me. I ain't want him on that porch wit me. But I guess he thankin I'm feelin close to him sence I fine'ly said I be joinin him tonight. Afta'while, he start talkin bout somethin. I don't know what.

I was starin out to the road studdin freedom.

Freedom.

Freedom seem to be jes ou'side of Mr. Tucker yard, jes down that there road a piece. That musta been what slaves useta thank, how near an far they freedom was an how they lived an died jes a few feet from it.

That git me to thankin bout the slave womens that was bought jes to make yellow babies wit they *masta's*. Them yellow an high-yellow babies fetch a higher price, I heard. I was wondrin what the woman musta been thankin bout when it come time for her to root round wit the devil what bought her jes so's he could make light-skinned sons an daughters to sell *down the river*. I was wondrin what kept her from killin that devil, or the babies, or herse'f? Was she too skeered? Was it doubts? Was it hope?

Then I was thankin, what kep her from runnin away?

I thank I'm feelin jes like they felt, ceptin I cain't imagine what they migh'coulda felt. So I jes set there tryin to.

Mr. Tucker alla time, jes yappin away bout somethin, then he tetch my arm. I jump an shoot him a look of pure evil that make him shy back some an say, "You ain't tetch yer tea, Princess."

I glance at my cold cup, then look back out to the road wit'out sayin nuthin.

Miss Johnson say Harriet Tubman was a slave, but she git tarred of that. So she run away nawth usin the map God put in the sky at night. An she wa'nt the onliest one, she jes the mos famous cause she kept comin back to he'p others git away. I was tryin to 'magine her firs' run. She ain't know whure she was goin. The patrollers was always out lookin for runaways. There was poison snakes, an poison oak an ivy, an rabid dogs. Plus, there was cold an rain an no food. But she went on anyways, an she come back again an again. She jes trust in God an say, "Yer will be done, Lawd. Yer will be done." It was her faith in God what made her s'strong.

I need more faith, I thank. I need to pray an make peace wit myse'f cause they's a war goin on inside of me that's gonna ha'f kill me ef I don't do somethin soon.

Mr. Tucker ain't a bad man. He don' want me to be his slave, even ef tha's what it feel like. He want me to be his wife. I don' wanna be married to him. I need to find out what God want. Yer will be done, Lawd. Yer will be done.

I do likes takin a bath in that deep tub wha's in the bathroom. We ain't never have a bathroom at daddy an mama's house, although they be gittin one fixed near good as this'un soon. I treats the bathroom like a chu'ch whure the tub kin baptize me clean. Wash away all my bad thoughts, steada spittin up my insides all the time. Sometime I soaks in that tub til I looks like a prune.

While Mr. Tucker up here jes yappin away, I'm thankin I'm gone run me a hot bath an have a long talk wit God to figger out His will.

****

"Our Father Who art in heaven, thanky for t'day an all the blessins You put in this an ev'yday. Thanky fer my family, specially my sister. Thanky fer my friends, specially Miss Johnson, even though I don' git to see her no mo. Thanky fer our health, the food we eat, the clothes we wear, the roofs over our heads. Thanky fer the good b'cause it's good an is a gift from You. But thanky fer the bad too, cause hard times make us to learn an grow, so tha's a gift from You, too."

When I was small, Sister Ruth at chu'ch taught us to begin our prayers by thankin God fer ev'ythang, the good an the bad. She say to specially thank Him fer the bad cause the lessons we learn from hard times kin only make us bettah. If we ain't learn our lessons, we gonna be repeatin 'em til we do... or til we die.

"Dear God, you gave us Yer Son to show us the way. He live a life full of sacrifice an showed us how all thangs are possible through faith. But I feel so lost now. You know I don' wanna be here. I never wanted to be here an never said 'I will'. But here I am. Please make me to know what I must do bout bein a wife to Mr. Tucker. You know my heart an hopes even b'fo I do. You know my fears an dreams. Make me to know Yers, my sweet Lord, please make me to know Yers."

I jes set there in that hot tub axin God to give me a sign or somethin. I got to thankin bout some of the crosses people been made to bear an how they was able to see they troubles through. Daniel in the lions den, Jonah in the whale, Lot an Sarah leavin Sodom an Gomorrah (only Sarah ain't make it cause she look back). Harriet, Sojourner, George Washington Carver, Booker T. Washington an Frederick Douglass. Nat Turner, too, only Nat ain't have no happy endin cause he use violence. Even though he read the bible an prayed, God would ruther you turn th'other cheek, I guess. Thankin bout all those famous ex-slaves got me to thankin bout the millions of unknown slaves, wit trials an struggles we ain't never heard bout an will never know. Specially the women that was raped to make babies wit a buncha men they ain't want or sometimes ain't even know. They was worked, whipped, bought, bred an sold like horses. They's lots of women round Smedley been raped an cain't say nuthin cause lots of times it's the law mens rapin' 'em.

Here I am in a fancy house wit a man I have known all my life. Mama say this man love me an he ack like it, too. Lease he ain't rape me. Am I makin a big thang outta nuthin? Mr. Tucker been takin care of me an my family sence fo'ever. God, di'ja send him to bless us so that he could find me an be blessed in return?

"Was that Yer plan? And ef it is, how come You give me Isaac? Why You let me git a full schola'ship? Why do I git sick t'my stomach at the thought of Mr. Tucker? Please he'p me t'be stronger an wiser an more givin an forgivin. Please flush alla my mean an ugly ways down this drain when I git out this tub an make me t'be the person You would have me t'be."

When I got out the tub bout a hour later wit my feet an hands wrinkled as raisins, I still din't know what to do. But sence I said I would go to his room, an my word is my bond, I did. Afta that would be afta that. I was still prayin to God in my head for His will.

****

Mr. Tucker lit a fire in the fireplace when I come in the bedroom cause I was shakin so hard my teeth clicked. He awready had hot toddy fixin's on the table by the bed. He told me that a toddy would warm me up right quick. I ain't never put corn in my tea to make it a toddy be'fo, but tonight I did. Mr. Tucker said he was gonna take a bath now that I done took mines. When he lef' the room, I poured ha'f a cup a corn an topped it wit ha'f a cup a tea. I tried to gulp it down, but I din't know it was gonna light up my mouth an thoat like that.

I took a big slurp an even though I din't like the taste, I tried to swallow it. It musta gone down a wrong pipe or somethin cause I end up coughin my fool head off.

I guess Mr. Tucker heard me, cause he come runnin in the room wit only a towel wrapped round his big ole Buddha belly. His chest was saggy to whure it look like he was growin li'l tits. His narrow shoulders sprouted stubby, skinny lookin li'l arms an a short, wide, stump of a neck that held his big ol head. His legs was his best feature, thick thighs an calves, even though they was a li'l bowed. My chokin on the corn turned into nausea at the sight of him.

I closed my eyes, put my hand up an gasped, "S'okay, ...really. Go on... go on back take yer bath."

"You sure, Princess?"

I stayed bent over so as not to hafta lookit him, an nodded my head fer "yes".

So he went back. When he did, I stole a glimpse of him walkin away. He din't look near so bad from behine.

His back look exter wide prob'ly cause his belly was pokin out on the sides, but the big bulby part was in front whure you couldn't see it. Then alla that gut was snatched into a tight li'l round butt, lease tha's how his butt look inside his towel. Jes b'fo he lef' the room it hit me what he look like... a frog!

93

He got that big ol' head on a stumpy neck wit a wide back an a big ol belly pulled tight into a li'l round butt wit pretty legs an no arms to speak of. From behine, Mr. Tucker look jes like a frog swimmin round in a pond.

I liked to hurt myse'f tryin not to laugh out loud. I thank bout the way he alla time be callin me *Princess* an be tryin to git me to kiss him. Maybe he really a young, handsome prince locked up in that old, fat, froggy body beggin to git freed wit a kiss. Omigosh! I wish Bertha was here so we could tell frog jokes an make froggy noises an git Daniel an Samuel t'play leap frog again.

I got a towel from the closet to clean up the toddy I had coughed up on the floor. I was still on my hands an knees tryin to keep from laughin myse'f silly, when Mr. Tucker finish his bath. He got on a robe this time when he come in the room an find me on my hands an knees wipin up my mess an gigglin like a ninny.

"Lemme git that fer you, Princess."

"Is awready got," I said usin alla my strength not to fall out from him callin me *Princess*.

"Well, I'll take that dirty rag then," he said lookin kinda funny cause he really want to know what I was laughin at, but he too skeered to axe.

Afta he lef' to take the dirty rag away, I poured a li'l more tea in my toddy an sipped it slow. I still ain't like the taste, but it did warm me up. I felt woozy an numb afta'while like the room was swayin in a gentle breeze. Sence I was in the room, I got swayed, too. I din't feel like movin round too much cause it felt like I was movin when I was jes sittin still, so I stretched out in the bed when I finished my toddy.

Mr. Tucker come back not too long afta that.

Now, it migh'coulda been the toddy or it migh'coulda been me over dreadin his touch or, more'n likely, it was God answerin my prayers wit one a His tender mercies, but to the best of my recollection, Mr. Tucker's affections was kinda quick an painless. Later, he tried to wrap me up in his arms.

"No Mr. Tucker, please. I'ma pro'bly be sick," I said.

"Okay. Tha's okay," he say, then rolled over on his side.

When I hear him snorin, I went to the bathroom an took a li'l bath. Then I went down the hall to my room, so's I kin git some sleep.

****

94

I mos'ly still sleep down the hall, but once or twice a month, I go to his room. In a coupla months, jes when I thought I was toleratin awright, I start gittin sick stomachs all over again. I was sick mornin, noon an night. I 'ont ever feel like eatin. But now when I be cookin, the smell of the food, the feel of it or even jes the thought of it, make me sick.

I was over to mama's helpin the twins wit they history lessons one afta'noon, when mama axe me to he'p her wit the chicken for dinner. They was awready plucked. She want me to cut 'em into they parts so she kin fry it up. Jes lookin at that bumpy, white-pink flesh make my stomach start to churn. I tried to tough it out anyway an went on ahead an picked it up. But feelin that cool, sticky, loose skin slidin over the thin slimy tissue that cover the thick, pink meat tha's wrapped round them fragile li'l bones... well, I dropped that bird like it was on fire an ran to the bathroom (that was fine'ly installed) an threw up all over the pretty yellow hook-rug mama made to cover the floor.

I heard Mama behine me when I was tryna sop up my puke wit a rag b'fo rollin the rug up to take ou'side an hose down. I'm thankin mama gonna be hurt bout her rug. She seen I was tryin my best to git t'the toilet so she cain't be mad, but I still messed up her pretty rug an I thought tha's gonna hurt her.

"I'm sorry mama. I'ma take this ou'side an clean it up good as new. I jes couldn't make the toilet in time," I said feelin real bad bout the mess I made of her rug.

Mama bent down, took the rag out my hands an pulled me up. "Tha's okay baby, I git the twins t'clean that up directly," she said real gentle-like.

"Mama..."

"Allie...I thank you pregnant."

"Huh?"

"You gonna have a baby!"

"Why you say that?"

"Cause I'm shore you is. You been throwin up ev'yday now, ain'chu?"

"Mama, I been throwin up ev'yday sence b'fo the weddin."

"When's the las' time you had yer monthly?"

I had to thank on that one, but I couldn't say fer shore. "I 'ont know," I say.

"Not this month?"

"Not yet."

"Las' month?"

"Uhmm...I 'ont thank so."

She hug me real tight then an start rockin me from side to side chantin, "My baby gonna have a baby! My baby gonna have a baby!"

Then mama called fer the twins an tole 'em, "Come roll up this here rug in the bathroom, take it ou'side an hose it down real good. Then wash it an hose it down again."

"Why we got to clean up afta Alice? We ain't the ones throwed up on it!"

"Y'all gonna do it cause I said fer y'all to, an cause y'all don' wanna git yer li'l backsides whupped for not lis'nin! Gone do it!... Now!"

Mama set me down at the table an she set down wit me still holdin my hand like we was girlfriends bout to talk some juicy gossip. But then I seen that chicken was still layin on the floor by the sink where I dropped it.

"I'm sorry, Mama. I dropped y'alls dinner on the floor, now it's gittin all germy." I got up to go finish my job.

"Girl don'chu worry bout that bird none!" She set me back down, then went an picked the chicken up off the floor, rinsed it good in the sink an lef' it there.

"That bird kin wait awhile," she said comin back to the table. "Mr. Tucker ain't said nuthin to yer daddy fer some time, so I figgered y'all done worked out whatever needed to be worked out."

I felt a wave a sickness wash over me alla sudden an mama musta seen it too, cause she quick tryna splain herse'f.

"I know you tarred a hearin it an maybe you don' b'lieve it, but yer daddy an me feel real bad bout marryin you to Mr. Tucker like we did. We really ain't thank it was gonna happen. But sence it did, we ain't know it was gonna turn yer stomach so much as it do. He a good man, y'know that, an he do love you dearly.

"The onliest thang he want as much as you... maybe even more'n you... is a son! Alice, ever sence y'alls weddin, he been talkin bout y'all startin a family an makin him a son t'venchally take over his mill when he git big.

"Yer daddy was jes teasin him one day wit small talk afta y'all was married a few months. He was axin Mr. Tucker ef his grandson was t'be expected anytime soon. Mr. Tucker tole him, 'I cain't see how you ever gonna git any grands from Alice, bein as she sleep in the bedroom on the other side a the house from me.' He wa'nt gossipin or complainin to yer father. He was jes ans'ern a question.

"But a man always wanna boy baby, Alice. They love they sons better'n they love theyse'f mos times. They plan fer that boy to do all the thangs they ain't never done or cain't do. They look at them boys like it's they own second chance at life.

"Mr. Tucker married late. Ef he had married at the same time as other people his age, he pro'bly be a gran'daddy by now. He ain't all that old, but ef you make a boy-child, that man gonna retire! Then you kin retire, too, Alice. You kin stay in the far bedroom an Mr. Tucker pro'bly won't be pesterin you no mo. When the baby git a li'l growed, you kin pro'bly even go t'college ef you still wanna go. Mr. Tucker ain't gonna be studdin you fer tryna remake his own life through his boy. Ef this baby be a son, you gonna be on Easy Street fer real!"

Dear Sweet Jesus, mama still tryna make out like bein Mr. Tucker's wife is a blessin to me. But ef I am pregnant an this *is* a boy I'm carryin an he come out lookin like his daddy an I got to be round *TWO* Luthern Tuckers day in an day out, good man or not, I b'lieve I ruther slit my thoat then to live on Easy Street one more minute...for real!

fifteen

Mama was right. I was pregnant. Afta he found out, Mr. Tucker couldn't do enough for me. So I din't hardly ever see him no more cause tha's what I really wanted. I ain't tell him that, but he knew. He ain't stupid.

Afta them few weeks of retchin over ev'y li'l thang, I spend mosta my days eatin, sleepin, readin the books in Mr. Tucker's liberry an eatin some mo. I start lookin an actin like daddy an mama's plow mule, Lazybones, gittin big as a house an movin kinda slow pokey like.

Havin a whole nother person grow inside you is truly one a God's miracles. It kin make you t'know that you a special wonder jes like sunrise an sunset, or the quench of rain, or the strength in light'nin, or the sweet in pure cane. Life is a blessin an brangin life make you a blessin to the life you brang.

Then again, I cain't he'p but to thank that this jes a li'l Mr. Tucker I'm carryin round. Ev'ytime this boy move, it's like he makin some kinda demand. So I got a big Mr. Tucker *ou'side* a me tryna pull me to *his* side an a li'l Mr. Tucker *inside* a me tryna pull me to *his* side. I feel trapped an torn like I cain't breathe. An I need to breathe.

When the baby move, I git pulled in two directions, feelin the miracle of life an feelin the fear of certain death.

This wa'nt a happy time fer me. Even though the sensation of a growin baby was innerestin an new. The thought of two Mr. Tuckers to take care of when the burden of one was awready so unbearable, almos make me lose my appetite. Almos.

****

Come August, I was over he'pin mama wit the clothes. I was hangin wet thangs on a line out back an only ha'f hearin voices an noises comin from the front. Mama called to me t'take a break an when I got in the house ev'ybody yelled, "SURPRISE!!" It was mos'ly my family an mama's friends, mos'ly women from the chu'ch. Mama an them was givin a surprise shower fer the baby.

I ain't no real big fan of surprises. To do it right, you gotta keep a secret from the friends or folks you gonna surprise. The last big surprise my family gimme was tellin me I couldn't go t'college, even though they knew I was tryin ev'y which way I knew how to do jes that. So my suspicions an fears to-ward surprises shouldn't surprise nobody.

Look like ha'f the women in the county was standin in my mama's house yellin "SURPRISE!!" An even though I kin see they all smilin an happy, I'm thankin, "Lawd, what now?!"

Ant Betty grabbed my hand an made me sit. She say, "Siddown Alice, rest yerse'f. We come by to give yer baby a shower!"

"Give this baby a shower?" I was confused. "The baby ain't even here yit. How he gonna git a..."

"Alice," mama stop me, "this a party. We jes givin you some thangs you gonna need an pro'bly ain't thought of ahead a time. Relax, baby. Jes relax."

So I relaxed an they was right. I wouldn't never a thought a none a this stuff cause I be tryin my best not to thank about this chile or how I

99

come to be carryin him. I'm jes dreadin the day he's born an there be two Mr. Tuckers bossin me round. The baby won't be no problem at firs', jes sleepin an eatin an bawlin when he ain't git enough of sleepin an eatin. But he gonna grow fast an learn that he is the son of the King of Smedley. He gonna be makin his demands an pushin me round jes like his daddy, who I b'lieve gonna be less patient wit me afta his son is born.

I jes set there while the ladies lined up to gimme gift afta beautiful gift. Knitted blankets an bonnets an booties, a big patch-work bear wit button eyes, a ton of diapers, hand-carved an painted toys an blocks, a crib, a wagon.

My favorite gift was a book Bertha an the twins made for li'l Luthern. They called it, "The ABC Book of Alice Tucker." It was a biography of me to he'p him to learn his ABC's an learn about his momma at the same time. There was a picture an a few lines fer each letter of the alphabet makin it twenny-six pages long. They punched two holes on the lef' side of the papers an painted a cardboard top an bottom fer the cover, then looped strang through the holes, an tied 'em to keep it all t'getha. You could tell they put a lotta work into thankin bout what to write an what to draw fer each letter. "A is for Alice, your mother's first name. She is the oldest of four children born to Grace and Nathaniel Ward, your grandparents on your mother's side. Alice was their first baby. Her name begins with the first letter in the alphabet. She was an A student in school. Alice is first in many books." They drew a body onto a picture of me as a li'l girl in pigtails smilin' big wit my two front teeth missin an labeled it "Alice". There were other bodies drawn onto labeled pictures of Bertha, Daniel an Samuel. It was so nice, tears come right to my eyes an I had to close it fore I boo-hooed an smudged up all the pages.

"Thanky Bertha, I love y'all," I said givin her a bear hug.

She said, "Thank Miss Johnson, it was her idea."

I held Bertha away from me by her shoulders, "I shoulda guessed that," I laughed in her face while tears rolled down mines. "All the grammar an spellin is right!"

Then Bertha hugged me close and whispered in my ear, "She want to be here, but it break her heart too much cause she thank she let'chu down."

I said, "Tell Miss Johnson I love her, too. I know she done all she could an tha's all anybody kin do. Tell her I want her to visit me sometime soon. Real soon."

"I will."

"You an mama come, too. Us girls gotta look out fer one another."

Janey came in wit her baby on her hip. All the ladies start makin a big fuss over the youngest girl in the room, her daughter. When they took her baby away from her, she come over to me.

"Hi Alice," she said handin me a big soft package.

"Hey Janey. You ain't hafta brang me nuthin. It's a gift jes seein you."

"It ain't nuthin," she said smilin. It was a needlepoint pillow that read *"Congratulations New Mother"* an had ducks, bluebirds, butterflies or flowers in each corner.

"It's jes a li'l somethin I sewed. Yer time aw'mos here ain't it?"

"S'poze to be next week, or the next."

"You skeered?"

"A li'l bit. But mos women git by wit'out no problems."

"Yeah, it's like tryin to poop a watermelon!" She said, then laughed at the faces me an Bertha was makin. "But afta it's over, it's over. Y'might say you ain't gonna do that no mo... but, b'fo you know it..." she looked down at her little bitty round belly an back at me.

"Oh Janey! You havin another one?!" I said.

"Yeah," she said lookin tired an sad.

"Wha's wrong?" Bertha axed.

"Makin a baby ain't nuthin, you know that," Janey looked at me like we had a secret. "Havin one ain't that much more work, really. But afta the baby git here, Lawd, tha's when you ketch it! Less you got a pile a money in the bank awready or you marry a rich man, you ain't never gonna ketch up. You gonna stay dirt poor an ev'y baby afta the firs' jes gonna he'p to make you poorer."

"Don'chu love Lucas?" I axed cause I was shocked that she was talkin like this.

"Yeah...but that ain't got nuthin to do wit it! You lucky, Alice..." she start to say.

"Whoa...!" Bertha say grabbin my hands. I guess she thought I was gonna slap Janey.

But afta Bertha jes seen me lookin nice an calm she let go.

"Y'thank I'm lucky?" I axed Janey, "Y'thank so?"

"Yeah."

Bertha smirked, "*You* wanna be married to Mr. Tucker?"

Janey's face scrunched up like Bertha jes farted or somethin, but she ain't say nuthin.

"Well, that's how *LUCKY* Alice is!"

Janey dropped her jaw an looked down at my swolled belly in a daze. She reached out an touched it light as a feather, looked into my face wit her jaw still hangin, then got up an walked away wit'out sayin a word.

****

Ant Betty an Miss Myrtle got to celebratin an raisin a ruckus afta'while. I thank they spiked they dranks wit a li'l corn. They was Ooooin an Aahhin ev'y li'l thang from daddy an mama's new plummin an 'lectricity to me livin in a big house on a hill an havin a *million doller baby,* tha's what they call him.

They volleyed a call an response back an forth to each other. Sometime one of the other ladies would agree wit a "Speak!" or "Tell it!"

"Yer mama raised you right, Mrs. Tucker! I hope you on yer knees ev'yday givin thanks t'the good Lawd what give you this woman to raise you!" Miss Myrtle say.

"Tha's right, cause mos colored people gotta work for a livin!" Ant Betty say.

"Not jes colored people in Smedley eitha!"

"Not jes colored people! An not jes in Smedley! Whites, Chi'nee an them reservation Indians, too!"

"Tell the truth!"

"But Alice Tucker ain't gotta work!"

"Oh no, not Alice."

"She got her a good man!"

"She got her a rich man!"

"The richest colored man in Smedley!"

"The richest colored man in South Carolina."

"Speak!"

"Mrs. Tucker ain't never gonna hafta sweat her brow or callous her hands!"

"Tell it, y'all."

"Not less she want to."

"Not less she want to!"

I wanted t'slap sense into both of those loud, stupid women paradin around my mama's front room ack'in like they know what they talkin bout.

WORK?! How you gonna tell ME bout work when the onliest thang YOU ever work is yer mouth, yap, yap, yap all day long. An the only people you impressin is people tha's stupid as you. WORK?! Try bitin yer tongue when ev'ybody up in yer face tellin you how *lucky* you is jes cause money ain't a problem fer you, naw...BUT BREATHIN IS!! You tellin *ME* bout WORK?! Try havin some great big, flabby gran'daddy toad lay on top of you, push up inside you, gruntin words in yer ear bout love when the thang you would love best is fer him to roll off you an drop dead on the floor! An not cause you really want him dead...YOU JES WANNA BREATHE!! WORK?! I work t'keep from grindin up a li'l glass fer his mashed potatoes. I work to keep from pushin his eyeballs out his head wit my thumbs when he gimme *that look*. An the onliest reason I don' is cause a the guilt I know I'd give my daddy an mama who sold me to the bullfrog t'begin wit! WORK?! When you git a li'l dirt on yer skin, in yer hair, under yer nails, you kin scrub it clean. But I got foul thoughts runnin in my veins, goin round in my brain, makin me choke on puke an scream! How do I scrub that clean?! I been robbed! I been raped! I thank bout murder a dozen times a day! Mr. Tucker squirted a seed in me that took root an is jes bout ready t'be borned. An y'all spect me t'be proud an happy bout THAT?! Y'all want me t'smile in y'all stupid faces an say, "What a lucky girl I am!" You thank that AIN'T WORK?!! I'm WORKIN right now t'keep from takin daddy's shotgun an blowin off y'all's loud, drunk, stupid mouths. I could wake up t'marra on death row an feel mo peace an freedom then I ever feel wakin up mornin's in the big house on that li'l hill. Keep pushin me... I'll stop workin so hard!

I ain't say none of that out loud. It was screamin in my head though, til my temples start t'throbbin an my heart start t'poundin. The next thang I know, I'm stretched out on the floor an mama's moppin my face wit a cool rag.

"She comin round now, y'all," mama say. "My baby comin round now,"

"What happen?" I axed.

"Shush up now. You jes fainted tha's all. You be alright directly."

"Grace," Mrs. Barnes say, "this the second time this chile done blacked out when she look pressed. Member she done it afta her weddin, too. She need t'see a doctor bout that."

"Okay, Mrs. Barnes. Thanky fer yer concern." Mama sounded a li'l put out wit Mrs. Barnes puttin in her two cents. We was raised b'lievin a visit t'the doctor was only fer the rich or the dyin. An ef you was dyin, you needed t'be bleedin out yer mouth or ears or somethin firs' fore people b'lieve it.

"I ain't tryna meddle none, Gracie," Mrs. Barnes caught mama's tone an splained, "Mr. Tucker got the money fer a doctor. Tell him t'git his bride checked up directly."

You could tell mama 'preciated bein reminded that a doctor wa'nt gonna cost them nuthin.

sixteen

"It is common, during some pregnancies, for other health conditions to temporarily arise and/or alert us," Dr. Drew splained.

Dr. Drew was the firs' colored doctor I ever heard tell of in these parts. I 'ont know how Mr. Tucker found him, but I'm glad he did. I plan t'axe him ef he's related to Dr. Charles Drew, the colored man that invented the blood bank then bled to death cause a white hospital wouldn't take him in afta he got banged up in a car accident. But I fergot all about that when he said, "You've developed acute cases of gestational anemia and diabetes, Mrs. Tucker. These conditions will more than likely pass after the baby is born, but it's good to know that you have a tendency towards them so you can continue to take care."

I shore did like hearin all them big, important soundin words rollin round in his mouth. "Gestational anemia, diabetes...acute cases." I bet they was real cute cases, cute as they sound rollin offa his tongue. It make me proud t'know a colored man got that much book-learnin. Isaac kin be a doctor, smart as he is, ef he put his mind to it.

"Your blackouts are a lot more serious. You have developed hypertension or high-blood pressure. It occurs often in older people, over-weight people and smokers. It occurs more often in the Negro race than other races, *supposedly*, because our diets are higher in salt and fatty foods. But you are only sixteen years old. You never smoked, you are slender and seemingly, otherwise, very fit."

"Why you say '*supposedly*' our diets? You don't thank so?" I axed.

"Our diet is the thing that's mentioned most when statistics show hypertension occuring in such high numbers in our race. But exercise has been proven to reduce blood pressure and our people are extremely hard workers, particularly in the manual or physical trades. Yet, this disease prevails in the Negro race. Why? Well, high-blood pressure is also caused by stress."

Dr. Drew quit talkin for awhile. He look down an seem t'be studdin the papers he been writin on in a folder. Then he start back t'talkin, but said thangs real low.

"You can leave out salt, all fried foods, pork and butter," he say to the folder, then look at the window even though the blinds is drawed, "but if you are living with the Klan and Jim Crow segregation, legal lynchings and the rapes of your mothers, wives and daughters... Well, let's just say, that's a lot of stress."

He lookit me alla sudden an seem t'be wearin a shadow over his face. I kin see his jaw bone movin whure he clenchin it, an maybe he raised his voice jes a mite.

"I have hypertension and I *know* it came with my medical degree. The discrimination I had to fight, along with the regular rigors of study..."

He stopped again alla sudden and it seem like he mighta been countin t'ten.

I start t'see Dr. Drew as a man for the firs' time. I know he a man an all, but firs' he was a *doctor* wit the power to heal. That made him differnt, special, in my mind, like he was more'n me. Now standin here tryna ketch his temper, he remind me of Isaac that day we was walkin home from school talkin bout the kids we knew that been lynched right round Smedley. He look mad an skeered an tarred like ev'ybody else. I

106

see now that he ain't that old. He ain't old as Mr. Tucker, I don' thank. He ain't wearin no weddin band neitha, but that don' mean nuthin. I don' wear mines cause it make me gag.

In a minute, he's calm an lookin at me. "You are too young to have that much stress in your life. But I can't think of what else may be causing your blood pressure to soar. And this condition is not temporary. It will not go away on its own. Do you feel much stress in your life, Mrs. Tucker?"

"Stress?..." I repeated thankin, sides you up here callin me **Mrs. Tucker**?! Somethin tha's unnerstood by anybody that know me, ain't nobody allowed t'call me... t'my face or behine my back!!

Instead, I said afta a pause, "Well, maybe some..."

"You've got to learn how to relax some, young lady. You're going to be giving birth real soon and with the kind of stress labor causes, you could suffer a sudden stroke or a heart attack that could leave you crippled for life,... or worse."

"You cain't do nuthin...?"

"A cesarian birth would spare you going through labor, but it is a major operation that would take a heavy toll on your body. I don't recommend it, unless it becomes necessary at the time of delivery. You need plenty of peace and quiet. It may be difficult to do, young lady, but you need to rest, rest, rest."

"I really don' do mucha nuthin now, but I'll try," I said.

"Is Mr. Tucker a problem for you?" He axed it gentle, like he figger this migh'could be a sore spot wit me.

I couldn't lookit him. I din't wanna scream. I din't wanna cry. I felt like I migh'could do eitha one or both right then an I din't wanna. He put that wrap back round my arm an took my pressure again right quick.

"Your pressure is rising right now, while you sit here presenting such a calm and peaceful picture. You hold things inside. Let it out, Alice. Let it go!"

It was the sound of my name, Alice, that fine'ly made this medicine man feel like a friend. A friend I could talk to cause he know all bout stress from when he was goin t'school. I figger he migh'could unnerstan ef I splained thangs cause he done awready figgered out Mr. Tucker ain't no big joy in my life wit'out me sayin nuthin. Mama said ef y'hold bad things inside they make you ugly an sick. I learn on my own they kin make you mean. Now Dr. Drew tellin me they kin kill you, too.

107

"Alice," he said, "you don't have to carry the burden all by yourself. Drop it now. Let it go!"

So I did. B'fo I could even think good on what t'say, the words come out my mouth so fast, they was trippin over each other in they rush t'be heard. I 'ont know ef I was makin any sense to Dr. Drew at all. I was rantin an ragin an blubberin all at once. My hands was flyin round in the air beggin an pleadin an punctuatin my sentences all on they own. Arms flung wide with open hands was a question mark. A closed fisted swang was an exclamation point. A backhand slappin into an open palm over an over was a buncha commas separatin a list of stuff.

Dr. Drew studied me hard. He stood leanin against a counter, not sayin a word. He had one arm wrapped cross his middle an his other arm bent, the elbow restin on that wrapped arm an that hand idly pullin on his top lip. He wa'nt standin far from me an I seen a few drops of my spit speckle his cheek an the hand pullin at his lip, but he ain't move til I was through.

Then he turn t'the sink to wash his hands an wet his face. He turn back t'me dabbin his cheeks dry wit a towel an say, "I'm going to recommend that Mr. Tucker make himself scarce for you, Alice."

****

I was prac'ly bedridden fer the last six weeks of my pregnancy. Mr. Tucker had mama t'come over an cook, an mama brung Bertha to clean.

It was always a point of pride fer Mr. Tucker to point out to people that I do all the house chores. I do them to take my mind offa whure I'd ruther be an what all else I ruther be doin.

Wit mama an Bertha doin all the chores, I spend my time thankin bout all the thangs I been tryin to avoid thankin bout. Tha's makin me moody an mad an it make me give ev'ybody stress.

The 9th of September I got to feelin too jumpy t'be layin round no mo. Mama an Bertha was hangin clothes out to dry in the backyard an I came down to git a cool drank. I started out washin the breakfast dishes an wound up startin to fix supper.

"Alice, girl... wha'chu doin?!" Mama say rushin inside soundin all worried like she thank I'm gonna hurt myse'f or the baby cause I'm standin on my feet. "Ef you hungry, I'll fix you somethin t'eat!"

"Is okay mama. I ain't hungry... I'm bored. An I ain't sick eitha, I'm jes pregnant. I'm tarred of jes layin round while you an Bertha do alla work."

"Well you know the doctor said you need to *rest, rest, rest.* You washed the dishes an started dinner. You done enough fer now. Set down an rest."

Mama picked right up where I lef' off. I watched her move round this kitchen like she right at home, an I know she is. Food is her second family. She mixin an choppin an stirrin an I start thankin what I always thank when I watch mama movin through life, how her name Grace fit her like a glove. I start to hummin "Amazin Grace" real low an Bertha, over by the sink mixin strawberries in some lemonade, start to hum along wit me.

Mama look over t'me smilin cause she love that gospel, too. Then she lookit my belly an say, "How you feelin, Allie?"

"Fine, mama."

She still lookin at my belly, she say, "I thank you might be in labor."

I look down an seen my smock movin round like somethin underneath is pokin it wit a stick. That boy always be runnin round inside of me like he rollin a hoop or playin stickball or somethin. But I ain't in no pain or nuthin an tha's what all the womens been tellin me bout when they was havin they babies.

"I 'ont thank so mama. I ain't havin no pains. The baby jes runnin his reg'ler relays b'fo he jump the big hurdle."

Mama crook her brow, still watchin my belly an say, "I thank you be in labor directly."

I thank she wrong, but I ain't say nuthin cause I 'ont know fer shore. I cain't jes sit there like that fer long. I went upstairs t'git somethin to sew or knit an brang it back down so I could be doin somethin while I'm sittin there.

While I was upstairs I used the toilet. Seem like this baby be layin on my kidneys or bumpin my bladder or somethin cause I gotta pee alla time. But when I'm in there, I jes had a li'l tinkle. Right b'fo I stand up though, a bucket a water come rushin outta me. I ain't pay it no mind. I finished in there an went back to the kitchen wit my sewin stuff.

Dinner was ready in bout a hour. Mama made potato salad, strang beans and salmon croquettes. Bertha baked sweet potato biscuits and mixed peach preserves in fresh churned butter t'spread on 'em. I thank Bertha oughta be fat wit that sweet tooth of hers, but she ain't much heavier'n a whisper. She cain't eat nuthin plain. She gotta add raisins, bananas or berries to her cereals, breads, butters an dranks. Dessert is her favorite part of any meal. She even have dessert wit her breakfast, a slice of cake or pie or fried apples wit sugar an cinnamon. "Wha's fer dessert?" I axed her cause I know how she like t'make you beg for it.

"I 'ont thank you should git none sence you awready big as a house," she say wit a silly grin.

"Okay, so what I'm gonna be missin?"

"Lemon puddin pound cake wit fresh strawberries an homemade ice cream!" I swear that girl start to shine like a new penny at jes the thought of somethin sweet, so she was all aglow now.

"When did y'all make ice cream, Bertha?"

"While we was washin clothes. Mama an me took turns scrubbin the clothes an churnin the ice cream. Do Mr. Tucker like ice cream, Alice?" She axe me like she care.

"I'll eat whatever he don'."

"You cain't have none," she teased.

"Then ain't nobody gonna git none," I tease back an jumped up like I was gonna fetch it from the freezer.

Tha's when the firs' pain hit me. It made me stop dead in my tracks an kinda took my breath fer a minute.

"What happen?" Bertha had been runnin to the freezer from the other side to beat me to it, but when she seen I stopped an was holdin my side, she come to me instead.

"It ain't nuthin," I said when I could fine'ly say somethin. "I'm okay."

"Yer labor comin Alice. Set down an take it easy now," mama say.

"Should I go git the doctor?" Bertha ask mama.

"Nah, not now. It's gonna be awhile yet. He'p yer sister sit down, then fix her a hot water bottle for her back," mama say.

"I'm okay mama. I b'lieve this baby jes poked me in my spleen, is all."

"That migh'could be. But a hot water bottle t'yer back'll feel right nice anyway," she say comin round to knead my back an shoulders like they was bread dough. It did feel nice.

Ev'ythang was jes quiet fer awhile, then while Bertha was fixin the hot water bottle, she start sangin, "A-maaa-zin Grace..."

"Ain't nuthin amazin bout me," mama say.

"Ain't nobody talkin bout'chu," I said.

Bertha stopped singin an mama give a soft little gasp, then I laughed. They ain't say nuthin an that make me laugh mo. Then they start laughin, too. We kept laughin harder an harder til we was all near to tears, then the second pain hit me. I stopped to ketch my breath, but they ain't notice cause they was still laughin at my rudeness.

When they start to quiet down I said, "Gone sang that song they writ bout mama, Bertha. Gone sang that song."

She start in again an mama take that bottle an wrapped it in a towel an strapped it low on my back wit a table cloth. I could feel that boy floppin round in me. I figger he was turnin round to face down fer his big swim out. I thank in his hurry he kicked my stomach cause alla sudden I felt a lurch then had a pow'ful hankerin to vomit.

"Move mama!" was all I could say for I pushed back from the table an threw up all over the floor.

Mama an Bertha was the best. They ain't say nuthin. Bertha jes quick gotta clean wash towel, wet it then gave it to mama who wiped my mouth. Then Bertha took the used towel an started moppin up my slop on the floor.

"Yer water oughta be bustin soon," mama say still rubbin my neck an back.

"I thank it might awready did a few hours back when I was in the toilet."

"Why ain't you tell me?"

"I wa'nt shure. I still ain't. But I had me a little tinkle, then right b'fo I got up a big rush a water come down. It ain't feel like I was pee'in, but it was hard to tell sence I went in there to make water."

"Tha's okay, Alice. You ain't know. You ain't never had no baby b'fo. Bertha when you finish moppin the floor, you kin call Dr. Drew an tell 'im Alice water broke a few hours ago an ef he kin come on out to the house, we preciate it."

Bertha say Dr. Drew say it sound like the baby gotta long while yet, so he be by this evenin. He say mama know what t'do til then. I ain't know, but mama used to he'p him birth babies when she was bout my age... my mama really is Amazin Grace!

Bertha call Daddy an Mr. Tucker afta she call Dr. Drew an they come out to the house directly. Wa'nt nuthin for them t'do, cept eat supper an wait. The pains was gittin stronger alla time an ev'ytime I thank this the worst one, the next one be worse. I ain't say nuthin louder then a grunt all this time cause I was savin my scream fer the great big pain.

Sence they kept gittin bigger, I kept savin my scream. Mama tell me it might hurt less an the baby might come sooner ef I yell out ev'y now an then. I don' tell her, but I ain't tryna rush this baby gittin here. The idea of two Mr. Tuckers have always turned my stomach. I'm jes tryna hold that up from happenin, ef only fer a minute more. But I know little Luthern is on his way. He been pushin my guts outta his way makin me lose my bowels in two or three big spurts, so the only thang lef' to come outta me is junior. I'm jes holdin my scream til I cain't hold it no mo, kinda like I been keepin my mind til I lose it.

Dr. Drew show up to the house jes in time. He come bout 7:30 an the baby come bout 7:45 that evenin. The doctor say I had the quietest labor he ever heard tell of. I never did scream, not even when he cut me to widen my passage to he'p the baby come out or when he sewed me back up.

"Congratulations, little mother," Dr. Drew said when he was puttin in a few stitches. "You just gave birth to a perfect baby girl!"

seventeen

A GIRL?! I couldn't b'lieve my ears! I don' thank I really b'lieved it til mama handed me the tee-ni-niest li'l bundle. I moved the blanket flap an seen the li'lest eyes tryna look back at me. She looked confused like she tryna figger out what jes happen. Her little mouth was smackin an suckin like she tryna axe, "Who you?" Ev'ythang about her was precious an I could feel my heart jesta flutter an pound, barely able t'hold all the love she was floodin into it.

Bertha musta run an told daddy an Mr. Tucker cause the twins an them all come runnin up to the room. They all stopped at the door though, like they was skeered to come all the way in. I 'ont know what it is bout babies that make men feel so shy, but there they was, two full-growed men an two big boys lookin wide-eyed an shy at the newest member to the family.

Fine'ly, Bertha pushed through them and come take the baby from me an hold her out to Mr. Tucker an say, "Come meet yer beautiful new daughter, Mr. Tucker."

Ef he was disappointed it wa'nt no boy, you couldn't tell it. He tip-toed up to her an say real soft-like, "Hey there Li'l Miss Purty. I'm yer papa."

She quick made a funny face like she might wanna sneeze or like a gas bubble jes popped in her li'l belly. It made ev'ybody laugh an I thought, "I know wha'chu mean, Sweetness. I know jes wha'chu mean."

"You should feed her some, Alice," mama say. "All that hard work to git her born wa'nt yers alone, y'know."

Mama put a towel over my chest an I put a nipple to my babies mouth. She went to suckin like she been doin it for years.

"You jes a li'l greedy gut, ain'chu? Yes you are! Oh yes you are!" I cooed.

"Wha'chu gonna name her?" Daniel axed.

"I ain't thought about that. Y'all say what y'all like an I'll know her name when I hear it."

"Cora!" Samuel shouted out. I know he sweet on a girl named Cora in his class, so I guess that name jes music to his ears right now. But he still young an got a lot more sweethearts to fall in an outta love wit. He ain't gonna wanna be callin her Cora no mo ef thangs tween him an his Cora don' work out.

"No," I say.

"Why not?" Samuel say soundin indignant.

"Tha's a nice name, but it ain't her name," I said.

"Clara yer grandmama's name," daddy said offerin his mama's name.

"Tha's nice," I said, but he could tell I wa'nt takin it jes yit.

"This baby look jes like you, Alice," Mr. Tucker said. "Why not name her Alice?"

She did look like me. She look *jes* like me, I thank, now that he point it out. But she ain't me an she ain't gonna be me. She gonna be better'n me, I hope. That surprised me. Mama said Mr. Tucker would feel this way bout his son an here I am thankin the same way to-ward my daughter. It ain't nuthin I planned, it jes hit me like that an that surprised me.

"Nah," I say.

"Well, she shore beat a paperbag. She got yer purty yellow skin. We kin call her Daisy," Mr. Tucker say puttin in the second of his two cents.

"No," I say. He alla sudden made me so mad, I almos blurted out, "Is my yellow color the root a yer *love*?! Is that what make you t'buy me from my family?!" But when I looked at him standin there lookin so happy like he jes give a good idea, I wa'nt mad at him no mo. He was too stupid to be mad at. Anybody stuck on a paperbag test is jes too lost an sad t'ever be mad at.

Some colored folks preach you should always marry somebody lighter'n you so yer babies come out lighter. Some thank lighter skin is bettah then darker skin. Some thank lighter skinned people git treated bettah then darker skinned people, an that migh'could be true. Eitha way, the point is tryna make yer baby's life bettah... easier. These people tell they kids, "Don'chu brang home nobody to marry tha's darker'n a paperbag. You got t'thank bout yer babies!"

I don' fault nobody for nuthin like that. I cain't. My own sister once talked to me like that an I 'ont know whure she got that from. All I know is ef I got anythang t'do wit it, this little girl gonna be free of all the chains people gonna try to put on her. My baby gonna be free! Free! Free! Free!

"Harriet," I say.

"Harriet?" Mama say, "Tha's a nice name, Alice, but why Harriet?"

Cause my daughter gonna be free! She gonna do whatever she wanna do wit her life. She gonna go to college ef she wanna go an she ain't gonna hafta wait on no schola'ship to do it cause her daddy got money. An even ef he lose alla his money or don' thank a girl oughta go, she gonna go anyway ef she wanna. She ain't gonna ever be shackled wit a man, young or old, that she don' want. She gonna know her worth an make other people to know they worth from watchin her fly. She gonna be brave an bold an brilliant an beautiful an free... like Harriet Tubman. Free an makin other folks free.

Tha's what I was thankin. That ain't what I said though, cause tha's what I want for my child, but The Lawd's Will be done. Sides ain't nobody need to know alla that. All they need to know is what I said.

"We gonna call her Harriet cause tha's her name."

eighteen

Mama an Bertha still come out to the house to he'p, but they ain't treatin me like no invalid no mo. Dr. Drew say I still need t'keep quiet cause my pressure is easy to rise, but I know he don' spect me t'be still an quiet all my life! Ef he do, he need to thank again.

I was ironin, Bertha was scrubbin the parlor winders an mama was waterin the house plants fore goin to tend the garden. I looked over at Harriet, jes a month old, holdin onto her foot like she tryna taste the toes she jes discovered an said, "Mama, Harriet is the mos perfect baby God ever made, don'chu thank?"

Mama smiled an said, "I thought *you* was the mos perfect when you was born, baby."

"Nah, really! I know all mama's thank that bout they chile, but I b'lieve it's really true bout Harriet! She quick t'laugh. She hardly ever cry. She so ser'us when you talk to her, I thank she really unnerstan wha'chu sayin. She jes cain't talk herse'f so's to make you to know she unnerstandin. She be talkin alla time too, but it sound like baby jibbers cause she ain't learn no words yet. She strong...."

"An you figger Harriet come to save the world!" Mama said, still smilin.

"Mama! Tha's blasphemin!" Bertha stopped scrubbin a winder to warn mama.

"No it ain't Bertha. Tha's every new mother's true feelins, ef she lovin her baby," mama splained an patted my back on her way ou'side to tend the garden.

Harriet couldn't quite git the grip she wanted on her toes, so she start suckin on the sugar tit Bertha made for her. I don' want her to pick up Bertha's cravin fer sweets, but I 'ont wanna hurt Bertha's feelins eitha. I let her have a sugar tit once in awhile an tell Bertha my baby sweet enough mos other times.

"Lookit her Bertha. You thank I'm wrong?"

"Nah, I thank you migh'could be right," she say lookin at Harriet like she kin see a halo shinin a warm light on her fat cheeks, too. Then she say, "Would'chu thank she was near so precious ef she din't look like you? Like ef she had'a been a little boy baby lookin jes like Mr. Tucker?"

Bertha wa'nt teasin either. She axin' cause she really wanna know. I got to thankin bout how I hated the idea of livin wit two Mr. Tuckers so much, I thought I'd ruther die. I even tried to make my labor pains last longer jes to keep from havin to face a little Luthern. God knew my heart, heard my pleas an ansa'd my prayers. He give me a little girl an turned my biggest fear into my biggest blessin. I know I wouldn't be praisin this baby ef it was jes another li'l Mr. Tucker.

"No, I pro'bly wouldn't be so happy bout a Mr. Tucker, Jr., Bertha," I said. "But God ain't gimme no li'l Mr. Tucker. He gimme Harriet an I thank she migh'coulda come here to lead us."

"She the mos perfect baby I ever seen," Bertha say lookin at me wit'out smilin no mo. "An I know mama say all new momma's feel the same. But it sound like blasphemin to me an I thank it's best to jes call her a pretty baby for now til she do somethin bigger later on."

I ain't gonna argue. Ain't nuthin to argue bout. I know what I know jes like I knew Harriet name when it come to me, an it ain't blasphemin. Ef don' nobody wanna hear it, they ain't gotta cause I know what I know.

****

Bout a week later, Mr. Tucker start to droppin hints bout tryna make him a son. He see me startin t'take back my chores an, I guess, he figger I'm strong again an all healed up.

Now I unnerstan why he wa'nt disappointed tha' this here baby come out a li'l girl. It give him another chance to try t'make him a boy. Mama told me ef Harriet be a boy, he pro'bly wouldn't be pesterin me no mo. But she ain't his son, so now he want me t'come visit his room again.

The thought of goin to his room nights gimme a bout of low spirits that hit me so hard, it knock me off my feet. I mean I couldn't git outta bed fer real! My head felt pressed, like there was a balloon bein blowed up inside that was pushin my brains against my skull makin me feel a heavy, throbbin pressure. Plus, I git so dizzy, I wobble on my feet when I'm jes standin.

Mama come over to the house an fix me a breakfast I ain't axe fer an don' want. A sick stomach come over me that made me throw up in the middle of tryna eat, so she took that away.

She ain't know what to do. I din't either. Mama brung in Harriet afta'while. I guess she thank the baby gonna make me feel better cause sence she been born, I seem to be so happy wit her.

But when she come walkin through the door wit li'l Harriet tryna blow spit bubbles an laughin, so happy an proud of herse'f, I bust out cryin. Mama froze ha'fway in the room not shore what t'do.

Then she come closer, holdin the baby up a li'l mo like a offerin or a shield, an she say, "It's yer baby, honey. Don'chu wanna see yer baby?"

I lookit li'l Harriet an wail away. I skeered her so much, she stop laughin an start cryin, too. Mama try to shush her, but she jes git louder an louder, so mama rushed her out the room.

I couldn't stop bawlin. I din't mean to make Harriet sad when she start the day so happy, but I couldn't he'p it. I felt as bad fer her as I did fer myse'f. She jes as beautiful an smart today as she was yestiddy, but she a victim jes like me.

I am sixteen years old an I feel older'n Methusela. I wa'nt never thankin bout no babies. Not fer me. Not no time soon. I ain't got *NO* say in my life. I ain't have Harriet fer me. I had her causa mama an daddy an Mr. Tucker an even Rev'ern Pritchett. I ain't never wanted her my ownse'f. Mr. Tucker don' want her eitha. He want a boy. I was so happy she a baby girl wit my face that people mistake me fer bein happy!

I start doin to her what mama say Mr. Tucker was gonna do to his son. I'm tryin to escape my life through hers an I plan t'do alla thangs I cain't do by hopin she do 'em. But life don' work like that an ef it could, I don' want it to. I WANT MY LIFE BACK!! I am sixteen years old! I ain't been nowhere! I ain't done nuthin! I don' know nuthin! And I never will! Why? WHY?!!

Mama an them prac'ly got a new house. Bertha an the twins git new clothes an books an gonna be goin t'college when they gradiate. Daddy got steady work an money now. Mr. Tucker got me. When do I git somethin I want? When do somethin good happen to me? An poor li'l Harriet, what do she git?!

I was thankin she was exter special, she migh'could save the world. She migh'could be the zample fer ev'ybody to follow. Tha's what I was doin to her, afta it been done to me. I wouldn't wish that on nobody.

My poor baby ain't nuthin but a baby. Ev'yone of us come into the world wit the possibility of bein anythang... a sap or a savior. Anythang is possible when you don' know enough to be afraid of nuthin. Then life start, an we learn to fear an follow rules people give us, people we call leaders. But real leaders is the ones that break the rules! Mary McCleod Bethune say, "I kin too start a college wit hard work an $1.50." George Washington Carver say, "Lookit what all we kin do wit a peanut!" Benjamin Banneker say, "I got the designs for the capitol!" Lewis Latimer put the ring in Alexander Graham's bell an the light in Edison's bulb. I named my baby Harriet an said she gonna be jes like Harriet Tubman, leadin ev'ybody around to wherever she want 'em to go. An maybe she will. But it's gonna be cause *SHE* want to, not cause I want her to. She kin make herse'f a zample ef she want, but I ain't gonna do it.

I need to find out what I kin do. Cause ef I don' do somethin, somebody gonna git hurt up in here. I'm bout to lose my mind!

I'm thankin alla these thangs, but cain't nobody tell it. All they see is me layin in the bed blubberin an beatin' on the sheets.

****

I cried so long an s'much, my face swolled up an it feel hot an tight, an not jes my eyes eitha, my nose, my lips, my cheeks. I was still cryin when Dr. Drew showed up, but I had been done run outta tears by then. He come cause mama call him an tole him how I was carryin on. He say he need t'give me somethin to he'p me sleep.

"I 'ont wanna sleep!" I told him.

He lookit me an say, "You need to, young lady, to get your pressure back down. You are putting yourself at unnecessary risk. You must stay calm and if you can't do it on your own, I'll have to help you.

"I'll give you an injection right now, but I've also brought some sleeping pills for later. Be careful with them. They are very potent. Now sleep, Alice," Dr. Drew say stickin a needle in my arm. "Sleep...."

I kin feel myse'f relaxin wit'out even tryin, like my body was shuttin down. In a minute, I couldn't feel my hands or feet. Then my legs an arms went numb. Then my body. My head. My eyelids was too heavy to liff, but tha's the only thang feel heavy on me. The rest of me feel light, like I'm floatin on a cloud.

I din't wanna go to sleep at firs', but now I don' thank I never wanna wake up.

nineteen

Hours later, when I was wakin up, I could feel somebody in the room. I acted like I was still sleepin good cause ef I open my eyes an see Mr. Tucker settin there watchin me, I ain't shore what I might do, but my guess is I wouldn't be very pleasant.

I hear a soft scratchin or a soft brushin noise, but I ain't open my eyes. I was tryna figger out the sound wit'out peekin, but I couldn't make it out.

Then a smell of flowers come to me, but they wa'nt any flowers I could put my fanger on. They was kinda strong an too sweet, like... *perfume*! I'm pretty shore a woman is sittin side me!

I decide to open my eyes, but it wa'nt no easy thang to do. When I fine'ly got my lef' eye cracked, the lady sittin there say, "Oh, you're awake."

"Miss Johnson!" I say tryna sit up. "You fine'ly come to see me!"

"Yes, I finally did," she say gently pushin me back down, "But you need more rest. I was writing you a note. You can read it after you wake. I'll come back later when you're well rested."

"Don' go, Miss Johnson...please," I feel like cryin again. "You don' never come to see me an I axe Bertha to brang you alla time. Now you here talkin bout later, wha's wrong wit now?"

"Nothing," she say relaxin back, then she take a cool wash rag from a bowl wit ice an water in it on my night table. She wrang it out an dabbed it on my forehead an cheeks. "There's nothing wrong with now. I just thought you should rest a little more."

She do a lotta little small talk bout school an whatnot. I din't care what she was talkin bout. I was so glad she was there, I jes laid there an listened to the sound of her voice wit'out really hearin what she was sayin.

"...a strong and beautiful name. Was she named after someone in particular?"

"Huh?"

"Was Harriet named after someone special?"

"Harriet Tubman."

"Oh yes. Beautiful and strong and so full of promise and potential."

"I woulda named her afta you ef I'da knowed yer name."

"That's awfully sweet of you to say, Alice. Ola. Ola Johnson is my full name."

"Oh la! Tha's french fer full'a promise an potential, too, ain't it?"

"Well, when you say it like that," she laughed. Then she got quiet, "But I broke my promise to you."

"No you din't. Mama ain't let the rev'ern axe ef anybody disagree, but I know you woulda. I *know* you woulda!"

"I should have anyway. Right in the middle of the vows, I should have just spoken up out of turn."

"It don' matter. That was a long time ago, now. Yestiddy seem like a long time ago to me."

"You are still young yet. The longer you live, the shorter the days will seem. We don't realize how brief life is, until we're old and gray, or sick and just about to lose it."

"I feel old an gray right now. Old an tarred an gray wit nuthin else to lose."

"You're too young to feel that way. One day when the weight of the world is no longer resting on your shoulders, you will look back on this challenging period in your life and love it for all of the lessons you will have learned."

"What I'm gonna learn from this?"

"You'll learn how to fly. You'll learn how to dump your burdens and fly away."

"How?!"

Miss Johnson gimme the note she was writin when I was wakin up. "Maybe this will help. I don't know. Read it at your leisure. Or read it when you're feeling your lowest. It may or may not not have an answer for you, but I think you will find it an inspirational and interesting read either way."

I din't know how to tell Miss Johnson I hate good advice wrapped in pretty metaphors that make for interestin readin an not much else. I need a nuts an bolts plan. I need real instruction. My good advice need to be naked so's the dressin don' distract from the point. "*Dump my burdens an fly away.*" What do that mean?! How do I do that?! I don' tell her how useless flowery suggestions are for me right now cause I 'ont wanna hurt her feelins an risk her not comin back.

"Thanks a lot," I say then buried her note in the Dunbar book of poetry, sence she talkin poetic poop. "I'ma read that later on."

"You do that," she say like she know I ain't plannin on readin it no time soon, but she really want me to.

We hear Mr. Tucker huffin an puffin up the stairs, that make us lose any mo private thoughts we migh'woulda shared. We both look to the door expectin to see him any minute. An fore you could say Jack Rabbit, he standin right there wheezin in the doorway.

He firs' lookit me all worried, then that worry-face drop off quick an leave a cold, stony face glarin at Miss Johnson.

"Hello Mr. Tucker," Miss Johnson say wit'out battin a eye at his rude stare. I know she pro'bly gonna leave soon. "I came to check up on my star student."

"Alice ain'chur student no mo. Ain't been fer over a year now."

"No, but the lessons never stop, do they? And Alice will always be my star," her mouth was all smiles, but her voice was all steel.

"Well, I thanky for stoppin by, Miss Johnson. I kin take care a my wife from here."

Miss Johnson jes stare at him wit'out sayin nuthin fer a long while, then she bend down, kiss my temple an say in my ear, "You make sure you get some more sleep, then have a nice leisurely read later, after you've rested. And write some too. Writing can help you understand and exorcise the demons you wrestle, okay?"

"Okay... When you comin back?" I axed, eager an anxious.

"As soon as I can. As soon as I can." She say it twice like that an give my hand a little squeeze, then walk pass Mr. Tucker still standin in the doorway.

I ain't never seed Miss Johnson again.

twenty

Mr. Tucker ain't brang up his son no mo so I ain't have another fit like that last one, but my low spirits kep on. I read some Dunbar afta Miss Johnson visit an I come cross one that seem to be writ for me called "Life's Tragedy":

What did you say was "Life's tragedy?"
"It may be misery not to sing at all,
And go silent through the brimming day...
It may be sorrow...
Never to be loved,
But deeper griefs than these beset the way.

To have come near to sing the perfect song.
And only by a half-tone lost the key,
There is the potent sorrow, there the grief,
The pale, sad staring of life's tragedy."
To have just missed the perfect love,
Not just the hot passion of untempered youth.
But that which lays aside it's vanity
And gives thee, for thy trusting worship, truth.
"This, this it is to be a curse indeed,
For if we mortals love, or if we sing,
We count our joys not by the things we have...
...but by what kept us from the perfect thing."

"To have just missed the perfect love,..." an "...what kept us from the perfect thing" is the parts that cause my spirits to sink. It ain't like I'm jes thankin Isaac was my perfect love. He migh'woulda turned out to be a big loser, I 'ont know. I never will.

It's the never knowin that make my heart to break.

At fifteen I was Miss Johnson's *star student*. At sixteen I got a beautiful baby an a rich husband. I live in a great big ole pretty house an mosta the womens in Smedley ack like I'm they envy. But I give it all away to anyone of 'em ef I could jes figger out how to *dump my burdens and fly away*. I 'ont know how to do that an it make me feel stupid. It seem like I'ma stay stupid an die dumb. Tha's the other side of life's tragedies. There's Dunbar's near misses an then there's me missin ev'ythang by at lease a country mile. Mama an Bertha keep comin to he'p, but they don' push me or nuthin. Ef I start dinner, they dust or mop or mend somethin. They cook only ef I stay in bed or sit quiet in the parlor readin. They talk to me, but don' none a us feel like we gotta fill up silences.

Sometimes daddy an the boys come over, too. Cept for Sunday's, I don' go to they house so much. Wit all the changes an add-ons, it don' feel much like home to me anymo.

Dr. Drew musta told Mr. Tucker to make hisse'f scarce again, cause I mos'ly see him in passin. Sometime he brang me somethin like a lemonade or a piece of pie sayin, "Thought you might like this," then he leave. Sometime he brang me a sleepin pill or two an say, "Git a good sleep t'night, Princess." He tryin so hard, seem like. I don' usually want nuthin, but when he brang me somethin, I take it cause he went to the bother. I keep hopin he gonna brang me my freedom one day an say somethin like, "Here y'go, Princess. I know you really been wantin this." I'll thank him, then dump my burdens an fly far away.

Harriet ain't never been no problem an I'm lovin her all over again jes fer her, wit'out tryin to make her be anythang fer me. Sence I ain't havin no mo fits an ev'ybody seem to find a way to put up wit me peaceable, I guess my pressure been steady an low enough, even though I don' check it.

When Mr. Tucker brang me a pill or two to sleep, I take it cause the doctor give 'em to me to take an they don' seem to hurt none. The only thang I don' like is it take me too long to wake up an sometime when I do, I got pains in my back an joints like I been sleepin hard. That ain't often, but it's enough to make me thank I migh'should stop takin 'em til I kin axe Dr. Drew ef they got a differnt kind.

One night when I was readin a good Richard Wright story, Mr. Tucker come in wit two pills an some juice tellin me, "Is gittin late now, Princess. I thank you should try'ta git some rest now."

"I'll take that later, thanky," I said, more'n a little bothered wit him breakin into the story right then. "I ain't tired jes yit."

He stood there lookin bout as bothered as I felt, then he put the pills an juice down, looked round, then said, "You don' wanna wake up li'l Harriet, it's late an she jes a bitty baby."

"Harriet over there sleepin jes fine," I said, thankin you couldn't come up wit nuthin better'n that! Then I added, "Ef she do wake up, I'll jes giv'er one a them pills, sence you brang me two." I was jes jokin an tryin to git rid of him so's I could git back to my story.

"You cain't do that, them's fer you!" He said all alarmed like I was gonna give my baby grown-peoples pills.

Then he realize, a shade late, that I was jes jokin an he give a little chuckle, "(Heh-heh) You jes funnin' me. Well, tha's a good one." He turn to leave an say over his shoulder, "Don' stay up too long. It's already late now, Princess."

While he walkin out I'm thankin, ain't nobody axe you what time it is. Ef I go to bed late, I wake up late. Mama be here in the mornin t'see bout Harriet. I got to wondrin what he tryna hide, cause blamin me fer messin wit the baby's sleep was jes too stupid sence she over there in her crib makin her like cat purr snores. She out like the light he tellin me to turn off. I decide not to take them pills no mo startin tonight, but I ain't gonna tell him. I put 'em in the drawer of my nighttable, drank the juice an kep on readin.

When I went to bed bout a hour later, I thought I heard Mr. Tucker in the hall. But he usually git to bed real early sence he gotta git up early t'be to the mill to open up, so I figger eitha it's my mistake or he jes went to the bathroom.

Maybe a hour afta that, I hear my bedroom door creak open. I was jes bout to sit up an scream bloody murder at the thief come to steal my baby an my thangs when I heard Mr. Tucker whisper, "Princess,...you sleepin?"

"Nah," I whispered back sittin up, scared that he was gonna say he heard a thief earlier an we better high-tail it on outta here.

But he jumped when I ansa'd an knocked down the wash pitcher an bowl I keeps on a stand by the door an broke it. Then he was stumblin in the dark tryin to find the light switch an stepped on some broken glass an start hollarin like a hound. That woke poor Harriet wit such a fright, she start right into screamin, too. I turned on my nightlight t'see what was goin on. Mr. Tucker was up there hoppin on one foot, his robe flappin open to whure I could see his big naked Buddha belly. He squint at me from the light bein in his face when he ain't used to it yet, an then he got the nerve to fuss an blame ev'ythang on me!

"I told you y'need t'go t'bed sooner...Now Look!"

"Lookit what?!" I was confused.

"What?! Don'chu hear li'l Harriet over there screamin her li'l lungs out!"

"You done that, not me!"

"Ef you'da gone t'bed when I said..."

"Wha'chu come in here fer?!"

"I was jes checkin on you cause yer light was on fer so long."

"My light been off!!"

"Don' worry bout me, Alice, see bout Harriet right now," he say hoppin from foot to foot an lookin disgusted. "I got t'see bout my cut feet an clean this mess up."

He lef' in a huff fore I got to say, I ain't worryin bout'chu!

Soon's he lef' wit his big ol loud mouth, Harriet quiet down an in no time, she back was to sleep. Mr. Tucker come back wit a broom, a pan, a mop an a bucket to clean up the mess he made. He ain't say nuthin when he come back an neitha did I, but I was still wondrin what he come in here fer in the firs' place.

****

I ain't mention it to him or nobody else over the next few days. I jes watch Mr. Tucker real close when I thank he ain't lookin. Afta three or four days, he come to my room all nice wit two pills an a juice an say, "Is gittin late now, Alice. You oughta take yer pills an go on t'bed."

"Tha's a good idea, I am gittin tired, thanky. Y'kin leave that right there," I nodded to the table, "an afta I finish this page I'ma go on t'bed."

"Okay, nighty-night," he smile an whisper over to Harriet, "Nighty-night, Angel!" Then he leave.

I put them two pills in my nighttable drawer along wit the other two, drank the juice, finish that story an turn off the light. But I ain't go to sleep. I wa'nt thankin bout goin to sleep.

Shore nough, afta bout a hour or so, my bedroom door is creakin an Mr. Tucker whisperin, "Princess,...you sleepin?"

I ain't say nuthin this time cause I wanna find out what he up to.

He ease on in the door an tiptoe cross the room to my bed. He standin right near my head an whisper again, "Princess?"

I ain't say nuthin.

Then he bend down, stroke my hair an axe, "You sleepin, Princess?"

It take everythang in me not to shy away from his hand strokin my head, but I wanna know what he thank he doin.

He stop strokin my head an he stand back up then I hear a soft rustlin sound. Next thang, Mr. Tucker come crawlin 'neath the sheets next to me, naked as a jaybird. I refuse to let myse'f git riled cause I know ef I blow my stack this time, I will blackout fer shore an I'm thankin tha's what he want me t'be.

I'm layin on my back an he layin on his side facin me an steady murmurin thangs like, "C'mere Princess, you know yer daddy want'chu." He talkin an strokin my leg, at firs'. Then he say somethin like, "Is been too long, baby. Papa bout t'bust!" An he try to pull my gown up. But I turn on my side to face him, slow, like I'm still sleepin. He quick freeze ev'ythang. He don' talk. He don' move. He don' even breathe, til he thank I'm in a deep sleep again. Then he start liffin my gown again an say even lower, "I want'chu, Alice. I need'chu, Alice. C'mere Princess. Come to Papa."

I snatched his hand up, reared my leg back an brought my knee up as hard an as fast as I could, almos buryin it in his crotch.

Mr. Tucker was howlin an retchin when I scrambled cross that mattress an outta that room. I could hear Harriet startin to scream while I made my way down the hall, but her li'l pitch wa'nt near so close or so loud as the blood rushin in my ears or my heart bangin in my chest. I took big gulps of air an counted to ten an told myse'f over an over to git a grip it's almos over, it's almos over, it's almos over, so I wouldn't blackout b'fo I was through.

My pulse was still racin an I was still seein red, but I felt a li'l calmer when I went downstairs to git Mr. Tucker's huntin rifle.

My hands was tremblin s'much, I was afraid I wouldn't be able to load it afta I found it. I b'lieved it was in the pantry. Tha's the last place I seened it an he din't use it but once in a great long time.

In the kitchen, I set down an forced myse'f to calm down. I wa'nt thankin too far ahead or nuthin. I only shot a rifle four or five times in my life when I was younger, but I figger ef I was close enough I wouldn't miss...EF I had to shoot.

Thankin *EF* made me feel a lot better. Maybe I wa'nt bout to ruin my life becomin a cold blood killer. This wouldn't be cold blood, this gonna be self-defense ef anythang. But could the woman call it self-defense when she tryin to keep her husband from sexin her? I 'ont know an right now I 'ont care!

Alla this thankin make me t'calm down enough to go to the pantry. I decided ef the rifle wa'nt there, then tha'd be a sign from God that Mr. Tucker ain't s'pozed to die tonight.

I opened the door an pulled the drawstrang fer the light. Firs' thang I seen was Mr. Tucker's Winchester standin upright in the far corner. I checked he barrel an seen it was loaded.

Thy Will be done, Lawd. Thy Will be done.

****

Standin at the bottom of the stairs I heard Mr. Tucker in the bathroom runnin water. Harriet was still screamin in her crib. Jes fore I decided to go up there an comfort my li'l girl, I heard Mr. Tucker leave the bathroom an rush down the hall to my room.

He was in there fer awhile an Harriet stopped cryin, but I wa'nt shore why she stop. Part of me say he rockin an cooin her like I woulda done, then another part of me say he migh'could be smotherin her cause he mad at me. An sence he ain't never gonna have no son, he don' want me to have this daughter.

That last thought got me to rushin up the stairs an down the hall, but I stopped at the door when I could hear him sangin real soft, soft like he had been talkin to me a li'l while ago. I thought, of course! He like 'em young! I was pro'bly Harriet's age when he struck the deal wit daddy an mama, tha's why they ain't never thank it was really gonna happen.

I cracked the door an seen him bendin over the cradle. I slipped in wit'out him hearin me an stood on the other side a the bed an pointed his rifle straight at his head, then I said real calm an low, "Turn round Mr. Tucker."

He did, real slow.

"Afta tonight, I ain't never gonna brang this up no mo an I don' spect you to eitha. I ain' gonna make myse'f sick wit pressure from studdin you. But, ef you ever put yer dirty, nasty, fat, grisly, old gran'daddy hands on me ever again... fer any reason... you better kill me. Cause ef you don', I will kill you. An ef you thank you cain't he'p yerse'f, I'ma kill you right now. So,... you thank you kin he'p yerse'f?"

"Yes ma'am," he like to choke, but I b'lieved him.

"Good. Now git the hell out my room an don'chu never come in here uninvited again."

"Yes ma'am," he said an slunk through the door.

When I closed my bedroom door that night, I felt the end of somethin an the beginnin of somethin else. I wa'nt shore, but I thought maybe I jes dumped a burden.

twenty-one

Jes like I said it was gonna be, ain't neitha one of us said nuthin bout that night to the othern an I spect he ain't told daddy neitha, cause mama ain't brang it up t'me. Thangs seem t'be goin along like b'fo til I hit a spell of sour stomachs an got to pukin up ev'ythang I put in my mouth.

I went to Dr. Drew to fine out what all the signs of high blood was beside headaches, blackouts and vomiting. I wanna know ef I kin take somethin sides sleepin pills to brang it down.

"Sleeping pills are specifically for sleep. All they can do is help you to get to sleep when you cannot otherwise do so. There are medications I can prescribe to lower your pressure, but your condition does not warrant that. Not yet. You can lower your pressure through diet, exercise and eliminating stress as much as possible which, I believe, is the source of your hypertension. Your levels today indicate that you are managing fairly well.

"When blood pressure rises to higher than acceptable measures, different people have different reactions. In addition to headaches, some people experience a pressure or tightness that isn't comfortable, but isn't painful either. Some people get dizzy and their eyesight becomes blurry, or like you, they faint altogether. Some people get nose bleeds, some experience numbness in their extremities, some get hot flashes, some experience nausea. It varies from person to person."

"So you sayin it migh'could hit me anytime in any kinda way? Cause see, I ain't feel headachy or dizzy in quite awhile, but now I'm pukin my guts out all over the place. You sayin I migh'could go numb an blind anyday now, too?"

"You talk in such extremes, Alice," Dr. Drew chuckled. "You may experience many things in time if you don't manage your pressure levels now, but you have been managing them apparently. As long as you keep following the regiment you've set, you shouldn't experience any old or new symptoms."

"Then why I keep throwin up? Tha's new."

"That's not from hypertension, young mother. You're pregnant!"

My mouth flung open to say somethin, but ain't nuthin come out. I was memberin the last time Mr. Tucker come to my room. I thought I had jes stop him from doin somethin. But what I did was stop him from doin some mo of what he been doin all along. Tha's why my back an joints useta be hurtin some mornin's! I could jes see that buzzard creepin in my room afta druggin me up an havin his way big as you please. Jes the thought gimme a pow'ful bout of the dry heaves.

I was doubled over an talkin to the Lord tween gaggin on my empty stomach spasms. "Is this Yer Will Lawd?! Is this Yer Will?" I din't wanna seem se'fish, but I couldn't he'p but to wonder when I was gonna git to have a say in my life. When do I git a turn?

It musta sound like jibbers to Dr. Drew. He steady tryna git me to lay down on the table I was bendin off of. He keep sayin, "Careful. Careful," in his quiet, concerned voice. Then I feel a prick from the shot he gimme to make me calm down. I could feel myse'f relaxin an I carried on a calmer li'l talk wit God.

So, Mr. Tucker gonna git his way afta all. He sneakin an creepin round his own house like a thief in the night an done plant another seed in me from I don' know how many rapes an he still git his way. Is this Yer Will? Lawd, I see why so many people follow behine the devil.

Or is this Yer lesson to me for turnin that rifle on Mr. Tucker? Is this Mr. Tucker reward for not seekin revenge on me, in all this time, for bein such a thankless wife? In The Bible You say vengeance is Yern.

I'm jes tryna unnerstan, Lawd. I don' unnerstan. That was my last thought fore I dumped the burden of my dumbness an flew away to the peace Dr. Drew's drugs always brang me.

****

Ev'ybody was shocked when I tole 'em I was expectin again. Of course, Mr. Tucker was pleased as punch. Daddy seem t'thank that this must mean that I done fell in love wit Mr. Tucker cause he start teasin, sayin thangs like, "Ef you an Luthern keep this up, y'all gonna make the firs' colored league team for Smedley!"

I couldn't tell daddy to shut the hell up like I wanna, so I jes leave the house when he start to talkin like that. Bertha look bothered an confused, but I guess she don' wanna seem to be meddlin in my bizness, so she ain't never say nuthin to me or to daddy. Plus, I thank she feelin a might guilty that she gonna be goin away to college next September, but she don' know, tha's the only sunshine in my future right now. She ain't git a full schola'ship, but she got mosta one. Plus, she got a whole nother year to maybe git a full one. Eitha way, wit daddy workin full-time at the mill, they kin afford to pay the rest. Knowin Bertha, an pro'bly the boys, gonna have a chance to be anythang they wanna be is the only bright spot to warm my day. It he'p me feel a little more hopeful... a little less he'pless.

I take Bertha hand one day when daddy start his teasin an make her t'come outside wit me. I kin feel my heart racin an a throb start thumpin behine my eyes an I know I bettah talk to somebody to he'p ease my pressure or I'ma have me a stroke.

"Bertha, I ain't tryna bad talk nobody, but I gotta tell somebody fore I bust! Mr. Tucker trick me so bad, I like t'kill him!" Then I tole her all about that night I said I wa'nt never gonna brang up no mo. I ain't leave out nuthin. I tole her it seem like rape to me, then I tole her bout the talk I had wit God axin' Him ef this His will.

"I don' know what t'do, Bertha. I'm damned when I do an I'm damned when I don'." I hate to whine, but tha's jes what I was doin. "What I'ma do, Bertha? I don' know what t'do!"

"I'ma thanka somethin, Alice. It ain't right we got ev'ythang so nice an easy cause'a you an you ain't got nuthin you want. I'ma thanka somethin. Y'hear me? I'm promisin, Alice, I'ma thanka somethin."

twenty-two

Mr. Tucker made a trip nawth for six weeks in the spring of 1950. I was five months pregnant, almos two years married an it was the firs' time I feel good wakin up every mornin an lookin forward to whatever the day migh'could brang.

I axe daddy to teach me how to drive.

"Yer husband git you where y'need to git to."

"Mr. Tucker ain't here an you over to the mill wit his truck so you kin run yer errands. Why I got to sit round waitin fer somebody t'come git me when they's a car sittin in the yard day in an day out doin nuthin that I kin be runnin my errands wit?"

I kin tell he don' wanna do it. Maybe Mr. Tucker tole him he don' want me drivin or somethin. I jes keep talkin.

"Wha'chu skeered of, daddy? You taught Daniel an Samuel how to drive an they five years younger'n me. Did Mr. Tucker tell you he thank ef I kin drive, one day I migh'would drive myse'f away from here? I still got feets! Anytime I wanna, I kin walk away."

Daddy ain't know how to tell me no. Me tellin him he got Mr. Tucker truck fer his convenience an plus he done awready taught the twins how to drive pro'bly make him feel guilty, like I want him to.

He ain't never say yes or no fer shore, but the next day, daddy take Bertha an me out for our firs' drivin lesson.

He splain bout the clutch an the differnt gears, then show us how t'work 'em while he doin it. Then he lemme change the gears while he still in the driver seat workin the clutch. When he fine'ly let me try it all by myse'f, I had that car jerkin an stutterin all up an down the road. It shore do look easy when you sittin in the ridin seat. Tha's jes what I kep tellin Bertha in the back seat laughin her silly se'f near to death over me an the sorry way I handled the car.

I took up so much time that firs' day, Bertha had to wait fer the next day to git her turn an she was worse then me! By the end of the week, though, you couldn't tell us we wa'nt ready! We thought we was both professional chau'furs ready to start up a jitney service fer the town!

We wanna teach mama how to drive, but she say nough people awready round her know how to do that to whure she ruther jes ketch a ride wit one of us.

Afta that one week, Bertha an me ride around whurever we want, whenever we wanna go. We went to town mo in them four weeks then I been to town in all my life. Downtown Smedley is jes a li'l place. There's a hardware store, a post office, a five 'n dime wit a drug store in the back, a restaurant wit a soda bar, a hat an shoe store, a men's shop, a lady's shop, three bars an two roomin houses. These places din't allow colored people in 'em, cept fer the Negroes workin there cookin or cleanin up. We ain't know that none of this wa'nt nuthin, cause we ain't never been nowhere else. An sence we wa'nt allowed in there, we wanna go there even mo cause it seem like we must be missin somethin.

But Berth an me ain't want no trouble. We drive over to the colored side of town that got ev'ythang the Whites Only downtown got, plus The Juke. The Juke is a dance, bar, club, restaurant where mos' ev'ybody either start out or end up they day or night. We usually stop to git a soda an visit wit whoever we see that we know.

We see Alberta an Mary two or three times. They live in the roomin house above The Juke. They a lot differnt from when we was in school. They smoke cigarettes, drank corn, laugh loud, dance raunchy an paint they faces. They look old to me, lease older then seventeen, but they still nice an friendly to Bertha an me.

We was all talkin outside The Juke one afta'noon when some ol ha'f drunk, pimple-face white boy park his pick-up truck an walk right over to us like he know us or somethin.

"Which one a y'all black tails wanna wrangle?" He axe lookin at Bertha like she a fresh beefsteak an he a hongry dog.

Mary step right up, slipped her arm in his and say, "Ten 'n two, I show you what t'do!" Then they both laugh an go on upstairs to her room.

I stood there gawkin at them goin up them stairs. They was strange as snowflakes on a beach. I heard of white mens ackin all familer wit colored womens they plan on messin wit. But I ain't never heard'a no colored woman ackin friendly back to'em. An I ain't never heard of no couple like that out in broad daylight laughin an walkin arm 'n arm! An Mary took that pitiful li'l white boy up to her room when me an Berth done seen her an Alberta a few times now an they ain't never invite *us* up to they rooms. An I ain't never heard of that kinda wranglin goin on *inside* of nowheres. Them white mens take the black girls out in the fields or the woods or in they trucks. Plus, I was wondrin what "ten 'n two" mean that ev'ybody seem to know cept me.

"Shut yer trap, Alice! An don' start ackin all high falutin mighty wit Mary an me. We doin the same as you, ceptin you married yer John an gotta put up wit some damn babies!" Alberta barked at me an rolled her eyes like I done done or said somethin ugly an now she mad at me. What she mean, they doin the same as me... What am I doin? An who's John? I married Mr. Tucker an I ain't *REALLY* marry him!!

I ain't say none of these thangs, though. I stood there gawkin at her wondrin what jes happen an why she mad at me? Then I felt Bertha pullin on my arm.

"C'mon Alice, is time t'go." Bertha was talkin to me, but lookin at Alberta. Bertha wa'nt mad or nuthin, she jes ready t'go.

Bertha was drivin the car on the way home cause I was too dazed. We was drivin along wit'out talkin fer awhile then Bertha start talkin like she done read my mind, "Mary an Berta is ho's, Alice. I din't know you ain't know that til you stood there starin at Mary an that boy."

"What Alberta mean, they doin the same as me? What I'm doin?"

138

"She talkin stupid. Lot'sa women don' love they husband. They git married so they be set, y'know, wit a house an food an clothes an stuff. Ho's call they customers 'John', tha's why they say you married yer 'John'. They thank tha's why you married Mr. Tucker!" Then Bertha laugh, "They don' know, do they Alice?! They don' know a damn thang!"

But I thank they right. Married or not, lovin my babies or not, they right. I am lettin myse'f be prostituted fer my family. Ef I picked to be a ho' myse'f, lease I be free an alone, livin life on my own. I be free like I wanna be.

You don' know, Bertha. I ride there side her thankin, *you jes don' know*.

****

When Mr. Tucker git back, I ain't let on that I know how to drive or nuthin cause I thank it migh'could git daddy in trouble. I member how daddy ain't really wanna teach me. Plus, Mr. Tucker seem to be in such high spirits. He keep busy runnin round ev'ywhere an I like it best when he be gone. I decide to leave good enough alone an not call no 'tention back to me that migh'would git him to stayin at home or watchin me mo.

When we was all havin our supper t'getha that Sunday afta'noon, Mr. Tucker start givin advice an makin promises like he answerin a wish list.

"Nate an Gracie, y'all kin rent out yer house an land an make a nice exter piece a change. Ef you do 'em seh'pert, I thank you git more money. You kin even save a patch fer Bertha an them boys t'raise a few vege'bles they kin sell to tourists in the summer. When Bertha be goin t'college next September, you boys kin work down t'the mill on weekends wit yer poppa to earn some pocket change."

"Where we gonna live?" Mama axed lookin pleased an puzzled.

"Y'all kin move into me an Alice house come the end a the month, ef ya like." He say into his plate, busy stuffin his face.

Bertha an mama lookit me an I shrug my shoulders cause I don' know nuthin! "Where Y'ALL gonna live?" They axe t'getha.

"Alice an me movin t'Cleveland." He say it like it wa'nt no big deal. Like me an him done talked bout it an agreed to it. He ain't got no blood relations that I know of, so I kin see whure it migh'could be easy fer him to up an move t'wherever, whenever he wanna go. But I got roots an they here. Ev'ybody an ev'ythang I know an love is righ'chere an I wa'nt never

139

studdin bout leavin Smedley, cept t'go t'college fer a spell. Lawd, I wished I hadda lef' wit Isaac!

I done loss my appetite. I drop my fork, wipe my mouth an start countin t'keep calm. When I thank I kin speak wit'out yellin or arguin, I say, "When was you gonna tell me, Mr. Tucker?"

He drop his fork an lookit me like he darin me or somethin an he say, "Today. Tha's what I jes now done." Then he wipe his mouth, pick up the rice bowl an he'ped hisse'f to mo. He ain't lose none a his appetite.

"Ain't this kinda sudden, Luthern?" Daddy try'ta ease the tension.

"Nah Nate," he say soundin like he migh'could be darin my daddy too, at firs'. But then when he keep talkin, it sound more like he beggin. "Now you know I been done tole you I want my boy t'have all the vantages a colored chile kin git. The nawth is way head'a us in some ways. I was thankin one'a them Great Lake cities be best cause they got s'many op'tunitites. All them fac'tries needin workers mean makin a livin ain't so hard an ev'ybody jes a li'l better off. Li'l Luthern don' need t'be round a buncha jealous, hard luck chirrens like mosta these ones round Smedley. Schools is bettah up nawth. They got lotsa colleges, Bertha migh'would wanna go to one a them stead'a one a the ones down here."

Round bout the time he include Bertha, he sound happy an proud'a hisse'f, like everybody gonna love his plan later ef they don' like it now.

"An they's jes more thangs t'do. I'm gonna take my boy t'all the ball games! The Buckeyes, The Indians, The Brown's, c'aint do that here. Plus, all 'ese southern negroes been movin up nawth, so's it ain't so strange or hard t'git along like you migh'would thank.

"I picked out a nice house in a real nice neighborhood. I figger you kin take over the mill, Nate, an jes send me my money up in Cleveland. I'm gonna take my boy on train rides t'Chicago, Detroit, Buffalo, maybe even Niagra Falls. We only gonna shop in the big department stores downtown. Lemme tell y'all, they got stores so big, all the shops in downtown Smedley kin fit on one a the floors of The May Company, or Halles or Higbees or Bonwit Tellers, tha's they big department stores. An they still be a buncha floors lef' over fer the other thangs they be sellin, perfume, furniture, fur coats, books, fancy candy, toys an jewelries...ev'ythang!

"Y'all kin come up jes t'go shoppin like some a them rich white folks be doin. An we kin come back down here for Thanksgivin an Christmas an some summers."

I 'ont thank anybody ever heard Mr. Tucker talk s'much at one go. Cept maybe daddy. Maybe. We all jes sittin there starin at him, not sayin a word, jes lookin. We studdin him like he a pastor up here preachin, describin what heaven gonna be like for the saved. And ef tha's the case, the twins was the firs' to be saved.

"I wanna go! I wanna go!" they chimed, hoppin round in they seats.

"Y'all kin come visit whenever y'all wanna, s'long as you git good grades in school an mind yer mama an papa."

That shut the twins rightup. Firs' they was hunched over in they seats rubbin they hands t'getha like they couldn't wait to git 'em on somethin. Then when they looked over to mama, they quick set ramrod straight an still in they chairs to show how good they was gonna be. It hit me right then how Mr. Tucker git people to jump through hoops fer him fer the promises he be makin. Daniel an Samuel gonna be good so's they kin come visit in Cleveland. Mama an daddy gonna be movin to the big house an gonna be makin money from rentin out this'un, plus daddy gonna be the new Mr. Tucker down to the mill so's ev'ybody gonna do whatever daddy say. Bertha ain't so impressed. But she know that her goin to college is cause a Mr. Tucker makin it so's we could go to grade school. So even though she ain't all for him, she cain't be all against him neitha.

"When you thankin bout leavin'?" Daddy axe.

"The end a the month is in two weeks. We oughta be hittin the road a few days b'fo that."

He ain't promise me nuthin cause he know he cain't make me jump. They ain't nuthin he got I want. I know he doin this, movin us outta Smedley up to God-knows-where, cause afta I done raised that gun to him, he thank I'm jes gonna be smellin myse'f howsomever. He still tryna control me. He figger ef I ain't round my family, I won' be feelin so high falutin, lease tha's what I thank he thank. He tryna break my spirit. It jes bout break my heart to thank I ain't gonna be able to see my folks whenever I want to, whenever I need to, anytime a day or night.

Afta a minute or more of ev'ybody sittin round thankin they thoughts, I decide I need some fresh air. But b'fo I go, I stand an start clappin, "Gradulations Mr. Tucker, or should we be callin you Rev'ern Tucker? That was a right nice sermon you jes give. Better'n Rev'ern Pritchard ever give. Yers is fulla prophesies an thangs... whoooeee, very enlightenin! We need to spread them good words of yern, Rev'ern Tucker! We ain't gotta die to git to heaven. The Promised Land is nawth an Cleveland is the capitol. Praise be, Hallelujah!"

twenty-three

We ain't hardly have time to separate what we wanna take from what we gotta take from what we jes c'aint live wit'out, no less box it up fer haulin.

Mr. Tucker say the same thang bout anythang I try to pack up, "Leave that fer yer family, we kin buy another one...*or*...we kin git a bettah one...*or*...ain't no need fer one a them in Cleveland!"

An really, he was right. But I din't wanna hear that. I was packin sentimental thangs, thangs that would brang me remembrance of the people an the place I was leavin behine. Smedley, South Carolina is the cradle of my life, where I was born, where I met ev'ybody an learned ev'ythang I know. I lived all my life in a twenny mile radius from my family home. Now, in less then sixteen hours of drivin, we gonna be ridin into Cleveland wit the trunk full of all the clothes, pictures an kitchen stuff Mr. Tucker would let me brang.

Sence I ain't never lef' Smedley b'fo, I wanted to go early in the mornin so's I could see all there was to see from here to up nawth. But Mr. Tucker said we gonna leave at twilight cause ef the po-lice see us long the road, they liable to give us a hard time an maybe even some tickets for nuthin. He thank ef we leave afta the sun done set an we ride mos'ly through the night, then we be in the nawth come sunrise an that'll make it be a shorter, safer trip.

I say, "Mr. Tucker, slavery been over for eighty-five years! The po-lice ain't the same as them paddy rollers useta go round lookin fer runaway slaves on the roads."

I thought that migh'would make him to laugh at hisse'f. But he lookit me then look out to the road we soon to travel on, "Yeah well," he say through tight jaws, "the more thangs change, the more they stay the same."

I ain't never wanna leave my family or the familer sights an smells of home cause of missin 'em all so much, but now I don' wanna go cause Mr. Tucker make me skeered to. We ain't movin nawth no mo. It feel like we escapin. An to make it worse, I'ma be travelin wit my jailer.

Mama an Bertha fixed a ton of food fer us to take to keep from starvin. They fried up two whole chickens, baked a honey glazed ham wit cloves an pineapples. They made sweet potato salad wit apples an pears, pickled beets, carrot/raisin salad, three-bean salad, a mess of biscuits, peach/strawberry muffins an Mr. Tucker's favorite dessert (my second best) sourmilk cake sprinkled wit powdered sugar an cinnamon.

It's too bad I wa'nt hungry. I din't thank I'd be hungry fer food ever again. I pined for my relations. We musta all fixed in our minds not to cry, but at the last minute, we was all bawlin like brand-new orphans. Even the twins was cryin an clingin to my sides. Harriet was wailin cause ev'ybody else was. Mr. Tucker even seem to have misty eyes, but it was hard to tell fer shore cause mines was all blurry. Bertha promise to write ev'yday. Mama say she gonna come up to he'p me when the baby come due. I was hopin Miss Johnson woulda stop by, but she ain't an that made me cry too.

Mr. Tucker was past ready to go when we fine'ly git goin. He put all the food up front wit him an fixed the backseat like a bed, best he could, so's Harriet an me could sleep mosta the way. I din't thank I could sleep a wink, but I guess all that cryin musta tuckered us out. Me an Harriet was sleepin b'fo we even reached the highway, an I was really lookin fo'ward to seein what a wide, fast road like that migh'could be like.

****

When I woke up, we was ridin down a street call St. Clair in Cleveland, Ohio. It's the widest, longest street I ever hear of. Mr. Tucker say ef he keep drivin on St. Clair for six or seven hours, we venchally gonna wind up in Buffalo, New York!

But we only rid on it for bout twenny minutes or so fore we turn down 105th Street. It ain't as wide, but it seem to be long as St. Clair, to my eye. They got stores, restaurants, chu'chs, banks, bars, fune'ral homes, gas stations, hunnerds of cars, an more people walkin down this one street then live in alla Smedley. Afta'while, we turn down Wade Park, a wide, tree-lined street wit big houses sittin back from the curb an they all got green lawns an blossomin hedges. It look like somewheres Alice an Jerry from my school books would live, or Callie an Jasper from the Sears Roebuck cadlog.

Mr. Tucker pull into a long driveway next to a big brick house wit two wide picture windows on eitha side of a stain-glassed door and say, "Welcome to yer new home, Princess."

I c'aint b'lieve my eyes! I was all ready to hate the Nawth, Ohio, Cleveland, an our new house in perticuler, but I love it. I love it all! I jes wished I coulda come here wit somebody sides Mr. Tucker.

Mr. Tucker unpacked the car while I run through the house wit Harriet to see what we gonna see. The inside look even bigger an better'n the outside. Every room is bout big as Mr. Tucker's bedroom back in Smedley, even the kitchen! They's three fireplaces an four floors an ev'y floor got a full bathroom includin the cellar, cept the cellar bath got a shower stall stead of a tub. Mr. Tucker say the cellar is called a "basement" an it's "finished" like the attic, tha's what he call 'em. The basement got fancy, dancy knotty wood panels on the walls an a glass bar that light up on one end an a fireplace on the wall cross from it at the other end. The attic got two big rooms an a full bathroom. It's hot an stuffy up there now, but I kin see one of these bein my sewin room an the other one bein my bedroom or a liberry. The two floors tween the top an bottom got bout five or six big rooms each, includin the kitchen on the firs' floor. There's a porch on the side of the house wit a green canvas coverin that collapses so you kin enjoy the sun or the shade, whatever you pleasure.

144

You kin git to the porch from two differnt rooms on the ground floor. Ain't no furniture yit, but I don' care. I kin sleep on that one mattress I seen in a room on the firs' floor, big pregnant belly an all.

"You an the baby muss be tarred, Princess. I'ma go git some groceries while y'all git some rest. Later on, I drive y'all round the neighborhood, 'kay?"

"You the one need rest, you been drivin all night. Plus, we ain't gonna need no groceries til bout a month from now wit all the food mama an Bertha fixed. Gone rest yerse'f, Mr. Tucker. I'ma git me an Harriet a li'l somethin to eat."

"Well I do feel a little pee-ked. I only got one mattress, though. Ef you don' mind... they's plen'y room for all three a us..."

"We been sleepin all night. We gonna git somethin to eat now. We migh'could lay down a li'l later."

Tha's how Mr. Tucker an me spend our firs' day in Cleveland, bein thoughtful an polite to each other. I kin keep this up long as he kin, so long as he know whether this his son I'm carryin or not, it's the last time he ever git to try... wit me.

twenty-four

We went drivin round every evenin for a week. The firs' day I seen how convenient ev'ythang was to us. Theys four hospitals kinda close to our house. Four! Mt. Sinai Hospital, University Hosptial, The Vet'rans Administration an The Cleveland Clinic. Smedley ain't got ONE, you gotta go to the next town. Mt. Sinai, right down the street, is whure I'm pro'bly gonna have my baby.

They's a bunch of museums an colleges near us, too; the Health Museum on Euclid is the first museum in the country devoted to the human body. The Art, the Science an the History Museums are jes round the corner on Wade Oval Drive. Case Institute of Technology, Western Reserve University an Severance Hall, where The Cleveland Orchestra play, is closeby, too. Theys a park across from Severance Hall wit weepin willow trees an wide, stone steps leadin down to a lake called Mirror Lake that got ducks an swans an make you feel like you in a differnt country or a differnt time.

The next day we went all round downtown. I believe Mr. Tucker been studdin the history of this place to try to impress me bout how smart he really is or to point out how wonderful Cleveland gonna be to live in, cause sometime he run off the history of it like it was his own. Like, The Terminal Tower is the tallest buildin in Ohio. It's in the middle of downtown an the tower part look jes like pictures I seen of The Empire State Building in New York City, the tallest buildin in the world. Come to find out from Mr. Tucker, that The Terminal Tower was completed in 1927 an at 708 feet tall, it *was the tallest building in the world before The Empire State Building*! Near to one side of the Terminal Tower is The Farmer's Market. It got every kinda fresh fruit, veg'table an meat you kin thank of. Near to the other side of The Terminal Tower is The Flats, right down there on the Cuyahoga River at the bottom of downtown. The Flats got warehouse stores an fac'tries. Mr. Tucker say the Cuyahoga River at Lake Erie was a point for all kinds of transportation afta the Civil War. In 1890, gov'ment funds made the river wider an made Cleveland a major transportation hub. John P. Rockefeller made his fortune here usin Cleveland's water, rail an pipeline links in The Flats to bring crude oil to his refineries. Whether he was tryna be he'pful or jes braggin an showin off bout what he know, I thought alla Mr. Tucker's information was interestin.

Cleveland got live theaters like The Hanna Theater that opened up in 1921 an ain't never closed down like mos other theaters did in the depression. The KARAMU House is the firs' theater to mix races on stage an is even older then The Hanna. KARAMU wa'nt always the name neitha, but it's the one that stuck. It opened in 1915, burned down in 1939 an the whole thang got rebuilt an renamed in 1941 to KARAMU, that mean "a place of joyful meeting" in Swahili. The Hippodrome downtown was the largest stage theatre in the world next to the Hippodrome in NYC. Enrico Caruso, WC Fields, Will Rogers an Al Jolson all worked there. In 1931, it changed over an now it's the largest movin picture theater in the world.

The Cleveland Stadium is whure the major league baseball an football teams play; The Cleveland Indians Baseball Team started in 1901 an went through a buncha name changes. "The Indians" was they nickname that stuck permanent in 1915. It was in honor of Louis "Chief"

Sockalexis who useta play for them when they was called the Cleveland Spiders.

The Cleveland Buckeyes was they colored baseball team that played in two Negro World Series and won the 1945 series. Afta hearin bout The Buckeyes an hearin the Indians was named afta a real Indian, I thought The Browns musta been fulla Negroes. But Mr. Tucker say The Browns was just named afta they coach, Paul E. Brown. He been they coach sence they started jes four years ago, in 1946. The Elysium Skating Rink is the home of The Cleveland Barons hockey team, an firs' *they* was called *The Cleveland Indians.*

Old Stone Church downtown is open alla time. Cleveland got big hotels, whole-in-the-wall jukes an fancy bars, plus The Euclid Arcade, the first mall in the country! It's gotta indoor walk wit a buncha specialty shops linin the upstairs an downstairs. Seem like Cleveland got so many stores linin' the longest, widest streets in the world wit names that sound like tall trees or tropical flowers... Euclid, Cedar, Chester, Carnegie, Superior an St. Clair.

The third day we rode round the Culture Gardens. Mr. Tucker say these gardens is "landscaped", that mean "groomed" like what we do to our face an hair an fangers an toes when we be dressin fancy. The Culture Gardens twist is a wide stretch of green lawn wit little ponds, big trees, flowers, bushes, fountains an sculptures of famous mens from Yerp. Mr. Tucker say theys more parks in Cleveland then any other city in the country! He say some of 'em got horseback ridin, hikin, boatin an all kindsa thangs so these Culture Gardens ain't such a much, but I love 'em. The Culture Gardens start cross the street from us an stretch all the way down to Lake Erie. Then the street turn into a highway called Lakeshore Drive (I fine'ly got to see me a highway!) that run along the lake. Lake Erie look more like a ocean. You c'aint see nuthin on the other side an wha's on the other side is Canada! They's a footbridge that cross Lakeshore Drive an take you from the pier to alla way cross where theys another big, pretty park surroundin the Aquarium. Lake Erie shoreline got a beach an a boat dock wit houseboats, sailboats an The Burke Lakefront Airport. When night fall, you see lights ev'ywhere. Big red letters blink on one letter at a time, *P. O. C.,* then blink off an back on all together. *P.O.C.,* it's a local "brewery" called Port Of Cleveland cause tha's where they make it. Them lights plus the Republic Steel mill fire an lights, the stadium lights, an the lights from houses an other biznesses shape the "skyline".

When night come to Smedley, it's jes black. It's so black you cain't see yer hand in front of yer face, less the moon is full. I love the Cleveland *skyline* an all the other new words I been learnin to describe what I be seein.

The next four days was jes like the firs' day, Mr. Tucker drivin me an Harriet round to see what there is to see. It all start to blend togetha in my mind for what was where. I migh'couldna found myse'f back to none a these places, but I seen the zoo, Hopkins International Airport (the first city owned airport in the country), John Carroll University, Oberlin College, the tomb of President James Garfield in Lakeview Cemetary who was assassinated like Lincoln, chinatown, a whole buncha schools from primary to high school, public to private, Euclid Beach Amusement Park, television an radio stations, the big General Electric plant where Garrett Morgan worked, the colored man who invented the traffic light an started The Cleveland Call, a newspaper for an about the city's Negroes. They's at lease one hospital or more in ev'y neighborhood. I seen a golf course, two prisons an a Horse Race Track... Hot Dog!

twenty-five

I guess they do be doin thangs differnt in the nawth then from the south. Come to find out our street got all kindsa people livin on it, Negroes, whites even folks from Japan an India! Mos'ly they doctors or nurses or teachers. Mr. Tucker an me is the only ones ain't workin at one of the hospitals, colleges or museums round here. Almos alla them talk like Miss Johnson or Dr. Drew. I decide I'ma try to talk more like these college gradiates, then maybe people thank I gradiated from college, too. Plus, it migh'could make thangs easier fer me ef I venchally do go to college. Ev'ybody real nice too, from a distance. They come over to welcome us an they wave whenever they see us, but they don' be stoppin by all the time. We be by ourse'f mosta the time.

Afta a week of ridin round, I ain't hardly know whure nuthin was, but I do know whure Mt. Sinai Hospital is an I went there that second week t'git my baby a doctor.

I ain't never seen a hospital b'fo, no less walked round inside of one. It was so big an cold, not the temperature, but how it make me to feel inside. I was feelin so important, at firs', walkin down them wide corridors, but ain't nobody lookit me or seem to even notice I'm there. That make me to feel smaller then small, like I don' exist. When I fine'ly found the waitin room of the maternity section, I was so early, it wa'nt open yet. They was one other lady come in afta me an I thought one of us was in the wrong place cause she was white an I ain't. But she ain't ack like nuthin was wrong. She wa'nt studdin me a tall.

When the nurse open up, she ain't shoo me away like I was thankin she migh'would do. I told her I jes moved from Smedley an I was needin a doctor. I brung the copies of my records Dr. Drew gimme to pass onto my new doctor. The nurse took 'em, long wit a buncha forms she had me to fill out, then told me to go home an somebody was gonna be callin me. That seem backwards to me.

"I'm standin right here," I said, "wha'chu wanna call me fer?"

"You haven't been assigned a doctor yet," she said. "Your records will be reviewed and the doctor that accepts you will have his secretary make an appointment for you." She lookit my records an say, "That's not the way it's done in Smedley, is it?"

"No m'am."

"Well, it's how we do it here. If you had called, I could've saved you a trip." She wa'nt very friendly, but I din't thank she was tryna smart alleck me either. She was jes tellin me how they do thangs in Cleveland, or in Mt. Sinai, one.

"Go home," she say an smile for the first time that morning, "You'll probably get a call before noon."

I went home an got a call from a Dr. Lepert office at 11:30 sayin to come back at 3:30.

****

Now, my experience wit doctors is limited to one, Dr. Drew. But still, what I heard bout how thangs go on round Smedley is mosta them don' treat coloreds cause then whites wouldn't go to 'em, an theys the ones that keep 'em in bizness. When colored folks need tendin to, it's usually

151

the animal doctors that see to us, tha's why Dr. Drew was exter special. He ain't no animal doctor. He colored an he good. I thank bein a Negro is part of what make him so good. He treat the sick by what they say an by what he kin see. He ain't figger he know somethin bout'chu that he don', like them animal doctors do.

Sence the animals cain't talk, I figger they doctor go by what they kin see an kin guess. So, ef you up there tryna tell a animal doctor somethin, they ain't lis'nin to you no more'n they be listenin to the brayin of a mule.

But Dr. Lepert ain't no animal doctor. He old an white an he seem to be good. He more like Dr. Drew cause he don' figger he know nuthin bout me. He read my records, took some tests an then axe me a buncha questions *an writ down what I say*! He don' even seem to notice I'm colored, I was jes his new patient. I like that.

twenty-six

Over the weeks, we did a little shoppin for a few key pieces of furniture like a sofa chair and ottoman, a sleepin sofa, some lamps, a kitchen table wit chairs, a big bed frame to hold the mattress that we had all been sleepin on, a crib for the baby and a coupla throw rugs jes to tide us over for now.

It was Mr. Tucker idea to git our first bit of furniture from the big Sears Roebuck store over on Carnegie Avenue. I ain't say nuthin then, but I couldn't wait to walk into the real life world of Callie, Jasper and Sadie.

Sears ain't let me down none neither. Seem like it was bigger'n all outdoors. Great big bright halls filled with clothes, shoes, lamps, couches, beds or whatever it is you want. I let Mr. Tucker pick out what he like cause I ain't really care. I was jes happy to be there.

Afta that, I wanna plant a garden in that big yard out back. Mr. Tucker ain't got nuthin much to do, sence he ain't got no mill to run, so he wind up plantin it.

"I'ma dig up the space you need. You jes show me how much yard you want. It ain't good for you to be doin a whole lotta work in yer condition," he say while he diggin up grass.

He fertilize a nice size plot, but when I went to drop the seeds, Mr. Tucker say he oughta be doin that, too. I let 'im, but I ain't shore how I feel about it. I like to do work to keep my mind offa him and thangs. But ef he gonna be settin me down in the shade to watch him do the work and have me jes to supervise, I ruther be inside readin or sewin or somethin. I don' wanna watch him do nuthin. But I don' say that.

Afta the garden is planted, I told Mr. Tucker it be nice ef we had some grapevines round the porch. Then we could jes pick 'em off they vines for jellies and juice. So he plant some concords along the side porch.

By the time I was about seven months pregnant, the garden was fulla little tender shoots. At this rate, I figger we be bearin our fruits round the same time.

I don' know what kinda person he gonna be, but I know he already a lot differnt as a baby from Harriet. It make sense, too, cause boys migh'should be differnt from girls. I ain't git temporary anemia or diabetes this time. Little Miss Harriet use to feel like she was runnin relays or hopscotchin up and down my ribs. I don' thank she ever slept more'n a hour or two any day. She din't hurt me none, but seem like she use to steady be movin to remind me she still there. This boy don' hardly move a tall, but when he do, it take my breath away. First time, as I recollect, he musta kicked me in my lungs cause it knocked all the wind outta me. Plus, he made me to fall fo'ward like I got pushed, only the push come from inside of me stead of from behind.

I had been worried that somethin was wrong at first, cause he was so still. But afta that first kick, I'm glad he ain't moved but three times in seven months.

Come August, the baby drop down so fast and hard, I'm thankin he migh'could split me in two when he come out, hard as he be pushin. Either that, or he gonna jes rest in my pelvis for another month or so, slow as he be to move. But Dr. Lepert say he gonna check me in the hospital on the tenth cause he thank the baby should be ready around then.

"You want me to come here even ef I ain't in labor?"

"Yes, I do. If you're not in labor when you come, you will be soon after."

I called mama and told her the baby done shifted down and she took the next Greyhound Bus outta Smedley, a big rush for nuthin the way it happen. They shore do thangs differnt in the nawth. I was *IN* labor that afternoon when Bertha called Dr. Drew and he still ain't come til that evenin. Now, Dr. Lepert tellin me, ready or not, to come check in.

So I did.

****

My labor started late in the evenin of the eleventh. It seem to be a lot harder the second time and I know one reason why is cause mama wa'nt wit me. My labor start way afta visitin hours was over and they told me not to bother mama cause she be here in the mornin, then in the mornin they wouldn't let her in cause they say it was too late and the baby was practically here. The other thang is they shoot me wit a needle in my back. It's s'poze to be for pain, but first they wait til I done had mosta all the pain there was gonna be. Then the nurse start yellin all up in my face, "PUSH! PUSH!" like she ain't jes gimme a shot that make me go numb. Plus, they tell me whatever the mama take, the baby take, too. So ef I was feelin numb from the shot, the baby musta alla sudden felt numb, too. Tha's bound to slow a birth down some. Despite alla that, the next mornin, August 12th, I had my second baby.

****

"Parents often ask if I think it's going to be a girl or a boy," Dr. Lepert said. "I never venture a guess because you never know. I tell them their guess is as good as mines. It's so hard to say because every pregnancy is different and, to my knowledge, there really are no telltale, through-line characteristics in an unborn child that are exclusive to either gender. Remember, I am an old doctor and I have delivered thousands of babies.

"But I would have bet cash money on this child being a boy. That strong, strong heartbeat and the fact that he barely moved, but when he did, it knocked the stuffing out of you. I never said, but I just *KNEW* you were carrying a boy. And not just a boy, but a future running-back for the Cleveland Brown's!

"But see, you never know," he said handin me the sleepin beauty I plan on callin Ola.

twenty-seven

Seem like everybody was kind of disappointed bout Ola bein born, cept for Harriet. That's cause she thought Ola was a gift to her. The biggest, newest baby doll toy ever!

I thank mama want the baby named for her, even though she ain't say nuthin. Mr. Tucker want a boy for sure, sence I done told him this was his last chance to make one with me. I was kinda hopin for a boy too, so's I wouldn't have to fight with Mr. Tucker alla rest of my life. Daddy and them didn't sound excited. They were happy the baby and me was okay, but they didn't sound excited like when Harriet was born. I couldn't tell ef they sound like that cause we talkin on the phone, or cause mama wa'nt there to take care of them, or cause they wished they was here, or cause Ola was a girl, or what.

Ola look more like Mr. Tucker then Harriet, mostly cause she got his rich, dark chocolate color. I know Mr. Tucker ain't like that, but he ain't say nuthin bout it. Which was wise. I thank she a lot prettier then Harriet. Her face is mostly big, brown, cow eyes with long curly lashes and a mess of curly little ringlets crownin her head. She kinda look like Bertha, who look like mama only browner. And she got deep dimples in her fat cheeks that they ain't got. She's quieter then Harriet was at her age. I wonder ef that's cause she can feel how everybody is kind of disappointed. Or could it be that numbin drug they give me fore she was born ain't quite wear off yit? Or maybe that's jes the way she is, sence she was still and quiet most of the time I carried her inside of me.

Mama say she gotta *old soul*. She splain that people call babies *old souls* when it seem they been through more lives then most other people, so they ain't impressed with jes another time around. The closer I watched Ola, the more I thank mama is right. This baby got a old, *old* soul.

She be studdin people like she seen them or know somebody like them from before. Harriet, not quite a year old, is jes a baby herself, but you can't tell her that. She always pullin on Ola, tryin to pick her up and her kisses are clumsy and sometime look hard, but Ola never cries or whines at her sister. She squinches her little face waitin for Harriet to stop and sometime she give a big sigh, like she thankin she be glad when Harriet grow up and stop worryin her.

****

Mama love this house more'n anythang. When I come home from the hospital, I don't never see her cept when she servin meals.

She say, "I thought Mr. Tucker house in Smedley was big, but you kin git lost in this'un!"

And everyday, she did.

She take Harriet with her and spend the day in a differnt room.

"Where was you and Harriet at all this time, mama?" I axed her one day.

"We was in the front guest room."

"What front guest room?"

"The one with the twin beds for Harriet and Ola's sleep over frien's."

They up there in a different room everyday, all day long. I don't know what Harriet be doin to amuse herself, but mama be decoratin in her mind. Finally, one day I got the hint.

"We need to go furniture shoppin fore you leave, mama. It be a big help. I'm gonna have my hands too full with these babies to do it afta."

"Well,... only ef is gonna he'p you out," she say with her eyes bigger'n saucers tryna act like Christmas ain't jes come early for her.

When I told Mr. Tucker our plan, he say right off that's a good idea, I thank cause he know mama ain't gonna be spendin his money all free and foolish like some people woulda done.

Now, look like mama was more excited then I was the first time I went to Sears Roebuck cause she was gonna git to see a television set.

Ain't none of us ever seen a T.V. before, I ain't thank of it last time I was here. The T.V.'s was in a big, dim room. I guess they kept the room dim so's the pictures would look even brighter. Mama liked to died when Mr. Tucker bought one settin in a big walnut cabinet with doors that look like a nice bookcase or bureau when the doors is closed. And like that wa'nt enough, Mr. Tucker went and bought a Hi-Fi console to go long with it bein as they was on the same floor as the T.V.'s and it jes seem like one wouldn't do without the other.

"You shouldn't be spendin all this money on these here thangs!" Mama say, and I kin tell she mean it, too. $350 ain't nuthin to be sneezed at. Lot'sa people in Smedley don't make that in two years! Mama was jes happy to *see* her a television, like I was happy jes to be inside of a Sears Roebuck store. She wa'nt plannin on Mr. Tucker *buyin* one.

"Tha's what money is fer, Miss Grace." Mr. Tucker say. "Plus, it look like my li'l angel ain't gonna let me leave here wit'out me firs' gittin her one a these here music boxes."

It was true, too. Harriet was standin in front of one of those High Fidelity consoles jumpin up an down and swayin from side to side to the music lookin like she in a trance or somethin. We got some of them records to go along with the hi-fi, too. We took Dinah Washington, Nat King Cole, Ella Fitzgerald and Eartha Kitt with us, but was havin the T.V. and the hi-fi delivered later on.

Only Ola was sittin cool as a cucumber. She look at the T.V. picture and the hi-fi box like she almost bored and thankin, "Oh yeah, I remember these." In five weeks, I ain't known her to git excited over nuthin. Even

159

her feedin time seem to be like a chore she know she gotta do, but ain't nuthin she look forward to. She take my breast when I give it to her, but she ain't never whine for it yet, she don't never cry or nuthin.

"Wha'chu wanna see next, Miss Gracie, livin room, dinin room or bedroom sets?" Mr. Tucker say to mama fore she even got over him spendin more'n $300 on thangs we ain't even need.

"You ain't spendin one more dime in this here store. You done spent enough money today to last all this year an alla next!"

"We still got to furnish the house," Mr. Tucker say with a little chuckle.

I thank it make him feel good to hear people makin a big to do bout how much he be spendin. I thank it make him feel important or powerful to be recognized for doin generous thangs. I know it make him to stand and walk a little differnt, a little taller. Ef you doin thangs from yer heart, I thank it should make you feel good, but it shouldn't make you feel so differnt that you start to puffin yer chest out and swaggerin when you stroll like Mr. Tucker be doin. Mama decide we gonna leave the store right now and Mr. Tucker went along with it like he doin her another favor, but I kin tell from the way he struttin, he feelin proud of hisse'f and the fuss mama makin over his purchases.

On the way out the store to the parkin lot, they got a house pet section full of birds and fish and thangs. When we start walkin through it, Ola start to reachin for thangs and makin little cooin noises, blowin through her lips makin 'em flap like she tryna say somethin.

We ain't never seen her light up like that over nuthin, so we got to git her some a these pets that she tryna talk to. We got her two parakeets with a cage, a cover and a buncha birdseeds, plus a mess of goldfish with a big aquarium bowl, colored pebbles, a sunk ship, seaweed, a filter, a net and a mess of fish food. They put the fish in a big clear plastic bag full of water. I sat in the backseat with the girls on the way home and held the bag up by it's knot so they could watch the fish movin around. They was jesta gigglin and fallin all over theyselves all the way home.

****

"Who hungry?" Mama axed goin through the backdoor.

"Me! Me!" Harriet start yellin and skippin round. She ain't hungry, she jes love to eat mama's cookin like everybody else.

Mama start fryin hamburgers and boilin corn to go with the potato and three-bean salads already in the frigidaire. While she doin that, she axe, "Where the Goodwill and Salvation Army stores round here? Colored neighbor of y'alls told me sometimes you kin find some nice used thangs for cheap in them stores. She say the Sunday Cleveland Press an Plain Dealer newspapers got housesales, where y'kin git real nice thangs aw'mos fer free."

"We ain't gonna be fillin up this house wit other people's throw aways!" Mr. Tucker say.

"Don' git too proud on me, Luthern. I wouldn't pick out nuthin that looked so used it couldn't be fixed up good as new. I jes wanna see what's out there, okay?"

"Okay," he say under his breath, knowin she ain't gonna jes look, then walk out without gittin a few choice thangs.

After we all ate, mama ain't brang up the used stores again and neither did Mr. Tucker. Me and the babies laid down for a nap and it was dark when we woke up.

twenty-eight

I could here talkin down in the basement. I went down there carryin Ola and Harriet followin behind holdin onto my pants leg. We was surprised to see mama sandin the finish off the frame of a oak chair and Mr. Tucker knockin the seat off another one, and four more waitin they turn to be worked on.

"Where these come from?" I axed.

"There's my angels," Mr. Tucker say lookin pleased as punch. "Y'all git a good nap?"

"Yeah they did. Where these come from?"

"Yer mama picked 'em outta Brock's Bargain Shop over on Quincy. They gonna deliver the table t'marra long wit a breakfron', a chaise lounge, a wardrober an a sleigh bed. Yer mama got a real good eye f'thangs an she handy!"

"How we gonna sit in them chairs with you knockin the seats out?"

"We gonna go fabric shoppin t'marra an pick out some material so's I kin upholster some new bottoms," Mama say without even lookin up. She jesta sandin away.

"Y'all don't go to the store t'marra without us, okay?" I felt kinda cheated, but we ain't even hear them leave so we musta been all tuckered out and needin that nap real bad.

"We wouldn'a lef' you this time, but y'all was down for the count!" Mama say and her and Mr. Tucker laugh like they got a secret.

I took the girls back upstairs cause the dust comin from mama's sandin seem to be gittin in they little noses and throats. Harriet start to coughin and rubbin her eyes and Ola start to sneeze.

We was sittin in the kitchen watchin the fish swim round in a pot. You c'aint put fish in tap water til it sit out for at least 24 hours. We had our water in two big buckets in a kitchen corner so's tomorrow we could fix the aquarium. But since we ain't have nuthin to do right now, I decide we kin fix everythang except the water for now. I had Harriet to hold Ola while I scrubbed and dried the tank good. There was half a wall separatin the livin room from the dinin room with a wide ledge that'd be the perfect place for the fish tank with a light over it. I put the tank there and put the colored pebbles in the bottom with the sunk ship. Ola started to fall asleep watchin me. I guess I was jes borin her silly since she musta seen this done a million times in all the lives she done lived. Anyway, I put her in the middle of the bed surrounded by a bunch of pillows, then come back out to fix the filter.

Without Ola to keep her hands busy, Harriet was tryna git into everythang. I let her wash and dry the filter. Then I let her put the charcoal in the bottom of it, but I told her, "I'm gonna handle the angel hair cause it's fiber glass an it'll sting you, even if it don't look like it." I scrunched up my face and pinched at my arm when I told her the angel hair would sting her, but she still ain't have no idea about what stingin really mean, so it wasn't no real threat to her.

I put on rubber gloves to handle it, but it was so fine and wispy, it was hard to work with. It looks like it would feel smooth and silky, but a few hairs got on my arm and after while I felt like scratchin there. No sooner did I git the filter all fixed up, then I heard Harriet whinin. I looked round and seen my little girl sittin on the floor with angel hair all over her chubby legs and arms and tween her fangers. She slappin and kickin at it to git it off of her, then her whines turn into cries of pure terror.

I swooped Harriet up and tried to gently shake her to git all the loose hairs to fall off, but she was kickin and screamin now so hard, it was all I could do to jes keep hold of her. That fiber glass was pricklin my arms, hands, neck and even parts of my face, so I know what she was feelin. I rushed her into the bathroom, stood her in the tub an scooped handfuls of cool water over her arms and legs to rinse off the glass hairs still clingin to her skin and cool the fires burnin there. It seem to he'p some, but she was still some kinda miser'ble

Mama and Mr. Tucker come rushin into the bathroom.

"What happen, Alice?" Mama axed lookin all around like maybe she kin figger it out before I answer.

"Poor baby got into that angel hair and it's stingin the mess outta her."

"Where's Ola?"

"I put her in bed awhile back. Mr. Tucker, would you check on her, please?"

Mr. Tucker left without a word. I know he pro'bly always gonna resent little Ola for bein a girl, but I wasn't studdin that right now. Mama took over for me and told me to git the cocoa butter in the medicine cabinet. Mama undressed Harriet while she still standin in the tub, wrapped her in a big towel and set her, still whinin, on the toilet seat.

"This angel hair is right devilish," mama said. "It's glass, Alice. No matter it looks silky an soft an smooth. It's glass an yer baby got hunnerds a li'l cuts we c'aint see cause they ain't bleedin. An she pro'bly got hunnerds a li'l glass splinters, too. They gonna cause her plenty misery for a couple days, I reckon."

After I took my rubber gloves off and rinsed off my arms and hands, mama told me to be on the lookout for more stray angel hairs on Harriet and gently pluck them off ef I see any while I'm pattin her dry and rubbin cocoa butter on her. Then mama put Harriet's jumper in the wastebasket to rinse out good with a hose in the yard later, then she rinse the tub out bout a million times.

Mr. Tucker come in carryin Ola, who look tired like she jes been woke up. Mr. Tucker actin like he wanna chide mama on wastin so much water. But mama shut him right up.

"I don' thank you want angel hair to be cuttin yer butt when you takin yer bath. You be screamin louder'n l'il Harriet!"

It was not an ideal way to end a good day, but we did all learn a little somethin. Harriet know what *stinging* mean, now. I ain't gonna do nuthin else in front of my kids that I don't want them to do. And Mr. Tucker ain't gonna be cryin bout the cost of a little extra water ef that little water can save him from a pain in his behind.

****

I knew mama couldn't stay forever, but when she told us she was gonna be leavin the end of the week, I panicked.

"What about the furniture? We ain't finish shoppin yet. Plus, I cain't reupholster stuff like you!"

"You know how to sew, Alice. You kin make drapes an beddin. We gonna git a sewin machine next an I'll show you how to do slip covers, cushions an frames. You a fast learner. You be fine."

"I don't know..."

"You be fine."

On Monday, we got us a Singer sewin machine that can do fancy borders and embroideries. Mr. Tucker ain't want the neighbors to see none of their throw away thangs in our house, so he say we gotta go way out to buy any secondhand stuff. That end up bein the best idea. We ended up in Shaker Heights and the Bratenahl section of the westside where most of the big money makers live. They change their furnishings sometimes jes cause they bored, not cause they need to. So some of their thangs look brand new and don't need new stuffin or covers. We got two brass twin beds, a big scrolled iron bed, a roll top desk, some wall tapestries, drapes, a black baby grand piano, some tiffany lamps, some coffee tables, two different fancy full china sets for dinnerware and some wicker for the patio. This stuff woulda cost a fortune new, but this way it was almost free. Matter of fact, a lot of stuff *was* free! They gave us crystals to git us to buy the china and lamps. They threw in silverware when we bought the fancy goldware. We got oriental runners when we bought oriental rugs and tapestries. We got beautiful gold-leafed, leather bound books includin the complete collections of Shakespeare, Dickens, Henry James, Bronte, Hemingway, Fitzgerald and Faulkner, all for free because of the bookcases we bought.

Mama showed me how to make covers for cushions with pipin and zippers. Mr. Tucker sanded down a desk chair on casters and restained and varnished the wood frame. Mama showed me how to repad the seat, the back and the arms with horsehair, then cover that with kidskin leather the color of oxblood and nail it down with shiny brass tacks. It went with the roll top desk. They gave us that chair cause it was in such bad shape, but it looked better'n brand new after we was through with it.

Mama and me moved most of our rich-lookin used stuff in the downstairs rooms and put the new stuff Mr. Tucker bought at Sears up in the attic. The kitchen table he bought is now my sewin table and I kept two of the six chairs with the table. We put two of the other chairs in the girl's room on the second floor with the twin brass beds and two chairs in my new bedroom with the big scrolled iron bed, on the second floor next to the girls room. Only I ain't tell nobody that was my new bedroom yet. We fixed up a liberry on the second floor with the bookcases, the fancy leather books, one of the coffee tables, one of the tiffany lamps, and a big over-stuffed sofachair and ottoman. We made a guest bedroom with the sleighbed in it next to the liberry. One day, I plan to make one of the other second floor rooms into a playroom for the girls, but that's after they git bigger and got a bunch of toys. We fixed up one of the first floor rooms to be a recreation room with a big oriental rug and the television and hi-fi set Sears delivered two days ago.

We were doin good buyin expensive thangs for cheap or gittin them free. We bought thick brocaded fabrics to sew slipcovers, makin sets out of unmatchin furniture, or makin somethin well-built and ugly into somethin well-built and beautiful. We were doin so good, then mama said it was past time for her to leave.

She been here for almost eight weeks. I know she had to go back, so I didn't complain because I ain't tryin to make her feel guilty or nuthin. But I c'aint imagine how I'm gonna manage without her.

Our backyard garden came in so lush, I was able to fix mama a basket of food that was near to bein packed as full as the one she made for me and Mr. Tucker when we moved here. She laughed and said she was gonna feed half the bus with all that food. We laughed about that and a dozen other silly little thangs.

But when she started boardin that Greyhound bus, I bawled like Harriet stingin from the angel hair.

twenty-nine

Mama made it home alright and so did we, if a little sadder. I figger the best way to git over these blues was for me to git back to work, lots of it. I decided to paint some rooms. I asked Mr. Tucker to git me some pale yellow and pale green paint for the girl's room.

"What kinda colors is that for they room?" Mr. Tucker axed.

"I'm gonna split the room down the middle and paint one half yellow and the other green, so's they can keep track of which side is theirs."

"This house big enough for them to have they own room, ef they want."

"They pro'bly will want that later, when they git older. But they'll be good company for each other now. Plus, they pro'bly gonna be afraid of the dark for awhile, like most little kids."

He ain't argue with me, even though I can see he don't agree. But he still bought me the paint. He even helped me paint when I asked him to. I needed his help paintin the ceilin green on one side and yellow on the other. They each had a window on their side of the room, too. So I made a frilly yellow curtain for one and a frilly green for the other, and hooked oval throw rugs, one yellow and one green, for the floor. I put pads on the seats and backs of those hard kitchen chairs and made green and yellow slip covers for them. I bought two great big old stuffed bears to sit in those chairs and put a green or yellow bow around their neck. And, of course, I got yellow and green sheets and shams to cover the beds.

Mr. Tucker loved that room so much when I was finished, he ain't never question my taste no more.

I painted the iron bed and the walls of the room next to the girl's room eggshell white. I made white curtains and white slip covers for the last two kitchen chairs I padded. I put in a small round table to go with the chairs and covered it with a white, laced tablecloth. I plan to keep white roses or calla lillies in a clear, round vase on that table. I had Mr. Tucker to put in a big brass hook in the ceilin over the bed, then draped yards of gauzy white material from the hook to cover the bed like a tent. I made about ten pillows in different sizes and shapes, all white, to throw at the head of the bed. And I put one of the red, blue and beige oriental runners on the floor for a splash of color.

I painted Mr. Tucker's room robin's egg blue and put navy and white striped bedsheets on his bed to match a striped loveseat I put in front of his window. I made drapes and a comforter with raw silk that was red and navy paisley and threw a bunch of different pillows of every shape, color and pattern at the head of his bed.

To keep Harriet out of trouble all this time, I set her on a canvas drop cloth with some paper and watercolors so she could paint and create along with mommy. I thought, for thirteen months, she came up with some pretty good swirls and thangs. I was just tryin to keep her out of my way, but I decided to save them and maybe frame them later on. I wrote her name and dated them on the back and set them aside to eventually decorate the walls of their playroom.

I put the wicker furniture on the side porch and sewed overstuffed cushions with lavender floral print covers to match the grapes that would soon start blossomin on the vines Mr. Tucker planted. When mama was here, she said we ought to keep the birds out on the porch since the weather was so nice most days. She brought them in in the evenings. Mama thought they liked it out there because they were always twitterin and hoppin around.

After mama was gone, I got back to readin when I wasn't workin. I discovered Chester Himes, Zora Neale Hurston, Albert Camus and Langston Hughes. I couldn't seem to git enough of them. I liked to sit out on the porch with my girls readin Dr. Seuss aloud to them and feedin them fruits til it was time for their nap. One day, after I laid them down, I went back out on the porch and started readin some of Langston's poetry. I love me some Langston, but this day I got to feelin low even when I was readin my favorites like *The Negro Speaks of Rivers* and *Dream Variations*. My spirits kept sinkin lower no matter what. I thought maybe if I read one of his blues poems, it would speak to me and perk me up some. So I read *The Weary Blues* because he describes a man croonin about his bleedin soul at a piano. Then I thought maybe I could sing my blues away or at least lull them to sleep.

I went to the front room and sat at the baby grand and stroked the keys, one at a time so as not to just be plunkin, waitin to be moved. I wasn't playin a song I knew, I was tryin to turn my feelins into song. I tried to empty my head of everything to git to the core of my somber mood, but something kept risin in my mind while I sat there tinkerin the keys. Afta'while I glimpsed what wouldn't leave me.

I know why the caged bird sings... I been sittin out on that porch with my babies everyday listening to those birds chirp and putter in their cage. I accepted mama's interpretation that the birds were happy out there and that's why they were movin around and singin like that. But *I know why the caged bird sings...* Dunbar told me why.

I was so upset with my stupid self. I called those birds happy when they were pro'bly cursin me for teasin them with the song and flight of their uncaged cousins, who were pro'bly laughin at them. Mama ain't read Dunbar, so she ain't know, but I did.

I DID!!

I jumped up from that piano in a panic, ran out to the porch and flung their little cage door open. When they wouldn't leave on their own, I got them out with a stick. When shakin the stick to git them off didn't work, I threw it in the air and forced them to fly.

They flew up and perched on the awning frame that shaded the porch, lookin down at me confused, like they thought I was mad at them, or I had maybe just lost my mind.

I would've kept shooin them away, but I didn't want them to thank I didn't like them anymore, or that they'd done somethin wrong, so I jes let them be. I didn't know it right then, but those birds were domesticated. They had no idea about how to survive on their own in the world. Freedom was scary to them. I didn't close the door on their cage, so they just flew back to it to eat their seeds and drink the water. They would sometimes perch outside the cage, too. Come winter, I'd keep them in the house full time because outside would be too cold and they didn't seem to know anything about flyin south for the season. But like I said, I ain't know all that right then.

I went back to the piano feelin slightly better thinkin I had set the parakeets loose, but feelin only slightly better. I got to tinkerin again. Ain't nothin come to me at first. Then I thought about the gospels I knew, and I tried to find their melodies buried in the keys. I struggled with Amazing Grace, but never did figger out what to do with my left hand. After puzzling and playin it through for an hour or so, I decided to take lessons with somebody and find out how to play this thang proper.

thirty

Miss Macaulley was a lady I met from goin over to Severance Hall where the Cleveland Symphony plays. I went there lookin for a piano teacher that would come to the house. They gave me a list of possibilities and I figgered she sounded as good as any of the people I called, and since she wasn't a man, Mr. Tucker pro'bly wouldn't mind paying her.

She loved the house, the girls and the piano, that she said needed tunin somethin awful. But when she found out I didn't work no job, she seemed to like Mr. Tucker best of all.

Miss Macaulley is old enough to be my mother, but I don't thank she was old as Mr. Tucker. She was pro'bly very pretty when she was younger, but she was on the decline. Her middle is thick, but she thanks she's hidin that by wearin belts pulled too tight, tryin to make a waistline that hasn't been there for years. Pullin them tight like that didn't hide nothin cause her belly pooched out underneath and spilled over the top of the belt. Plus, it looked like it hurt, especially when she sat. She's got nice legs though, long and shapely. She must have known it because all of her skirts were too short. Her wavy hair hung to her shoulders and she wore bangs with a side part. She had a little mustache over her full top lip. Her posture was ramrod straight and everytime I looked at her, I thank her bra must rear her shoulders back like that, the same way it hikes her breasts and molds them into pointy cones.

She ain't met Mr. Tucker yet, but I know she liked the idea of a man providing for all of his family's needs. I read lots of books about women who'll do anythang to git a good man to take care of them. These women don't care what the man looks like or if he's kind or if he's married to their best friend, their sister, their mama or their daughter. They plan to take that man for theyse'f ef they have a mind to. I try to encourage Miss Macaulley so she'll make her move to take Mr. Tucker away from me when she does meet him, because she looks like a woman on the prowl.

I say thangs like, "I don't know why Mr. Tucker puts up with me! There is so much I don't know and cain't seem to learn. He's got a lot of patience, but I bet he'd be a lot happier with a smarter, more experienced woman."

She don't never say nothin more than, "Really...?" But her mouth gits fixed in a little crooked smile and her eyes git a dreamy, far-away look to them.

In the meantime, she's been comin for an hour twice a week for ten weeks and she tells me I've got a lot of talent. I think I'm doin pretty good too, cause I practice all the time bein as I got so much time on my hands. I go through one whole beginner's practice book and a half of another one everyday. I don't never stop with just the pages she assigns me to learn, that's why I git so good so fast.

She brung me some sheet music with songs one day. I started singin the words while I was playin and she said I've got a real nice voice. She said she could give me voice lessons too, to develop my singing. I told her that was okay because I knew she was just tryin to git more money. I figure I can just sing these songs and do the scales with my voice like I do with my fingers.

One day, Mr. Tucker came in when my hour with her was just about up. And like I knew she would, Miss Macaulley started squirmin and blushin like a schoolgirl. She started talkin in a high voice and let loose a giggle every three or four words or so.

"Little Alice is coming right along! (heh heh) Today, I learned she has a sweet little singing voice, too. (giggle giggle) It sure would be nice, if you can afford it (snicker), to give her voice training as well. I'll have her properly serenading you in no time. (giggle squirm blush)"

Mr. Tucker looked at her like she was some strange new kind of bug that he wasn't sure if he should squish or set out in the garden to breed. Then he looked at me like he wanted to axe my advice on what to do about this here exotic insect. But I quick found a reason to leave the room.

"What y'all want to drank? Hot tea, hot cocoa, coffee?"

"Whatever Mr. Tucker pleasures is fine with me. (eye bats)"

"Nuthin for me, *Princess*." It sounded like he kind of stressed *Princess* for some reason, I thought.

"I'll make coffee to go with that coffee cake you like, *Mr. Tucker*." I stressed *Mr. Tucker* the same way and for the same reason he emphasized my name, whatever that was, then left.

I took my time in the kitchen brewin the coffee and slicin the cake so Mr. Tucker and Miss Macaulley could have a nice long gittin-to-know-you visit, but when I went back into the livin room carryin the refreshements on a tray, Mr. Tucker wasn't nowhere to be found.

"Your husband went to one of the rooms out back," Miss Macaulley said lookin kind of sad.

"He's pro'bly in the den. Let's go join him," I said tryin to sound cheery, unlike I was feeling. Mr. Tucker must've been tryin to git rid of this music lady, to just leave her all alone like he did. I could be about to mess up, pressin him with her like I was. But she looked so hopeful when I said let's go join him, I tried to feel more hopeful myself.

****

Mr. Tucker was in the den listenin to Eartha Kitt singin "My Heart Belongs To Daddy" on the hi-fi.

I set the tray on the coffee table and was pourin Mr. Tucker a coffee. Miss MaCaulley stood over by the hi-fi with her back to us, swayin her butt from side to side to the rhythym of the music while she studied the album cover of Miss Kitt.

"Oooo, can I put on my favorite La Kitt song?!" Miss Macaulley asked all of a sudden in that young, perky, schoolgirl way that made her sound and look so ridiculous.

"Play whatever you want," I said.

"Oh Mr. Tucker, I know you would *loovve* to hear Alice sing '*My Heart Belongs To Daddy*!' But my favorite is '*I Wanna Be Evil*!'"

She got to singin the song and she sounded alright, but when she got to the end she started bumpin her hips and shakin her legs and runnin her hands through her hair like she was Jackie Wilson or somebody, while she wailed, "*I wanna be evilll....little eeevvill meee! Just as mean and eeevill as IIiii ccaaan Bbbbeeeee*!!!!"

We sat there watchin like she was a show we had paid for. When she was finished, we ain't know what to do. She was lookin at us and we were lookin at her for a while, then Mr. Tucker suddenly burst out laughing. Miss Macaulley looked confused, then hurt. When I saw pain then shame come in her face, I started clappin fast and hard.

"Good, Miss Macaulley! That was real good! Mr. Tucker and me loved it!!"

She went from hurt to confused again, "You...liked...it?!" She asked, lookin dead at Mr. Tucker whoopin it up on the sofa across from her.

"He's havin a good time, ain't he?!!" I said still clappin and wishin Mr. Tucker would stop the hysterics.

He quieted down afta'while and, still chuckling, got up and left the room. But right before he went out, he said over his shoulder, "You funny, Miss Macaulley! You *real* funny!"

If there's a simple way to ease the pain of somebody that just got their feelings crushed, I don't know what it is. I started fiddling with the food. "How you like yer coffee, Miss Macaulley?" I asked, pouring her a cup.

"I don't drink coffee," she said.

"I made this for you and Mr. Tucker, but I can make you somethin else."

"You didn't make that for me *or* Mr. Tucker. I said I'd have what he had and he said, *Nuthin for me, Princess*. You need to pay closer attention to things, little girl," she snapped. "Mr. Tucker *would* probably be happier with a smarter, more experienced woman. But there's no reason that woman can't be you!"

Well ain't you nothin! Here I am trying to do you a favor, because you obviously want to take Mr. Tucker from me. But now, since he rejected you, you want to git all snippy with me, tryin to give this *little girl* advice on how to keep a man I've been tryin git rid of and wouldn't have for myse'f even after Hell froze over!

I didn't tell her none of that. I thought it, though. She stalked out of the room after snapping at me before I could say anything back. But I know I wouldn't have said nothing no way. I wasn't raised to sass my elders, even if I'm right. Plus, I understand that she blamed me for encouraging her. My crime, if I'm guilty of one, was not knowin how pathetic this woman was. I had no idea the pitiful moves she would make could cause a charging buffalo to backdown.

She must have let herse'f out of the house because I didn't see her when I took the cake and coffee back to the kitchen. I did see Mr. Tucker, though.

"What'chu thank you was doin, Alice, tryna push that old fool off on me?!"

"I ain't trying to push nobody on nobody. That's yer style, Mr. Tucker. But it would be nice if you could see the goodness and beauty in Miss Macaulley. Plus, since you ain't seem to notice, she ain't *that* old. She ain't old as you. Y'all got a lot more in common then you'll ever have in common with me!"

I wasn't tryin to argue with Mr. Tucker or hurt his feelins. But it seems like I'm the one always pussyfooting around, goin out of my way to spare somebody's feelins when nobody ever seems to think of mines. Plus, hurt, mad, like it or not, I was tellin the truth.

"Well, little Miss Cupid," Mr. Tucker was tryin to hold his temper, but he couldn't. His eyes were bloodshot and little white patches of spit collected in the corners of his mouth, I thank from him tryin not to yell when he said, "I ain't gonna be payin fer no mo music lessons fer you, sence what you really wanna do is match me up wit yer teacher!"

I didn't say nothing to that. Wasn't nothing I could say. That dollar he paid per lesson is his money and he can spend it, or not spend it, like he wants.

Plus, I doubt Miss Macaulley planned on comin back here anytime soon.

****

I was right. I never got to tell Miss Macaulley I wouldn't be continuing her lessons because she never came back, or even called to

175

quit. But I figure I had a big enough start that I could keep on teaching myself, so that's what I did.

Mr. Tucker knew he wasn't paying for any more lessons, so he must've known Miss Macaulley wasn't coming over any more and nobody else came by for him to think I was trying to push them on him. Yet, whenever he came into the house and found me singing and playing the piano, he got a scowl on his face, like he thought Miss Macaulley was about to pop out from somewhere and start one of her schoolgirl serenades.

I don't pay him no mind. I'm thinking maybe he don't like the way I sound. Or maybe he's jealous because I'm teaching myself and don't seem to need a teacher any more. Or maybe he thinks I'm neglecting the kids, even though I only practice while they nap. Whatever his problem is, I don't pay him no mind.

thirty-one

Mr. Tucker decided we ought to go back to Smedley for Christmas and New Years since we had a quiet Thanksgiving with just the babies and us here in Cleveland. This was just a little while after Miss Macaulley's final appearance.

We were back home in about nineteen hours instead of the sixteen hours it took us to move nawth, and that put Mr. Tucker in a real foul mood. But, we left in the day. I think if we had left in the middle of the night, like we did when we moved to Cleveland, then the girls and me would've slept through most of the ride and we may have made better time. But Mr. Tucker didn't want to take my suggestion, so the extra long ride was really his fault.

We got to Smedley on the eve of Christmas Eve.

We had to ride past daddy and mama's old house to get to Mr. Tucker's big white one. My old home looked real nice with a fresh coat of pale yellow paint and a stuffed Santa sittin in a rocker on the porch.

But it felt strange lookin up the drive from the street at the lights on in the house knowin it wasn't my family living there. So, we didn't stop for long and I felt a little relieved to leave it behind.

When we drove up to Mr. Tucker's big white house, it seemed like every light must have been lit, bright as it was. There was a big Christmas tree in the front left window and little candles with light bulb flames lighting all the other windows, upstairs and down, maybe because they were expecting us. The front porch light was on and there was a huge candy wreath hanging on the front door so anybody that came by could help themselves.

We had barely gotten out of the car good when we heard somebody shoutin, "Alice an Mr. Tucker an 'em is here!!" Then while we were comin up the walk, the front door banged open and my whole family came swoopin down on us like bees on a hive. They even sounded like bees, with everybody talkin at once, their voices blended into one loud drone.

"Y'all fine'ly got here!" "Here y'all is!" "We was worried bout y'all!" "How was y'alls drive!" "Whure's my new grandbaby?!" "C'mere Harriet, member me?!" "Y'all hungry? Y'all tarred?" "Hey Ola. We's yer uncles!"

Somebody took the baby. Somebody else took Harriet. Somebody else took everything out of the front and back seats of the car. Everybody seemed to be moving around us in such a frenzy, getting things done while leading us to the house. I thought this must be how it feels to be in the eye of a tornado, a whirlwind going on all around you while you're sitting easy in the center of calm.

After we finally got in the house, they showed us to our room. It was the one I used to sleep in down the hall from Mr. Tucker, only they planned on us sleepin in there together.

"I hope you don't mind this room, Luthern," daddy said, "Grace and me is kinda settled in the big bedroom."

"And y'oughta be!" Mr. Tucker laughed. "This room be fine, Nate. It's more than fine."

"Bertha, where you sleepin?" I asked, changing the subject.

"I'm in the sun parlor, come see it an brang Ola!" Bertha said like she was real excited to show me something, but I know she knew I

178

planned for me and the girls to stay with her. She swooped Harriet up and spun her around in the air, makin her squeal, then she ran downstairs to the parlor with my oldest girl riding her hip.

"I'm gonna go visit with Bertha awhile."

"Well, don' stay up too late," mama said soundin a little concerned. "We got a big day aheada us t'marra."

"Okay mama," I said, knowing she knew I planned for the babies and me to stay with Bertha this whole trip.

****

Ain't nobody say nothin later that morning at breakfast about us sleeping in the parlor. After we ate, we got our gifts out of the trunk of the car and put them under the tree in the front room. Then we strung popcorn, walnuts and dried apples to wrap around a little pine tree outside for the birds and squirrels. Then Bertha and me went visiting. Mr. Tucker still didn't know that I knew how to drive. Bertha drove us downtown, then I took over just to dust off the rust.

We went lookin for Miss Johnson first, because I wanted to invite her out to the house to meet her namesake. But she wasn't home. Bertha said she pro'bly went away for the holidays. Then Bertha asked if I wanted to go down to The Juke. I said maybe, but first I wanted to go see Mrs. Petty.

Mrs. Petty's house was close to where we used to live. I ain't been over there since I was a little speck of a girl, but walkin up to her front door and hearing the sweet, crystal tinkles coming from her wind chimes brought back memories that were clearer then yesterday.

"Bertha, Alice, what a nice surprise! C'mon in an git some of these sweets I jes fixed."

I don't know why I wanted to see her so bad, because I didn't have a word for her once we got there, but she acted like she didn't notice. She seemed to be expecting us, or somebody. She gave us pecan shortbread cookies, still warm from the oven, and had just finished makin fresh whipped cream to top steaming mugs of hot chocolate.

"Thank you ma'am," I said when she handed me a cup of chocolate. "We're sorry to just be dropping by like this. I told Bertha I wanted to see you, but you're expecting company."

"I wa'nt expectin anyone. I try to always be ready for anythang an anybody that might happen along. I got blind-sided once... but not no

179

mo." She looked at me strong like I knew what she was talkin about, then she sipped her chocolate and asked, "How's life treatin you, Alice? Bertha?"

I dropped my eyes from hers. I didn't want to lie and couldn't if I wanted to. I felt like she was looking straight through me and already had the answers to any questions she might ask. I didn't want to bawl or rage and I was afraid if I opened my mouth, one of the two would happen. I wasn't quite sure what I wanted. What was I expectin comin here? I never just dropped by to see her before. I guess it was just to be in the presence of someone who *knew* what I was goin through, who maybe could comfort or counsel me in some way as to how I could... escape.

"I be goin t'college in Septemba," Bertha finally said to answer Mrs. Petty's question and break the uncomfortable silence. "I'm thankin bout goin somewheres up in Cleveland. They got a buncha schools up there."

"Oh, that sounds nice Bertha. Then you kin be close t'yer sister an the two of you can run all around Cleveland t'getha."

I could feel Mrs. Petty's eyes on me. Nobody was sayin anythin. I guess she was still waiting for my answer since Bertha gave hers, but I sat mutely staring at my hot chocolate. After awhile, Mrs. Petty started answerin the questions I brought, but couldn't voice.

"Life is strange, but we all got choices. We make plans and sometime other people make plans fer us that we don' know bout. Then we gotta choose which plans we gonna follow. But it don' stop there. Ev'yday is differnt. Ev'yday is brand new. We mighta went wit our own plans an come t'find out they wa'nt no good. Is okay. Y'kin change yer mind, do somethin differnt. We might go 'long wit somebody else plans fer us an find out one day, we cain't do that, not fer one mo minute. Is okay. Y'kin change yer mind, do somethin differnt.

"Life is a journey. Y'set yer destination, then y'travel 'long the road you picked t'git there. Some roads is smooth an straight, some are rough an crooked, some are fast highways, some are slow li'l country lanes, some got lotsa traffic, some ain't hardly got nobody on 'em, some roads got plenty detours an dead-ends. You kin change direction or y'kin git on another road anytime. Y'might find a better one, or maybe not. But y'keep yer focus on yer goal an keep mappin out a way t'git t'whure you goin. You kin change whure you wanna go, too, ain't nuthin set in stone.

"Now, ef you axe ten differnt people how t'git whure you wanna go, they all gonna tell you somethin, but they gonna be tellin you from wha's bes' for them. Do that enough times an y'learn not to axe nobody nuthin.

You got t'make yer own way an find wha's the bes' route for you so's you kin enjoy yer journey, cause now see, y'might not never make it t'whure y'thank y'wanna be. Lotsa people don', leastwise seem like mos' colored people don'.

"Life is jes a short li'l journey. An ef you ain't gonna make the place y'set out for, that mean all you really got is the road you travelin on. Some folks like t'run, some folks like t'stroll, some folks like a challenge and some don' wanna struggle none atall. Ef you gonna enjoy yerse'f, you got t'choose where you goin an how y'plan t'git there. Do I make any sence to y'all?"

"I'm tryin," Bertha piped right up, "But I don' know wha'chu talkin bout!"

Mrs. Petty laughed til she cried, she was so tickled with Bertha. Berth and me looked at each other and smiled, but I didn't know what was so funny.

"Oh, you girls are precious. I love you both. I do!" She said winding down and wiping her eyes.

"Take me, for example," she said after her tickle faded. I thought she must have had something important she wanted to share with us. Otherwise, why was she bein so persistent with what first sounded like idle chit chat? I got to thinking that she was really talking to me and maybe this was the reason God gave me such a powerful hankering to visit Mrs. Petty today. I decided to listen a little harder.

"I live alone," Mrs. Petty began the example she told us to take. "I am alone all day, mos days. Bein alone s'much, sometime I gits lonely. But I gits lonely sometime when I'm with somebody, or even when I'm with a buncha people at a party or a picnic or whatnot. I thank the loneliest I ever felt in my life was on my weddin day."

I knew just what she was talking bout. I remember how packed the house was inside and out with so many people that came to bless or bust the proceedings. Wasn't nobody payin me no mind. If they had, they would've seen I was sick to my stomach, heart and soul and they would've known ahead of time I was gonna puke my guts out all over Mr. Tucker before the day was done. But it was like I was all by myself outside in a cold, empty yard chained to a post, watching a houseful of folks having a good old time in a warm, bright house. I wasn't welcome to come inside, even if I wanted to, and I couldn't get away because I was chained up like a dog. Alone, forgotten and crucified and they didn't even know what they'd done.

I glanced over at Mrs. Petty and she was lookin dead at me. I felt her gaze hypnotizing me in the same way I've seen snake charmers in pictures hypnotize a snake.

"I was miser'ble," she said. "I ruther be alone than to ever feel like that again, cause y'see, as lonely as I gits sometime, I ain't never made myse'f miser'ble. By bein alone s'much, I keep myse'f free of misery."

The way she stopped right there still starin at me gave her last words a special meanin, like if they were written, they'd be underlined or all capital letters or somethin. I figured that was the big point she was tryin to make, so I ran them through my head a couple more times to save them for later when I could puzzle out their meanin at length, *By bein alone I keep myse'f free of misery.*

"I know some people talk bad bout me here in Smedley behine my back. They make good people that ain't studdin me, wonder bout me. A few people have told me what they done heard, so I ain't imaginin' none'a this, but ain't none'a these bad news buggas bout t'say nuthin to mah face. So I pay them no mind. None.

"Ef you wanna be free, you cain't be studdin stupid people. Pay nonsense no mind, chile, pay it no mind!"

"Why you stay in Smedley ef you ain't got no friends here no more?" Bertha asked.

"I got friends here, baby, an more'n that... mah family here! My mama an poppa gimme to Mr. Petty t'try t'make they life easier, cause see Mr. Petty had lotsa money. So I gotta stay t'make they life easier, don' I? I mean, they went to all that trouble fer theyse'f an all. Lease I kin do is make shore they reap some'a what they sowed, right? Like seein that my brothers an sistahs is took good care of til they growed. Tha's the lease I kin do.

"Mr. Petty got mosta his money from a IN-surance policy his last wife lef. People talked about him when he firs' come t'be a widow, too, not two years afta they hitched. People come sayin, 'She wa'nt sick fore she married him!' He ain't pay them no mind. Now they talkin bout me, an I was married to Mr. Petty almos' *FIVE* years. But I don' pay them no mind. Ef you gonna be free, firs' y'gotta learn t'pay stupid people no mind.

"Then, y'gotta figger out jes what it is you want. You wanna go t'college Bertha?" Mrs. Petty asked my sister, still lookin straight at me when she wasn't nibblin a cookie or sippin her hot chocolate.

"Yes, ma'am."

"Good. Go. I bet'chu be good at it." Mrs. Petty said.

"What bout Alice?" Bertha asked, I guess because she noticed how Mrs. Petty was watching me.

"What bout Alice?! Alice is young, strong, pretty an pretty clever I hear." She ain't never take her eyes off me. "Alice gonna be fine."

"Well," Bertha looked around like she was expectin to see spies takin notes and said, "bein as you alone mos' the time, I guess you kin keep a secret..." Then she lowered her voice to nearly a whisper and said, "Alice don' really wanna be married to Mr. Tucker. She jes wit him cause'a mama an daddy."

"Chile, *that ain't no secret!*" Mrs. Petty blurted out, this time lookin straight at Bertha instead of me. It sounded like she was shoutin after Bertha's timid little murmur. "An as I recalls, Alice *ain't* marry ole Luthern Tucker," she snorted. Then she looked back at me with that snake charmer's concentration and said, "An even ef she did, Alice still got choices. Ev'yday is brand new. Yer life ain't set in stone, cep'in yer headstone."

"Well I only axe you," Bertha sounded hurt and defensive, "cause it seem like Alice is in the same sit'ation you was in wit Mr. Petty. But Mr. Petty died so you ain't hafta be wit him all tha' long no way. I'm sorry I axed you."

"I'm not," Mrs. Petty said real gentle. She was tryin to let Bertha know she wasn't mad at her. "I wa'nt wit Mr. Petty all that long, but it seem like fo'evah t'me. Tha's how it is when you find yerse'f some place you ain't wanna be, doin thangs you don' wanna do. It feel like a noose round yer neck. But we all got choices an I made one. Cain't nobody *MAKE ME* do nuthin. Not no mo... not for long."

I got a chill from the way she spoke that last, looking at me like she was tryin to will my freedom into being.

We stayed about thirty more minutes before Bertha announced we needed to be on our way. I know she was still upset at the way she thought Mrs. Petty spoke to her. Bertha was wrong, but there was no way of tellin her that just now.

"'I made a choice!'" Bertha was on a roll soon as we got in the car. "'Cain't nobody *MAKE ME* do nuthin. Not no mo... not for long.' I see why they call her The Black Widow. You thank she killed Mr. Petty, Alice?"

I shuddered when she said those words Bertha now mocked. Words, I know, she offered as a key to somehow unlock the doors that barred me.

I recalled that last time Mr. Tucker tried to put his hands on me. I leveled that rifle at his head and offered to he'p him with his difficult decision. I know I was not bluffin then, like I know I will still he'p him into Kingdom Come right now, if he ever thinks about puttin his hands on me again. He cain't *MAKE ME* do nuthin neither! Not no more... not for long! I don't doubt for a second that Mrs. Petty may have easily rid herse'f of Mr. Petty once and for all, if he pushed her one time too many.

But since I didn't know, I said, "I don't know, Bertha. I don't know," and left it at that.

thirty-two

When we left the pretty, young widow wavin at us from her front stoop, the air barely stirred enough to play its compositions on her chimes. She had the quilt I made and gave to her wrapped around her shoulders like it was freezin. In addition to the Christmas gifts I brought for my family, I brought quite a few things for anybody in general. Folks I may run across during my visit that I forgot about, but didn't want them to know I'd forgot. These things were mostly quilts and pillows that I made, and a few choice paintings of Harriet's that I had framed like rare art treasures. I gave Mrs. Petty a patchwork quilt after our visit so that whenever she got lonely, she could wrap herself in it like a hug, and know that she is loved.

I was driving. We had quite a few stops we had planned to make and I didn't have any particular destination in mind. But, I wasn't surprised when we wound up on the colored side of town in front of The Juke.

I realized after awhile that I had a powerful urge to see Alberta and Mary all along, second only maybe to my seeing Mrs. Petty.

The Juke was extra lively this Christmas Eve. Long strings of tinsel crisscrossed the ceiling with candy canes hanging off of them. There was a huge tureen of egg nog at the back of the bar and anybody comin through the door got a glass for free. But if you bought a shot of corn to spike it, Tennessee, the bartender, hung a candy cane on the side of yer glass.

"Well look what the wind jes blew in!! Merry Christmas ladies!" Tennessee gushed at Bertha and me. "Y'all ain't been round here in a spell! C'mon git you a glass a this 'ere nog," he said dippin up two glasses. "Is virgin so y'all kin par-take." He gave a little wink when he handed us the glasses.

"Thanks, Tennessee. We brung you somethin too," Bertha said and we handed him our small wrapped packages.

"You girls is so thoughtful," Tennessee said, truly touched by our gestures. Then he grinned like a chesire cat and asked, "Kin I open 'em now?!"

"Open 'em when you wanna. They yers," Bertha said grinnin big as Tennessee.

He started unwrappin his gifts before Bertha finished her sentence. I gave him one of Harriet's framed paintings. The way he carried on, you'd have thought Jacob Lawrence had painted it. Bertha made a banner to hang across his bar with "This Juke Is Jumping" embroidered in colorful needlepoint.

Tennessee wanted them both hung right then, but he couldn't take the time to do that. So, Bertha and me did it for him. We put Harriet's picture next to a framed dollar, the first one The Juke had ever made. We were hanging the banner across the back bar wall over the mirror when Mary and Alberta came strolling in with dollar bills pinned to their bosoms, holding mistletoe over their heads saying, "Ho Ho Ho!"

Bertha nudged me hard in my side, like she thought I might have missed them. It occurred to me for the first time that Bertha may be holdin a grudge. From the way she pursed her lips and went straight back to tackin up the banner without speaking, I think Bertha was still mad about that time Alberta got snippy with me because she thought I was passing judgement on Mary and her.

This was all so stupid in my mind. Alberta said *I* was like them, so if anything, I should be the one with a grudge. But in my heart I agreed with them, so I wasn't about to side with Bertha's nonsense.

If they noticed us, they gave no sign. After their entrance, almost every man in the Juke was running to pin another dollar on their breast so they could get a kiss. I thought about it for a second, then jumped down off the bar and lined up with the men, holdin two dollars in my hand.

"Merry Christmas, Berta! Happy Holidays, Mary!" I said handing each a dollar before kissing them each on a cheek.

I could tell Alberta wanted to get ugly, but she couldn't. If she thought I had judged and sentenced them before, she must have suddenly felt pardoned now because after a little pause, she grinned and squeezed me tight. Mary never hesitated. She yelped and fidgeted like a puppy, waitin for Alberta and me to stop hugging so she could get one.

"Ooooo, don' this remine you a spinna bottle?" Mary laughed in my ear and tried to crack my ribs in a bear hug. "How you doin, li'l mama?"

"I'm good, I'm good. Y'all look good, too," I said holding her back and looking at her and Alberta. They looked healthy, young and pretty underneath their gaudy getups.

"Bertha and me just makin our rounds, givin out our little Christmas tokens," I said motioning to Bertha nailing the last tack in her banner.

"'This Juke is Jumping'! You got that right Bertha," Mary said and started jitterbuggin with Alberta.

"We got y'all a little somethin, too, out in the car. C'mon get it an take it upstairs," I said knowing Bertha didn't get them anything and hoping she wouldn't say that.

We went outside to the car trunk and I gave each one of them one of the pillows I made with "You Are Very Special" embroidered across the front and one of Harriet's framed paintings. I didn't say, but I know they probably thought that the pillows were from Bertha since the banner she made for The Juke was a needlepoint, too. And I let them think it.

"Yer l'il girl draws like this?" Mary cooed like it was a Rembrandt. "She cain't be more'n, what... a year old?"

"She 16 months now, goin on 16 years," I said cause I heard so many mothers say that about their kids. But Alberta tried to make it out to be something else.

"Sound like she gone be a l'il fast tail, don' it Mary? Don' let'er tail git too fast now, Alice," Alberta smirked and bumped her hip into Mary trying to get her to smirk, too. But Mary took a little step to the side and looked down at the ground and then at me with a pained expression.

That made me hurt for Alberta. I hurt for her because she wasn't happy with herself. She needed to try to recruit Mary to join her little joke about my baby. Alberta can't stand alone. She needs a crutch, but she likes to come across like a big-shot.

That's when I realized Alberta didn't want to be a whore. She probably feels as trapped and helpless as I do being forced to be with Mr. Tucker. Mary seemed to be right at home in their trade, but Alberta wants something else for herself. She doesn't seem to have the backbone or the imagination to strike out on her own. I bet she wound up prostituting because that's what Mary picked and she figured she could lean on Mary and limp along through life that way. I bet she wished her family had arranged for her to marry some rich old man to take care of her.

Mrs. Petty had just given my sister and me wise words about choice. It's really just common sense and pretty obvious when you're on the outside looking in, but it's not so easy to see when you're in the thick of something to know that all you've got to do is try something else if this ain't working for you. I guess you've got to see a way out before you can take it.

"Alberta," I started out slow and low so she wouldn't mistake what I was about to say for insult or aggression. "I been thankin bout what you said bout me bein jes like you an Mary, only I married my *John*. I was confused when you said it, but Bertha splained thangs to me, and I thank you migh'could be right."

I wanted her to hear me and understand not only my words, but my intentions, so I slipped back into the country speech I was raised on. I thought it might help her to understand that I was speakin *to* her as a peer, not talkin *at* her like a judge from some lofty perch.

"You an Mary are better off then me in a way, cause y'all are free to change yer mind an yer life ef you wanna, anytime you wanna. I'm only wit Mr. Tucker to he'p my family. Ain't no reason I cain't he'p my friends, too.

"Ef y'all is tarred of what'chall is doin, ef y'all wanna change yer mind an yer life right now.... y'all kin come nawth, to Cleveland, an try somethin new. We got a big house an y'all kin stay wit us til you git on yer feet. They got stores an fac'tries an more places whure y'all kin work

188

then I kin even start to splain. Ef y'all been savin yer money, maybe y'all kin start y'alls own bizness. There's a mess of schools there, too, ef y'all wanna go there. Case Institute an Western Reserve University is right close to our house. You might could git a schola'ship or work yer way through college. Yer still young and yer more'n jes pretty, y'all useta be smart in school.

"You kin do somethin else, ef you got a mind to. Thank bout it."

Alberta stood there lookin at me like she wasn't sure if she should laugh at the big joke I just told, or if she should fall to her knees and kiss my feet like I was her personal savior come to deliver her from evil. Mary looked confused, too. But more than that, she looked concerned for her friend. She put her arm around Alberta's shoulders and started shushing in her ear like she was trying to console her. Alberta seemed oblivious to Mary, crushing her pillow and picture to her chest, trembling from trying to control the conflicts of hope and doubt battling in her heart. Her mouth clenched shut, she let her eyes plead for her that I was sincere and serious.

Bertha came out of The Juke, looked around and walked over to join us. She soon quickened her pace at the picture I realized we made. Mary looked like she was holding Alberta back from going upside my head. Bertha reached us just as Mary asked,

"You ser'us, Alice?"

"I'm dead serious."

"Wha'chall talkin bout?" Bertha asked.

"I jes invited Mary and Berta to move to Cleveland an stay with me so they kin change they life, ef they wanna."

"You cain't jes move people into Mr. Tucker house wit'out him knowin bout it, Alice!" Bertha said and she seemed angry when she said it.

"It ain't jes Mr. Tucker house, Bertha. I live there, too! An Mr. Tucker *will* know bout it, soon as they come." Then I said to our friends, "An I hope y'all do come."

I scribbled my address and telephone number on a piece of paper for each of them and pressed it into their palms.

"I hope y'all do come. Merry Christmas."

Those were my last words before hugging them goodbye and driving away.

On the ride back, Bertha wanted to argue with me, but she waited til we got downtown and switched back to her driving again before she started, and then I stopped her before she got started good.

"Mary an Berta are ho's, Alice!"

"Yeah, and tha's yer fault."

"My fault?!"

"Yeah, Bertha, yer fault! But for the Grace of God, we might be doing that, too. They think they doing the best they can with what they got. That's all anybody does. But the difference is *WE KNOW* we can do better. We know it first of all, cause we got a father and mother that raised us to know our worth. Then second, we *listened* when Miss Johnson told us we can do better.

"Lotsa people don't get the kind of encouragement we did. Apparently, Mary and Alberta didn't. So *we* need to coax and encourage them. Sometimes all it takes is reminding somebody that they *can* do better. That they *need* to do better.

"You knew they were ho's when we first started coming over here. *I DIDN'T*!! They are our *FRIENDS*! Friends help friends, Bertha. Friends help friends. If you had tried to tell them they were too precious to be sellin theyse'f so cheap, and they turned around and told you to mind yer business, then at least you would've tried. That's all you can do. After you do everything you can, then it ain't yer fault.

"But, if you talkin to them and laughin and actin like they ain't doin nothin wrong, then for all they know, you approve and accept their whorin. But if you don't approve, and it sounds like you don't, you should be tellin them...not me, Bertha. You should tell them."

Bertha was driving and she didn't say a peep for the whole time I talked or after, so we rode the rest of the way back to Mr. Tucker's house in silence. Then after she parked in the yard, neither one of us moved. We just sat facing the house wrapped in quiet. I'm not sure what she was waiting for, but I was waiting for her reaction to what I said, if for nothing else but to know she heard me.

She finally sighed, "I never thought of it that way."

"That's okay," I said. "Now you know. Now you can do better." I reached over and hugged her. "We can all always do better."

thirty-three

I thought Christmas and New Year's would fly by, but tension made the air thick and hard to move through, so the days dragged. I guess it started with me spending my nights with Bertha in the parlor, but that was just the beginning.

After all the gifts were opened and after we went to the special service at church to sing Happy Birthday to Christ and reflect on how His life affects ours, we came home for Christmas dinner.

"It be a mighty fine day to hear the gift a my gran'son is on the way," Daddy casually remarked.

I felt my temperature rise and thought, it'll be a mighty fine day *FOR ME* when you're satisfied with what you got! You won't be getting another one of Mr. Tucker's babies out of me, so stop begging! I would rather slit my wrists right now and let you suck the blood out of me *ALL AT ONCE*, instead of in fits and starts like you do!!

Of course, I didn't *say* that out loud... I don't think.

It seemed like everybody got quiet and stiff at the table. They were polite enough on the surface when passing the peas, but something had changed. Before, when I felt really strong about something and held it in, I passed out. I didn't faint this time. As dinner went on, I felt my pressure dropping like I had expelled the stress.

The only way I figure I could've done that is if I had spoken my mind out loud. But since nobody said anything, I decided that I didn't. And maybe I didn't. I just didn't want to ask and find out, otherwise.

****

From the holiday dinner on, time dragged for me like a weight tied to my ankles. Momma was always smiles and sunshine, but I could see hurt in her eyes and I prayed I hadn't put it there. I told myself she was still feeling guilty for making me marry Mr. Tucker in the first place, not because I disrespected her husband. But not being sure was a weight.

Bertha and me went back to The Juke almost every day. Mary and Alberta would ask me all about Cleveland. Mary wanted to know about the nightlife and Alberta wanted to know everything. I think they might come for real and now I got to feeling that maybe I shouldn't have been so quick to tell them they could stay with us. But I couldn't take it back, so my invitation to them was another weight I dragged around with me while I was back home.

Then, I was in Benjamin's, the colored hardware store, the day before New Year's Eve buying some firecrackers for Daniel and Samuel to set off the following evening when Isaac walked in the door.

I was so stunned, I dropped the box of bombs and sizzlers I'd just bought. He saw them slip from my hands and caught them right before they hit the floor. When he stood back up, holding them out to me, I saw it wasn't Isaac... at least, not a present day one. This was some future Isaac, still handsome but older, still limber and strong but not quite as, still serious but much quicker to smile. This was Isaac at my daddy's age, maybe. Then I realized this was Mr. Freeman, Isaac's daddy.

"There you go l'il lady," he smiled and big dimples burrowed deep into his cheeks. "You gotta be pertic'ler careful wit this box, heah."

"Thank you,... Mr. Freeman."

He looked surprised and satisfied that I knew who he was, then briefly searched my face for something recognizable. Finding nothing, he said, "Sorry but... we met?"

"No sir, but I b'lieve I know yer son, Isaac. I heard he was yer spit."

"Tha's what I know! How you know Ikey?"

"We went to school t'getha here in Smedley. Did he come home for the holiday's?"

"No, he workin over to Howard. He wanna make a little money an git a little exter study in, so he stayed over to Howard."

"Howard?"

"Howard University," he puffed his chest out a little, "in D.C., the cap'tal."

"Would you tell'im, please, that Alice said hello."

"Alice...?" Mr. Freeman began, then he sighed and gave me a look of great sympathy. If my hands weren't holding the box, I believe he would have hugged me and I would have hugged him back. But that's just speculation because we didn't hug.

He gave a little nod and said, "I will shorely do tha', Miss Alice. I shorely will."

I thanked him and wished him and his family a Happy New Year and left with the burden of memories and lost possibilities, like the weight of the world, nestled between my shoulders.

Back in the car where she was waiting, I asked Bertha what she knew about Howard University, like how far it was to drive to from Smedley.

"I 'ont know how far D.C. is, but I bet y'all kin ride through it on y'alls way back to Cleveland."

At first, I thought Bertha was joshing me and knew that I really wanted to go visit Isaac. But, she looked so innocent and honest like she had just given a helpful suggestion, I realized she had no idea about where Isaac was or what he was doing. So, I let it go. I wasn't about to make a trip to The Capital a Tucker family outing.

I started half hoping that Bertha might attend Howard, then I could visit her sometimes, alone or with the girls. I could maybe see Isaac that way. But then it hit me that I would just be setting myself up for a fall and putting misery in everybody's life. What came to me was that Isaac hasn't been trying to get in touch with me! It would have been a lot easier for him to send me a word through Bertha, or write to me up in Cleveland with some kind of code name. But he ain't try nothing like that. He's probably found hisse'f a girlfriend up in Howard and I would just be in the way confusing everything and everybody, and for what? Trying to resurrect some old childish romance?

I am not a child anymore and I don't think Isaac was ever one. I need to respect him and respect myself by learning to let go and get on with the rest of my life. What was is what *was* and since I can't change the past, dragging it around with me has made it another load I need to dump. Thinking of Isaac as something unwanted seemed impossible and ridiculous, but here the truth of it was staring me in my face. I must embrace it and move on.

That's what I told myself, even though I know fantasies of us will come back to me, bouying me up whenever I find myse'f sinking from the heaviness of my life. Then, what Miss Johnson said a thousand lifetimes ago came to me, "writing will help me to understand and exorcise the demons I wrestle". So I decided to manage my miseries by scribbling them away.

thirty-four

I wrote about our last days in Smedley when we got back to Cleveland. How mama tipped in the sun parlor early on the morning of New Year's Eve and woke me without disturbing Bertha or the babies and beckoned me to join her outside the door. She looked strong and broke-down, tired, timid and determined while I shifted from one barefoot to the other because of the cold, hardwood floor. I wondered if the gift of looking so many ways all at once had rubbed off on her from daddy. Then with the thought of daddy, I knew what she was about to say. I guess I knew it all along.

"You owe yer daddy a 'pology, Alice. It been a week t'marra an you ain't said word one yet. I hope you ain't plannin to leave here wit'out showin some kindness t'yer daddy. We unnerstan the strain we put you under an b'lieve me, it eat us up ev'yday, but he don' deserve this. Not from his daughter. Not from nobody."

I *had* spoken my last outburst out loud. That's why, I guess, I didn't faint after. What's worse, I went right on and finished my holiday meal like everything was okey dokey after putting knots in everybody else's stomach. Now it was time to apologize, or at least explain myself, before I breezed on out of here like it was a perfect visit without a hitch.

"Where's daddy now?" I asked looking over her shoulder toward the kitchen where I thought he might be having coffee.

"He out to the barn or the field broodin, I 'spect. He been broodin round here sence Christmas."

Since Christmas, letting me know just how long I had turned a blind eye to the misery I caused her man, my Papa. My model of a perfect man.

I did a quick wash-up in the bathroom sink and threw on a pair of Bertha's dungarees, somebody's sweater and Daniel's (or Samuel's) shoeboots parked by the rear door. Everybody's things were too big for me. I felt like a little girl playing dress-up in her parent's clothes.

I found daddy standing in the middle of the field that bordered Mr. Tucker's fortune, the forest of trees that kept his mill going.

I didn't know what I was going to say. I hadn't planned anything. I thought I'd just say the first thing that came to mind and prayed it would at least be appropriate. But it turns out that daddy was the first to speak.

He must have heard me coming, because he turned around. Then all of a sudden, his eyes got big and he said, "Oh my Lord,...!" and laughed in one big burst. He bent down and opened his arms wide so I could run into them like I used to do as a child. And I ran into them clutching his narrow waist, laughing with him, happy that he was happy to see me.

But when he pulled back to look at me, his laughter stopped and his smile faded. He brushed my hair in soft, slow, backward strokes with his hands. Then a world of grief pooled in his eyes and he looked up to the heavens, I guess to help stay the tears that began trickling down his high, smooth cheeks.

"I thought for a minute you was my li'l girl an I had a second chance t'take it all back. I been prayin e'vyday. I promise God anythang! I beg Him to take mah life an give yers back. But I cain't take it back. Ah'm so sorry, but I cain't."

I never saw a grown man cry, and I *never* thought I would see my father cry. I felt my heart sink, my whole low being sunk. To witness his grief was bad enough, but knowing that I caused it made it unbearable.

"Don't cry daddy," I said. "I don't blame you an mama for nuthin. Y'all was jes doin the best y'all could and that's all anybody can do! Don't cry daddy, please don't cry."

It seems like I'm always causing somebody pain and regret when that ain't never my point, just like I am sure my parents never meant to make me hurt or regret. But here we are again, cutting and bruising each other with good intentions. Maybe that's why they say the road to hell is paved with them.

I can't apologize anymore for anything I do and I don't want anybody apologizing to me. When did everybody get so sensitive? When did I get so harsh? I can't take back what's done, but I can try to help him understand.

"Daddy, there ain't never a need for anybody to apologize for doing their best," I explained. "It's a blessing having you and mama for parents. Most people ain't so lucky. But y'all is still human, and being human means you gonna make mistakes.

"Mr. Tucker been a godsend too, to all of us. He gave y'all everythang he promised in return fer y'all keepin y'alls promise. That deal was signed and sealed a long time ago, and it's been delivered. Now that's over for everybody. I went along to git along back then, but now that's over, too.

"You said jes now you thought I was yer l'il girl... I am, daddy. I will always be yer l'il girl. But I'm a woman, too. I got two babies of my own an I hope I'll be half as good in raising them as you an mama been in raising us. That's my goal an promise to keep til they grown, so that won't be over no time soon."

I said all that with my arms still draped around his middle. But then I let go and backed up a bit to give him a good look at me. My hands were hanging by my sides so he would know I wasn't puttin a sugar coat on my words.

"Y'all can do whatever y'all wanna do with the twins or Bertha or yerselves. But it would be a mistake to try to make another deal with Mr. Tucker, or anybody else concernin me."

I felt like I was talking to Harriet or Ola, not my father, trying to soothe them over some punishment I have to give.

"I mean no disrespect, but I will not be making anymore babies with Mr. Tucker. He knows it cause I already done told him. Now you know it, too. Y'all will git yer grandsons from Bertha or Samuel or Daniel, if you git any at all. Expectin one from me is just a waste of time."

Daddy didn't look sad no more, he looked puzzled. He slid his hands into his back pockets and bent towards me with his head cocked to the side like he wanted to make sure he was hearing me right. I'm sure what I said sounded disrespectful even though I already said I didn't mean no disrespect. Since daddy ain't say nothin, I finished what I wanted to say, but I said it to his belt buckle, cause otherwise it might seem like I was makin a threat.

"I love you an mama, daddy. I always will. But no more favors. I prayed that I ain't hurt yer feelin's. If I did, I'm sorry. But you will git over it... or you won't."

I only added that last part cause it told the *whole* truth.

My father was always *The Perfect Man* to me. He was everything I would have ordered from a menu if Man was a thing I could have made to order. Isaac put me in the mind of my daddy and I just know that's why I think he's such a much. Now here I was trying to tell my father... what? That nobody can breathe for you. You have to do that for yourself. And I can't breathe for me, if I can't live for me. I was just trying to tell daddy how I couldn't breathe and I want to. I want to *breathe*. But it came out all wrong. It sounded like I was smart mouthing or daring my father, and I was losing him.

He knit his brow and flinched like I had slapped him, then he stood up straight, his big hands hanging by his sides and asked me, "Who you thank you talkin to?"

"I love y'all more than anythang," I repeated, "I do. But I cain't breathe. So no more favors, okay?"

We just stood there like that for what seemed like forever, then I stole a little glimpse. Daddy was still standing tall, but he was staring at a spot between his wide planted feet and he looked like he just got the stuffing knocked out of him.

I didn't know what else to do, so I hugged him. He hugged me back, tight. After standing like that quietly for a while I asked him, "You ready for breakfast?"

He gave a chuckle, then we went back to the house, arm in arm, to get something to eat.

****

After a brief, but brilliant display of fireworks at midnight in the yard, we went inside and toasted the New Year with mama's homemade apple brandy. Mr. Tucker wanted to leave early the next morning, so he didn't stay up much past midnight.

Before retiring, he said, "Should I leave the light on for you Princess," with a little sneer.

"This Alice las' night to yap her mouth wit Bertha," daddy piped right up. "I b'lieve y'kin turn that light off, Luthern."

Mr. Tucker looked a little put out with daddy because he was so used to daddy agreeing with him. But my daddy just stood there siding with me wearing a big innocent grin on his face. It defused and confused Mr. Tucker til all he could do was grumble goodnight to everybody and go on upstairs.

thirty-five

Back on Wade Park, I wrote about all the things I could ever remember starting from the present going backwards. I was overwhelmed with pride for my father and mother when I wrote about daddy siding with me staying with Bertha that last night in Smedley.

Daddy moved so easily back into the role of my protector, like the way he was before Mr. Tucker became my sole provider. We'd just had our little talk that morning when I thought my words had wounded him, but that evening he was defending me and my right to make my own choices. I wondered for the first time if he had felt pressured all these years to always accommodate Mr. Tucker. I wondered if he felt free now, like he'd just dropped a load, standing there grinning in his boss' face, taking my side against him. And that only came about because we spoke on it. And that only happened because mama said I needed to talk to daddy. Boy!! January 1, 1951 marked the beginning of a new year *and* a new day!

****

Mr. Tucker developed a subtle mean streak towards me back in Cleveland. I suspect his occasional acts of hard-heartedness were born the night I leveled that rifle at his head and dared him to ever touch me again. He usually tried to maintain an appearance of peace, but he did go off on me after Miss Macaulley's tragic tease. Now that my parents have taken my side, I guess he figures he doesn't have to pretend to be kind anymore. This was his way of telling me like I told daddy, that he won't be doing me anymore favors.

Whenever I practiced on the piano that first week we were back, Mr. Tucker rolled his eyes and ha-rumphed like he was trying to dislodge something painful or distasteful in the back of his throat. That second week, he created urgent little chores that had to be done *right away* and *only by me* whenever I sang or tickled the ivories. The third week, he out and out waged war on my happiness by installing a padlock on the baby grand to keep me from it and forbidding me to sing within earshot of him.

"Sence you wanna be so se'fish an stingy," he whined, "not pleasurin yer husband like The Bible teacha to. Well then, I ain't gone be givin you the *pleasure* of playin on *my* pee-ana!"

Although I didn't think so at first, it was a blessing. I reveled in the freedom I was forced to find. The only reason I stayed around the house as much as I had up to that point was because I could lose myself in music. Now that harmony was a domestic no-no, I searched for it elsewhere and found it just a few blocks away at Our Saving Grace Baptist Church, a struggling little storefront congregation that had just lost their pianist and thought they couldn't afford another. I wasn't as accomplished as they may have liked, but because I was a hungry, self-teaching student and a quick learner, they gave me keys to the church so that I could practice at my convenience.

It became my second home.

Nearly everyday I packed up my girls and we would trudge through the frigid winter weather to our little haven down the street where I played the piano to my hearts content and taught songs to Harriet and Ola, who couldn't even talk.

Our Saving Grace was thoroughly satisfied with my work, especially since my services were free. I tried to organize a little choir and wound up with a quintet that sang three to four hymns every Sunday, featuring a solo by one of us.

Mr. Tucker knew about my new church home, eventually. But there was nothing he could do or say about it, so he didn't say or do anything.

For quite awhile.

****

I was preparing for the coming Easter holiday one Thursday afternoon in March during an early thaw. Outside, the ice and snow had melted into slushy, black/gray pools of dirt along the curbs and in the cracks and depressions of the sidewalk. I was inside the church watching Harriet help Ola practice walking by strolling her around the "sanctuary," a big empty room with folding chairs lining one wall. All of a sudden, we heard Mr. Tucker banging on the door outside and yelling at the top of his lungs, "Open up this'ere do' Alice, Damn you! Yer li'l ass bet open up this'ere do' right *Now* or I'll bust it down!!"

At first, the girls were frozen in shock in the middle of the room. Harriet stood stock-still in a trance of pure terror. Then Ola, losing the strength to stand, buckled at the knees and sunk to the floor whimpering before she wailed. I had never given this man cause, or the right, to yell or curse at me. I couldn't imagine what his problem was now.

I ran to the door, flung it open and barked, "What is yer problem, Mr. Tucker? Why're you banging on the door of the house of the Lord like you ain't got good sense?!"

"You done gone too far this time Alice!!!" Mr. Tucker said pushing past me to get in. He reared around and fixed me with his eyes bloodshot and bulging, speechless but snorting and panting, looking like a bull working himself up to charge somebody.

"WHAT?" I rasped. "What have I done to make you come down here and scare the girls half to death?" I pointed to the children right behind him. They were too afraid to breathe, gaping at him like he was the boogey man.

He turned around and, seeing them for the first time, staggered back then softly and tenderly inquired, "Oh my goodness, did daddy scare the babies?"

He bent down on one knee and beckoned them to come get a hug. "I'm sorry. C'mere, I ain't gone hurt you. I wouldn't never hurt my little angels."

The girls didn't know what to do. I could see they wanted to believe him, but weren't sure that they could. Harriet looked at Ola and helped pull her to her feet, then slowly led her to their daddy, offering her sister like a test or a sacrifice. If he was lying, she could still bolt away.

He enveloped them both in his beefy embrace then looked at me with the agonized expression of the broken-hearted and asked, "How can you expose these here angels to the filth of them two harlots you done invited into our home? How you do that, Alice?"

That was how I learned of Mary and Alberta's arrival. I thought they were going to write me first. I planned on warning Mr. Tucker. But they just dropped in like we weren't hundreds of miles away. Like they just took a notion to stop by and say hello since they were in the area. I told Mr. Tucker that I had meant to tell him.

He released the girls and slowly rose. He approached me talking low at first, but gradually raising his voice to match his temper, "You was gonna tell me? *Tell Me*? How bout axin' me? You *AXE ME* ef you can invite some two-bit, backwood ho's into *MY* house, Woman!"

If he thought I was going to back down, he had another thing coming. I didn't get loud, but my words came fast and furious, and no longer consciously correcting pronunciation, my speech reverted back to its comfortable country roots.

"It ain't jes yer house, Mr. Tucker! You ain't the only one livin there. I ain't never axe you for nuthin! I shore ain't axe you to move me away from my family an frien's! Them girls is my frien's, Mr. Tucker, and I ain't gonna be axin' yer permission for me to he'p my frien's when I kin an cares to. As far as them bein backwood ho's, tha's jes wha'chu made of me buyin me off like you did, makin me yer baby bride! Nah, I ain't never *axe* you for nothin! An I ain't bout to start now. But I will *tell* you this... don'chu never raise yer voice in anger t'me in fronta my babies!" I stepped around him to tend to the girls huddled together and gawking at us like we were some amazing and terrible moving picture show.

Because I kept my volume conversational, my children's fears were quickly soothed, but I believe it sounded all the more ominous to Mr.

Tucker's ear when I said, "Don'chu never raise yer voice in anger to me *at all*! Not less you wanna feel some of this rage I be chokin down ev'yday!"

****

Some folks will never stop surprising me, like when Mr. Tucker came to the church to tell me off, he *drove*. Our house is just down the street from the church and that fat man *drove*! No wonder he looks like he's gained forty pounds since moving here. After we pulled up in the driveway, I rushed out of the car and up to the backdoor. I wanted to get in the house and give an extra warm reception to our houseguests to try to make up for the rudeness I know Mr. Tucker showed them. But while I was fumbling with the lock, I heard Mary and Alberta calling from the side of the house, "Yoo-hoo! Yoo-hoo!"

That man had left them *outside* when he came and fetched us. *OUTSIDE*! These were two southern girls born and bred. They weren't accustomed to this freezing temperature. I couldn't imagine a meaner more cold-blooded, selfish, self-centered, spoiled little petty person… unless he be the spawn of Satan. Luthern Tucker, Lucifer's li'l boy. Another day, another time, that thought would have struck me as funny, but I was too busy fuming. The only thing that saved the moment was my concentrating on showing surprise and delight for my visiting friends.

I turned around and gayly answered their yoo-hoo's, "Mary? Alberta? Is that y'all?"

They rounded the corner of the house wearing tight, thin coats trimmed in cheap fur, maybe rabbit or squirrel, no hats or gloves, and high-heeled shoes that made their walking slippery and slow. They looked prettier than I remembered them being. Their smiles were huge and their eyes were full of what looked like relief or gratitude. If they recognized the insult Mr. Tucker gave them, leaving them out in the cold, they paid it no mind.

"Watch yer step," I needlessly warned. They were stepping as quickly, but as carefully as they could. I had on flat boots so I reached them first, still slipping and sliding in the driveway not far from the house corner they'd just come around. I hugged Alberta and Mary hugged me from behind and then when I switched to hug Mary, Alberta hugged me from behind. I had forgotten about the children until I heard the high, clear, music of their laughter dressing the air. The three of us turned towards the car and watched them scurrying to us over the slushy macadam, eager to be a part of our affectionate trio.

Then Mary began pointing in mock amazement at Ola and Harriet kicking and laughing in the pile of shoveled snow they'd just fallen into.

"Omigosh," Alberta laughed and teased, "is them the two biggest, wiggliest snowflakes y'all ever seen or what?!"

Seemingly from nowhere, Mr. Tucker came from around the front of the car and lifted each child high in the air by an arm out of the snow grumbling, "C'mon now, fer you ketch yer death a cold."

After we all had shed our snowy overcoats and boots… or heels, I fixed blueberry muffins and hot chocolate Mrs. Petty-style. The girls were absolutely enchanted by our guests. Harriet kept trying on the different costume trinkets they wore on their arms, ears and necks. And Ola, usually unimpressed with anything, was so amused with her sister's clumsy attempts to display the baubles and bangles that she sat in Alberta's lap cooing and gurgling her delight.

Mr. Tucker stood brooding by the backdoor reluctantly sipping his hot chocolate like I'd put vinegar in his cup. He flinched at the children's antics as though their laughter stung. I could tell it took a mighty effort, for him to wrestle his demons and keep them inside so as not to spoil his daughters fun. I sympathized with his internal battles some, but then again I thought, now you know how I feel.

When he couldn't take it anymore, he announced, "Nap time!"

"No, no, no," Harriet whined and Ola made little baby grunts in support of her sister's protests.

"Yeah, yeah, yeah," Mr. Tucker insisted. "It's time for y'alls nap. Y'had a big day and now the grown folks got to talk."

After he left to tuck them in bed, Mary and Alberta looked as uncomfortable as I felt.

"I hope us comin here ain't causing you no trouble," Alberta said.

"Nah, not atall," I lied, then added sincerely, "I'm glad y'all is here."

We sat not speaking, uncomfortably anticipating what might be on Mr. Tucker's mind for a minute, then I decided to start supper. It always made me feel better to be doing something. Just sitting there wrapped in my thoughts felt stagnating and burdensome, but moving around making supper felt like progress. Maybe it's just the way of country people, an idle mind or hands or something, being the devil's playground and all, because shortly after I started taking food out of the refrigerator, they joined me. And they didn't even know what I was making.

Mary moseyed over first, picked up one of the onions I had laid on the counter and asked, "Diced or sliced?"

"Diced."

Alberta lifted a carrot out of the bunch and asked, "What you doin wit these?"

"I need two of them shredded, the grater is on the top shelf of the counter right behind you. The rest of them you can julienne slice."

"Juli-who?" She asked, and that got us started.

"Cut'em long and thin," I said with a chuckle.

After a few minutes, I noticed Mary silently weeping in her little corner of the counter. I went over, turned her around, wiped at the tears running down her cheeks with the back of my hand and gently asked, "What's the matter, Mary?"

Even though I raised her head by the chin, she kept her eyes down. Her bottom lip was trembling and her nose started to run, which got her to sniffling. But eventually she managed enough control to finally explain, "Onions."

Well after that we were no good. We laughed until we were all crying and clutching our sides.

Finally I said, "You so stupid. Chile, go snap them beans and I'll finish the onions."

"Oh, so you gonna wait til I'm bawlin mah brains out fore you offer to he'p," Mary said, still laughing and pushing me away. "I migh'could be stupid, but'chu late Alice. You jes a tad late. Go on snap them beans yerse'f. I'ma keep dicing."

Mary continued to pretend to be offended as I continued my attempt to rescue her from the onions. We were falling all over one another laughing and crying from the pungent vapors.

"Let *me* chop them onions," Alberta said joining the struggle. "One a y'all kin Juli-who the carrots."

Laughing and pushing and making silly vegetable jokes, I guess we were having too much fun for Mr. Tucker standing in the doorway watching.

"Sound like y'all is havin a reg'ler hootchie ball in heah!" He said with a derisive chuckle. "Tha's nice. Y'all go on an whoop it up for a week or two. Tha's all the time I'm givin y'all to git yer bizness straight."

I started to protest, "Mr. Tucker, you..."

"Alice! You don' like it, you kin go wit'em!"

And that was the end of that.

thirty-six

The next day Mary wanted to peruse the Jukes on Euclid Avenue between 105th and 107th Streets and find out who was playing at Leo's Casino, one of the many nightspots I had never heard of before and wondered how she had. Alberta kept asking me about Mr. Tucker like she thought he might really throw me out with them when they left. She was in a big hurry to get them their own place so as not to get me in too much more trouble. Through all of my bravado about my rights and what I will and will not do, that was a real concern of mine, too. If I were by myself, I would have welcomed that independence. But I have to think about my girls, too, and that made staying a necessity, for now. I couldn't leave my babies and I would never have them go hungry and living poor as church mice on the street with me, if I didn't have to. And if Mr. Tucker wanted to fight me over their custody right now, I couldn't afford a legal battle. So while I took my friends around looking for jobs and rooms, I was also looking for the girls and me. I had the same feeling as Alberta, that inviting them to stay with us may have been a step too far.

I asked Mr. Tucker to watch Harriet and Ola while I took Mary and Alberta around, getting them accustomed to the area so they would feel comfortable travelling about alone looking for work and whatnot. We rode on the bus all the way downtown to the Terminal Tower. I pointed out places of interest on the way down. Of course, they nearly lost their little minds when we passed the Sears Roebuck Co. I told them they could spend the whole day in there come tomorrow, but I wanted to cover as much ground as we could today.

We got a Cleveland Plain Dealer and looked through the classified section to find out what kind of work was available. The paperman said the Sunday edition would be best for that type of thing, but Sunday was three days away, so we bought Thursday's paper anyway.

They searched the paper for houses to buy as well as lease, although they obviously didn't have the money. There were homes with rooms to let pretty close to ours, but Mary wanted them to live in a seperate apartment, not to just get a room in a private house. I think she means to keep plying her trade and figures the easiest way to avoid complaints or arrest is to bring her Johns to her own, separate dwelling.

They found half of a two-family house available not too far from us on Pasadena, on the other side of 105th street. They explained to Mr. Thompson, their landlord, that they were new in town so they didn't have the entire first payment, but they would have it within two weeks. He took their $25 and their word to return with the $60 balance in two weeks. $85 a month to rent only half a house sounded unreal to my ears. I told them all about the opportunities moving north would afford them, but I had no idea what high price tags these opportunities wore.

The next day, Alberta found herself a job in a shirt factory over on 55th Street starting Monday morning, and was checking coats in a downtown bistro starting tomorrow night. Mary refused to work in a factory, but she got herself a dancing job right off at The Naked Truth, one of the clubs on Euclid, not too far from the house.

****

That Sunday we all attended the services at Our Saving Grace Baptist Church to give thanks and praise to The Lord for seeing us through another trial. I should have anticipated some unpleasantry since Mr. Tucker came with us. He rarely ever attended church anymore since he regarded me as a Christian hypocrite for refusing him intimate relations. It also irritated him to no end that I found an outlet for my musical leanings without using his old padlocked baby grand.

I sat up front playing the piano, of course. Our quintet's sound was so rich and perfectly pitched that we usually did two numbers completely a cappella. Those, plus the two songs we perform with my piano accompaniment during the collection of tithes and the three hymns done with the entire congregation, makes our musical contribution substantial to the services.

It seemed to be the habit of Reverend Pope to choose scriptures he made relevant to the local, national or even international events. I suspected him of having political leanings like Adam Clayton Powell, Jr., the Baptist minister turned congressman out of Harlem in New York City that I've been hearing so much about. The theme for this Sunday's sermon was "How Wives Must Submit To Their Husbands." I felt a déjà vu stir up. Until now, Reverend Pope kept his text out of the bedroom, but this was another omen of things to come.

Meanwhile, Alberta and Mary couldn't have been more ecstatic with my choral direction had they taught me. They puffed out their chests, strutted and crowed like proud mother hens, "Tha's our frien', y'all! Tha's our Frien'!"

From the corner of my eye I saw Mr. Tucker and Rev. Pope shaking hands and smiling like old friends, but I was so full of myself from my friends adoration that I thought the good reverend was congratulating Mr. Tucker on my talents.

So I had no right to be thoroughly floored when Reverend Pope warmly hugged me and said, "You certainly have developed into a formidable Choir Mistress, self-taught at that, quite commendable! You've been a blessing to our little congregation. We will sorely miss yer music here from now on."

"But..." I began.

"I tole the good rev'ern here," Mr. Tucker was all sugar-coating, "how you was jes over-workin yerse'f comin here alla time on toppa raisin' two li'l babies *an* he'pin out yer childhood frien's an all. He unnerstan's, Princess."

I wondered if I was the only one smelling the stench of his foul and bald-faced lie. No good can ever come to this man I thought, bearing false witness, breaking one of the ten commandments right here in the house of the Lord.

"Reverend Pope, I am not..."

"Now, now. Don't you worry about us! Your husband said you would. Luthern Tucker certainly knows you. He's made a *significant contribution* so we can afford another pianist to fill your space, but no one will ever take your place. Thank you so much, Mrs. Tucker. Now you'll have time to relax some, before we see you next Sunday."

There was no use in protesting so I didn't. I wondered how long Mr. Tucker took to plan this. Was it just since Mary and Alberta's arrival, or since I first started playing for the church, or since before the beginning of time? I wondered how much of a contribution he had made to cause Reverend Pope to quiver so when explaining, "He's made a *significant contribution.*"

Reverend Pope was dead wrong. Luthern Tucker doesn't know me at all, not if he thinks this is going to stop me... or even slow me down.

****

I volunteered to be the Sunday School teacher for the few children that attended Our Saving Grace. The reverend tried to protest, but I explained that Mr. Tucker's concern was with me being away during the week so much, but Sunday School would be an additional hour or two just on Sunday's. I asked some of the working mother's in the church what they did with their small children when they went to work and they told me about a pre-school on Yale Ave. I went there that Monday and enrolled my children and myself as a volunteer, since there was no paying position available. I decided I would do this with them all the way through high school, if need be.

Mary and Alberta were gone all day and most of the night with their new jobs. I never knew or cared about what Mr. Tucker did as long as he didn't interfere with what I was trying to do. And I never told him where I went or what I was doing. I just left in the morning with the children and came back in the afternoon. He never asked about my comings or goings either. I guess he expected resistance or rebellion of some kind from me as a response if he were to ask, but I would have told the truth. I have nothing to hide. People see the world as they are in it, and because Mr.

Tucker was such a two-faced, underhanded, backstabbing, vindictive old buzzard, simple truth would never have occured to him.

So I left in the mornings with the girls and Alberta on her way to the factory, and came back in the evening in time to fix dinner for everyone. This routine only lasted eight days before Mary and Alberta left.

Mary made a lot of money in tips from dancing. I thought she was dancing for dimes like they did in the Depression. Back then, the men wore suits and the ladies wore nice dresses and every dance was ten cents plus tips, if the man particularly liked the dancer or wanted to insure future numbers. The lady's carried cards for making reservations and there was even a saying that was made popular from that ritual, "Is your dance card full?" I thought that was the kind of dancing Mary was doing.

Silly me.

There's another type of dancing, it's called "shake dancing" because that's what the women basically did. Girls dance solo for a group of guys who pay to watch. If they really like what they see, the men stuff dollar bills in her waistband or down her brassiere. Sometimes the woman will take a man in a back or side room to have a "private" dance - a tangled tango no doubt. It's considered one or two steps above whoring, so I guess Mary was moving up in the world.

But I can't judge.

Anyway, from all of her tips at The Naked Truth, plus Alberta's tips from checking coats and her first paycheck from the factory, they were able to leave in eight days. Alberta said they were going to try to buy the duplex if they liked it well enough.

I took the girls to school and dropped them off that day, before helping my friends. They only had the few bags they'd brought with them so moving was a breeze. It took one trip with the three of us walking over there. Mr. Tucker could have driven us, but he didn't volunteer and we didn't ask.

On the way back to the day care I felt warm tears chilling on my cheeks in the frigid February air. I was going to miss having those two with me. They weren't moving so far away, but they might as well be on the other side of the moon.

When I returned, Leone, one of the aides at the school, dabbed at my cheeks with a tissue and exclaimed over the cold. She thought the brisk outdoors made my eyes water.

I let her think it.

thirty-seven

It's strange how days drag on, but years fly by when you're stuck in routine.

The girls did well in school and seemed to be reasonably happy, but they'd somehow picked up the most annoying habit of pretending to be weaker or dumber than certain boys when it came to friendly competitions.

I noticed it first during a lunch recess in the playground when Harriet was about six years old. I was still volunteering at the day care with Ola, but I'd check on Harriet at Columbia Elementary School, a block away on Empire, during her lunch break. With her long little lanky legs, Harriet could always run as hard and as fast as the wind. So I knew she should have left all of her classmates behind in the schoolyard relay races. But I watched her give the lead to Anthony Barnard, one of her classmates and a real cutie pie, three times in a row. The first time, I didn't let her know I was standing just outside the fence, but the other two times she knew.

I thought if she knew I was there she would do her best to try to impress me, but she gave the race to Anthony anyway. I wondered what other concessions she may have been making, perhaps academic ones as well. I decided to get to the bottom of this in one of our girl talks after school on our way home.

"Who's the young man that beat you racing this afternoon?"

"That's ol' Tony Baloney," she said with a smirk, but blushing all over herself from just the mention of his name.

"Tony Baloney, Tony Baloney, Tony Baloney..." Ola began skipping around, chanting and kissing the air, teasing her sister. Harriet stuck out her tongue and swatted at Ola, trying to mask the warm flush that made her look all aglow.

"Stop it Ola..." pretending frustration or anger Harriet threatened, "you better quit it!"

"Ola, stop," I said, then got back on the subject. "I bet you can run faster than him."

"He's really fast!" Harriet said with stars in her eyes.

"Yeah, but I bet you could beat him."

"He likes to win."

"Most people do. Don't you?"

"Yeah, but he really *really* likes to win."

"Is that why you let him beat you?"

We had been walking down the street, but when I asked Harriet this last, she slowed to a crawl becoming sullen and pouty as though I'd accused her of an unforgiveable act. And I suppose in a way, I had.

"I was running fast," she mumbled.

"Yes you were, but I bet you could have run even faster."

She was silent.

"If you tell me you ran as fast as you could, I'll believe you. But right now, I think you let him win."

Harriet kept quiet.

"It's nice to share with your friends. It's nice to give people things, too. But first you need to develop your own talents and gifts and become the very best person you can possibly become. Then you will have more to share and more to give. That's why we have schools. That's where we go to learn and develop our skills. You like to read, don't you?"

No answer.

"I've got a book at home to show you. Okay?"

She wanted to stay aloof, but curiousity got the best of her. She peeked at me briefly and said, "Okay."

When we got home, I took out a book on Harriet Tubman from the top shelf in my bedroom. It had plenty of pictures in it, but I thought the language was too advanced for her reading skills, so I hadn't shown her this book before.

When I bought it, I thought I might hold the gift of her namesake for some Christmas, but she seemed to need it now.

"This is a book on a famous lady named Harriet Tubman. I named you Harriet after her. She was brave, bold, beautiful and brilliant, but she couldn't read or write because she had been born a slave. Less than a hundred years ago, there were laws against colored people learning how to read and write in this country."

Ola and Harriet both were looking at the pictures in this book with a fascination I rarely saw on their faces. But when I mentioned the laws for colored people, their little heads jerked around and they looked at me dumbfounded.

"A hundred years sounds like a long time, right?"

Their expressions remained blank, but nodded so I knew they were listening.

"Well, it's not so long ago. I bet there are thousands of people alive in the world right now that are a hundred or more years old. Well, the Negroes that are that old and were born and raised in America, mostly can't read or write because it was against the law to teach them when they were young. It's against the law for Negroes to go to white schools right now in some places, if they don't want us there."

Their little jaws began to slowly drop open.

"Harriet Tubman couldn't read the alphabet, but she could read the stars. And in the middle of the night, with the sky as her map, she found her way to freedom."

"Where's freedom?" Harriet asked like it was a place she might like to visit.

"It's here," I said, resting a hand over each of their hearts. "And here," I said, moving my hands to their heads.

"True freedom is in your heart and in your mind. But hundreds of years ago before our country was a country, evil people calling themselves *Masters* said that Negroes weren't entirely human and were created to be their slaves. They passed laws that made it legal for them to keep colored people in chains and caged like animals, sell babies and children away from their mommy's and daddy's, beat them, maim them and even kill them if they couldn't force them to live as slaves. Slavery times were very scary times and fear made many Negroes give up their freedom or bury it deep inside, hoping to be left alone. They did what they were told, when they were told, hoping to stay alive long enough to see better days.

"After The Revolutionary War, the war that made this country the United States of America, the states in the north ended slavery as a way of thanking Negroes for fighting so hard in their battles. See now, the first person killed in the Revolution, Crispus Attucks, was a colored man. But the south didn't care about that. They kept slavery going until 1865. That's less than a hundred years ago. Well, Harriet Tubman was born a slave in the south and she was afraid too, but she didn't give into her fears. She prayed to God for the strength to keep the freedom she hid deep in her heart and help guide her when she was most afraid. When the evil man calling himself her *master* threatened to sell her away from her family, she ran away to the north where there were no more laws of slavery.

"But what made Harriet Tubman different from all of the other runaway slaves was that she kept running *back* down south to get her family and friends, and anyone else that wanted to live free. She didn't allow anyone - man, woman or child - to change their mind after they were on the road to freedom either.

"I named you after Harriet Tubman because I wanted you to be that bold and brave... that free."

"I am, mommy!" Harriet said. "I not a slave."

"Harriet Tubman would never settle for second place. If you let someone else win a race, when you know that you could've beaten them, you're *choosing* to be in second place behind someone you know doesn't deserve to be first."

"I ran fast, mommy," she said, tracing Tubman's face with her finger in the back of the book.

"Yes you did. But if you weren't running your fastest, you were just wasting your time and that doesn't help anyone. Especially not Tony Baloney. He'll never try to do better if he thinks he's already the best.

"Harriet Tubman made others do better even when they didn't think they could. She gave them strength when they became weak or afraid. You know how you can help Tony Baloney?"

"How?" Harriet asked.

"In the next competition - spelling, math, writing, or running race - do your very best. If it means you win, then win!" I said and hugged her and kissed the top of her head. "Beat Tony Baloney and anybody else, every time you can."

"What about me?" Ola asked. "Why I got my name?"

"Ola was my teacher's first name. She was another brilliant lady who was as bold, brave and beautiful as Harriet Tubman. I hope you'll both get to meet her someday," I said, then hugged them both and kissed their heads.

"You got her picture?" She asked.

"No, I don't. I wish I did"

She looked disappointed then, but I lifted her face by her chin and told her, "You do your best too, little lady, in everything all the time."

I guess because I told Ola the same thing and in the same way, Harriet felt less put upon and she became her old, happy self again.

"Can we make some cookies?"

"Yeah, let's go make some cookies," I said, tickling their tummy's until the music of their laughter rang through the house like the songs ol' master Tucker forbid me to make.

****

From that point on throughout their school years, I relished every opportunity to make history relevant to now. Pointing out the injustices and inadequacies of our social, educational and political systems. I was hoping to spark a fire in my girls to become leaders and help drive the changes that would surely be made. Emmett Till's lynching, the Reverend Congressman Adam Clayton Powell, the Reverend Dr. Martin Luther King, The Civil Rights movement, Chief Justice Thurgood Marshall and the 1954 Supreme Court ruling desegregating schools were all discussed in our after school girl talks. I constantly reminded them that education was a gift that had been denied to most Negroes and that the fight to make our lives better begins with ourselves. Whenever we visited mama and daddy in Smedley, I would parallel the Jim Crow laws of segregation in America with the apartheid laws in South Africa. I'd point out how the

"Whites Only" and "Coloreds" signs were everywhere to my eye now, yet I couldn't remember seeing a single one when I was living there. I wanted them to know how sometimes removing yourself from a picture may help you recognize a situation you blindly accept.

Miss Johnson was never home when we dropped by. We only travelled during the scheduled school recesses and I suppose she took her semester breaks to travel, also. But we exchanged letters from time to time and I sent her photos to keep her updated. If Miss Johnson was rarely in Smedley, Mrs. Petty always was and my kids loved her like a second mother.

Once when the children were amusing themselves playing some game in her yard, she asked, "Are you happy Alice?"

"I'm happy for those girls."

"I am too. But those girls are gone grow up one day soon. Then what? You got t'do somethin for yerse'f, Alice Tucker, beyond yer chirren. Less you lookin fo'ward to spendin the resta yer life wit Luthern."

thirty-eight

It was 1959 when Mrs. Petty dropped that pearl of wisdom in my ear, shaking me to my core. It shook me awake to recognize the gravity of my blind living, the freedoms I hid and the ones I gave away.

I could no longer content myself with the happiness and well-being of my children alone. I knew they would be fine, but what about me? I hadn't thought much about what I would do after they were grown, except for some vague notion of leaving Mr. Tucker to begin the rest of my life. Mrs. Petty challenged me to face my future and plan for it now.

Not knowing where to start, I did what I found comforting, I consulted the wisdom in the words of Dunbar and Hughes.

I didn't find a poem that could help me, but I did find Miss Johnson's letter buried in the back of Dunbar's book eleven years earlier. I must've seen it a thousand times before, but I never read it. Now I remembered her words when she gave it to me; "*Read it at your leisure or when you're feeling your lowest. It may or may not not have an answer, but I think you will find it inspirational and interesting...*"

My heart stopped the first time I read it. It was just a brief note. I read it again and again, in case I read it wrong the first time. Then I knew my heart had started beating again because I felt it break. Tears of joy, intense pain and unfathomable regret rained down my cheeks. Timing is everything and eleven years after the fact, I knew this time I was too late.

Despite my very bad timing, I wrote the longest, most impassioned apology ever written. I explained to Miss Johnson how I'd *just* read her note of Oct. 16, 1948. I thanked her for being such a good friend. I told her if I'd read her note back when she'd written it, maybe I wouldn't be living in this black hole I call home. I asked if that was why she was never in Smedley when we came to visit, and if so... then I went into another long bout of how very sorry I was. I knew none of this would make a difference. But however late, I needed to let her know how appreciative I have always been of her concerns and attempts to make me happy.

I took it to the post office and sent it Special Delivery so she'd get it the next day. Then I went home and soaked in the tub for the rest of the afternoon. And long after the bath water had turned icy as Lake Erie's, I wrestled against a nearly unbearable desire to discover what peace I may in drowning.

****

I didn't want to feel sorry for myself and I could never imagine putting myself or *my* welfare and happiness before my daughters. But nearly paralyzed with remorse from missing the infinite possibilities of Miss Johnson's note, I couldn't do anything. I couldn't talk. I couldn't listen. I couldn't eat or sleep. I couldn't help my children with their homework, not that they ever needed help. Harriet was eleven and Ola was nine, so they weren't little girls that needed their mother walking them to school or picking them up. I think Harriet may have even been a little embarrassed by it for the past few years. So, she was probably more relieved than anything else when I first stopped showing up to school. But Ola seemed to clamor for my attention even more.

I had long ago developed a real skill for ignoring Mr. Tucker, so if he was more attentive or concerned for me in anyway, I failed to see it.

But somebody must have said something to somebody who got word to Bertha, because she was on the next bus to Cleveland from New York City where she attended Columbia University working on her doctorate's degree in some kind of exotic and important sounding finance or marketing field, which to me is just a fancy dancy term for sells. I don't know why Bertha would waste her time trying to *develop* skills in one of her strongest natural gifts... I swear my sister could sell RAID® to roaches.

****

"Alice...? I fixed you a little something to eat."

I thought I heard a familiar voice pierce through the gray miasma of memories recalled and relived inside my head where I have retreated and now reside.

"Bertha...that you?" I said in a raspy whisper.

"Yeah Allie, it's me. C'mon now, you gotta eat."

I felt her pulling me up to sit straighter in the leather library lounge chair. I don't know how I got there or how long I'd been there. I felt weak and fatigued. I thought I could remember drinking water, some nature calls, rising, sitting, walking, but I was unsure and unable to grasp the point to any of it.

Bertha slowly spooned chicken/vegetable/rice soup and cornbread into me. I felt stronger with each spoonful, but uninspired to do anything other than sit and be fed. She talked to me, too. She brought words from mama, daddy, the twins and Miss Johnson. I liked the sound of her voice and every now and then, a word or phrase would register. After I ate, she ran a bath for me, got me washed and changed into clean clothes, then took me for a walk. The fresh air and her constant prattle made me feel more like my old self, but I still had trouble focusing for long on any one thing.

She only stayed a week, but when she left I was better than I recall ever being. Bertha sold me on living again. I wasn't so hesitant to spend Mr. Tucker's money. I wasn't going to be suddenly extravagant or foolish with it, I wasn't raised that way. But I was determined to fill more of my basic needs, including a second-hand car to get around. I decided to start an Adult Learning Clinic on Tuesday and Thursday evenings at Our Saving Grace Church and to volunteer in some of the other community-based organizations like the YMWCA up on St. Clair Avenue.

thirty-nine

"What we s'poze to do wit Bertha's car?" Mr. Tucker asked looking out the kitchen window at the '52 Chevy parked in the backyard the morning after she left. Alberta, Mary and I drove Bertha to the Greyhound station downtown. Mr. Tucker wasn't around then, so I guess he thought one of the "harlots", as he called them, drove me home.

"That's not Bertha's car. It's mine."

"Wha'chu need a car for?" Mr. Tucker looked stunned. "You cain't drive!"

"You don't know what I can do," I said without malice and continued ironing bedsheets.

The phone rang about thirty minutes later. Harriet and Ola wanted to know if they could go skating at the Playmor with their friends Niecy and Yasmine. I told them I'd pick them all up in about twenty minutes. I wanted to go skating, too. Mr. Tucker heard me say I'd take them and decided to pick a fight with me.

"How you gonna volunteer mah time like that? You don' know what I got t'do!"

"I didn't ask you for anything. You go on and do what you have to do," I said putting the ironing away.

"How *you* gonna take the kids anywhere?"

"I'll drive."

"You *cain't* drive!"

"Watch and learn," I said putting my temporary driver's license, some money and the house keys in my jacket pocket. Then tossing my car keys in the air, I left.

Out in the driveway, I got in the car and started it up.

"I'ont know wha'chu tryna prove, Alice Tucker!" He ran out the backdoor shouting, "You gone keel yer fool se'f tryna…"

I didn't hear what else he said. Or, it may have been that his shouting stopped mid-sentence watching me back out of the driveway. My last look at him, before driving away to get my girls, was of him standing stock-still in the driveway, eyes bulging, jaw dropped low and gaping. He looked amazed and disbelieving, like he was seeing me walk on water instead of driving a car.

****

My life changed for the better after that. Mr. Tucker barely questioned me about anything. I'd sometimes catch him eyeing me and looking puzzled like he wanted to ask, "Who are you and what have you done with *Alice*!"

Harriet and Ola were bright, balanced, getting older and more independent, running around with their own set of friends and refusing my offers to help with nearly everything saying, "I can do it." So without neglecting my motherly duties, I went where I wanted and did what I wanted, whenever I wanted.

I taught adults much older than me basic math and grammar and how to read and write. Some of them found work and others, already employed, got promotions because of my lessons. I also started an after school youth program at the church, to help kids with their homework and provide wholesome social activities to keep them out of trouble. I think these programs were so successful because they weren't limited to church members, but open to any and all who came. Harriet and Ola blossomed into quite a tour de force in the youth groups. They organized the fundraising committee to finance extracurriculum outings and usually led the talks and votes that chose the monthly trips.

The Y had a yearly membership that some people couldn't afford, plus their scheduling wasn't conducive to a lot of interested folks, so I enrolled and took classes; pottery, quilt making and african dancing to name a few. Then we started an arts and crafts group for people interested in learning what they taught at the Y and from what the seniors shared of their expertise. We made quilts, pottery (bowls, mugs, plates, candle holders) and flower arrangements that we sold at our fundraising spring and winter bazaars.

I was rarely home, but I left evidence of my having been there like dinners in the oven, washed laundry and brief notes of chores for my daughters.

I laughed and sang and danced and had friends outside my Wade Park residence, but I never brought any of that home because I knew Mr. Tucker would take it from me.

Life was a great gift, not to be taken lightly or wasted… ever again.

****

July 4, 1961, the Youth Committee organized an Independence Day field trip to Euclid Beach Amusement Park. It was their most ambitious project to date because of the overwhelming response from the neighborhood. Everybody knew somebody, but nobody knew everybody because our church functions were dedicated to outreach. With the success of each outing, the next was always larger, and this was by far the largest yet. We chartered four buses to take the toddlers, children, teens, adults and seniors. Plus, there were several carloads of people following the buses.

Before setting out, we broke up into twenty sub-groups with three leaders in each group to help keep a tab on who was where at all times. When we reached the park, we set up a "home base" in the picnic area. One of the three leaders from each group had to be there at all times. The other two leaders would trade off with them periodically, so no one felt stuck in any role and no one escaped K-P (kitchen patrol), the affectionate alias for home base. The group leaders could also switch from group to group, mostly to give the toddler leaders a chance to ride some rides.

There was a ton of food: Fried chicken and barbequed ribs, hot dogs, hamburgers and corn on the cob wrapped in foil and grilled, baked beans, cole slaw, potato salad, tossed salad, carrot/raisin salad, macaroni salad, string beans, deviled eggs, fresh fruit salad, watermelon wedges and every kind of cake and pie known to Negroes... sweet potato, apple, pecan, strawberry/rhubard, peach, bean, cherry and coconut custard pies and 7-UP, red velvet, carrot, coconut/pineapple, lemon pound, butter pound, chocolate and german chocolate cakes and a huge tub of banana pudding.

I volunteered to lead a group of toddlers first thing because I didn't want to get stuck with setting up all that food or grilling the meat and corn.

So, most of my morning was spent at the merry-go-round and the caterpillar (the baby roller coaster) rides. Toddlers have so much energy. I got tired from just watching them. Two grandmothers were my other group leaders. Dottie, a short, stout lady volunteered for K-P. So, Miss Mildred and I were on our own. After two hours, I couldn't wait to trade with an older, less tiring crew. My relief came when LaVerne, the reverend's wife, volunteered to switch with me. I declined at first, in deference to Miss Mildred. I figured if I was tired, she must be feeling half-dead... Wrong!

"I won't be riding any rides today, so you go on Alice. Have some fun. I like watching the babies whoop it up. They just like fleas on a stray dog's back," Miss Mildred laughed. "They give these tired old bones a lift, bouncing around for hours without breaking a sweat!"

It was amazing how the very thing that wore me out, boosted her senior spirits.

LaVerne had been supervising a high school group and when we switched, they were standing in line for the Flying Turns, the fastest, scariest ride in the park. I joined them just in time to get on board. It's hard to describe the Flying Turns. It's like a sideways roller coaster that you and a partner ride toboggan-style stretched out, one between the others legs, instead of sitting up. It flies around the tracks, twisting and turning, giving the sensation of a falcon in flight. It made my stomach churn and flip flop, but not quite like a roller coaster with its dips and turns.

After it ended, the kids laughed and punched the air ready to do it again. They weren't paying me any attention until I veered toward some bushes when they got back on line.

"Miss Alice, where you goin? We ridin this one again."

Waves of nausea made it hard for me to speak. "Y'all go ahead," was all I got out before I puked my breakfast.

Doc, the other group leader, immediately jumped out of line announcing that everyone would have to forget the ride and escort me back to our picnic area.

"Aawwww!!" Moans and groans rose in unison.

"No, no," I said, wiping my mouth with the handkerchief he offered. "That won't be necessary. I don't have to ride. I'll sit over there on that bench. Y'all go on and have fun."

Doc, who was a real doctor, looked a little worried, but then agreed. "Okay you all go on then. When it's over, meet us by the bench."

"You ride, too," I said.

"No. I really don't want to," he smiled through his concern. "I'm just using you for an excuse."

That's how we spent the bulk of the afternoon, strolling around or sitting on benches while the kids rode the rides and checked with us before going to the next ride. I hadn't intended to boycott all the fun, but sudden attacks of nausea would hit me unpredictably and I didn't want to be stuck on a ride spewing vomit on innocent bystanders. So, for the most part, I opted to watch.

After a couple of hours, they'd worked up an appetite so we headed back to the picnic grounds. I started wondering about how old my breakfast eggs were because the sight and smells of all those delectable dishes made me queasy. Once, I wondered if I had a touch of food poisoning while rushing to the restroom to throw up yet again.

Harriet and Ola were in a different group that happened to be in the lavatory when I rushed in to wretch the last of my breakfast in a toilet bowl.

"You okay, Alice?" One of their group leaders called out.

"Flying Turns," I answered and everyone laughed. As a group, they were shorter than the minimum height allowance so it'd be awhile before they could attempt that terror, but they were very familiar with its reputation.

"You wanna take my place with this group?" she asked when I finally emerged from the stall to rinse my mouth and wash my hands. "I'd like to fly me a turn or two."

"Sure. My group is at the picnic area right now. Tell Marie and Doc that we switched."

I rode all of the rides my daughters did, except anything that went in circles or that plunged in any way... which wound up being most of them.

On a whole, it was a very good day.

forty

Mr. Tucker never went with the girls and me anywhere. If they asked him, he would take them places and do things for them. But they hardly ever asked him for anything, aside from his affection. They were the only reason I stayed and probably the only reason he let me stay, since we barely ever spoke three words strung together to each other.

But late in the evening of July 6, 1961, I gave him more than words in the den where I found him sleeping in front of the television test pattern. I brought two glasses, two beers and a fifth of scotch. I put Eartha Kitt on the stereo and turned the TV off.

"Mr. Tucker...Mr. Tucker," I said nudging his knee with mine.

"Huh?" He grunted still groggy with sleep.

"Have a drink with me."

"Wha...?" I felt his shock as he slowly came around.

"C'mon, drink with me," I urged.

I poured two fingers of scotch in each glass and handed him one.

"To life and living it at any risk," I toasted, gently clicking my glass to his before tossing it down.

Fire water.

I heard somewhere that that's what the Indians called liquor. Fire water. Good name. It's liquid, many a brand is clear and it's often served over ice. An iced beverage usually implies something cool and quenching. But this stuff burns like a hot coal in the back of your throat in spite of the ice, if you chug it down like I just did. Even in sips, if you're not used to it, it'll burn your tongue.

Fire water.

The pilgrims pumped the Indians full of their burning spirits creating a formidable screen to mask their lies and robbings and pillages.

Through teary eyes, I watched Mr. Tucker watch me gag on the scotch in the shadows. He didn't move or say a word. I could barely make out his features in the dim light from the stereo console, but I knew his brow must have been wrinkled in puzzlement trying to figure me out.

"Drink," I said in a hoarse whisper.

He did and I immediately poured him another drink. He tossed that one back, too, then took a long swig of beer from one of the chilled bottles I handed him.

I was glad he didn't say anything. That made it easier to pretend I was alone and talking to myself.

"I'll be twenty-nine on my birthday coming up. Twenty-nine. An old lady. Harriet will be thirteen on her next birthday. She'll be fifteen in two more years, the same age I was when daddy walked me down the aisle to you. You think we should be trying to find a husband for Harriet?"

He didn't answer so I asked with a little more force, "Do you!"

"No," he answered quietly, then poured himself another scotch.

"Good. Me neither."

We sat there listening to Eartha purr for a while. I'm sure he was wondering what was my point. I know I was. Then something occurred to me.

"I never thanked you, Mr. Tucker. I've been so mad with so much for so long, I never thanked you for putting us all through school and giving daddy a job that truly made him able to provide."

"Well, princes..."

"Sshhh," I put a finger to his lips to gently quiet him. "Let me finish. I know you never meant any harm. I knew it then, too. There are so many more things you could have done to make life a lot harder for me, but you didn't. I wanna thank you for that now, because I never have."

I heard him gasp and saw him fall forward like he was bending to pray.

"You never seemed to realize that I never meant you any harm either," I continued. "I always wanted you to be happy Mr. Tucker, just not at my expense. Remember Miss Macaulley?"

He snorted, but didn't say a word.

"She was nice... enough... sort of. But if you didn't want her, if you thought she was too old, or too pathetic, or what have you, you should have laughed."

Chuckling, he said, "I did."

"But you stopped laughing after she left and that's when you should have laughed the hardest. I wasn't trying to hurt you. But you acted like I was, padlocking the piano then paying off the reverend to keep me from playing in church. You could have done a lot worse than that, though. That's why I'm thanking you now, for the restraint you did show. But you need to know that I never meant you any harm."

Those three quick shots, plus that beer seemed to have gone to his head. He wasn't drunk, but he wasn't clear either.

His speech was slurred, "I know it. I know you din't. I do know that. You nevah..."

"Sshhh, it's okay," I said softly. I liked it better when he didn't speak.

We sat there listening to Miss Kitt. The heat from my one shot slowly bleeding through my body, first warming my mouth, then my chest, then my head and stomach. It blurred my senses and thoughts. I felt lazy. If I felt like this from one drink, I wondered what Mr. Tucker must have been feeling, even though granted, he does drink occasionally and I never do.

When Eartha started crooning about how evil she wanted to be, I said, "Singing your song!"

There was a pause before we both doubled over laughing, and then crying from the effort to keep quiet. I got up on the first refrain and started wiggling my behind to the beat and softly emphasized "Eeevviilll". Mr. Tucker joined me running his fingers over his half-bald head like he was combing them through long curly locks. I thought for sure we must've been loud, but every now and then we'd stop to listen and never heard anything.

When the song ended we were still standing and Mr. Tucker, swaying unsteadily on his feet said, "I wanna thank you too Alice, cause I never did."

"Don't mention it," I said and gave him a little hug.

He returned my hug.

Then I pulled my head back and gave him a small kiss. When I felt his groin stiffen, I sat him down and straddled his lap.

forty-one

My son, Dunbar, was born March 15, 1962. The Ides of March. He was a big, strong, healthy, happy baby with semi-sweet chocolate colored flesh, big black cow eyes and two deep dimples that sunk in his chubby cheeks whenever he laughed, which was often.

Mr. Tucker was proud as a peacock with the birth of this boy. True to his promise, he *retired* from the Mill completely, leaving his buisness in the more than capable hands of my parents and accepting whatever monies they sent north as absolutely fair and correct. He could have done that all along. My folks never needed his long-distance supervision and they would only be fair and correct with his finances. It's how they turned every leaf of their life. But truth be told, Mr. Tucker didn't want to feel unnecessary so he'd call them all the time and make little trips to *check on things*. Now he said he needed to retire to *rear his boy*. He was eager to pass on what he considered to be his great wealth of knowledge.

The only grudge I could tell Mr. Tucker held against me was that he expected this child to be a junior. I told the hospital to put "Dunbar" on his birth certificate and so saved him from the moniker "Mr. Tucker II".

Dunbar flunked the paper bag test, but his midnight hue didn't bother Mr. Tucker at all. It was further proof to the world that, "That boy is my spit!"

"He looks more like Ola than anybody right now," I'd counter, but it fell on deaf ears.

Christening my boy Dunbar didn't stop Mr. Tucker from calling him *Junior*. I had to fight in order to get to spend any time with my youngest baby. It was always, "Ah'll bathe junior!" or "Ah'll watch junior!" He never said, but I know he would have nursed Dunbar, too, if he could have.

In fact, one day he brought home a *gift* (his words) for me. "Surprise!!" He beamed.

It was a breast pump!

I thought, if he thinks I'm going to pump the milk from my breasts so that *he* can feed my son, he was dumber than dumb and I told him so.

"Princess, I jes thought… well, y'know sometime junior git hongry when we out..."

"You need to stop taking him out so much! I will not be pumping my milk to give you even *MORE* time with him!"

"That's not..."

"Give him to me...NOW!"

Mr. Tucker handed him over with a trembling bottom lip, so intense was his effort not to balk. You'd think Dunbar was his good luck charm or favorite toy, or his security blanket.

Actually, in a way he was Tucker's *social* security blanket. Everything Mr. Tucker lacked himself, he'd point out as one of the baby's attributes that, "He got from me!"

Dunbar didn't get anything from Mr. Tucker and saying it wouldn't make it so. But saying it, made old Luthern Tucker walk, talk and feel younger. It was like Miss Mildred had said, just associating with youth gave old tired bones a lift. What was tedious or draining for a younger person reinvigorated Mr. Tucker. He was jumping on that second chance mama said a son would make him feel he got.

Mr. Tucker wanted to go everywhere with the children and me now. Everyone clearly knew this was just because of little Dunbar. Nobody ever saw him at church before, or at the Learning Clinics, or at any of the Youth outings. But now, you couldn't beat him back with a stick.

I got tired of his monopolizing all of Dunbar's time. I never planned to share my daily church time and space with Mr. Tucker. It had to stop. To do that, one day I challenged him.

"Mr. Tucker, can you read?"

"Why you axe me somethin like that?"

"Because I want to know. *Can you?*"

"What differnce do that make?"

"You've been spending so much time in the Learning Clinic lately, I figure you need to be teaching or learning. Helping someone else, or helping yourself. When you come over this afternoon, be ready to do one or the other."

"I come to he'p out with junior!" He sounded flustered.

"Dunbar is fine *alone* with me. I'm teaching him his ABC's and his numbers, like I did his sisters. You see how smart they are. I don't go to the barbershop or the numbers hole or wherever else you take him when you go out, and I will *not* have you moving in on my time with him. So if you come to the Clinic today, be ready to teach, or be ready to learn."

I never saw him read anything and figured if he could, he more than likely didn't do it well. His pride would keep him from trying to improve in a place where everyone who knew him assumed he was highly educated already and looked up to him for the money he's made.

Thank God, it worked.

As soon as I pried Mr. Tucker away from Dunbar's every waking moment, here come Harriet and Ola to take their daddy's place. They were crazy about their handsome little brother. Ola was the worst. I understood. She seemed to feel vindicated through him. Mr. Tucker had given her a color complex with his paper bag test. He never said anything directly to her. But she'd heard him mention skin color more than once regarding other people, back in Smedley mostly, when she was more often in his company. I don't think he even realizes how aware and affected she is by some of his stupid off-handed comments. But now, everyone agrees that Dunbar is the beginning and the end of gorgeous and everyone agrees that Dunbar looks like Ola the most (except for Mr. Tucker who claims "Junior is my spit!"). Therefore, everyone must also agree, even if only to themselves, that Ola is also the beginning and the end of gorgeous.

Dunbar raises her self-esteem, self-appreciation and self-worth in a way no one else ever could. Heaven knows I've tried.

So, it's only when the girls are in school that I get to have my son all to myself. His sisters are together with him at the learning clinics and on some church trips. Mr. Tucker takes him Lord-knows-where in the early evenings and most weekends. It wasn't an ideal arrangement, but you take what you can get, for now.

forty-two

Against all odds, Dunbar was growing into quite an unspoiled and precocious little man. I know Mr. Tucker wanted to be his hero, but he wasn't at all. Dunbar indulged his activities with tolerance and understanding. That was about it. Dunbar liked everybody so I think he liked him, but I don't think he liked Mr. Tucker as much as I did at his age. He didn't see him as his personal Santa Claus because everybody gave him everything. His being precocious - barring accidents, illnesses or undetected birth defects - was unavoidable. I began teaching him the alphabet and numbers when he was weeks old. He started reading when he was two-years-old. The pre-school suggested that I enroll him into primary school at four, but Columbia Elementary adamantly required that he be five-years-old. Then about three weeks into kindergarten, they skipped him to the first grade. As a matter of fact, the most amazing thing about him was how unspoiled he remained in spite of how willingly everyone doted on him.

If he had a hero, it was Doc. He taught him that everything was connected in the universe and that for every action there was a reaction. He gave Dunbar a view of the world under the microscope and compared the lives of amoebas to ours when espied from God's point of view. For this reason I think, Dunbar appreciated the importance of everyone and everything, seeing nothing and no one as greater or less than anything or anyone. He seemed to understand and look for the subtext in different levels of living. It made him wise beyond his years, deep and introspective, thoughtful and sometimes provocative for a five- year-old. He was a miracle to call son and a joy to call friend.

****

Harriet married right out of high school. She was eighteen. Her husband was a twenty-two year old graduate student from John Marshall Law School. She'd met him at Cory Methodist Church when Malcolm X gave his famous *Ballot or the Bullet* speech. She's a Muslim convert and I expect they'll start adding to their little family directly.

I am truly happy for them. I hope they stay in love and stay together, against the many statistics that maintain they probably won't. But most of all, I wish they had waited. Harriet was too young. They both were.

I tried to get her to postpone her nuptials for a year or so, but they were too caught up with romantic notions of love and lust.

They had a small, elegant African ceremony in our livingroom. Dunbar made a dashing ring bearer in his little tux and tails with kinte cumberband and bowtie. Ola was a striking beauty in her African wrap dress and gelee, the colorful print reflecting her warm mahogany hue eclipsed the splendor of her sister-bride. I could tell by the moony look in Ola's eyes that she could hardly wait for her turn to stroll down the aisle.

Society insinuates that a woman isn't much without a man. I never taught my daughters that and have tried to make my life an example to the contrary, but they seem to have fallen prey to that popular dictate. So, I said what I could to the newlyweds, *Congratulations* and *As Salaam Aleikum*, then gave my fears and regrets to God.

My daughters are young women, free to pick and choose their life journeys. If I am disappointed by any of their choices, I hope the disappointment is mine alone.

On the other hand, there is solace in the plans I've made that will make life different for my little Prince, Dunbar.

OLA

forty-three

Her name is Ola Tucker, but she always felt like a Nelson... as in Ozzie and Harriet. The fact that her sister's name *was* Harriet just served to strengthen her identification with that perfect, white, upper middle-class, Hollywood American family.

Although The Tuckers lived in the "ghetto", Wade Park and its immediate neighboring streets remained untouched by the storm of summer riots that marred so much of Cleveland's Glenville area in 1966 and '67. The peaceful Civil Rights demonstrations launched by the Southern Christian Leadership Conference led by Dr. Martin Luther King, Jr. had been met with violent resistance by the local authorities throughout the country for years. Young impatient urban protesters ran out of cheeks to turn, having only the two to start, and for the past two summers embraced the edicts of their more aggressive leaders. They started tearing down social and economic barriers everywhere, *By Any Means Necessary*, that meant *Burn Baby, Burn!*

Now in 1968, after the recent assassinations of Dr. King April 4th in Memphis and Bobby Kennedy June 5th in Los Angeles, 105th Street, was again poised and ready to host The National Guard tanks. They would keep nightly patrols to enforce an eight p.m. curfew for all but a few with jobs or emergencies.

But the spacious abodes and landscaped yards of Ola's street had nothing to do with the fright and flight circling all around them. Her beloved Culture Gardens were even insulated against the Civil Rights protests and uprisings, until those nights when vandals tarred the sculptured busts of European artists. That was an act Ola secretly felt was pure and poignant since the demands were that the rights of America's black citizenry finally be acknowledged and instituted as promised by the Constitution. So far no blacks, not even Cleveland's own elite, rated recognition in those public gardens or in the museums she loved to frequent.

All of that aside, Ola felt like one of the television Nelson's because her family was like no other real-life family she'd ever known.

Her mother was young, petite and beautiful. All of her friend's pretty mothers looked older than her mom. Alice Tucker was talented in a variety of areas, but she never had to work a day in her life outside of the home. Her friend's mothers usually worked at leas*t one job* and blamed their miserable housecleaning or lack of cooking on working so much. Ola's mother kept their home economically yet richly decorated, and so clean you could eat off any floor. Her mother made sumptuous meals with only the freshest ingredients. She even baked all of their breads. Her friends regularly dined on canned, frozen, leftover or take-out foods. Ola and her sister and brother were always immaculate in the latest fashions, bell-bottoms, hot pants, tie-dyed dresses and tops. It certainly helped that her mom could sew like a tailor, but what she didn't make, she cheerfully bought. Her mother helped them with their homework and Ola knew for sure that a lot of her classmate's parents could barely read or write. And Ola's mother never discriminated when it came to her children and their friend's, she treated all of them like they were her own.

Ola wanted to continue the fairy-tale lifestyle her parents created for her. She wanted to be like her mother and marry a man just like her father because in Ola's mind, they were perfectly matched.

Her father was a distinguished, older, gentle man who, like Ozzie Nelson, never worked a job. Huge profits were sent to him from a lumber mill he owned down south that her grandparents managed.

Luthern Tucker used to dote on his daughters, well Harriet at least, which used to make Ola jealous and proned to cruel and petty revenges. But ever since Dunbar was born, old L.T. mostly ignored his girls, which was right in Ola's mind because boys were always the favored children of men. Everyone knew that! The sons would carry the family name through generations so it only made sense. Plus, Dunbar came along twelve years after her, so he was pampered and spoiled by everyone in the house, whenever they could get him past his father. It was an unspoken familial fact that Dunbar was to be affectionately ruined.

The most remarkable thing to Ola about her parents was that they never argued... *NEVER*! Her friend's parents, even the happiest couples, could be heard having heated discussions over some disagreement from time to time during her visits. Some even went so far as to curse or physically fight one another, the homes that still had two parents in them. More than a few of her friends had parents that lived apart either from divorce or abandonment, usually by the father.

Ola could tell her mother and father didn't always agree, but neither disagreements nor their resolutions were ever expressed in words. It was often just a look or the crooking of a brow or the raising of a finger that served to call attention to and correct some small offense. And since it was usually her mother quietly admonishing her father, and because he *always* deferred to his wife, Ola thought her father to be a gentle man. She hoped to marry a gentle, giving man like her father, but she strove to model herself in the image of her strong, silent mother.

That's why Ola volunteered to cook and clean and sew and garden. She learned how to determine the best produce by smelling for the sugar-rich aromas in ripened fruits, to search for the deep green-purple coloring on the healthiest brocolli stalks and asparagus tips, and to gauge the freshness of fish by the clarity and color of their dead eyes. She learned how to shop for weekly promotional bargains offered at the big chain grocery stores and how to always buy certain necessities, like toilet paper and soap, during huge sales. Because everyone always uses them, they are rarely overstocked. She canned and pickled foods, redecorated rooms with tossed furnishings she found and refinished or repaired, and sewed a closetful of "new" garments from refashioning her old discardable things. Ola learned every conceivable craft, trying to force her mother's image on herself. Her deep ebony complexion was her complex and she just knew that her skin would always work against her, even though black was now officially beautiful if you listened to James Brown. And lots of people must have believed him because they kept his hit single, "Say it Loud, I'm Black and I'm Proud," pumping from WJMO and WABQ, the black radio stations.

But none of this hard work would mean anything unless she found herself a man... preferably a wise, rich, older, light-skinned (for their children's sake) man. He would recognize and appreciate Ola's home economist talents and would marry her and maintain for her a lifestyle similar to her mother's.

Harriet had already married a man with great husband potential. She was working now, but not for long. Abdullah Latif was working part-time and studying to be a lawyer. He wasn't old or rich, but he was very smart and made all the right promises of providing future wealth and leisure for his young wife.

Her mother didn't approve. She thought Harriet had wed too young. But, Ola thought, Harriet was *eighteen*! She was a high school graduate who'd only wanted what Ola wants, what Alice Tucker has; a cushy comfortable life provided by a man with whom you never argue because he always defers to you, as befits a queen.

But then again, Harriet was light-skinned like her mother. She never worked hard to improve herself because, Ola reasoned, she didn't have to. Harriet's color was sunny and acceptable. She met and married her pretty, promising, Nation of Islam man without any seeming effort at all, but that was the hand life had dealt her. Being sun-kissed like her father, Ola felt she always had something to prove, little to expect and everything to be grateful for from whoever gave her the time of day. Those were the cards she was dealt from life's deck and she would just have to graciously work them the best way she knew how.

Ola's boyfriend, Aldo, wasn't always kind or thoughtful. Actually he *never* was. He was lazy and soft, about three pounds shy of fat. He was not old, but a prematurely receding hairline made him look it. He was also unemployed, unambitious and slow. Okay, stupid is more like it. But his skin was lighter than a paperbag, which was important to her father and her. In fact, he was bright enough to carry the coveted nicknames of

Yellowman and Redbone. His eyes were gray and the thin, wavy locks scantily adorning his scalp were considered *good*. These were the premiums that made Aldo such *a catch* in her mind... and in his. So, even though he didn't recognize Ola for her beauty, wit or talents, after investing nineteen months she was determined, God Willing, to have him.

****

Following her high school graduation, Ola was floating down the street idly wondering what to do with the rest of her life. She didn't want to get a job because she had no real desire to ever join the workforce. She planned to be a housewife, a mother, and a homemaker. But Aldo had not as yet proposed. The only other viable alternative to her seemed to be college, which may pose a different problem.

Ever since a few A & T University students staged a peaceful sit-in in North Carolina, student Civil Rights efforts have become more aggressive and government retribution has been increasingly and disproportionately brutal. February 8th earlier this year, 1968, the National Guard and the local police in Orangeburge, South Carolina killed three and wounded three hundred unarmed students on the campus of South Carolina State University.

So Ola thought her parents might worry if she suddenly announced plans to attend college. Then again, northern universities were much less volatile in these tumultuous times and there were plenty of colleges in and around Cleveland, plus because she was reasonably certain that eventually Aldo would ask her to marry him, she didn't want to venture too far away lest distance cause her to lose him. She weighed the pluses and minuses of Cleveland State against Case Western Reserve, Kent State, Oberlin and a handful of other schools in the immediate area. Two schools sounded flexible and open to unrestricted opportunities to Ola. Cleveland State because of its newness, having just opened in 1965, was bound to be progressive. And Oberlin College, founded by abolitionists, was the nation's first experiment in racially integrated coeducation maintains an unorthodoxed curriculum. This is what was on her mind as she after graduation.

Rounding the corner to her block, she noted a minivan in front of the house. The handsome doctor from the learning clinic was rearranging cardboard boxes and vaguely familiar suitcases and paraphernalia in the back. Soon after, her mother came out of the front door with a suitcase and Dunbar, struggling with his own large box of toys.

Her father stood mute and idle in the middle of the frontyard, bent slightly forward with his hands jammed into his pockets, staring dazedly ahead. He looked small, old, lost and worthless, like an ancient, over-sized lawn jockey. It was a disturbing picture. As she approached, Ola felt an unnamed dread flood the pit of her gut causing her stomach to flip-flop and her bowels to churn.

Despite not wanting to know, she heard herself ask, "Mama, what's going on?"

"Ola! Oh good, you made it back. I left a note for you inside. I'm leaving Mr. Tucker. I'm going to marry Doc," she glowed. "He is the love of my life. Dunbar is going with us because among many things, he is still a minor that I am responsible for. We're moving to Arizona. I left the number and address for you. Come kiss your brother and me goodbye."

She was radiant. Ola had never seen her mother look so young and vibrant. Doc was classically tall, dark and handsome, but so what? This was wrong! Her mother was throwing everything away for a pretty face? When did she become so shallow and frivolous? Did she say, *The love of her life*? How long and how well does she know him beyond the Learning Clinic? What about daddy? And what about her?

After a long and confusing silence, the most disturbing thing about this bad, new situation surfaced. It was all she could do to condense her fear, pain and anger into one simple heart-of-the-matter query without crying.

With panicked indignation Ola asked, "What about me?"

"What about you?" Her mother asked, bright and happy.

"*Mama*, I just graduated from high school!" Ola said as though *that* explained everything.

"That's good Ola. What do you want to do?"

"I was thinking I might go to college."

"That'd be fine. You can go to college if you want."

"But mama," Ola figured she had to say something to put things into perspective. "I'm eighteen!"

"That's right, you're eighteen. You're a high school graduate. You're a woman now, Ola. You're free to do whatever you want to do. You can go to college, or you can get a job, or whatever. You are grown. Do whatever you like."

Her mother made eighteen sound old and wise. But eighteen is still a teen. It's insecure, inarticulate, unfocused, inexperienced and usually finds the limitless options of life overwhelming and scary. Ola's abbreviated explanation for all that was to repeat...

"Mama,... I'm *eighteen!*"

"That's right, you're eighteen. You are three years older than I was when I was forced to marry Mr. Tucker. But I'm not forcing you to do anything. You are free to go to college, go to work, or to even join us if you like. You decide and enjoy choosing.

"I am thirty-five years old and I have never lived any of my dreams... until now. I am leaving Mr. Tucker. I am going to marry Doc. I am taking your brother with me. These are *my* choices. I know I'm going to enjoy them," she said with a starry-eyed grin to the doctor.

Alice Tucker couldn't wait for her youngest daughter to gather her senses and kiss them good-bye. So, she wrapped one arm around Ola's waist and brought her over to the van to get a hug and kiss from her brother and a firm but friendly handshake from the doctor. Then she led her back to the sidewalk in front of the house. She gave Ola a kiss, a bear hug, and a promise to keep in touch before getting in the van like Cinderella entering her pumpkin carriage to be whisked away to happily ever after.

****

Ola walked in a fog after that. Up until that point, life seemed pretty set for the members of The Tucker household. Now, Ola found herself questioning and reassessing everything she thought she'd known.

If *her* mother, the tranquil model of a content and comfortably provided for woman, a position to which her daughters fervently yearned and aspired, could so easily abdicate her position as the fairy-tale matriarch, then what was *that* to yearn for and aspire to be? Did her mother really say, *You are three years older than I was when I was forced to marry Mr. Tucker!*? *Forced* to marry... at *fifteen*?! Who forced her? Grandpa Nate and Grandma Grace? The coolest, nicest grandparents she could image, still running the mill from which all of her family's worldly possessions flowed? Could they have done that?

Her father was no help. He'd quickly aged and shrunk in the weeks immediately following his wife's absence. Always a quiet man, he continued his customary taciturn references to Ola; *Mornin, Evenin, Pass the rice, please, Thanky.* Even though she'd assumed all the tasks of her mother in running the home, including shopping, cooking, and cleaning without complaint, they had grown no closer. In fact, Ola felt more and more that she was in the way. The few times she had tried to question her father, he grunted some vague disapproval, silently rose and walked away, thickening the fog of confusion that enveloped her.

But as some things became cloudy, others became abundantly clear and she thanked her mother for opening her eyes to finally *see* Aldo.

After her mother left, Ola thought she needed a hand to hold, a shoulder to lean on or some tender, whispered reassurances to keep her from falling apart. Standing on the curb in her frontyard she watched the van roll down the street, make a left turn onto 105th and disappear. Then she turned to her father, the huge, empty shell ornament decorating the yard. She didn't think she could expect much comfort from him right then, so she ran inside to call Aldo.

On her bed was an envelope addressed to her in her mother's neat handwriting. She opened it and read:

Dear Ola,

I know that after today you will be confused, hurt and maybe even a little angry for quite awhile. But I have faith that in time you will understand and appreciate, if not agree with, the difficult decision I made to end the many sadnesses in my heart. As your mother and your friend, I will always love you and be in your life as much as you want and allow me to be. I will be there to help you with any and every obstacle and difficulty you may face. You are a brilliant, brave and beautiful young lady. You deserve the best that life has to offer. I'm leaving you with a brief list of "Life's Don'ts" to help you understand and avoid some of the pitfalls I am only learning now how to handle: Don't sell yourself short. Don't compromise. Don't settle for less in love ever. Don't settle for less in any other part of your life when it's not necessary. Whenever you get the notion, don't hesitate to call me collect, write, visit or relocate to 123 Arbo Blvd. Scottsdale, Arizona 555-6768. God bless and keep you forever. Love, Mama.

Ola wanted her mother beside her on the bed right then, to calm the rage of emotions making her feel so helpless. "*I will be there to help you with any and every obstacle and difficulty you may face.*" HA! Her mother was the reason she was in this quandary, and her father had problems of his own. So, she called Aldo.

"Hey li'l mama. What's happenin'?"

"Oh Aldo, I don't know. My mother just left my dad for this young guy and she took my brother with them! She left me a note, but it doesn't explain anything. I don't know what to do!"

"You gimme a call if you think I can help."

"Well... that's... why I'm calling you... now, Aldo."

"Oh. So what'chu want me t'do?"

"I don't know... I've never been in a situation like this before."

"Well neither have I, you know. I'm a busy man, I can't be wasting my time. You figure out what'chu want me to do and if I can, I'll help you. But don't be wasting my time, babes, okay?" Aldo sounded perturbed.

Ola was shocked. She knew Aldo had never been particularly sensitive to her wants and needs in the past, but those were usually little requests of hers. Like, would he go with her to the movies ("Your treat, sweet cheeks. *You* asking *me* remember."), or would he escort her to the prom ("If your pops'll spring for my tux and a car. He got big bucks, babes. I'm low man on the totem pole.") It suddenly occurred to her that Aldo *never invited her out anywhere* except to make-out in the backseat of his brother's car at an occasional drive-in movie or to make-out in the woods in Garfield Park. He was a selfish, stingy, boring jerk. But what shocked her right now is that she never realized that before.

Now he wanted *her* to figure out what *she* should be doing about her problems. If she could do *that*, she wouldn't have *called him*! What a stupid jerk! She thought. What a stupid jerk I've been! Well no more.

"No Aldo, we don't want to waste your *time*. Goodbye," Ola said right before hanging up.

That lazy little doughboy wasn't busy, she thought. He never does *anything*. He wasn't in school, he had no job and he wasn't looking for one. She decided not to ever call him again, then see how long it took before they spoke or saw one another. Never would be too soon.

forty-four

Her SAT's weren't high enough to win her a scholarship or significant grant, so Ola got a job. She'd put in applications at a few places and accepted an offer from the telephone company because they had an employee college reimbursement program that would provide her with free college courses, as long as she passed.

Ola stopped trying to communicate with her father. She wasn't any less concerned about him, just tired of beating her head against a brick wall. She continued to cook and clean, doing all of the chores her mother once did, but she didn't extend herself socially to her father beyond the usual mechanical salutations during certain periods of the day; good morning, afternoon, goodnight. If he wanted to crawl up in a shell to lick his unmending wounds, fine but she wasn't going to stick around to watch. She was saving her money to move out. Her father didn't charge her, but she paid rent every month anyway. She put the approximate amount she thought she'd have to pay for rent, utilities and food, into a savings account that she never touched or even thought about. She squirreled that away, creating a healthy nest egg for herself. It was a good habit to begin now, so that it wouldn't be such a shock to her budget when she'd really have to do it.

Her father's lack of attention and appreciation made her feel helpless, hopeless and worthless. Nowadays, she only felt good *outside* of her father's household. It was the promise of possible happiness somewhere out in the wide world that kept her poised for flight.

                              ****

After more than a year at work, Ola got a strangely familiar phone call one Saturday afternoon.

"Sweet cheeks, what's happening?" Aldo wanted to know.

Her surprise was pure. She was caught entirely off guard, not happily nor angrily. She hadn't planned what she would say if this ever happened because after the first seven months, she was sure this call would never come. But here it was and she had no idea what to say. So she opened her mouth and trusted it to say something halfway intelligent of it's own volition.

She was absolutely delighted when she heard herself ask, "I'm sorry, you are...?"

After a long silence, the answer was a timid little, "Aldo."

"Aldo...Aldo...Aldo...," she mumbled.

"Aldo... McKenzie," he hesitantly added.

"Aldo...McKenzie!" Ola loved the lofty assurance in her voice that she'd never heard or felt there before. There was also a subtle touch of condescension that made her positively tingle when repeating *Aldo*, as though she knew a ton of Aldo's and needed the surname to know exactly which Aldo this one was. She was suddenly two people, her autonomous and unpredictable talking voice, and the real, silent Ola who was quickly becoming overwhelmed with hilarious images of how she once pampered and doted on this worthless, not-such-a-pretty-boy simpleton.

"How have you been, Aldo?" Barely able to contain the bubbling laughter in her voice made the inquiry sound enthusiastic.

"Fine, baby cakes. I'm *fine!*" Hearing what he mistook for eagerness, he continued with his old cockiness from their relationship a year earlier. "Calling to see if you wanna ride with me up to Garfield Park a little later on?"

"Oh, wow," she feigned disappointment, "another time maybe." When hell freezes over, she thought. "You just caught me in the middle of packing."

"Packing? You going somewhere?"

She had no idea what made her say that, but her alter ego, *The Mouth,* apparently did because it never hesitated, "Yeah. I'm gonna go visit my mother for a couple of weeks in Phoenix."

"Oh good. So y'all patched up that little misunderstanding awhile back, eh?"

"We're right as rain. Thanks for asking," Ola heard herself say. "Omigosh, look at the time! I gotta go. Take care of yourself, Aldo. Stay in touch."

Before he could say another word, and without saying goodbye, Ola hung up.

A few moments after digesting what had just happened, she popped up from the couch she'd been reclining on in the den watching television, and began doing a little nonsensical victory dance. She felt so light and free and kept running over and over again in her head, the music of their dialogue. When he spoke in her mind, she'd sway, strut or sashay around the room. But for her answers, she would twirl, kick, jerk, leap into the air or freeze dramatically. She felt so spontaneous and elegant that she thought maybe she'd become a choreographer.

Hey sweet cheeks (sway) I'm sorry (twirl) You are...? (freeze) Going somewhere? (sashay) Yeah... Phoenix (kick, kick, leap). She danced that dialogue over and over with different movements each time. Soon, the den alone could no longer handle her solo performance and she went lunging and strolling, spinning and strutting through the diningroom, the livingroom, all around downstairs. She wound up in the kitchen exhausted and slumped in a chair with a glass of juice at the breakfast table when it hit her... it's not a bad idea.

Ola didn't call her mother often and never spoke that long, but her mother always accepted her collect calls and usually ended their talks with, "When are you coming out here?" She thought her mother was being polite and that the inquiry was not a real invitation. But now Ola had two weeks paid vacation coming to her from work and she had saved

251

up a little money aside from the rent and utilities she paid to herself each month, maybe enough for a plane ticket and a few sight-seeing excursions. She'd never flown before. The prospect of her first flight was exciting. The whole idea was exciting! She wondered if two weeks would be too long... or not long enough. She knew her father could do without her. He barely seemed to notice she was even still here. If her mother was willing, she decided she would do it!

Caught up in the moment, she wanted to call her mother right then, but what would she say? Plus today was Saturday. She never called on Saturday. Would her mother be alarmed or concerned... would she even be there? Ola gave it all a lot of thought.

She never asked about her mother's second husband. He was some kind of research doctor whose work took him to conferences around the world and her mother often accompanied him. This is how her mom discovered that she *loved* to travel. So much so that sometimes she'd stay away longer than the doctor after a business trip, if she hadn't explored the place quite enough, and sometimes she made short trips alone. Ola didn't ask about him, not only because their sudden marriage still confused her, but because she didn't know what to call him. Her mother never brought him up, Ola thought possibly out of respect for *her* feelings, which was okay, but it didn't help her to know what she should be calling him. The dilemma of his name was not such a big deal before, but if she's going to be staying in the man's house on vacation, she should call him *something*. She decided she might continue to call him Doctor if anything, not only because that's how he had been addressed at the learning clinic at church, but because that is probably how formal her mother was with him. She always called daddy *Mr. Tucker*.

Ola felt odd about Dunbar, too, because their relationship was forced into a separation that he seemed to have perfectly adjusted to. When Dunbar spoke with her, it was about his new friends, or the sports he played or school activites. And he often cut their conversations short to run off to some pressing engagement. She didn't want to bring Dunbar's spirits down with her melancholy moods, so when they spoke she kept it light and upbeat. But since she wasn't asking anything she really wanted to know or cared about, she felt pretentious and false. Maybe a visit would bring them closer together. Or maybe it would confirm her fear that they've grown irrevocably apart.

Maybe this was a bad idea, she thought.

Then she thought again immediately changing her mind, maybe you think too much. Call first and figure it out later.

"Collect call to anyone from Ola Tucker, will you accept?" She heard the operator ask.

"Certainly!" She heard her mother's customary happy response.

"Hi mama."

"Ola, what a nice surprise! I'm used to you calling on Sunday's. How are you, baby?"

"Fine. Are you planning on taking a trip anytime soon?"

"We'll be going to Singapore the end of next month on a business trip. Why? You wanna come out here?"

"Yeah, I was thinking about it."

"Wonderful! I hope it's real soon. I think you'd like the fund raising parties coming up. What size do you wear?"

"Huh?"

"What size dress do you wear? Two of these functions are formal. If you can't wear something of mine, we'll need to go shopping."

"I don't have a lot of money to..."

"Of course you don't, baby! I wasn't suggesting you buy anything. It's on me! Forget about clothes, just come. Come as soon as you can. As a matter of fact, you make the reservations and I'll buy the ticket. It'll be waiting for you at the airport. We are going to have so much fun! Make those reservations right away, okay... or would you prefer I make them?"

Ola was stunned and more than a little disbelieving that it had been so easy. For a moment she couldn't speak.

"Hello? Ola?"

"I'm here. I'll make 'em...I'll make the reservations."

"Okay. Try to get them for the middle of next week at the latest, if you can. But *anytime* you come will be fine. If you have any problems, call me. And don't forget, I'm paying for it on this end, so you've got to call me with the details as soon as you get them, okay?"

"Okay," Ola paused, then said, "There's one other thing, what should I call... your husband?"

"Well, you used to always call him Doc. You can call him... Doc," her mother said brightly then added, still warm but more soberly, "In time, maybe you'll call him dad."

"Doc it is," Ola quickly interjected.

"Good. Don't forget to call me with your flight info."

"Okay, mama. Thanks."

"You are most welcome. Thank *you*! You've given me something so nice to look forward to. Talk to you later. Love you. See you soon."

****

After her initial shock, Ola got out the Yellow Pages searching for the nearest travel agency. She found one close to downtown, but they said she had to buy the ticket from them if they wrote up the ticket. She didn't understand the business about the commissions they got from the tickets they issued. She was nineteen and didn't understand a lot of things about a lot of things, so she called her sister.

"Oooo, girl I wish I was going with you!" Harriet sounded happy for her sister.

"I'm still trying to figure out how I'm going," Ola said. "Mama said to make the reservations and she would pay for them, but the travel agency said I had to buy them from here."

"Just call the airline direct and make a reservation. Mama can call in your confirmation number and pay for it on her end."

"I thought you buy the airline ticket through a travel agency."

"*They* can get you the ticket that way, or *you* can get it yourself. Go get the Yellow Pages, I'll wait," she told her sister. When Ola returned, Harriet told her to go to the Airlines Section and start calling all the major airlines for direct flights to Scottsdale or the closest city to it in Arizona.

"Tell them you're flying 'coach'. Call them all because they have different fares and you want the cheapest one. After you make the reservation, they'll ask how you wanna pay for it. Tell them your mother is gonna call back from Arizona and buy it for you and that you'll pick it up at the airport."

"Thanks Harri. How's the baby?"

"Be glad you don't have one yet. Now, I know what mama meant about rushing things. Enjoy your freedom, O."

"You make it sound bad."

"Sorry, I didn't mean to. The baby is beautiful. I love her to death and Abdullah, too. But if I had it to do all over again, I wouldn't. At least not so soon. I'd live a little first. Meet more people. See more of the world. Maybe go to Scottsdale with you and meet mama's new man."

"I wish I had somebody that loved me enough to want to spend their life with me." Ola wistfully mused.

"Yeah, we both wanted mommy's life remember? And the first thing she did when she could was dump it like a dead weight! Life is too beautiful and brief to waste any of it. I'm not saying my family is a waste, but they are a lot of work and sometimes I wanna play.

"You're about to take a vacation, O. I never had one of those, and right now I can't *imagine ever having one.* That was my choice and I'll deal with it. But if I ever get another chance, I'm gonna play."

Life was always easy for Harriet, Ola thought. She never had to work to get the attention of boys, so she doesn't appreciate her blessings like she should. She takes things for granted. And now that she has to work the tee-ni-niest little bit, she's grumbling and crying about wanting to *play.* Ola knew from experience that there was nothing she could say to make Harriet more understanding or accepting of the charmed life she leads. Here was the same brick wall they often hit ending many a conversation.

"Thanks for helping me with the flight, Harri. I'll talk to you later, bye."

forty-five

Harriet offered to give her a lift to the airport, but Ola said she'd take the Rapid Transit after work on Tuesday. It would be rush hour and she wisely figured the train would be her quickest, easiest ride. Just last year, 1968, Cleveland opened the first rapid transit in the country to connect a downtown business district with a major airport.

Ola kept waiting for some unforeseen catastrophe to stop her plans. But she had no problem getting the days off that she wanted though she gave virtually no notice. She got the train to the plane and was at the airport over an hour before her scheduled flight. Her pre-paid ticket was waiting for her at the ticket counter. After checking her one large piece of luggage, she sat stirring the coffee she'd ordered but didn't want in a booth of a lounge waiting for her flight to board.

Ola worried about her father. He had been quiet and moody ever since her mother left, but after great effort, she was hard pressed to remember him being any other way... ever. He was always a quiet man. But now she interpreted his silence as brooding because he looked so little and lost, whereas before he seemed so comfortable and confident.

She didn't tell him that she was going to visit her mother, or even that she was going to Arizona. She would have, had he asked, but he didn't. She said, "Daddy, I'm gonna go away on vacation for two weeks. You wanna come go with me?"

She didn't really want him to come, or expect him to say yes. She only asked to be polite. But had he expressed any interest at all, she would have changed her plans immediately, just to see him perk up if only for a minute.

But his absent-minded response was, "No... no." She wasn't even sure if he'd heard her correctly until he added, like an afterthought, "Enjoy yerse'f."

****

The flight was nearly empty, so she got a chance to kick off her shoes and stretch all the way out, which was probably as perfect as a first flight could be. She was also scared to death so she threw an extra blanket over her head. Turbulence created sudden rises and dips, as though the air mirrored the earth with invisible hills and valleys that planes rode like cars. And like the earth, the sky roads had pits and potholes that caused the plane to sometimes bump bump bump along in all too frequent and frightening successions.

Ola stretched out with a blanket over her head and another covering her feet and prayed that they'd soon touchdown on solid ground. But in the meantime she diverted her fears with pleasant thoughts of yesteryear.

She remembered the impeccable home, healthy meals and rich wardrobes her mother created and kept on a shoestring budget. Alice Tucker sitting calm, quiet and serene like a Madonna. Luthern Tucker, the strong, silent guiding force in the family's life. Paving the way for their every need.

Why did mama have to mess things up? How could she just walk away from daddy like that when he always provided? What was missing in that marriage for her? What is so great about this one? Was she just feeling restless one day like Harriet, and decided to go play! I bet daddy would've taken her to Singapore if she had told him that's somewhere she'd like to go.

"Excuse me...?" A tentative voice softly interrupted.

Ola peeked out from under the blanket just when the plane began to rock and roll.

"Would you like steak, chicken or fish for dinner?"

Ola tried to look at the stewardess, but her eyes kept darting involuntarily just beyond her whenever the plane shook.

"Air pockets. They can be scary, but it's really quite safe," the attendant reassured her.

"I'm sorry," Ola tried to calm down, "you were saying...?"

"Steak, chicken or fish."

"How much is the steak?"

"It's included in your flight." She managed to make the question sound like a normal mistake, instead of something really stupid. Then she added brightly, "The steak is really good."

"Okay, I'll try the steak, thanks."

****

It was pretty good, but she could only eat a little bit. Her stomach was reeling from both the ride and anticipating this half-family reunion. The closer she got to Scottsdale, the more agitated her indigestion became.

Then she arrived.

forty-six

Her mother was beautiful standing by the gate when her flight disembarked. It had been announced that the temperature was 101 degrees, but Alice looked as crisp and cool as the cucumber green linen slack suit she wore. Seeing her mommy for the first time in over a year, Ola realized how much she had missed her, and saw in her mother's eyes how much she had been missed. They hugged for about five minutes before going to claim her bag.

"You hungry?" Her mother asked at the luggage carousel.

"I ate on the plane."

"Yeah, but they only give you snack-sized portions."

"Well, I could eat a little something. My stomach kinda flipped everytime the plane flopped."

"Good," Alice said hugging Ola, then reached to take her bag from her. They eventually settled on sharing the load, a strap apiece.

****

Dunbar was playing tennis-for-tots with some neighbor friends and Doc was at work, so they had time to catch up over tuna/apple salad on toasted pumpernickel bagels.

Ola was looking through a family photo album feeling pretty eerie since it had no pictures of her daddy and only a few of Harriet and her — when they were babies, as high school graduates and Harriet's wedding. On the other hand, Dunbar was on practically every page. Ordinary acts immortalized forever in seemingly thousands of snapshots: Dunbar bowling, fishing, skiing, eating a peach, drinking lemonade, at a birthday party, on the beach, from close-up and at a distance, sometimes alone, sometimes with the doctor, a few shots with all three of them. Her mother, no doubt, was the photgrapher and so she was in very few.

It struck Ola, who'd always thought Dunbar was her twin, how much he resembled the doctor, especially the older he got. Particularly in one close-up shot of Dunbar sitting in a park swing with the doctor behind him, bending down to make their faces level. They were looking straight into the camera wearing identical grins. The color of their skin, the size, shape and slant of their eyes, the flare of their nostrils, the high sharp ledges of bones for cheeks that sheltered deep dimples. These two men, the young and the old, were unmistakable clones.

While Ola puzzled what this could mean, she was startled back to the present by a sudden, loud burst of noise coming from the kitchen where she'd left her mother making dinner rolls.

"Mama?" Ola set the photo album down and called to her mother.

She was answered with another loud, staccato burst of noise. Alarmed, she jumped up and rushed into the kitchen.

Her mother was sitting on a kitchen stool holding the phone in her hands, doubled over, laughing.

Laughing.

Her mother was laughing.

Ola needed to see it in order to recognize it. And it wasn't of a particularly strange variety either. What was strange, was that her mother was doing it.

Ola thought back and quickly realized that she'd never heard her mother laugh before. Not once. Not in all of the eighteen years they'd lived together.

Then she understood... everything.

Everything!

She sat and watched this animated woman she'd never known or even met before. It made Ola feel light...almost high to see her mother so young and happy.

"Who was that, mama?" She asked smiling almost as big as Alice.

"That was old, crazy Monica. She's always got some silliness going on." Then she relayed the story acting out an array of colorful people that made Ola scream, more from the performance than the story.

After that, they went upstairs to see which one of her mother's gowns she might be able to wear to the dinner/dance the following evening.

Her mother was shorter than she; otherwise they were practically the same size. The only difference was that a gown touching the floor on Alice fell mid-shin on Ola.

****

Ola found her mother mesmerizing. So youthful and radiantly happy. When she and Isaac danced everyone gave them the floor. They were like Fred and Ginger, Alvin and Katherine, Buck and Bubbles. She could never remember her parents dancing. Even if they had, her mother wouldn't have glowed like she was doing now.

Yesterday's Alice, Ola recalled, was a homemaker, industrious, efficient, quiet and calm. Today's Alice was a firecracker! Efficient and industrious, but so nimble and quick, you had to run if you planned to keep up. Quiet and calm no more, she was a woman of passions. She loved to laugh, loved to hear a joke and was quick to tell one. Her wit was as explosive as Moms Mabley. Her dance was as sensuous as Josephine Baker's. Her singing was a stirring cross between Shirley Horne and Shirley Bassey. And she played the piano like Eubie Blake. She was wonderful to behold, breathtaking and brilliant.

Ola was meeting her for the first time. And she liked her. And she loved her. They felt more like best friends, than mother and daughter.

Ola loved Isaac too, mostly for the wonderful transformation he caused in her mom. He was usually at work and after school, Dunbar eagerly accompanied him.

Dunbar was another breathtaking wonder. At seven years old, he had more sense than Aldo would die with. That thought tickled Ola beyond measure.

Two weeks was much too brief. Ola left with two big bags instead of the one. The second was filled with any items she had looked at twice in her mother's closet and in a few stores.

Their goodbyes were a reaffirmation of love and devotion mixed with many teary promises to visit soon and often.

Promises that were for the most part kept, whenever Ola could catch her mother in the country.

MR. TUCKER

forty-seven

Luthern Tucker never meant any harm. If he could have foreseen the pain and repulsion his child-bride would suffer as a result of their union, he never would have done it.

Mr. Tucker had always been alone. He was the only child born to parents who were themselves the only child, so little Luthern didn't have much family to be around. When he was coming up, their immediate neighbors were white and he played with their children until he was about ten years old. Then their parents ended the friendly rapport with the li'l darky. It was time for them all to acknowledge and embrace time-honored traditions.

Like most locals, Mr. Tucker didn't get much formal schooling. He learned the lumber business from his father and became proficient at it, just before a pile of rolling logs crushed his papa to death. His widowed mother never got over the loss of her love. She died a slow death from a broken heart three years later. With no parents, no other family and no friends, Luthern started reaching out to his employees and latched onto his best worker, Nathaniel Ward.

Nate took his boss home and he became part of their family.

Mr. Tucker loved Grace. He thought she was a beautiful woman with her pale fresh butter complexion lightly dusted with cinnamon freckles across her nose and cheeks. A wonderful cook and able seamstress with quiet congenial manners made her Luthern's dream woman. Although unavailable, it was a joy just to watch her in the kitchen and fantasize that the plate she set before him was for her husband, Luthern Tucker, not her husband's boss.

Since he had to eat and keep himself groomed anyway, he thought why not hire this fantasy female to fix his meals and darn his socks. Being a shrewd businessman he realized that the young couple was so appreciative, he didn't always have to pay them in cash. He could barter with wood, fresh meats and little conveniences, like loaning them his car. It was a good arrangement for everyone all around.

When Alice started growing up, he could see that she was going to blossom into the similar beauty of her mother. Being raised by this woman, chances were likely that she would acquire her mother's talents and temperament, Mr. Tucker thought, and so put in his bid for marriage.

The young struggling parents surprisingly resisted his proposal at first, but he showered them with gifts and favors and promises of more. Knowing they would never be able to afford much without his continued help, they eventually accepted his offer. It was a common practice at the time. The understanding was that these types of agreements were binding, barring any unforseen circumstances like an incapacitating illness, bankruptcy, or death. Luthern Tucker had the patience of Job. Seven to fifteen years would be nothing since he would see both of his brides, the intended and the fantasy, everyday. It made good business sense.

If that damned Isaac Freeman hadn't come along, they might be happily wed right now. But Freeman's boy did come along and he showed Alice what she would be missing.

Mr. Tucker thought that after Isaac ran away, and after Alice graduated from school where that teacher-witch filled her little head with lofty ambitions, and after Nate and Grace drilled into her the true sense of her responsibilities to her parents, her siblings and her husband, then maybe they could settle down into a nice life. But she was never happy and Mr. Tucker couldn't pretend that she was, or that he didn't care.

Then all of the waiting was made worthwhile when Alice came to him that first night, trembling like a little bird. All of her trepidations, he thought, were the sweet fears of a virgin facing her defloration. And although it wasn't often, she did return, making each visit a treasure that was not yearned for in vain.

She was a wonderful cook, a meticulous housekeeper, a talented seamstress and an unbelievable mother who almost seemed happy at times. But any illusions he'd entertained about Alice's elations were shot down the night she pointed that rifle at his head.

He was not a violent man. He fought back, but he never started a fight. And fighting a woman, even in self-defense, was incomprehensible to him. So he never retaliated. He understood and empathized with her rage from his having tricked her for sex.

He puzzled over what to do and came up with... *move her away!* Alice was only so feisty and self-assured, he reasoned, because she had family and friends to call on or run to whenever she felt the need. The good book tells a woman to cleave unto her husband and a man to cleave unto his wife. If they were both in a brand new place, unfamiliar to everything and everybody except themselves, she may find herself cleaving to him in spite of herself. Then they could grow closer naturally, and settle into a nice life.

But first there was the Macaulley fiasco, then Alice's leanings toward that little piece of a church, and then her inviting Sodom and Gomorrah themselves in the flesh *to stay with them*! Oh, that was the last straw.

Mr. Tucker was not only outraged with Alice's invitation, he felt betrayed by Alberta. He'd been paying that yellow heifer well as long as she kept her big trap shut about him sexing her. A man had to have his pleasures, and if the wife was unwilling, plenty of *working women* were. Their presence was particularly unnerving because he couldn't tell if the idea truly came from Alice, or was a clever manipulation by Alberta to move his wife out of his life. He really didn't think Alberta was clever enough to think of blackmail. But the only way to be sure was to get the tramps out of his home.

He gave them the money for the down payment on that house on Pasadena. He told them to wait a week before moving so Alice wouldn't get suspicious.

He thought with her friends gone, eventually Alice would feel lonely enough to come to him and then they could settle into a nice life. And Alice did get lonely. More than lonely, she became dangerously depressed, until Bertha came for a week and pumped new vigor and purpose into her sister's life. And then Alice created a whole new world for herself and the children outside of their home, starting those infernal clinics for the ill... the illegitimate, the illiterate or something else he could never seem to get straight!

Luthern Tucker was tired of fighting. Alice still maintained an impeccable home and cooked sumptuous meals. And he still got his fill of pleasures, if not from a warm and loving wife, then from the skilled technicians over on Pasadena, which was decidedly closer than Smedley.

He loved his daughters, but they were girls. In his upbringing and in his mind, girls belonged to their mothers and sons to their fathers. Since Alice made it abundantly clear that she would be having no more children, Mr. Tucker resigned himself to not having a proper heir.

Then, years later, without pleading or promises or negotiations of any kind, Alice came into the den offering him pleasant memories and laughter, libations and love. And even though her gift was for that single night alone, from that union free of trickery, lies, deals, obligations, fears, resentments or remorse, his son was born. He was a perfect boy, beautiful inside and out.

His girls had to pass the paperbag test, but not his son. *Junior* (Tucker didn't care what Alice called him) was a chip off the old block. Little Luthern made Big Luthern feel young and invincible... immortal. The boy was Mr. Tucker's second chance to get life right. Not that he thought he'd done so bad the first time, but he was going to have more fun through his son this second time around.

Mr. Tucker tried to take Dunbar everywhere, but Alice got in his way. He couldn't balk about it either. She was right when it came to his daughters. He hoped his son would develop even half as well as his sisters. And with Alice's careful ministrations, he did. Dunbar was fearless, frugal and fair. Mr. Tucker made sure his boy knew that he could have anything. Still, Dunbar never took for the sake of taking. He chose what he needed first and what he liked second. And he would always do without until his sister's needs and wants were granted.

Everyone loved Dunbar. Everyone wanted to be around him. Everyone catered to him. But he remained aloof without snubbing people. He seemed to recognize the dangers of easy gains.

Junior's questions weren't like the endless prattle of other toddlers either. When he asked a question, he appeared to have a hidden agenda, as though he already knew the answer. Like the time Mr. Tucker thought his young son was confusing *spoiled* with *soiled*, then later realized that "little Luthern" was teaching his daddy something. Big Luthern lived for those lessons.

Then one day, a minivan pulled up to the house from completely out of the blue. And Alice began loading boxes that Mr. Tucker never even realized were packed.

"Wha'chu doin Alice?"

"Dunbar and I are moving?"

"Dunbar...?"

"Yes. We're moving to Arizona. I'm going to marry Isaac Freeman. You remember him don't you?"

Since the birth of his son, he thought they had been slowly settling into a nice life. Now she dropped this bomb on him. Well, he was too old to fight some things. But he would not be denied his son.

"Ah'm tired of fighting, Alice. You go on and make a fool of yerse'f wit Freeman's boy ef you wanna. But'chu gonna live in sin an burn in hell cause I ain't givin you no divorce!"

"We were never married Mr. Tucker. I never said 'I do', I never kissed you, and I never signed a license. I've been living in sin and burning in hell for twenty years. But not anymore."

He hesitated for a second before barking, "Well take yer li'l ungrateful behine on way from here then, but junior gonna stay righ'chere wit his daddy!"

"*Dunbar* is going to live with his *daddy*! He was never *your junior*, except in your mind."

"Damn you woman! Wha's yer problem?! Ah'm gonna put a stop to this right now!!"

For the first time, Luthern regretted leaving his Winchester behind in the Smedley home pantry. But he could not risk Alice getting so upset that she would actually shoot him like she'd once threatened. He would love to pump a shot or two into Isaac's butt, that nervy upstart! Pulling up in front of his house! Come to steal his wife and namesake! Mr Tucker planned to give him a good piece of his mind, and maybe a swift kick besides.

"Ikey Freeman," Mr. Tucker roared rushing out of the front door, "git yer tail on roun'here damn it!"

Isaac jumped down out of the back of the van, wiping his hands on a rag and grinning like they were old friends.

"Luthern Tucker," he hailed from the curb, "What's shaking, baby?"

Mr. Tucker was midway the yard with his fists drawn and jutting like pistols when truth delivered a low hit that knocked all the steam and breath out of him. It made him retract his threat and return his pistol fists to the holsters of his pockets.

There stood Isaac Freeman with his politician's smile looking exactly like a larger, older, carbon copy of juni... *Dunbar*.

Mr. Tucker froze with all the possibilities and probabilities spinning around in his brain. Beginning with Alice saying, "*Dunbar is going to live with his daddy!*"

That Isaac *was* his father could not be denied. But that meant that Alice was seeing Isaac while being married to him! Only she never was married to him... not really. So that night she came to him, the night he thought was pure and voluntary, was an evening full of trickery, lies, deals, obligations, fears, resentments and remorse. But then why come to him at all, he wondered? Why play cruel tricks on an old man whose only crime was to love you? Where's the triumph? What was the point?

It was the weight of these unanswered questions bearing down on him with no chance of relief that made him feeble and dotering and old. It killed his spirit and his hope of a nice life. Everyday he prayed and waited for death to take him.

It would be many years before he got his wish.

ALICE

forty-eight

When Mrs. Petty forced me to think about myself, daring me to make a change, I turned to the poetry of Dunbar and Langston that usually enlightened and inspired me to act.

But Miss Johnson's letter from eleven years earlier fluttered out of Dunbar's pages, like manna from heaven, although that's not how I took it at the time. I thought it was pointing an accusatory finger at me, "I told you what to do, but did you do it...Noooo!!"

It read: *My Dearest Alice, do not despair. God never gives you a load you can not carry. Just when you think you can't take another step, He sends His angels to carry the weight. You are a real angel in the lives of everyone who knows you. You've helped me out in school through the years so many times, as a teacher and as a person. I can't begin to repay my debt to you. So just consider this a deposit.*

Isaac Freeman told me that he loves you. He loves you so much that he refuses to interrupt what he believes to be your choice to marry Luthern Tucker. He loves you enough to let you go. I told him he was wrong. He said, 'If you find out for sure that I am wrong, please give Alice my address in D.C. at Howard University where I have a job and plan to study. Tell her to write me anytime and let me know if she wants me to rescue her from her awful predicament.'

The same goes for your sister Bertha and me. If you want to be rescued, let us know. But we can't help you unless you take the first step to help yourself. Here's Isaac's address. Write him today. Loving you like a mother, Ola Johnson.

****

Bertha told me when I fell into that last great depression that Mr. Tucker called mama and daddy scared to death because I wasn't responding to anything, not even the kids. Mama and daddy didn't know what to do, so they called her. Bertha didn't know what to do except to ask me what I wanted, so she hopped on the first thing smoking and spent that week with me.

She talked on and on about I don't know what. The messages that got through the fog in my mind were: *If you don't like your life, it's your fault, Alice. I learned that from you! Ain't no mind readers amongst your family and friends. Don't nobody know how miserable you are when you keep all quiet and to yourself! When did you get so timid and scared? What you mean Mr. Tucker don't know you can drive? How you been getting around? Why you call it Mr. Tucker's money? It's your money, too, just like this house. Don't you remember? You told me that when you invited Mary and Alberta up here? I can get in touch with Isaac. Are you ready to get in touch with him? It's been awhile, so I don't know if he's still interested or even available. Are you ready for that?*

She told me I needed to find a place that Mr. Tucker would never suspect was a rendezous point. She told me to let her know as soon as I figured something out. She said she couldn't promise anything beyond getting a message to Isaac.

After much thought and worriment, it finally dawned on me... The church! Mr. Tucker hadn't been in there since he bribed Reverend Pope to fire me as the choir director and pianist. I could teach there everyday in peace. If Isaac and I didn't work out, teaching is something I'd like to do anyway.

I set up the Adult Learning Clinic and swallowed my heart everytime the door swung open thinking that anyday could be the day Isaac showed up. But nothing happened.

I finally gave up hope of a reunion and contented myself with waging a battle for literacy in our community.

One evening, shortly after the last of my senior students had left, a militant looking Black Panther-type brother with a bushy afro, mustache, sunglasses and fatigues ala Fidel Castro, marched into the empty sanctuary.

"All Power To The People," he declared with a fisted salute.

"All Power," I half-heartedly indulged.

The hours were posted on the door, but I thought if he couldn't read, he may have missed that sign.

"I was just closing up," I said. "We're open tomorrow from 1-9pm."

"I can't register now?"

"Not tonight. Come back tomorrow."

"Okay, then I'll come back tomorrow," he said still approaching me.

"Fine," I pointed behind him, "the door is that way,"

"I know where the door is," he said, coming even closer.

I was so afraid, but I didn't want to show it. I slipped an ink pen as discreetly as I could into my right hand thinking, *Try me and I'll stab you in the eye.*

But instead, I said with unfelt bravado, "Good, then use it."

"I will," he said when he was almost upon me. Then slowly removing his shades he added, "but not before I git the rest of my spinna bottle kiss."

forty-nine

Eventually he transferred to The Cleveland Clinic continuing his work as a research doctor. It was fairly easy for him to relocate, having no patients to disappoint or reassign. He tutored for the Adult Clinic everyday and the after-school program occasionally. He went on as many field trips as he could and everyone knew him as "the doctor" or "Doc". So I got to see him all the time. After other volunteer staff and tutors were recruited, we were able to sneak away sometimes and spend quiet moments together.

I was afraid of the debilitation divorce may have on the girls. They seemed so well-rounded at home, in school and with their friends. I couldn't rob them now, like I was robbed when I was taken away from my home. I was also afraid that Mr. Tucker would somehow manage to take my daughters from me out of spite, if I left him before they graduated from school. I promised Isaac that as soon as Ola graduated, I would leave Mr. Tucker and marry him, if he still wanted me.

I was twenty-seven then and he was twenty-nine. He didn't want to wait. But he said, "Well, I've waited this long."

Then in '61 when I got pregnant, he changed his mind.

"He'll kick you out and keep your daughters for sure now." Isaac argued. "Go on your own terms!"

"He won't if he thinks this baby is his."

"What do you mean, Alice? Are you saying what I think you're...?!"

"No! Oh, no. Isaac, the man drinks. If I get him drunk and talk nice to him and he falls out and I come up pregnant, pride will make him think it's his!"

"Why do all that, Alice? Just leave him!"

"I owe Harriet and Ola, too. They deserve all of the happiness and security they can get before they strike out on their own."

It was the closest we'd come to breaking up. I think he only stayed because of the baby. If I weren't pregnant, we would have continued as we had been without a word. But I *was* pregnant, so he wanted to quit the farce. I insisted on continuing to protect my daughters. Now he was threatening to leave because of the baby, when the baby was his greatest reason for wanting us to stay together, which made this a strange conundrum.

****

That night, I plied Mr. Tucker with drinks and memories. I hugged him, kissed him and sat in his lap so he'd remember something suggestive of romance. I opened his shirt, loosened his belt and told him I'd be right back.

He fell asleep.

Then I brought him cereal in the morning and called him *Tony the Tiger*. I wasn't sure if he'd fallen for it at first. I was prepared to get us all out of there in case he leveled an ultimatum.

But when Dunbar was born, Mr. Tucker lost his little mind with delight. To think that this perfect little boy could spring from his seed was beyond his greatest imaginings... It was also against the laws of nature, but I didn't point that out until six years later.

When I made Mr. Tucker back off from coming to the clinics by demanding that he come to teach or learn, Isaac and I resumed our regular routine, as much as possible, with our child. I swore again that I'd leave with Dunbar as soon as Ola graduated from high school.

Isaac was afraid that I was sacrificing our son for my daughters. He thought Dunbar's spending so much time with Mr. Tucker would have a negative effect. But as our amazing little boy grew older and displayed an uncanny comprehension for what his father taught, Isaac's stronger influence helped us both decide to continue with the charade.

****

I never wanted to hurt anyone. But I'd been living in the bowels of hell for too long praying for relief, or death. I still think that waiting like we did was best, even though I knew it would hurt Ola. She was blind-sided along with Mr. Tucker. It was shocking, but I thought she'd get over it.

A year later, when she spent those two weeks with us here in Arizona, I knew it was the beginning of the beginning of something good and brand spanking new for her.

For me, it was like a new lease on life, like a beautiful awakening, like the resurrection promised to all who die believing in our sweet Lord's return.

Special Thanks and Acknowledgments

I apologize in advance to those I may have forgotten to include in this list of people and organizations whose ears and efforts have made this book possible. Your enthusiasm and faith were sometimes the only things that kept me trying to make the finished manuscript a published piece. First, I want to thank my sisters, blood and otherwise; Leslie, Debbie, Loretta, Pam, Marsha, Norma, Marjorie, Sandra, Christine, Sherri, Joyce, Lateefah, Vickie, Michelle, Grace and Delaine for years of ears and encouragement. Joyce Carol Thomas, my especially vigilant guardian angel. Cobi Narita, my sister-mother, for loving life and living and putting unfathomable energies and efforts into making *everyone's* dreams come true. Second, I want to thank my *brothers*: Donald and Marvin, my true love (Donald's alter ego); Paul Laurence Dunbar for poetry that inspires and informs; Mr. Ken and Ron Dean Wells Out-of-Cleveland-Ohio for marrying my sisters and changing the good name and reputation of our family forever! Gil and Dune for always having my back and daring me to be the me they see; Ron Bunn who published me first. Dr. Gregory Johnson who first told me to write, write, write; Carl for sharing his visions of my tomorrows; Lenny and Yusef, my brothers in deed; Eric a gifted and talented young soul, it's time to fly; Archie, Sidney, Lawrence, Harvey, Ajene, and Ronny just because. I also thank Philip for designing the cover for me at the 11th hour; Jesse, Preston, Beatrice and Norma (again) for smoothing the jagged edges; the enthusiastic nurturings of Tuesdays @ Nine.

Finally, thank you thank you Dwight and Lucy Smith. Dwight, everybody-needs-this-brother-man, for his eyes and ears, for his computer skills and instruction, for getting the book to the printers in my absence, and for always being so helpful and available in all things without complaint. And lovely Lucy, his beautiful and patient bride, for sharing him so generously with a world of people endlessly vying for his talents on their projects.